Maisey Yates is the ~~...~~ ...ing author of over one hundred ~~...~~ ...ce novels. An avid knitter with a dangerous yarn addiction and an aversion to housework, Maisey lives with her husband and three kids in rural Oregon. She believes the trek she makes to her coffee maker each morning is a true example of her pioneer spirit. Find out more about Maisey's books on her website: www.maiseyyates.com, or find her on Facebook, Instagram or TikTok by searching her name.

USA Today Bestselling Author **Jules Bennett** has penned more than fifty novels during her short career. She's married to her high school sweetheart, has two active girls, and is a former salon owner. Jules can be found on X, Facebook (Fan Page), and her website julesbennett. com. She holds competitions via these three outlets with each release and loves to hear from readers!

New York Times bestselling author **Vicki Lewis Thompson**'s love affair with cowboys started with the *Lone Ranger*, continued through *Maverick* and took a turn south of the border with *Zorro*. Fortunately for her, she lives in the Arizona desert, where broad-shouldered, lean-hipped cowboys abound. Visit her website at vickilewisthompson.com

A Cowboy Christmas

MAISEY YATES

JULES BENNETT

VICKI LEWIS THOMPSON

MILLS & BOON

First Published in Great Britain 2024
by Mills & Boon, an imprint of HarperCollins*Publishers* Ltd,
1 London Bridge Street, London, SE1 9GF

www.harpercollins.co.uk

HarperCollins*Publishers*
Macken House, 39/40 Mayor Street Upper,
Dublin 1, D01 C9W8, Ireland

A Cowboy Christmas © 2024 Harlequin Enterprises ULC.

Rancher's Snowed-In Reunion © 2023 Maisey Yates
A Texan for Christmas © 2018 Jules Bennett
Cowboy Unwrapped © 2016 Vicky Lewis Thompson

ISBN: 978-0-263-36260-2

This book contains FSC™ certified paper and other controlled sources to ensure responsible forest management.

For more information visit: www.harpercollins.co.uk/green

Printed and Bound in the UK using 100% Renewable Electricity at CPI Group (UK) Ltd, Croydon, CR0 4YY

RANCHER'S SNOWED-IN REUNION

MAISEY YATES

Chapter 1

After

Flint Carson had to hand it to his brother. His recent move in life had inspired Flint. And he couldn't say that he was often inspired by his little brother. Not that Jace wasn't a decent guy, it was just that Flint, in general, didn't want what Jace had. He had settled down recently, and that wasn't in the cards for Flint.

But when his brother had become a part owner of the hotel that his fiancée bought, it had gotten Flint thinking. And then he had done more than think. He had been content for a long time competing in the rodeo. Working his family ranch, giving to them in a way that he could. His father recognized rodeo triumphs, and he took them as credits to who he was as a father, as the rodeo commissioner.

He also recognized contributions to the ranch. His mother appreciated that his father felt appreciated. He didn't do emotions, so that kind of physical involvement was what he had to give, so he gave it.

At least until a couple of years ago. It had started being profoundly not enough.

And after...

There was just so much anger in him. There had been, for a long time. For a lot of reasons. But after that song had come out...

He gritted his teeth. It infuriated him every time.

But what didn't infuriate him was his brand-new purchase. Pine Creek Resort. Nestled in the mountains of central Oregon, a couple hours away from his family home of Lone Rock.

He'd seen it and just felt drawn to it. He didn't give much credit to fate or feelings—not these days. But he believed a man ought to trust his gut.

So, he was trusting his.

It was practically off-grid, and solar panels, generators and other things kept it going with the iffy power running to the place. But it was pretty seamless, and he had done his due diligence on that. Because while he thought it was great that Jace and Cara were running the hotel at the end of the main drag of Lone Rock's main business center—which was just a few businesses, surrounded by mountains—he wanted more. Bigger.

The thought made his mouth curve into a smile as he looked around the highly polished lobby area. It was all logs and wooden beams. Rustic sort of luxury.

He could remember back when he'd said he didn't have ambitions or dreams at all.

But that was before.

Back then, everything he'd done had been to burn the rage out of his blood. To push himself to the edge so that he could ride out the simmering hatred that turned his blood to poison.

He'd chased adrenaline because it made things feel clear. Pure. Clean.

Could have been worse.

Could have been heroin.

Maybe it wasn't all that different now. Maybe this wasn't all that different. Maybe he was still trying to climb impossible mountains, just with more financial risk than physical.

With the weather being what it was, almost every guest had canceled their reservation for the weekend. There was a huge storm coming in, and while usually the hotel was accessible year-round, there had been some warnings and questions about whether or not it would be possible over the next couple of days. He didn't mind. A little bit of quiet in his newest acquisition while he looked to the next one was fine by him.

And since there was only going to be one guest, he'd let the staff go as well. The guest had declined maid service, and there was enough food that all he would have to do was heat and deliver. And he didn't mind that.

A little bit of manual labor didn't bother him at all. In fact, he thought it was good. Another way to burn out that rage. He had to do it.

And as if just thinking had brought it all to him, he suddenly became aware of the fact that there was music playing in the lobby. And not just any music.

You were the cowboy my mama warned me about
And I thought I listened, I thought you were different
I gave you my heart, and you gave me good-luck charms
I gave you my body, and you kept my scarf
I gave you my body, and you kept my heart

For God's sake. Was it destined to follow him everywhere? Even when he quite literally owned the damn place?

He growled and stalked toward the reception desk. The guy had told him how to control the music, but as his own personal level of hell played around him, he couldn't quite remember how.

I gave you everything to the sound of crashing waves
You knew you were the first one
I wanted you to be the only one

It made him think of her.

The song always made him think of her.

The way she'd looked at him, like she was searching his eyes for the answers to all of her questions. Wordless questions he'd wished he hadn't understood. Questions that still echoed inside him.

In the end, she'd said that he was right. She had said that they needed to finish the whole damned thing.

She was the one that had called it a fling.

She said she loved you too.

Yes. She had said that. And then she had taken it

back. She had said that it was just because of the sex. And he'd been more than willing to believe it because hearing her say that she loved him had done things to him. Terrible, intense things that made him feel like his chest was being cut into.

He needed to find the volume. Or a sledgehammer.

Before the next part.

But then it was the next part, and it was in his head, his heart, his soul.

You took the clothes off my body
I gave you my yes and I love you
You took the skin off my bones
You gave me nothing at all
I prayed for our sin to disappear
But I didn't mean for it to end in blood

He found the speaker right then. He found it just a lyric too late. He crouched down, reaching for the knob on the speaker behind the desk. And as he did, he heard the door to the lobby open. He hit the off button on the speaker just as the next part of the song started.

He couldn't explain the way it made him feel.

He could remember where he was the first time he heard it. The first time he'd heard his ex-girlfriend— was she his ex-girlfriend? He'd never had a girlfriend in his life. And they weren't supposed to be that, but he'd also never ended a physical relationship with someone and felt like their connection was still there. And yet.

The simple truth was, he'd gotten in deeper with her than he ever had been with anyone else. Much deeper than he'd intended to. And he wasn't going to say he'd covered himself in glory at the end of all things. But she had seemed to accept it. He'd been up-front with her, from the beginning, about what they were, about what they could be.

So imagine his surprise the first time he'd heard that song. Documenting everything. The most personal, deep feelings he'd ever had in his whole life turned into a sing-along.

Even if no one else had ever heard it, it would have felt too raw and personal for him to listen to.

But people had heard it. So many people.

To make matters worse, her fame and his own niche notoriety in certain circles had made it so there were theories out there on the internet about who the song was about.

Her fans were nuts. They spent all day weaving together theories about what every lyric meant. And he knew that because he'd googled it, because he'd wanted to know what the lyrics meant too.

Dammit.

The terrible thing was, her fans made points. Points he didn't like, but points nonetheless.

That would have been bad enough. But it didn't stop there.

Strangers sometimes accosted him on the street and asked him how dare he break Tansey Martin's heart? Country music's sweetheart. Barrel-racer-turned-overnight-singing-sensation.

She was beautiful and beloved, and he was the expertly cast villain in her narrative. Set to music, which meant that people could hum his humiliation as a catchy tune.

He could remember clearly the way that she had

looked up at him. The way that she had looked up at him when he'd said all those things. The awful sort of things that he'd warned her he would say. As everything had broken apart inside of him, the walls that he had erected around himself beginning to crumble, she had looked up at him, and she had said that he was right.

That he was right, and they shouldn't be together. That he was right and they should forget everything.

Yeah. He knew that. Because he knew his limitations. And then… And then four months later, completely and totally blindsided by this song. And he'd known it was about them. That it was their story.

It was like she had crawled beneath his skin with those song lyrics. Like she had described his own pain. Like she'd dug into his soul and carved clear arrows to his own motives. To things he'd denied even to himself.

He'd pretended that he wasn't hanging on to her scarf for any particular reason, and she had immortalized it in song and made it impossible for him to pretend.

But it was the pregnancy scare.

That was what destroyed him the most, because it shone a light on the way that he had fallen apart most profoundly.

The worst, cruelest way he'd failed her.

When something like that happened, you had to take a good look at yourself. Even though there hadn't been a baby in the end, it had been a come-to-Jesus moment. A look-hard-at-the-man-he'd-become moment.

He didn't like that man.

It was one reason he'd changed everything. One reason he'd started…working. Really working. Not just on his father's land, not just on being rodeo champion yet again. But building something that was entirely his.

And he couldn't let that song into his head. Not now. Because it was the only thing that could get beneath his skin, just like *she* was the only thing that ever could.

He was pretty good at staying stoic in the face of difficult things.

It wasn't the fans yelling at him. That was actually fine. That made him *mad*. Anger, he had found, was fantastic fuel.

It was the pain.

The pain he wasn't supposed to be able to feel anymore. The pain that ambushed him when he didn't expect it. When he was alone. The pain that took him right back to the place that he'd been when he was a boy, a place he couldn't even think about, much less fully remember or relive.

And so he pushed the song to the back of his mind, and he stood up. But then he froze. The predator spotting prey. That was what it felt like. Like everything in him went quiet. And the edges of the empty lobby blurred.

Her.

There she was. Standing there at the center of the room, strawberry blond hair curling and cascading past her shoulders.

She looked like he remembered her.

Not the way that she dressed up for the public. All fake eyelashes and red lipstick.

This was just her.

The way that he had seen her that first day. Coming in from barrel racing, her cheeks bright red, her smile exuberant. Though she wasn't smiling now. She looked storm tossed, her hair full of snowflakes, and a couple of twigs. Her face was wet, likely from melting snow, and it forced him to remember how hot her skin could be when he put his hands on it.

She looked just like she had the first time...

Before

She wasn't his type.

Flint Carson had interacted with more than his fair share of the sort of women you met at a rodeo. From rodeo queens to buckle bunnies, and everything in between. He tended toward the queens and the bunnies. Soft, pretty rhinestones. The sort of glamour that wasn't necessarily subtle or classy, but he liked it. He was a man, dusty, hard and full of grit. He liked a woman who was the opposite of all that.

That was the point of women, as far as he was concerned.

Bring on the glitter, the lip gloss, the long fingernails. Flashy, maybe even bordering on what some would call trashy. He didn't think it was trashy.

He liked it.

Now, some of the barrel racers had a little bit of flair to them, but they still weren't his thing. Felt too much like coworkers, really. He didn't like it.

He was also very careful to choose women close to his age and level of experience. He didn't have forever in him. Hell, he didn't even have more than a couple of nights in him, so it didn't do any good to go after a woman who was expecting something more. To go after the kind of woman who wanted something more.

He needed the women that he hooked up with to want exactly what he wanted.

Which was why, when the pint-size, barefaced barrel racer tripped on unsteady legs on her way out of the gate after a ride, and landed right in his arms, the first thing he told himself was, she wasn't his type.

She had freckles all over her face. Her eyes were green. Her hair was strawberry blond, curly, he could tell; even though it was in a braid, there were wispy tendrils that had escaped. She was thin but athletic, wearing a plain white tank top and a pair of torn blue jeans. She was young.

And something in him burned.

He set her back on her heels.

"Careful there."

"Thanks, Ace," she said, brushing some dust off of her jeans. "I'll do my best to be more careful."

"Darlin', I just saved you from doing a face-plant, and you're going to get sassy with me?"

"A face-plant never hurt anybody."

"Neither has spending a few minutes in my arms. You can ask around."

She laughed. But it wasn't a particularly kind or warm laugh. "Of course. Somehow that doesn't surprise me."

"What's your name?"

"Tansey," she said. "Tansey Martin. You're Flint Carson."

She knew who he was. He supposed he shouldn't be surprised. She was…young. He was sort of an elder statesman of the bull-riding circuit, and in addition to that, his dad was the rodeo commissioner. Practically everybody around these parts knew the Carsons.

"Guilty," he said.

"Of quite a lot of things if the gossip is anything to go by."

She could walk away. That was the thing. She could walk away, but she was antagonizing him instead. *He* could also walk away.

Neither of them were doing that.

It would almost be interesting except she wasn't his type.

She wasn't his type, and wasn't charmed by his whole facade. Which made him wonder if there was any point to the facade at all. Made him tempted to drop it. And he never dropped it, not ever.

"Now," he asked, "did your parents ever teach you not to listen to gossip?"

"My mom taught me that gossip could be useful. If something is said often enough, there's probably some truth to it. And maybe a person should listen to it. All my daddy taught me was the way 1999 Ford pickup taillights look going out of the driveway."

"Sounds like a country song," he said.

She smiled, and it was unreadable. Not flirtatious. Not friendly. He wanted to know what the hell it meant. "Yeah. It kind of does."

She was standing with her horse. He had kind of only just noticed. The big animal that was right next to her. Funny.

It was like she took up all the space.

"Nice," he said, patting the animal on the flank.

"Thanks. Cinderella has a thing for cowboys that are too charming for their boots."

"I take it her owner does not."

"No, she doesn't. Like I said. Taillights. I'm familiar. With cowboys. Do you know what they're good for?"

"What?"

"Leaving."

That made him want to do something. Surprise her. Climb a mountain.

Stay.

"That is true. We are very good at that."

Except, he didn't leave. Neither did she. Neither of them pointed that out. They just stood there and marinated in the irony.

"You want to get a drink?" he asked.

Her lips twitched, like she was pondering that. "Sure. I'm not having sex with you. To be clear."

The way she said it was a gut punch. And good thing she wasn't his type, or his mind might have wandered somewhere it shouldn't.

"I'm not asking," he said. "To be clear."

Her face went scarlet. Well. He'd succeeded in getting something other than a cool, snarky reaction out of her.

Though, he had no idea why he was asking her for a drink. Except they were standing there, right near the gates, cluttering up the space, taking up too much room.

So, obviously they needed to move to another venue. It was the last night in this particular stop on the rodeo tour, and he didn't know how he hadn't noticed her before. He didn't really stand around watching all the other events. He had once, when he'd been new to the game. When things had been shiny and bright and he'd been excited.

At least, in his memory he was excited. It was entirely possible that he was painting the whole thing with a varnish that had never actually been there.

Always easier to look back on the glory days.

Mostly, he had been young and angry, and the adrenaline had felt good.

Now he was old and angry, and the adrenaline made his muscles hurt.

Okay. He wasn't old. He was thirty-four, but that was getting on in rodeo years. And that was a fact.

Especially when you'd been doing it since you were eighteen years old. It was a lot of years of abuse. More than not.

"Are you old enough to drink?"

Her face went red. "Yes."

"Okay. I don't want to be out there buying alcohol for a minor. I don't have a criminal record, which is a miracle to be honest. So I'd rather not get one now."

"That's kind of a surprise. I thought all you guys had a slew of DUIs."

"Sorry to disappoint."

"Well. I'm happy to be surprised. I didn't think your kind could surprise me."

"What exactly is my kind, Tansey?" He started to follow her out of the arena area and toward the stalls where the horses would be kept until they were ready to load up and head to the next event.

"Smooth talker. Probably never met a woman you couldn't con out of her clothes."

"Now, that sounds vaguely predatory. This here being the modern era, I am a huge fan of consent. I don't con anyone out of anything. Now, if they get a look at me and decide they'd like to take their clothes off, that is another story altogether."

"Good to know. A respectful womanizer. But a womanizer nonetheless."

"You do have my number. But then, I don't go around claiming to be anything other than a bad bet. I assume your daddy did."

"He thought he'd try to be a family man for a little bit. Didn't work out."

"Well. There's a difference between me and your father, right off the bat. I'm never going to pretend to be a family man."

"Well, I suppose that's something."

He watched as she took all the tack off of her horse—he didn't figure she was going to accept any help from him. She probably had a million reasons for it too. Something about being independent, he was sure. And while it would be fun, maybe, to engage in that banter, he figured he would keep going in the direction of the unexpected banter. Because he liked it.

He liked talking to her.

And hell, he'd had a great idea how this night was going to go. He'd won his event, kept his top spot on the leaderboard, and he'd been planning on going out to the bar with all the other guys, including his brother Boone, and having drinks. Which would probably devolve into taking shots, which would inevitably end up with him finding a woman to hook up with…

He'd go back to his motel room, they'd have sex, she'd go her way and he'd sleep for a few hours before getting on the road the next morning.

He could see it all play out in his mind. And it bored him.

Tansey didn't bore him.

And anyway, she wasn't his type.

So it wasn't like it was going to be anything but a conversation. He couldn't remember the last time he'd wanted to engage in a conversation with anybody after an event.

He didn't engage in a lot of conversations, really. He did a lot of drinking, a lot of physical things.

Didn't talk all that much.

This felt like a novelty. And... Hell. He was in the market for one. Hadn't known that he was until she'd fallen into his arms. But then, maybe that was a sign.

Not that he believed in that kind of thing.

Still, he found himself jerking his head toward where he parked his truck. "Want to take a ride with me?"

"I'll drive myself," she said. "Which bar?"

"Cactus," he said. "It's right across the street from the Okay Motel. That's where I'm staying."

"Me too," she said.

"How about we drive there, park across the street. Then nobody has to watch the drinking."

"I don't get drunk," she said.

"Why not?"

"Because. I like to have my wits about me."

"Well. There is the difference between you and me. I prefer to make my wits a bit blurry."

She looked at him, for a long moment, and he had the uncomfortable feeling that her green eyes could see more than just his face, his shirt, his jeans. He had the feeling that she could see something deeper in him than he even knew was there. And he didn't like it.

And still, he wanted to go get that drink with her.

"Okay. Meet you there."

After

She was standing completely still. Like she was the prey. Like she knew it. Like she knew that she had been scented.

Like she knew exactly what he felt.

Because hadn't she always?

Until that last moment.

And hadn't he always? Until then.

When they had both pretty spectacularly lied to each other's faces and broken down the world.

He stood by it.

Because the fallout had proved that he was right. His own behavior after the fact, and hers.

He would never have said he was sensitive. Far from it. He was a man who didn't do feelings in the slightest. But he felt like she had taken a layer of his skin and peeled it off with a paring knife, pulled it back and showed the world everything that was inside of him. And he didn't even like to look at all the things that were inside of him.

Hearing the pain in the song was like being stabbed through the heart.

Because as much as it was about her own pain, it was about his. As much as it was about him breaking them up, it was about him breaking himself. As much as he was the villain to her…

He'd been that for himself too.

If he believed in fate, he'd have been certain it had come for him today.

He didn't believe in fate.

It was just that life was a bitch.

So he had to be a bigger bastard.

He put his hand up to his head, and reflexively, without thought, touched the brim of his cowboy hat, and tipped it. "Howdy."

"What are you doing here?" She looked around, shocked, and he realized that she had gone as white as the snow outside.

He slowly moved from behind the counter, and began to walk toward her. She was the only thing. The only thing. "I might ask you the same question. Because I looked at the books, and your name is not on them."

"I don't check into hotels under my real name," she said.

"Oh right," he said, "because you're fancy now. Because everybody knows who you are. Everyone knows everything about you, don't they, Tansey?"

"Yes. I know you're trying to be mean, and trying to make it sound like maybe I'm above myself, but it's true."

"It seems there's something else you don't do. You don't look to see who owns the hotel you're staying at."

Her mouth dropped open. "I've been here before. You've *never* been here."

"I just bought it. It's mine. And you're the only guest." He spread his arms wide. "Looks like it's just the two of us."

Chapter 2

Run.

That was all Tansey could think. She needed to run. Because she'd never, ever wanted to come face-to-face with Flint Carson ever again. Not in her whole life.

But there he was.

Maybe if she closed her eyes, she could be not in this moment. Maybe if she concentrated really hard, he would disappear.

Maybe this was a dream.

The whole drive up here had been a nightmare, and maybe it hadn't even been real. Maybe that was the thing. Maybe the whole drive, with the intense, freezing snow, the white stuff piling up on the road and making it slick and almost impossible to keep her tires on the road, had been part of a nightmare. Maybe the branches falling across the road, the tree that had fallen down after her on the soft ground, and the lack of cell phone service, had all been an elaborate nightmare.

Ending with Flint. Standing right there in the lobby of the hotel.

Like it was *The Shining*. Except, it wasn't a crazy groundskeeper; it was her way-too-hot-for-anyone's-own-good ex-boyfriend, who had absolutely destroyed her and broken her into tiny pieces.

Ex-boyfriend. He was never your boyfriend. He was a guy who had sex with you. And you were an idiot.

Yes. She had been an idiot. And she'd had grace for that young idiot. That young idiot who had known better, whose mother had told her better, who had purposed to not act out her daddy issues in that way, but had done so because Flint was just so charming. Because she hadn't actually had any experience.

Because she had told herself that she knew getting sexually involved with a man who wasn't going to fall in love with her could hurt her, but she hadn't really understood it. Because she had told herself she could handle a fling, and then she had let herself believe that she had been convinced on some level she could change his mind about it being a fling.

She had been like every other dumb twenty-two-year-old who didn't want to believe that she was, in fact, like all the other girls.

Well, she'd made her peace with that, because she was more than two years past all that, and a heartbreak sure offered a lot of clarity. She didn't waste her time being outraged at that girl.

No. She knew where to put her outrage. It was on him. And there he was.

If this was a nightmare, she could take an umbrella out of the umbrella stand by the door and start whacking him with it.

She pinched her arm. It hurt, even through her heavy coat. But he was still standing there.

"What the hell are you doing?"

"I'm trying to see if I fell asleep on my way up here. Or maybe hit a tree and I'm unconscious in a ditch, so I'm hallucinating the ghosts of back-when-I-was-stupid past."

"Well. If you're hallucinating, then so am I."

"Great." And she had fantasized about running into him before, even though she had never wanted to see him again.

That seemed like a pretty normal thing.

In her fantasies of seeing him again someday, she had imagined herself in a beautiful designer dress—not looking soggy from her tramp through the snow up to the lobby, and being caught off guard.

No. She had always imagined they would run into each other at some soiree, not that Flint would have any reason to be at a soiree, but it was her fantasy.

Realistically, she hadn't thought it would happen, so she could imagine whatever scenario she wanted.

She had imagined that she would be dressed meticulously, looking every inch as wealthy as her music had made her, maybe with a handsome man on her arm—forgetting the fact that she hadn't been on a single date since she and Flint had broken up—and the look of regret that would wash over him would be profound.

But she would be happy. And she would drink champagne, and she would *show him*.

Because the best revenge was living well.

She had written it into the song because he had said it to her. He had said that to her about handling her own father's abandonment. And when she had written the song, she had hoped that he would hear it and appreciate the irony.

And now she found herself horrified by the realization that he had undoubtedly heard it.

Because all the self-protection that she had engaged in when he had broken up with her suddenly didn't matter. Because she had put it all in a song.

She had known that, but knowing it and coming face-to-face with it were two very different things.

And this was in no way what she wanted. This was way too real. She preferred the glossy fantasy.

This was him. And it felt like the first time…

Before

She had no idea what the hell she was doing. She didn't do this kind of thing. Didn't go out and have drinks with extraordinarily handsome cowboys. He was extraordinarily handsome. She'd known that, though. Ever since she first started riding with the rodeo two years ago.

She'd gotten into it hoping to see her dad again.

It was so stupid. All of it.

Her little pursuits to try and make a connection with a man who didn't give a shit about her at all. But she'd thought… Their paths would have to cross. Even when he wasn't competing in calf-roping events, he was often doing odd jobs around the rodeo. It was his whole life.

Plus, she'd figured… He paid attention to the rodeo circuit; he was bound to see her name.

Those were the two things her dad loved. The rodeo and country music. She was bound and determined that she was going to reach him through one of those ways or the other.

Funny that Flint had mentioned the taillights thing sounded like a country song.

She already knew it. She'd already made it one.

Of course, it wasn't the demo that her manager was shopping. It felt too personal. She hadn't played that song for anyone.

The frothy little love song that she'd recorded a couple of months ago when she'd found somebody who wanted to take a chance on her and push her to the labels was easier for her.

Not that anyone had shown any interest in it. But she did all the open mics that she came across while traveling for the rodeo, and that worked out pretty well for her.

Everything she did had a purpose. She'd joined the rodeo to find her dad, being in the rodeo let her travel, traveling helped her get her music out. That was how she did things.

But this… Having a drink with Flint Carson accomplished nothing. She didn't know why she had kept talking to him. Didn't know why she had stood there, unable to drag herself away. And she did not know why she'd said yes to this. But when she pulled up to the motel at the same time he did, and got out, crossing the dusty, two-lane Arizona highway to the little dive bar across the street, she stopped questioning it.

He opened the door for her, and she looked up at him, at his chiseled face, square jaw, strong chin. He had dark stubble over that jaw, and it looked rough, and she couldn't deny that she felt her fingers itch slightly with the urge to touch it.

Which was very stupid. She liked to think that she was smarter than that. That her body was smarter than that. Because it knew the memories of what it felt like to be abandoned. Remembered what it was like to crumple down on the ground, on her knees, with the gravel biting into the denim as her father's truck got farther and farther away and she gave in to her anguish. That was embedded into her soul. It was more keen, more real, than any desire to touch a handsome cowboy's stubble could ever be. That moment of it being the last time she ever saw her father would always be more burned into everything she was than…than the dark blue of his eyes. Like worn denim. So compelling and enticing…

She took a deep breath and pressed on into the bar.

The floor was rough wood, and there were neon cactus signs all over the place. And also a pink flamingo. She admired the commitment to tackiness, even if it wasn't totally following a theme.

There were a lot of cowboys and cowgirls already in there, people that she knew. She felt slightly embarrassed to be coming in with Flint, because why would anybody be with him unless they were going to sleep with him? She had never known Flint to hang out with a woman that he wasn't going to hook up with.

Well. Allegedly.

Maybe she had sort of noticed him from across the bar before, and that was what some of the girls she was with had said about him… And maybe she had committed some of that to heart a little bit more than she ought to.

Maybe she had gone back to her room and scribbled down a few song lyrics about unobtainable men who were nothing but bad decisions wrapped in dust and denim.

Maybe.

She was an artist, though. She often wrote about things that she had no desire to experience. She often wrote about things that she would never do. Things she didn't even want to do. She wrote about the human experience. Not necessarily her own.

The love song she'd recorded was a prime example of that.

She'd never been in love.

She thought about the song she'd written about her dad again, and shoved all that to the side.

"What will you have?"

"Uh. Beer?"

She just really wasn't a big drinker.

"Sure. What kind?"

"I don't know."

"Okay. That helps me make a decision."

He went over to the bar, and she sat down at one of the little tables in the corner. He came back a few moments later with two beers, one in each hand.

"How did me not knowing tell you anything?"

"I got you something easy. Something friendly. Since clearly if you don't know what you're drinking, you don't have a lot of experience with the drinking. So… mainstream it is."

"Are you insulting me?" she asked, drawing the glass toward her.

"Not at all. I'm giving you something accessible."

"Out of deference to my inexperience?"

He cleared his throat and took a drink of his beer. And far too late she realized the potential double entendre with that. Of course, he didn't know how inexperienced she was. Anyway, her experience, or lack thereof, when it came to things other than beer was immaterial to this moment and this conversation.

"What exactly are we doing?" she asked, lifting her glass up and taking a sip. Damn him. It was good.

"Having a beer."

"It's just… You have a reputation."

"That I do. Though, you're going to have to tell me which one you mean. Because I have a reputation for being a very good bull rider, as it happens. Maybe you missed it, but I'm in first place right now."

"I didn't miss it. And that isn't the reputation I'm referring to."

"You mean that I like to have a one-night stand. Many, many of the people who travel with the rodeo do."

"Right. Well. I don't."

"Great. Good to know."

"So why are you talking to me?"

"Why are *you* talking to *me*? Because as you said, I have a reputation. You seem to know it…"

"I don't know why I am talking to you. It's just that I wanted to."

"Well, I wanted to talk to you too. I can't say that I know why either." He huffed a laugh and took another drink of his beer. "I'll just tell you, I've known what I was doing for a long damn time. I joined the rodeo when I was eighteen. I knew that I wanted to be the best. I knew I wanted to win. I *have* won it all. Several times. I knew that was my goal. I achieved it. On a smaller scale… I tend to know what I want out of a given day. I knew what I was going to do tonight. I was going to leave the arena, I was going to come to this bar. I was going to go over there," he said, gesturing to the corner where there was a jukebox, and a gaggle of women dressed to the nines, their hair done up, their best push-up bras doing admirable work.

"I was going to strike up a conversation with one of those women, and we would've both known from the very beginning exactly where that conversation was going. We'd have had sex. Sorry. But it's true. I would've said goodbye, and she would've been on her way." He shrugged. "Yeah. I usually know exactly what I'm doing. I have no idea what I'm doing right now. No idea what's happening here. And I guess maybe that's part of why I like it. Why I'm interested. Because you ran into me… And changed the course of my evening. I think I'd have to be a particular kind of fool not to see where that went."

"It won't be bed."

"You've been very clear on that. And I have no interest in pushing."

She sat with that for a minute. Did that mean that he would have liked her that way if she'd said she wanted it? She had never been particularly flattered by the attentions of cowboys. In fact, just the opposite. Her mother had always made it very clear that cowboys had absolutely no standards. *"Darlin',"* she'd said. *"Men will stick it in the hole of a hollow tree. Don't you ever let yourself feel flattered because they want to put it in you."*

She knew that it came from a place of protectiveness. A little rough around the edges though it was. Darlene Martin was rough around the edges. It was part of what Tansey loved about her.

Her mom had taught her how to arm herself, protect herself, where she hadn't been able to do the same. Tansey was appreciative of that. She learned all of her mother's lessons, so she didn't have to learn her own.

If she wasn't careful, a man like Flint Carson could be a very difficult lesson.

But you know better. And this is just a conversation.

"What are your dreams?" he asked, leaning back in his chair. "You want to win it all in the rodeo?"

"I wouldn't be opposed. But… My dad is Huck Jones."

He frowned. "I know that name."

"Yeah. He's done roping and a few other events, plus general setup and teardown work, with the rodeo for a long time. I got into the rodeo to be closer to him. To find him again. Because I was a kid when he left and…"

"Taillights," he said.

"Yeah. And I guess I thought that I was going to change something. Redeem something, fix something by finding him. But you know what? He's never around. Even though I tried coming to him, I haven't ever encountered him. He hasn't been competing. I… I thought at least he would see me, and he would want to get to know me. If I was doing something that interested him.

I thought that I would matter. I thought that I would matter more. I really did. I guess I thought maybe the hearth-and-home thing wasn't for him, but if I took myself out on the road…"

"Right. Well. What a prick."

And that made her laugh. "Thanks for that. I think so too."

Except it hurt. It hurt a lot. And there was a reason she didn't go around just talking about this, but it was such a strange thing. To be sitting here like this with him. She had felt like she didn't want to leave his side from the moment she fell against him. This felt natural. And maybe that was why she felt compelled to ask him what it was they were doing. Because it shouldn't feel natural. Not to her, not to him.

They shouldn't just want to sit and talk to each other with no ulterior motives. In this world, in any world, it didn't seem to be a thing as far as she could tell.

And yet.

"What else? You didn't say that your dream was to win big here."

"I enjoy barrel racing. But no. It's not my dream."

"What's your dream?" he asked.

"I… I just recorded a demo. I… I want to be a singer. Well, I'm a songwriter. Really. And if what I end up doing is selling songs, that's fine too. It's okay if I don't actually end up being famous or anything like that." Except she kind of did want to be famous. She kind of did want to show him. She wanted to buy her mom a big house and end up on TV. She wanted to force him to see exactly what he'd walked away from. He acted like she was an anchor. Something that was dragging him down, holding him back.

She wanted to prove that she would've been the thing that got him ahead.

Better than he could do for himself.

Maybe that was bitter and toxic. But she couldn't help herself.

"Well. They do say the best revenge is living well," he said.

That was like balm.

He understood. He got it. She hadn't even had to say any of those dark, ugly things that rolled around inside of her chest. He just knew. He understood.

"Yeah. Well. That would be about the favorite revenge, I have to say. Especially because that version of revenge involves some pretty nice cowgirl boots."

"If you win the overall prize barrel racing this year, I'll buy you some boots."

"I don't need a man to buy my boots," she said. "That's the point."

"I get that. But maybe it would be nice if there was a man who wanted to buy you boots?"

"Sorry. I don't think that's a very good goal either."

"Why is that?"

"My mama raised me to be independent. At the end of the day, the only person you can depend on is…you."

She felt sad for herself just saying it, and she waited for him to look at her with pity. But he didn't. That was the interesting thing about him. He looked her straight in the eye. He looked at her like an equal.

He was a strange sort of man. Not exactly what she'd thought.

Though she was wary of him all the same.

"Can't you depend on your mom?"

She hesitated. "Yes. Though she is also an independent woman, so she has her own life. We stand for each other, but we mostly stand alone."

"I see."

"You have a lot of family, don't you?"

He nodded. "Yeah, I'm lousy with brothers." He hesitated for a moment. "And you probably know my sister, Callie. She was barrel racing until pretty recently."

She nodded. "Yeah, I do know her a bit. We're close to the same age."

He winced. "Right."

"You must never be lonely."

He chuckled. "I didn't say that."

"Oh."

"I respect that you want to stand on your own feet," he said, his tone switching abruptly. "But you can't stop me from buying a pair of boots for you to stand in if you win."

"I'd have to win," she pointed out. "And I'm not number one right now. Or did you not notice?"

"I didn't notice. I was too busy catching you when you tripped."

He met her gaze for too long. She looked away.

"Okay. So tell me how to win."

"You have to love nothing more than the moment you're in. Think about nothing more. Care about nothing more. You didn't ask me what my dreams were."

"Okay then... What are your dreams?" she asked.

"I don't have any."

"Oh."

"But that's why I win. Because it's very easy for nothing else to matter to me. Nothing but the moment. Nothing but the ride. Nothing else tugging on my attention. Nothing splintering my focus. There's not a single damn person out there that I care about more than I care about that moment. Not a single thing. Not a truck, not a house. Nothing. That's how I do it."

"You don't… You have a really big family…"

"Yeah. I mean… I love them. I do. But… I'm very good at putting a wall up over my emotions. In fact, I'm not entirely sure that I could get to them now if I wanted to."

He said it so casually. But she had a feeling that it was true. A deep truth. And one that he probably didn't go around speaking out loud. And he told her because… because they were able to talk to each other. Because it just worked.

If he wasn't going to question it, then neither was she.

"I'm not sure that I can do that. I care about too many things. Sometimes I feel like I care about… Everything," she said.

"You just have to learn to shut it off. Don't burn so bright with passion that you let it smoke you out." He snapped his finger. "You have to remember it can work for you. It can get you where you're at right now. But don't let it sabotage you either."

"Thanks."

She finished her beer. And the two of them stood.

They left together, and she was keenly aware of the fact that people were watching them. She made a show of putting a lot of distance between their bodies as they walked through the parking lot, and across the street.

"Bye," she said, waving.

"See you at the next stop."

"Yeah. See you then."

After

"So we're the only two people here?" she asked.

"That's about the size of it. And I don't know what's going on, if a tower got knocked out or something, but there's no cell service. We've got a landline, as long as that holds."

"Are you letting me know how easy it would be for you to kill me and bury me in a snowbank?"

His lips quirked up on the side. "I wouldn't do that. You're famous. Too many people would miss you."

It was the edge to him that surprised her, though.

Does it? If he's heard the song... You know him. You know how private he is, how protected.

Yes. And on some level, she knew that if he ever did hear the song, he would probably view it as a betrayal. And maybe part of her wanted that. Had wanted to pour out her own pain and anguish, to make everybody understand the intimacy of it. What he had taken from her. Not her virginity, it was deeper than that.

She had never slept with another man before, and she hadn't slept with one since, because she had been afraid of being hurt.

That was the part that got her.

That he knew what it had meant to her to give herself to him.

Yeah, she could see how maybe he would be upset that she had advertised that. But hell, people didn't know that it was him. Well. They did know that it was him. There were entire online forums dedicated to analyzing every single part of the song. If her scarf was a metaphor, or if it was real. If she was writing about the bull rider that she had been seen with on the coast that summer she'd gotten famous. Or if it had been a whirlwind affair in the studios with Harry Styles.

She had never met Harry Styles. But somehow, there were rumors about the two of them. Imaginary Tansey had a way more interesting love life than actual Tansey, who had one lover and a broken heart.

Your heart is not broken anymore. You just feel fragile because you are facing down your problematic past.

But yes, there were a lot of rumors. And many of them were true. It had been especially jarring to read a thread about lyrics where somebody had correctly identified the blood was about a miscarriage or a pregnancy scare. And it wasn't like it was subtle; it was just reading people trying to get deep into her words, rather than just applying their own experiences to it. Because to an extent, she had imagined that the song itself and what it could mean to people would be more interesting than what it had meant to her.

But somehow, she herself had become an object of fascination and… And that meant that people had wanted to know what the song meant for *her.*

But she had never said his name out loud. His name hadn't passed her lips once since they had parted that last day.

All that to say, she felt like she didn't fully deserve

his rage, but she also couldn't deny that she had known it would be there.

Deep down, she had known, because she knew *him*. If he hadn't thought she would write a song about it, then he had never really known her. Hadn't been paying attention. Not even when she had played him the song about her dad, the first song that had made her famous. The one that he had encouraged her to record. He had been an audience of one the first time she had ever played a song that had come so deep from her heart like that. And he had been the one who had said it was the key to her fame.

He'd been right.

As famous as the song about her dad had made her, the one about her heartbreak had taken things into the stratosphere.

That forced her to think about why she was here, and she'd rather not do that. So she focused instead on the blazing blue of his eyes.

She'd seen those eyes look a lot of ways.

But never angry. Not like this.

"Well. Good for me then. Because yeah, it would be kind of a bad idea for this to be the last place that I was headed, with you being the owner and all. That is a totally traceable murder. I wouldn't attempt it."

"Lucky for you, I'd rather have the notoriety of having you have stayed here, than I would getting rid of you."

His voice was hard, and it was like some of the anger was slowly beginning to subside. There was something flat there. Something unreadable. Except… She didn't trust it.

"What?"

"You're going to make sure that everybody knows that you stayed here. Wrote a song here or some shit."

"Right. So I'm going to tell everybody that I stayed at my ex... Sorry. Is it better if I just keep your name out of everything? Because we can go ahead and address the number-one hit in the room if you want."

"I don't want to talk about that shit. Except to say that you and I both know that whether you ever confirmed it or not, people know it's about me. I'm the one that gets yelled at by crazy fans walking down the street. You can deny it, you can refuse to address it, but the best thing you could do is show everybody that we're fine."

But they weren't fine. Nothing in her was fine. She felt utterly and absolutely rattled. And this was her retreat...

And it was never going to be again after this. Because he owned it now. She could never come here again.

If this was fate, fate was a bitch.

Or maybe this was all balancing the cost of what she'd been given. Maybe poor country girls didn't get to have fame and money if they weren't also given heartbreak and exes they couldn't forget.

"You know, that's quite the weird, blackmail-sounding thing that you can't make me do, but I think I would rather just leave."

"You're welcome to try. But the weather has picked up. Everybody else was smart and didn't come up. All my staff left. Because it was the smart thing to do. You were the only fool that decided to make the trek up."

"And I can make the trek back down." She turned around and started to head for the door. She pushed it open, and the wind just about blew it back. She shoved it, and headed back out into the night. Fuck all this, and him too. Him *specifically*.

Maybe there was a song in this.

That was the real problem. She couldn't think of a song. And she didn't want anyone to know that. She was completely dried up. She had written the greatest breakup album of all time. With a song that had reached into people's souls and taken hold of them. Had taken on a life of its own. She had done the same writing the song about her dad. She knew how to grab on to pain. She knew how to grab on to pain and turn it into something real and relatable.

And now she was famous and successful and…

And she was still sad. Because it had given her money. It had let her buy a house for her mom. But it hadn't given her a relationship with her dad.

And she was alone. And she couldn't figure out how to trust people any more than she could before.

Hell, it was even worse. Because the only person she had ever trusted was Flint. The only person that she had ever hoped might be more than he seemed was Flint.

And he had proved that he wasn't. And then she had gotten famous. And her ability to trust people had become even more compromised because people could actually get things from her. They actually wanted things from her, and that? That made everything feel fraught. It made everything feel impossible.

And now it felt like there were no more songs. Because all she had was old, lingering pain that she didn't want to keep writing about, and the thrill of a success story that she couldn't quite access. It made her feel ungrateful. It made her feel small and sad. To be standing in the spotlight and still feeling like she was shrouded in darkness. She was beginning to feel terrified that it would all go away. Because the only thing worse than the idea of staying in the spotlight, bombarded with all the fame, was what would happen if it went away.

Because one thing was sure. It was exposing to write a song like she had about her and Flint. But it gave her a way to expel some of that pain. It gave her a way to talk about it. She didn't have anyone in her life that she could talk about it honestly. The only person had been... Flint. And then it had ended. So she had written songs about him instead. And talked to the world about how he had let her down. There was a catharsis in that.

She battled the wind and walked down to her truck, forced the door open. All of her bags were still inside. The door to the hotel opened, and she saw Flint, up the stairs, looking down at her, backlit by the lights from the inside.

And he came down the stairs, heading out after her, the wind whipping the T-shirt he was wearing, tightening it over what she knew was a very firm body. And she did not need to be looking at him right now; she was trying to run away from him.

"What the hell do you think you're doing?" he shouted. "You were lucky to make it up here okay—you are not driving back down in this."

"You lost any right to have an opinion on what I do," she yelled back.

"Did I lose it, or did we agree to dissolve it?"

Well. There was the rub. With the wind and the snow blowing between them, and ferocity and fear burning in his blue eyes.

"I was protecting myself. If you were worried about anything other than your own feelings in that moment, you would've known that."

"You should've said it all to *me*," he said.

The song. That was what he meant. That she should have said all those things to him, and not the world.

It hurt, because it wasn't unfair.

"What would it have changed?" she asked.

She was breathing hard, and so was he.

"Nothing," he said, his voice rough.

It was hard to hear. For one moment she'd forgotten. For one moment she'd hoped. But this was the reality of it, of them.

"Okay then. Don't lecture me. Don't lecture me on what I should've done. Don't lecture me on what the right thing to do would have been when I told you that I might be having your baby and you looked back at me and said you didn't want it."

"If you had…"

"You never even texted me back."

"Because you said that you weren't."

"I wasn't. Or maybe I was. But I lost it either way. I never took a test."

"I'm sorry. If you had been…"

"Is this what you do? Tell yourself if I'd been pregnant you would have handled it well? You didn't handle anything about it well. What makes you think you would have been better if there was a baby? You're rewriting the story."

"We all get to write our own stories, Tansey, you of all people should know."

The words hit hard, and he stood there, blue eyes blazing.

"I'm leaving."

"Don't," he bit out. "It's too fucking dangerous. You're not leaving just because you don't like me."

"I have to leave."

She just had to. She couldn't stay, not with him. It was too much, too real.

Nothing had been real like this since him.

And she couldn't stand it.

Chapter 3

She got into the truck and started the engine, and he stood there in front of the vehicle, the headlights pouring over his body. She found some joyful irony in that. That she was the one driving away. When she had written a whole hit about the taillights on her father's truck, and watching him leave.

This should be a triumph. As soon as she started back down the winding road to the main highway, she regretted trying to leave.

There was snow all over the road, and her tires were slick. She had four-wheel drive, but this was solid ice. The temperature had dropped with the passing of time, and the movement of the storm.

Her truck was slipping and sliding, and her heart was pounding. She tried to drive slow, tried not to put herself in a position where she would have to brake suddenly, which would cause her to slide right off the road and over the edge of the embankment. Her palms were slick. She rounded the corner, and had to slam on her brakes, because there was a giant tree down in the middle of the road. Stretching from end to end. Her breathing was ragged, and she could barely hear it over the sound of the wind whipping against the side of her truck.

Shit. What was she going to do? She couldn't even turn around. The road was too narrow. And she would have to…to walk back up and…

There was a pounding on the door of the truck. She jumped, and turned toward the passenger side, and saw Flint standing there looking in the window. "Come back to the hotel," he shouted.

He was shouting because of the roar of the wind; she knew that, except he still sounded angry.

"No, thanks."

"Fucking hell, Tansey, don't be suicidal because you don't want to see me."

He didn't understand. It felt like suicide to see him. To be sharing air with him. To be sharing the same space with him. Because the problem was, he was still beautiful. And no matter how she had rewritten him into the perfect storybook villain, no matter how she tried to make herself remember only that terrible moment when he had shut all of his emotions off, and had been a blank wall she couldn't see through, couldn't reach through, couldn't get through, when she saw him, she had to remember that he was a whole human being. A man. Flesh and blood.

A man who had kissed her, touched her, given her pleasure.

A man who had held her, and cared for her, and given her things that no one else ever had before. And then taken them away from her.

Yeah. It was easier to remember him as the collection of truths she had put into that song. Because every line had been true. But he was right. It had been a story. Carefully chosen details designed to create a neat narrative. One that highlighted the things that had been so good they were painful, the things that had cost her. The risks she had taken. But none of his.

She hadn't put in all the ways he'd helped her, respected her, listened to her...

Hadn't put any of his risk, any of his vulnerability into it. Because even though he'd never opened up to her, not all the way, even though he'd never told her why he was the way he was, she'd seen how he was. That being with her scared him sometimes.

All the fear, the vulnerability in her song... It had all been hers. And so in the end it had been about her pain, because she hadn't given any credit to the idea that he might have had any.

But looking at him now, she knew the man. The whole man. Not just the one from the song.

And it made her ache.

It was why her little fantasy about running into him and coolly walking away could never actually happen. Because it wasn't really Flint in that fantasy. Just a hollow stand-in that looked like him. Not one that embodied his heat, his life. Everything he was.

"Come on," he said.

"I can't turn around," she said.

"I know," he said. "If you get in the ditch right now,

you're never getting back out of it. And it's too slick to try. So just get out of the truck and leave it here. No one else is getting past that tree either. We are going to have to get a chainsaw out and cut it into pieces to move it. And we could do it now, but to what end? There's just going to be more obstacles down the road. There's a hotel a quarter of a mile back that way."

"We have to…walk back?"

"Yes. We both have to walk back. Because you were playing the part of idiot in a horror movie. Congratulations."

"You're being such an asshole," she said.

"You too."

And it was only then that she realized they were literally shouting at each other over the howl of the wind and through the window of her truck. And her own voice was ringing sharply around her, and she didn't like it.

Reluctantly, she got out of the truck.

"Where are your bags?" he said, his voice hard.

"Just behind the seat…"

He reached back there and grabbed her duffel bag, and her guitar, slamming the door shut with his elbow.

"You don't have to carry…"

"If I were you, I would give it a rest. You can stop telling me what I can and can't do, and what I should and shouldn't do, because people who run off into blizzards don't get to make proclamations."

He wasn't wearing a coat. He had come after her in only that T-shirt, and she was so aware of how the wind was biting at him, but he just put his head down and kept walking forward.

It made her feel small, and strange. She was walking

directly behind him, and she realized that she was using his body to help shield her from the wind.

And that was sort of a humbling realization. She couldn't say she cared for it.

She was freezing, and she was wearing a coat. His arms were bare.

And this was the problem with Flint. There were these moments. Because this was exactly who she'd begun to believe that he was. The man that would shield her from everything. The man that would carry it all on his shoulders. And that was more, and different, than the sharp heartbreak she had been carrying around all this time. It was a deeper, more fully realized regret.

All that she didn't have because of what she had wanted him to become.

Because she hadn't been wrong about everything. Because that was the problem with a heartbreak anthem. It didn't give credit to the good things. And it was the good things that made losing love sad.

It was the fact that he was the man who would chase her down in a snowstorm, block the wind and carry her bags, while he was wearing only a T-shirt.

There was good in him, that was the issue. When things were wonderful, they were just amazing. But when he shut down, it was like he was a blizzard all by himself.

She couldn't reach him.

When he was cruel, it cut deep.

There was something in him that made him like this and she didn't know what it was. Didn't understand what had shaped him into this man who was so perfect in so many ways, until he wasn't.

Of course, the fact that she didn't know what his issues were was his fault. He could have shared with her. He could give her something. He could tell her more about himself. But he had never wanted to. He had told her what he couldn't give, but he hadn't told her why.

Maybe there was no *why*.

Except, she had one. Her reasons for not being able to trust were specific, and ample. And he'd added another layer to it. It was neat, explainable. Easily written into songs, and easily folded into stories.

Him? He hadn't given her those pieces. But she knew enough about people to know they must be there. And to know that he wasn't sharing for a very specific reason.

But she didn't actually want to feel charitable toward him. And even though he had just saved her from a storm, he had also been the reason that she had run out into the storm. Because he hadn't even bothered to not be a jackass to her.

He did ask you to stay.

Fine. He had. But it was much too little, too late, and it wasn't when she had wanted him to ask her to stay.

The walk was icy and cold, and her boots were not equipped for the task. She slipped as she tried to get up the hill, and a squeak came out of her mouth, and he whipped around, dropping her duffel bag and grabbing her arm, keeping her from falling. She looked up at him, and their eyes met. And she was brought right back to that first time they'd met each other.

When she'd stumbled coming out of the gate.

And everything in her went still.

The terrible thing was looking up at him and knowing exactly what she'd seen in him. Knowing exactly what she'd been thinking. And knowing that if she had been put in that exact same position all over again, she would've made the same mistakes. Over and over again.

Because there was something about him. Something about him that was her own personal brand of favorite mistake.

It was horrifying.

"I'm fine," she said, pulling herself out of his hold.

"Right."

Words bubbled up inside of her. Ones she shouldn't speak. But… They had been apart for two years, and there were endless wells of unspoken words between them.

Why should she give him the benefit of leaving it all unspoken anymore?

"It might make you happy to know I don't need my mom to warn me about cowboys anymore. I have my own warnings."

"Good. Listen to them," he said. "Because God knew mine weren't enough."

"Excuse me?"

"It's not like I didn't tell you." He picked up the duffel bag.

"We were…whatever we were for how many months? You gave me warnings, but you never gave me reasons."

"Why do I have the feeling that's going into a song?"

"It already is," she said.

"Wow. Quoting your own song lyrics at me. That's something."

She growled, and went ahead of him. She didn't need him to shield her from the wind. She didn't need him to shield her from anything. She didn't need anything from him.

"You don't know your way around here as well as I do," he said.

"You don't even know how many times I've been here," she said.

Three. But she didn't need to tell him that.

"Yeah. But I've actually been staying up here for the last couple of weeks," he said. "Making sure the transition went smoothly. There are some changes that I'm going to make."

"What are you…? What are you doing, anyway? You never expressed any interest in owning hotels."

"Yeah. Well. My brother and his fiancée bought a hotel in Lone Rock. He's more of a silent investor, but I found the whole thing really interesting. So I started looking around for properties. And this came up. I thought it was perfect. But I'm also looking at a hotel in downtown Portland. And considering something in Nashville."

"Right. Why Nashville?"

He shrugged. "Music city. Exciting."

"You know you don't have to tell me that."

"I do know," he said, his voice heavy with irony.

"Why would you buy something in a place where you might actually be in proximity to me? Since you hate me so much. Apparently."

"Why do you sing about the end of our relationship every single day?"

Ouch.

"Because it makes me a lot of money." He didn't say anything after that. Neither of them did. Finally, the lights of the hotel came into view.

"I'm surprised there's still power," she said.

"There's a backup generator, and some backup solar as well, with energy stored that we can feed off of. Because this is so rural, these kinds of things are a problem, even when the weather isn't this bad."

She huffed, and pushed through the lobby door. It wasn't a huge hotel, but it probably had about one hundred rooms. All in a big, gleaming log-cabin-style structure. The furniture was made of rough-hewn wood, with big geometric-patterned rugs over every surface.

She had always found the place restful. And had also found that nobody here was overly impressed with celebrity even if they did realize who she was, so she enjoyed the peace that came with it.

There was no peace now, though. There was Flint.

"What brought you to Oregon? Because you know this is where I am."

"Weirdly, Flint, I didn't think of you at all." She had enjoyed staying in Oregon when she had come with him, and they'd done quite a bit of traveling around the state with the rodeo. The Pendleton Round-Up and the big event in Sisters were both huge, and she had enjoyed being there every time.

That was all. She didn't necessarily think of Flint when she thought of the state.

Liar.

"Right. Fair. So maybe I didn't think of you when I thought of Tennessee."

"Except you sorta said you did."

"Maybe it was because a certain song came on the radio. Tough to say."

"Which room am I in?"

"Well. You can take your pick," he said. "The one we have you down for is the suite, though, and I imagine, given how fancy you are these days, that's what you want."

She scoffed. "What do you mean how fancy I am?"

"Don't tell me those aren't six-hundred-dollar jeans."

She blushed. Because yes. Her jeans were expensive. She had never imagined she would become that person. It was the weirdest thing. The way her money meter had adjusted. How she had gone from spending thirty dollars on a pair of jeans to one hundred, to more. And each incremental increase, as her income had gone up, hadn't really seemed like much of anything at all.

And to think, she'd once been so disdainful of people she thought of as excessive. But she hadn't done much to keep herself from enjoying certain kinds of excess that had come with her success.

She didn't drink, she didn't do drugs and there had been absolutely no sex since parting from Flint, so surely expensive clothes and a new truck were reasonable. Also a new house. And a house for her mother. *Of course* a house for her mother. That had been the most important.

"There's no reason for me to not take the suite," she said.

"Full-service. I'll walk you there."

"You don't need to," she said, holding her hands out for her bag and her guitar. "I'm going to go get settled in."

"All right. Do you want some dinner?"

Her stomach growled. And she really wished it hadn't, because she would like to say that she didn't need dinner, but she had been planning on eating here. The food was wonderful; she remembered that from her last visit. Except…

"Where is the food going to come from?"

"There was a certain amount preprepared by the chef in anticipation of the weather."

"Great. I'll have some of that after I get settled in."

"Well, let me get you your key."

He went behind the counter, the counter that he had been behind when she had first walked in, when he had stood up and nearly given her a heart attack. He took out a key card, and ran it through the device that programmed it before handing it to her.

"Thanks," she said, but his fingertips brushed hers, and she hadn't expected it. And all of the air in her lungs felt like it had been removed. Evaporated.

They just stood there for a moment. And memories swirled through her head. Memories she'd rather not have.

She took a step back. Decisively.

She needed a shower. She needed to get her head on straight. This was all unexpected, and a little bit too much.

She walked up the big, curved staircase—made of the same sort of log as the rest of the big lobby area—and headed down the hall toward the room she had stayed in before.

She unlocked the door, and let herself in. There was a large four-poster bed at the center of the room, done with plush bedding. There was a window seat, which she had spent a lot of time in last time. And a desk in the corner. She set her things down, and opened up her bag. She found her writing notebook, well-worn, but not used recently, and set it on the desk. Then she took her pen out, and…

She pulled out a little neon cactus key chain. It didn't light up anymore—the batteries were dead, and she hadn't been able to bring herself to replace the batteries, because that would be admitting that it mattered to her.

She ran her fingers over it, staring. And then she set it down next to the notebook.

This was the situation she was in. So she might as well embrace it. Might as well live in it.

What else could she do?

Chapter 4

He waited an hour, and then he went into the kitchen and dug around for one of those preprepared meals. There were strict instructions on how to reheat the steak without overcooking it, and how to plate the meal and all of that. He ignored a good portion of them, because he didn't care about whether or not it looked fancy. But for some reason, he did feel compelled to serve her something that tasted good. Hell, if he was too petty, she'd write a song called "Overcooked Steak" and he'd never hear the end of it.

He stopped for a second, and simply stood there. Tansey was here.

Tansey Martin. The only woman who had ever gotten under his skin.

The woman he had told himself he was outraged at for the last two years.

Outraged because she reminded him of all of the things in himself he hated.

And she was still beautiful.

Hell, it was no mystery why he'd gotten involved with her.

Remember when you didn't think she was your type?

Yeah. He remembered it vividly. He also remembered the first time he had tried to hook up after he and Tansey had parted ways. And hadn't been able to muster up even the tiniest bit of interest in the beauty queen he was chatting up. He had ended up going home alone. As he had every night since then.

Two years. It was a hell of a dry spell.

But he was too filled up with demons to want sex. That was the problem.

What you need is an exorcism.

He tried not to think about her, or how beautiful she was, or the fact that they were alone here, and it was pretty much prime time for the sort of exorcism that he was thinking of.

No way. Never again. Not her.

He already knew how that ended.

But you can only ever have relationships that end. So why not?

The carrots finished reheating and he put them on the plate, not caring at all how they were arranged, and then he covered the plate with a big domed lid, and started up the stairs.

He knocked on the door, and a few moments later, she opened it.

Her hair was wet, and she was wearing a white plush bathrobe. It covered everything. From the base of her throat down to her ankles. It was huge on her. But he was so very aware of the fact that she had just been in the shower. He could remember showering with her.

His hands moving over her slick curves... "Dinner," he bit out.

"Oh. I didn't realize it was room service," she said.

"Yeah. This is a fancy ass establishment, Tansey. I figured you knew that. Since you're the resident expert on the place."

He walked in, and looked around, then he saw that the desk had space. But he stopped when he got over there, because her notebook was sitting there, and beside it...

Beside it was the cactus.

Before

He didn't know what possessed him to buy a little neon cactus, didn't know what possessed him to stick it in the cab of her truck before they departed for the next stop. But he did.

And when she came to find him when they got to Sedona, with the little light hanging from her finger, and a strange expression on her face, he felt something expand inside of him. "What's that?"

"A reminder," he said. "A talisman. Stay prickly. And remember to put a wall up when you get on that horse. Don't think about anything but the ride."

"What does a cactus have to do with a wall, Ace?"

"Because we were in the Cactus when we talked about it," he said.

"Okay. Your symbolism sucks. But I'll hang on to it."

He watched her ride that night; she won. He went

to find her after, and gave her a high five. "It was the cactus," he said.

She rolled her eyes. "It was not the cactus."

"It was the damn cactus. You can't prove that it wasn't."

That was how he found himself asking her out for a drink again. This time, they had two beers. Not just the one.

And she didn't put quite so much space between the two of them when they left.

They had three nights in Sedona. She won every single one.

On the last night, it was three beers.

"Okay. So now I'm in the second position. But that doesn't mean you're going to buy me boots," she said.

"The hell I won't," he said, jamming his finger on the table. "Have you not figured out that I don't let anyone tell me what to do?"

"I don't know. I haven't really pondered you all that much."

"Liar," he said. It was a little bit more flirtatious than he had been with her.

She wasn't his type.

That was the thing.

But she was awfully damn pretty in the bar light. And just after she finished her ride, even with those fluorescent lights shining down on her. She was pretty in every light—that was the thing.

But not his type.

"I never lie," she said. "Not ever."

"Because your daddy was a liar?"

"I assume he still is. He's not dead, and his mouth is still moving."

"Fair."

"What about you, Flint?" She rarely called him by his name. She usually called him Ace. He didn't know why. He liked it, though. "Are you a liar?"

"I try not to be."

"That's not very definitive."

"How about this. I don't know if I'm a liar or not. Because I don't get close enough to anyone to need to lie."

"I'm not sure I follow."

"You lie to protect yourself, right? You lie to make people think better of you, mostly. I've never needed to do that, because I've never cared enough to do it."

"Well," she said, and suddenly, the bar seemed quieter. "I guess that's about as honest as a person can be."

"Like I said. I try."

He downed the last of his beer and they both got up, walking out the door. This time, it was a little bit farther of a walk to the motel, but they'd decided to walk so they could drink. They took the walk back kind of slow.

For some reason, he stopped. But she seemed to have the same idea he did. He turned to her. The sky above was lit up only with stars, and he could see them reflected in her eyes.

He couldn't remember the last time he'd wanted to kiss a woman. Just kiss. That was what he wanted to do then. He wanted to reach out and cradle her cheek in his hand and feel how soft her skin was. He wanted to lean in and press his mouth to hers, but slowly.

He just wanted to kiss her.

He didn't want to take her back to his motel room.

He didn't want… He didn't want anything but to kiss her. She hadn't said that he couldn't kiss her.

"Ace," she whispered. "Please don't."

He took a step back. "Okay."

They started walking again.

"Did you only stop because…because I asked you to stop? Were you going to…?"

"Yeah. To both."

She nodded. And then they reached the motel parking lot. And she beat a hasty retreat toward her room, which was at the opposite end of the complex. And he wondered if he had ruined whatever this was. And for some reason he felt…torn up with regret over that.

He didn't want to lose her.

He knew that much. So he wouldn't let himself be that stupid again.

After

"You still have this," he said.

Tansey looked at him in horror. She hadn't meant to leave that there. But then, she hadn't known that he was going to come here. She hadn't realized that he was actually going to come to her room to bring her dinner. And she felt exposed. She felt unmasked in some strange way.

"Everybody needs a good-luck charm," she said, her heart pounding hard.

"I would've thought that this wasn't a good-luck charm to you anymore."

"Well. That's the thing. You don't know me. Maybe you never really did."

"I think I did," he said, his voice rough.

"Well. Well." She took the lid off the food. "I'm actually not… The thing is, Flint. That was the first relationship that I ever had. You know that. Because I told you a lot of things about myself. It was the first relationship that I ever had, and the first heartbreak that I ever had. Of course I wrote about it. I'm…" She was trying to decide if she was going to outright lie to him or not. "I'm sorry. I didn't consider how it would make you feel when I released the song." That was partly true. Because if she had considered it at all, she'd hoped that it would make him *see*. She'd hoped that it would upset him.

She had hoped that it would show him.

She'd hoped that it would hurt him.

"I only thought about how I felt." What she had felt had been the only thing that mattered. "And I'm not actually invested in people yelling at you on streets. I've never asked anyone to do that, and I've never confirmed that the song is about you for that reason. I don't like any of that. I never asked anyone for it."

She sat down, and took a bite of her steak. "Do you want to have dinner?"

"What?" he asked.

"Let's just have dinner together." She didn't know why she felt compelled to do this. Except…here they were. Thrown together for a reason.

There had to be a reason, right? Fate, or Christmas magic or something.

She did still have the cactus. She needed…something. She needed something to jar her inspiration loose. Being with him these past couple hours she'd had more complicated feelings than she'd had in the past two years.

She felt more alive.

And she might be angry, that was for damn sure, but at least she felt something.

That feeling of wistfulness that she'd had when she'd been watching him walk in front of her—the feeling he might be a better man than he'd been when they'd broken up, but the man that she had always imagined he *might* be—was the beginning of a song. Was the beginning of something.

It was what she was here for.

And anyway, she knew better now. She wasn't in love with him anymore. Yes, she was still kind of angry. Yes, the hurt was still there. And yes, he was still beautiful. But she knew better now. Intensely, and wholly.

"We can eat downstairs," she said.

She resolutely picked her plate up. "Come on."

"Do you want to get dressed?" he asked.

She suddenly realized she was still in her robe.

"Oh. Yes. I do." She set her plate down. "I'll meet you downstairs?"

"Yeah," he said.

By the time she'd gotten her sweats on, she was resolved. Determined. She was going to use this to find a new angle on their relationship. She was going to use this as a way to heal.

And maybe it would also heal whatever was happening with her music.

Because she needed that. Otherwise that would really mean that the most exciting and wonderful part of her life was over. She had fallen in love and lost it. She had success and it was slipping away…

She pushed those thoughts away.

There was more for her. There was.

Flint Carson was not the end of her road.

But he might be the key to her reclaiming some of her creativity. And she was going to run with that.

Except thinking like that forced her to think back, and the whole time she headed down the stairs, she was thinking about him. And about how tonight paralleled another moment he'd come to her rescue.

Before

She felt like a coward leaving the motel as early as she did, a coward for avoiding Flint. But he'd been about to kiss her. Or he'd at least been *considering* kissing her.

And she'd…she'd panicked. Because she wanted to kiss him. She wanted to kiss him so much it consumed her every waking moment. She couldn't do that. Because…

He's not just a cowboy, though. He's Flint.

He's your friend.

Yes. He had become her friend over these last few days. It seemed improbable and strange. But she liked him. He was the highlight of every day. She…

She was headed down the highway when her truck started to overheat. Persistently.

"Shit," she shouted. She hit the steering wheel with the palm of her hand. "Shit."

Smoke started to pour out the top of the engine and she pulled to the side of the road.

She sat there. And she looked at her phone. No service. No damn service. What the hell was she supposed to do? It was Arizona, and it was hot.

She squinted and looked up ahead. There was a call box, blessed be. She got out of the truck, panic making her move quickly. It was hot, and she had Cinderella in the trailer, and she needed to get gone.

She was halfway between her truck and the call box when she heard the sound of another engine. She stopped and looked behind her. It was a sleek, shiny Chevy pickup, and it pulled sharply off the road behind her.

She ran back toward her truck, ran back... And realized exactly who it was.

"Flint," she said, not knowing if she sounded scared or relieved... Relieved. Overly relieved.

"What happened?"

"I overheated. It's this...this shitty truck. I need a new truck. It's fine."

"Well, if you win..."

"Do not offer to buy me a truck, Flint Carson," she said.

She stuck her finger out toward him, and he grabbed it, and shook it, the contact of his skin against hers making her tremble. She pulled it away, and took a step back.

"Okay, I won't offer," he said.

"Flint..."

"I have an idea. I'll unhitch your trailer, we'll get it hooked up to my truck, and we'll call someone and have them get yours. Then we'll get on the road together so you and your steed aren't sitting here in the heat. How does that sound?"

There was no way to argue with this. She'd tried to avoid him, she'd broken down. He was the one who'd found her.

Maybe it was fate.

"Thank you."

About half an hour later, they were driving down the highway in Flint's truck, with his superior air-conditioning keeping them both cool.

"Lucky I happened down the road when I did."

She could argue. She could say that it wasn't lucky, because there was a call box, and while it would've been a whole thing, she could've handled getting out of there herself. But this was better. And not just because she had been rescued sooner. Because she was with him.

"Yeah. I was lucky. Look, I… I'm sorry." She wanted to fix what happened last night. The way that she had freaked out and overreacted.

"You don't need to apologize to me for anything."

"I was weird about last night. And I was avoiding you. It's why I tried to leave really early today. But apparently we both had the same idea. And thank God," she said.

"It was my mistake. You made yourself clear. I was trying to give myself a loophole. You know, a kiss isn't a one-night stand."

"Now that's a song title," she said.

"It would be a good one."

There was nothing but the sound of the tires on the road. "You really just wanted to kiss me?"

"Right in that moment, yeah. Now, what I would've wanted thirty seconds after that…"

She leaned across the cabin and pushed his shoulder. He was solid and warm, and she could smell soap and his skin, and she regretted all that a little bit.

The touching. It was dangerous.

Why?

She shoved that to the side. She shoved that ridiculous question right to the side, because she knew that it was dangerous. She wanted to be friends with him. He had helped her; their friendship was valuable to her. She enjoyed talking to him, and he had given her the cactus, which now—against her will—seemed to function as a good-luck token.

He had rescued her from the side of the road.

It didn't have to be dangerous, this thing. It didn't have to be wrong or bad. It could be good. But she had to be… It had to be *not* kissing. It had to be friendship.

"I really like you," she said. And she felt so stupid with those words coming out of her mouth. He was a man. A man who had one-night stands. A man who probably didn't have silly girls saying that they liked him.

And when she had said it, she hadn't meant to be confessing that she *liked* him. It had started out as a speech about how he was a really good friend. But the truth was…she liked him. In all the middle school glory that it implied.

It was just that she wanted to be his friend more.

"You're the only real friend that I've made on the circuit," she said. "You're the only friend I've had in a long time."

"Same," he said, his voice sounding rough.

"It just matters a lot to me. This."

And he didn't say anything for at least an hour of the drive.

Chapter 5

After

When she came down the stairs, he had his own dinner ready, and had sat down at one of the tables in the dining room. He was still wearing jeans and a short-sleeve shirt, and she was in sweats, no makeup on her face.

He wondered what her adoring fans would think of her now.

They would probably love her for this. Classic Tansey. So down-to-earth.

If he happened to look at the things that people said about her, well. He was only human. He didn't have an endless amount of resistance and restraint where she was concerned. But then, he never had. It had always been... It had always been fraught. She had always been someone that he couldn't look away from. No matter how he couldn't explain it.

"Why exactly did you want to have dinner together?" he asked.

"Because this is ridiculous. Because…because you were an important part of my life, Flint. And now we don't even talk."

"As far as I know, that's how breakups go. Admittedly, I'm not an expert."

"Oh. So you admit that it was a breakup?"

"Yes," he said, his voice rough.

There was no point denying it. Because there was no point denying that they had been entangled in each other in a way he wished they fucking hadn't been. In a way they *shouldn't* have been. In a way he never had been with anyone else, and never would be again.

But here they were, and somehow it was like something entirely different and something altogether the same. Because he hadn't been charming for a single moment since she'd walked into his hotel, and he had no intention of being charming.

He didn't put up the performance for her.

But then, he never had.

She'd never believed it. She didn't buy into the facade that he had put up to interact with the world.

What he knew about himself was that he was a bigger bastard than most people realized.

Boone knew.

Boone knew better than anybody else, and seemed to forgive him for it, but that was kind of what younger brothers were for, he supposed. They had to see you better than you saw yourself. They had to see you better than anybody else did.

Didn't mean that *he* should.

Because Boone knew the truth, and he was still the brother that Flint was closest to.

And Tansey knew the truth.

Without even knowing any of the details of his life, she knew the truth.

Because he had shown her. He had shown her what he did when the chips were down.

Even with all that discomfort, there was something… undeniable about it. His connection to her. The same way there always had been.

Because he was himself when he was with her. Unvarnished and raw and not even bothering with the face he tended to show the world. And it was true now too.

Except she took that and she wrote a song about it. And she might do it again.

"I want… Do you want royalties from the song?" she said, as if she read his mind.

Everything in him rejected that. Everything in him was disgusted by the offer. Outraged by it. "No, I don't want to make any money on that shit," he said. "I don't want to make any money off of the things that you told everybody about us."

There they were, eating really good steak, and not getting along at all, and he had a feeling that wasn't at all what she had expected out of having dinner with him. Or what she had wanted. But here they were. And he was committed to the lack of facade. Because why couldn't they just be honest? Because he had been telling his brothers for two years now that the song wasn't about him. He'd been telling anyone who asked that it wasn't about him.

Part of him had told *himself* that it wasn't.

That she'd made it up. Because she hadn't fought him. She hadn't said any of those things *to* him. So maybe there *had* been another man.

Except he knew he was the first. Except he knew that he was the one.

And he knew that he had her scarf.

He had it here.

Just like she had the cactus. So whatever other stories they told, whatever they had told each other the moment that it had all ended, there were lies buried in there. And that much he knew. Even if he didn't know himself well enough to know what the hell all the lies were. Or what he was supposed to do about them. Because he hadn't known what to do then, and he knew even less of what he was supposed to do now.

Except his feelings were carefully kept behind the wall in his chest that he normally kept them behind. She was here and he was angry. She was here and he thought she was beautiful.

She was here, and they were having dinner in this fancy dining room, with her in sweats and him in his mud-covered boots, and they were fighting.

Whatever it was…it was real, and it was them.

So he was just going with it.

"Is that how you feel? That it was wrong for me to make money off of it?" she asked.

"Yeah. I fucking do. Because it was…"

"You told me it was nothing, Flint."

"And you told me it was fine. So are we going to be angry with each other now for a lack of honesty?"

"That was never why I was angry with you."

"Why *are* you angry with me then?" he asked.

"Because you ended it. I didn't want it to end. And you know what, I was too afraid to tell you that. Because I knew it wouldn't make a difference, and I knew that it would just…expose me. But now here I am sitting with you, and you might be mad at me about the song, but I'm kind of mad at myself about it too, because now you *know*. All the things that I didn't say, all the things that I couldn't say, you know what they are now. The song is the truth."

"The song is *part* of the truth," he said.

She winced. "The song is *my* truth. My feelings. It isn't yours. Only you could write that song."

"Good thing I'm tone-deaf."

"Can I at least do what you…demanded, asked, me to do first? I'll promote the hotel. I'll tell everybody how much I loved it, and that it's under new ownership and… I can make a big song and dance about the fact that I was here during the snowstorm and it was wonderful."

He shrugged. "Yeah, because I might as well get something out of it. And maybe if people know that you were here with me, they'll stop yelling at me on streets."

"Yes. Fine. That seems fair." Silence lapsed between them, and she stabbed the carrot with her fork and took a bite of it. "You're going to quit riding rodeo, aren't you?"

"What makes you say that?" he asked.

"Because of what you told me. About focus. About goals. About how you couldn't want anything else as long as you were trying to win. So this is what you want now? This is what you're trying to win?"

"Yes. You know, I have a trust fund. But I wanted to make sure I didn't use it for this. I don't want my dad's success. I want my own. And inescapably, my success is going to be built on some of that. I can't erase the advantages I got from him. Because my winnings that come from the rodeo... I was in the rodeo because of him."

"But you won because of you."

He didn't know quite what to do with that. With that kind word from her, because it was as real as any of the mean ones, but he wasn't sure why she had bothered to give it to him.

"I didn't really choose it, though. So now I decided to have something that I chose. I decided to make sure that it could be something that I wanted. That I was..." He was going to say that he was proud of. He wasn't sure that he was proud of a damn thing. Because what everything came back to was... This was something he *could* do.

He was fine enough at doing things.

It was why he'd worked for his family all those years. Because he could.

Feeling? Being there for someone emotionally? That was beyond him.

Something had broken inside of him a long time ago, and he didn't even have the desire to fix it. If something could have, it would've been Tansey.

But he hadn't wanted her to fix it then any more than he wanted it fixed now.

So maybe proud was a bridge too far for anything that he was going to do.

"I wanted something that was mine," he said.

And that much was true.

Because a man had to have land. His own. And his own achievements to stand on.

She nodded. "I understand that. You know...you know that I joined the rodeo to show my dad. And you know that I... I wanted to be successful and famous to show him. He doesn't care, Flint." She swallowed hard, and looked away. "He asked me for money. He found me, of course, not when I was barrel racing, no, nothing like that. He found me when I was really successful. When I might have something to give him. And you know... I couldn't figure out what I wanted to do. If I wanted to hold the fact that I had money and he didn't over his head and deny him. Or give it to him so that he would need me." She wasn't looking at him. She was looking past him. "Neither reason was very good motivation. Both make me...kind of a terrible person."

"What did you do?"

She swallowed hard. "I gave it to him. But not so I can hold it over his head. I gave it to him because... I just wanted it to not mean anything. And for him to not matter. If I withheld it, it was admitting I was angry. There was no way for me to really win. So I gave him money. Payment for the emotional scarring that produced the music, except I didn't say that. I didn't want to give him any credit for it. He never mentioned it. I think if he had known that the song was actually about him, like if he had known that it was autobiographical, he wouldn't have asked for money."

"He knew you were famous, but he's never listened to your music."

"No."

"Well. He's a special kind of asshole. Even I listened to my expert takedown."

"You thought *he* deserved it, at least that's what you said when you heard the song."

"I didn't say I *didn't* deserve it, Tansey," he said. "I said I didn't like it."

And that was the truth. It was a strange thing, this conversation. These honesty pitfalls. The fact that he remembered too keenly how much he had liked her.

It was easy to let all the pain that had come after that erase the friendship. His genuine affection for her. It was easy to tell himself it had all been some kind of sexual fever dream, followed by an immature tantrum on her part.

That was a lie.

He'd been in too deep with her. And it had not been his imagination. He couldn't deny it. Not now.

It was way too easy to remember the good times. To remember that friendship as the foundation, and the way that had shifted. The way it had shifted under his feet without him making the decision to let it.

Because he knew better. That was the thing. He had never in his life let himself get drawn into a relationship with a woman because he knew he didn't have the capacity to give a woman what she needed. He had always known that marriage and children weren't for him. He had known that since he was fourteen years old. And he had never, ever crossed those lines; he had never done anything that he was ashamed of with a woman. Not until her.

But he knew why it happened.

Because of her. Because there was something about her. And in the end, he supposed it wasn't all that surprising that she'd ended up famous. If he couldn't look away from her, it stood to reason the whole world couldn't look away from her.

He gritted his teeth. And he tried not to remember. He really did try to not remember.

Before

It turned out that her truck was effectively blown up, and while she absolutely refused to let him buy her a new one, she did concede to the fact that while she sorted it all out, she was going to need a ride. And he offered to be that ride. They would be driving from Utah to Nevada over the next few days, and they'd be taking the road trip together. All that would be fine if he didn't still want to kiss her. And if she hadn't been very clear that it wasn't going to happen.

I really like you.

He couldn't remember the last time a woman had said that to him.

I want you, sure.

But not *I really like you*.

He liked her too.

It was a hell of a thing.

He took his position back behind the gates to watch her event, and his heart was pounding harder than it did when it was his turn to ride.

When she rode, she rode spectacular, and it put her right up in the number-one spot.

When she got off, and came out of the gate, he pulled her in for a hug, lifting her up off the ground.

"Easy there, Ace," she said, her arms wrapped around his neck. He put her down, and kept holding on to her. She kept holding on to him.

"Tansey…"

She looked around, then stretched up on her toes, and kissed his cheek.

It was so innocent. A butterfly kiss. A whisper.

And it made him hard as a rock, instantly.

She was not his type.

He would do well to remember that.

She turned beet red, then ducked her head and extricated herself from his hold.

This time, when she went back to put her horse away, he did help with her tack, and he didn't accept any argument. He was driving her back to the motel. Because they were riding together. And once they were safely ensconced in the truck cab, all the tension that bloomed between them felt like too much to handle.

What was this? He had no idea what the hell it meant. No idea what the hell was happening. He wasn't…

Did he have a *crush* on this woman?

That was the weirdest damn thing.

He couldn't accept that.

They pulled into the motel parking lot and he put the truck in Park, then turned the keys off and pulled them out of the ignition.

"Wait."

Tansey put her hand on his. He froze. And looked at her.

She scooted across the distance of the truck cab, and put her hand on his cheek.

He just sat. Perfectly still. And he let her decide what to do next. He let her choose.

She leaned across the space, and she pressed her mouth to his. Tentative. Soft.

He sat completely still. And waited. She lifted her other hand, held the other side of his face and pressed more firmly against him, and that was when he wrapped his arms around her waist, pulling her closer to him, angling his head and deepening the kiss.

She made a muffled sound, wrapping her arms around his neck.

She kissed him back, all enthusiasm, no skill. He slid his tongue between her lips, and she returned fire, kissing him like she would die if she didn't.

It was all he could do to keep his hands still. To just keep holding her, rather than letting his palms move over her curves, not pushing his fingertips up beneath her shirt.

It was a temptation. It was a real damn temptation.

But there was something beautiful about letting the kiss just…be a kiss.

He thought he might drown in it. Thought he might die. He had no idea how long it went on. Just kissing her. Holding her. Lust was a drumbeat through his whole body. But the moment…

The *moment*.

He lifted his head. "You don't happen to have that cactus on you, do you?"

She laughed. The press of her breasts against his chest as she giggled making him groan.

"Why did you ask about the cactus?"

"Because nothing mattered but the moment."

She let out a long, slow breath. Her eyes looked a little unfocused, her lips swollen. And they were very close to his motel room. Normally, that would be the assumption. He didn't kiss a woman just to kiss her.

But he had to let the kiss with Tansey just be a kiss. Because it needed to be. It just did.

"You did good tonight," he said. "The barrel racing. I'm not grading you here. But that was good too."

She laughed and lowered her head. "Thank you."

He leaned in and kissed her. Shorter this time. "I need to tell you good night," he said.

"Why?"

He gave her a meaningful look. "Because I need to. I'm trying to be good."

"Oh," she breathed.

"I'll see you tomorrow."

And he didn't know how any of this had happened. How they had gone from friendship to this.

They might be… Hell. He might be dating her.

He didn't know what he thought about that.

But he also knew that he wasn't willing to let her go. And that told him quite a bit.

After

Yeah. That was the problem. He had known. He had known that he was getting in too deep. He had known that he was walking into something he had no right to walk into.

And there was no excuse for him. There was no getting older and wiser. Because it was about him. It was about what he had to give.

And sitting across from her now, he could feel the echo of unfinished business inside of him. Except it wasn't. They'd drawn a line under it because that was what they'd had to do.

Maybe that had always been one of the issues with the song. Maybe one of the issues with the song had always been that it showed him the line hadn't actually been drawn where he thought.

Because he'd been convinced that he got out of it before he devastated her. And it was a lie; he knew that. But that was part of the problem. He thought that he had a pretty good handle on who he was. But it turned out he wasn't as strong as he thought when it came to his resolve. And he'd been convinced that he just knew himself. That his resolve was what had kept him from those relationships, when in fact his resolve had had nothing to do with it. There had never been a woman that compelled him. And the minute she'd been there…he turned away from everything he knew. Everything he knew that he had to do to keep someone safe from him.

Maybe the real issue was that as much as she hated him, it had made him hate himself even more.

"I keep waiting," she said. "To feel triumphant. I keep waiting. I had pretty great revenge on you, you have to admit that."

"I thought you said you didn't think about how I would feel."

"I did. I wanted to hurt you. I wanted to find a way to hurt you, because I looked at you in the face and…

I didn't hurt you. I couldn't hurt you. And I hated that. I wanted to."

"That's the problem," he said. "You can't get to me like that."

"That's what I don't understand. I don't understand why."

"Let's just call it a night," he said, pushing his plate back to the center of the table.

"Why?"

"Because the point of this wasn't to rehash what we were. I thought the point of it was to find some common ground now."

"Yes. I guess so. But I… I gave you everything, you know that. I gave you everything. And…" She swallowed hard. "I guess it just doesn't matter, does it? But part of me wanted to hurt you. To take even half of what you took from me away from you."

"If you want the fucking scarf, you can have the scarf."

"I don't care about the scarf," she said. "It was never about the scarf."

"Are you going to tell me the scarf is a metaphor, because I *literally* have your scarf, so I think you know it isn't."

"No, the scarf doesn't matter. It's just part of a lie that you told. That I didn't matter, because if you do have it, if you can really give it back to me, then why? Why do you have it at all?"

Rage welled up inside him. And other emotions he didn't want to examine.

Couldn't.

"I have it," he ground out. "Because the idea of getting rid of it feels like cutting my arm off. Are you happy about that? Is that what you want to hear?"

She sat back, and he just stared. He didn't know why the hell he'd said any of that.

"I will go get you your scarf."

He pushed the chair back, and stepped away, and he didn't look back at her.

Chapter 6

Before

She held her breath while she watched him ride. She always did. But he was always perfect. But last night she'd kissed him, and somehow things felt…really tangled up now. But that kiss had been…everything she'd ever imagined a kiss might be. No, she had never kissed anyone before that night. Before him.

She hadn't wanted to.

Was that really all she was going to do? *Really?* Was she *really* just going to…kiss him?

She couldn't afford to be distracted. Not right now. She couldn't afford to be derailed.

Maybe she was even on the verge of something with her music. And the last thing she needed was…

All the dire consequences her mother had ever told

her about what happened when you got with men who were far too pretty for their own good rolled through her.

She knew better. She did. They opened the chute, and the bull with Flint on his back tore out of there.

She held her breath, but he didn't make it eight seconds. It was only four. And he was on the ground.

"Oh shit," she said, her hand going up over her mouth.

Sure, he got another chance. Another ride.

But she'd never seen him fall.

He got up and shook it off, went back and got back on. The gate opened again, and out he went. This time he stayed on, but only barely. And his score was… It wasn't good.

It hadn't been a clean ride.

She greeted him at the back of the gates, right when he came through. "What happened?" she asked.

"I was thinking about something else," he said.

And everything in her went still.

They just stood there and looked at each other. There was space between them, but it felt filled. With something. Something big. Bigger than maybe the two of them.

"Oh," was all she could say.

"You better win," he said. "One of us has to."

She did win.

It didn't really matter that much. And maybe that was the thing. It didn't matter; he did.

They ended up in his truck again, kissing like they might die if they didn't.

This time, his hands moved. Rough, up under her shirt, moving along the line of her spine. She arched against him, and when he pushed his fingertips beneath the band of her bra, she stopped. "Flint... I have to... I haven't done this before."

He froze. "You haven't done what?"

"I haven't had sex. I'm not... I'm not ready."

He slowly released his hold on her. "Okay," he said slowly. "I didn't... I didn't realize that."

"I know. Because I didn't tell you. Can we still kiss?"

"Yes," he said. "Definitely can."

"Okay. I don't... Just not yet."

She just needed to be more sure. Of her feelings. Of his. Of everything. She was just afraid.

"My dad really hurt me," she said. "And yes. I get that I'm a cliché. I get that it's like...a whole lot of daddy issues. But I'm aware of them. I'm trying to not..."

"Okay. It's okay."

But they didn't kiss again. Not that night. Instead, he walked her to the door of her room, gave her hand a squeeze before he left her there.

But the following night, they were right back in his truck, and just before his mouth met hers, she tried to lighten it. "No sex yet, Ace."

"Noted."

But the kissing was hotter this time. Longer. A wildfire that seemed like it was on the verge of burning out of control.

She wasn't aware of when she had pulled his shirt off of him, but at some point she did, and was moving her hands over his chest, down his back, and that was how she found herself laid across the bench seat in the pickup truck, her legs parting easily for him to settle between, and she could feel the hard ridge of his arousal up against her. She rocked herself against him, and then shook her head. "I'm not… I'm not ready for…"

"Okay," he said, breathing hard. "It's okay."

"I'm sorry," she said, terror warring with need. She wanted him so much, but she already cared about him far more than she was able to deal with or admit. If she actually let him inside of her body…

She just had to be sure she knew what she was doing. Sure she knew how she was…arranging all this inside herself.

And what if…?

What if she got pregnant? That was what happened to her mother.

It had just been an endless stream of heartbreak not only for her, but for Tansey as well.

There were consequences to this, and for the very first time, she felt somewhat sympathetic toward her mother, and her place in all of this, because apparently, charming cowboys were a lot harder to resist than she could have ever imagined. She had thought that *knowing* was enough.

But knowing *about* cowboys was different than knowing Flint.

"Do you want to come?"

It took her a second to realize what he was asking. His voice was hard like gravel, and she was desperate. Sensitized all over.

"Do I want to…? Oh. But I can't… Flint, I'd… You…"

"Not about me. I want to make you feel good. But only if you want me to. We don't have to have sex. But do you want to come?"

"Yes," she said.

"Can I?" He put his hand on the button of her jeans. She shivered. "Yes."

He undid the button, then the zipper, and moved his hand slowly beneath the waistband of her panties. She wiggled as his rough fingertips made contact with her very, very slick flesh. She moaned as his skin made contact with hers. As white-hot desire rolled through her. He began to stroke her. Her hips moved in time with his fingers, and she let her head fall back. "You're so pretty," he said.

And that was it. It sent her straight over the edge. She cried out as her climax slammed into her. She found herself immobilized by it, as wave after wave pulsed through her.

She was left spent and breathless in the aftermath.

He buttoned her jeans, zipped them back up. And then moved away from her, straightened up, there in front of the steering wheel, and put his face in his hands.

"Flint…"

"Just a second." He let out a slow breath. "You might kill me," he said.

"I don't want to kill you."

"I don't think you're going to have to try." She pushed herself into a sitting position. "Are you okay?"

"I'm great. I'm…" Her voice came out unsteady. She felt like she was going to cry. But she was good. She felt good. Well. Her body felt good. She felt like she needed to go lie down on the floor and curl up in a ball and wail about all these emotions that she didn't fully understand. That was what she felt like.

"I've never had sex with a virgin. I mean… Not saying that's what… I just don't want to do anything you don't want. I don't want to push you."

"You didn't push me. You didn't push me at all. You… I wanted it."

And she felt weird about it. And like she should've maybe offered him something. Except she knew that if she did, he would get irritated. It would sound like a transaction. She knew that he didn't want that.

"I'll walk you to the door."

They got out of the truck, and her legs still felt like Jell-O. She still felt unsteady.

And so she turned to him, and just pressed her body against his. He wrapped his arms around her, and just held her steady. And she had never felt quite so safe in all her life.

And she pushed against the emotion that was rising up inside of her.

"What is this?" she asked.

He shook his head. "I'm not really sure."

"We should call it something."

"Wilbur?"

"Oh, shut up."

She punched him in the shoulder.

"What did you have in mind?"

"A fling," she said, her heart pounding.

"I'm not sure you can have a fling without sex," he pointed out.

"Well…well, I'm not saying we won't. But maybe we should agree that it…that it will run its course and when it does, we're both okay with it. You said you don't… And I mean, I have all those goals."

"And you don't want to depend on a man," he reminded her.

"No, I don't," she said.

"Then it's a fling."

She nodded.

"Good night," she whispered.

"Good night."

After

She just sat at the table, immobile. Frozen. Her mind caught in a cascade of memories from the past. When things had been easy with him. When things had been beautiful with him. When they had kissed like it was inevitable, and she had hoped.

But he had her scarf.

It doesn't matter. None of it matters. Because you know where this ends.

Yeah. And she was beginning to feel like one of her favorite genres of country song. The one where you felt tempted to sleep with an ex that you shouldn't touch. But…

Yeah. It was tempting.

Not that he'd made any kind of gesture that indicated he was interested in doing that. She had to make sure not to confuse the intensity of the feelings that she felt around him, and the way that it picked at her creativity with actual desires.

She was smarter than that. She knew better than that. She was not the same girl that she'd been the first time she met him.

She heard footsteps and looked up. He was standing

in the doorway of the dining room, and he was holding it in his hands. And it was the weirdest thing. Because she had actually forgotten what the scarf looked like.

Because it didn't really matter.

It wasn't the point. It had been literal, but it had been a metaphor.

It was the one thing she had put in the song that held hope.

She'd hoped he'd kept it. That he hadn't just thrown it out. That it was everything he'd said. That he hadn't been able to throw it away because it had felt like finishing something.

Ending it.

And yes, they had ended it.

But it wasn't over for her. Not really. And she wondered if it wasn't really over for him either.

"Here," he said. He extended his hand and she stood up, walking over to him. Her footsteps were somehow muted and loud at the same time. And she reached out and took hold of the edge, but he didn't release his hold on it easily. Or quickly.

Until he did.

"Feels better to give it back to you than to get rid of it."

She studied this man, and tried to figure out…who he really was. Because he claimed he didn't do emotions or connections. And he claimed he wasn't sentimental. And God knew she had experienced the destruction of what it was like when he was finished with the relationship.

Yes.

She had been destroyed by that.

But this man… The one standing there holding on to

her scarf like it meant something. The man who had it with him on… He didn't live here. He had packed it to come here. For this day. For this business trip.

And you have the cactus he gave you.

Yes. And everything else.

She wondered how many women he'd had. How many women he'd kissed since he'd last kissed her.

There hadn't been anyone for her.

Suddenly, it was far too easy to remember all those old feelings. Far too easy to feel them. Far too easy to simply exist in them. Like no time had passed at all. Like he was still her lover, and not the man who had broken her.

She had tried so hard to turn it into a kind of complicated destiny. That if she hadn't been with him, she wouldn't have the song. She had turned it into an integral step in her life.

But it didn't feel like that here. It just felt like regret.

And like unfinished business.

Except maybe that was the story she was telling herself now because he was there and he was beautiful. And she still wanted him, no matter how much she tried to tell herself she didn't. It was painful. It immobilized her. She suddenly ached with it. Was on fire with it. And thought that it might burn her alive.

But it wasn't the kind of heat that they'd experienced when it had been new. When she'd been terrified and trembling, but so in need of it.

She knew. And she wanted it anyway.

Wanted *him* anyway.

So she took a step back, clinging to the scarf. "Thank you. For this." She wanted to forget everything. Everything that she knew.

About him. About heartbreak. About pain. She wanted to forget all of it. And jump into something she knew she shouldn't.

But she kept remembering all those times back then. When he'd made it very clear when she brought up sex that he wasn't offering.

Except he had wanted it.

No. Don't go there.

"I'm tired," she said. "I'll go… I'll go to my room now."

"Yes. See you tomorrow."

"See you tomorrow."

Chapter 7

He couldn't sleep. He couldn't sleep because all he could do was think of her. He couldn't sleep because everything kept rolling through him like a thunderstorm. Memories, things from the past, and need from now.

He got out of bed quickly, and went over to the window, looking out at the snow falling below. It was coming down thicker and harder now, and the wind was unforgiving.

They could be stuck up here for days. And he...he didn't know what the hell he was supposed to do with that.

He didn't know why he'd shown her the scarf, except... Maybe it was the penance that he needed to make. Because he could see that he hurt her.

Not that he didn't know that. He'd known that ever since the song had come out.

You knew it before.

But the fact was, this was another of those moments. Where he could turn back, or he could take a step forward, a step into something he knew wasn't a good idea.

Just like he'd done back then.

Before

They did a little more talking than kissing after that. It was a good thing. Because she needed to take it slow, and he understood that. He still wasn't quite sure what was happening between them. Not really. What the point of it was. Where it was going.

He didn't want to think about it. He was good at that. *Not* thinking about it. He hadn't lied to her when he'd said he was very good at putting up walls.

He was so good at it, he didn't quite know how to take them down. And he figured that was all right.

They both ended up winning top spot in their events for the season.

And he bought her the boots. Before they ever left the final event in Vegas.

"I told you not to do that," she said.

"Yeah. Well, I did."

"What are you going to do now?" she asked.

"I'm headed out to the coast for a few days." He always went and stayed in one of his parents' properties when the season was out. A little time to breathe between going and working the ranch and all the hard traveling and riding that happened all season long. "You should come with me."

He didn't know why he asked her to do that any more

than he knew the why of anything from the past couple of months. Why he was making out with this girl who wasn't his type. Talking to her for hours every night. Thinking about her all the time.

"Yeah, all right. But I'm still not having sex with you, Ace."

"Didn't ask you to." A smile tugged at the corner of his mouth. He wasn't even upset about it. He was a little physically frustrated, but he wasn't mad. Not even a little.

Because like everything else with her, the fling was unpredictable.

And he liked that best of all.

After

She couldn't sleep. She paced around the room, and then for some reason, opened the door. She crept down the hall. It was silent. The building was huge. She didn't even know where he was sleeping. And the odds were, it wasn't anywhere near her.

It was strange to be in such a big place like this with nobody in it.

Nobody but him. And somehow she felt his presence looming large as if they were staying in a tiny house.

She huffed. And continued down the stairs, into the lobby. The lights were off.

She looked around, up at the tall, arched ceiling with beams extending across it. The dim chandelier. And then she continued on toward the large windows that faced out over what she knew was a beautiful view in the daylight.

She could hardly see anything, it was so dark. But she could make out the swirling of snowflakes coming down.

She touched the window, and felt that it was freezing cold.

They had never been in snow together. They had spent the summer together. A summer that had been full of heat and longing.

A summer full of lies that she had told herself. But the truth was, he'd never lied to her.

She'd broken her own heart.

Even after two years she couldn't quite figure out how to make it beat normally again.

She sat down on the couch by the window, holding her notebook in her lap. And she started to write.

A prayer, really, more than a song. For what she wished could have been. For who she wished he could be, and who she wished she could be for him.

Somebody, someday would be enough to tear down the walls in his heart. She was only sorry that it wasn't her.

A tear slipped down her cheek. She had really thought that she was done crying over Flint Carson.

She'd thought that it had scabbed over.

That she had come to a place of reconciliation with it.

But he was here. And the problem was finding out that her feelings weren't anywhere near as different now from then as she would like them to be.

She closed her eyes, and she let herself remember. Because maybe that would jolt her back to reality. Maybe that would remind her.

It was so easy to remember that summer. To remember the beginning. To remember the end.

Chapter 8

Before

The house was beautiful. They had driven separately, so that they could go their separate ways after, because it made the most sense, after all. They still weren't claiming to be a couple or anything like that. They were friends who kissed a lot.

And she was still trying to sort through her feelings for him. Or rather, trying desperately to come up with something to call him that wasn't as terrifying as the word that seemed to echo inside of her whenever she thought of him.

She'd brought her guitar, and she was looking forward to spending a little bit of time working on her music. They'd reached pretty much a dead end with her demo, but she knew that was just how it went. They had gotten a couple of completely unknown internet radio stations to play her songs, but nothing big. And definitely no interest from labels.

She wasn't used to being on the coast. She got out of her truck and looked around: there were big, tall pines surrounding the house, and it was up on the edge of a sheer rock face, overlooking the great, pounding sea. The roar of it was intense, beautiful.

The front door to the house opened, and Flint stepped outside. Barefoot. She didn't know why that was notable. Only that it was. It felt intimate. She was wearing her boots. The ones he had bought her. She hadn't been able to help herself. But at least she hadn't let him buy her a new truck. She just fixed the old one. That was reasonable.

"Glad you're here."

She smiled. "Me too."

Her room was on the second floor, and had a breathtaking view of the ocean. It was also not his room. Which was fair. Because she had told him that she wasn't having sex with him. So of course he'd given her a separate room.

But she was starting to feel like holding on to her virginity was more of a habit than anything she actually wanted.

She wanted him.

And it was so difficult to figure out how much of that was weakness or giving in to something, or being just like all the people who didn't know better. When she was supposed to know better.

Know better than what?

He was a good man. He'd been nothing but a good

man to her. He hadn't pressured her into anything. Quite the opposite. He was being so respectful it was… It wasn't like anything she'd ever been warned about; that was for sure. Her mother had told her that men only wanted one thing. But Flint seemed to want to talk to her, buy her cacti and boots and kiss her. Let her stay in a beautiful beach house. Share meals with her. Share drinks with her. Flint seemed to want a lot of things from her. And he gave a lot of things to her.

There was no map for this. Not in her experience. And maybe not in her mother's experience either. It was okay that her mother would be wary. Upset about this. There were reasons she hadn't told her mother that she was here. Reasons that she had never mentioned Flint to Darlene Martin.

But she had never known a man like Flint. Tansey never had before either. She couldn't compare him to dire warnings that had nothing to do with him. He wasn't just a cowboy. He was Flint Carson.

And he was everything.

But he couldn't be what she stood on, what she leaned against. That didn't mean he couldn't be everything for right now.

For their fling.

She wanted to laugh and cry.

By the time she finished putting her things away and came downstairs, he had set a beautiful dinner out on the terrace. Right over the ocean waves.

"Did you cook?"

"My parents had this house for a long time, and knowing what to do with fresh seafood is awfully helpful. So yes. I did. But doing a crab boil is pretty basic."

"This does not seem basic. This is extremely fancy."

He poured her a glass of wine, and she felt like this was a life she had never even dreamed of. She wanted to know more about him, though. He was very good at asking her questions about herself. And he certainly alluded to certain things about him. But he didn't open up all that easily.

"So you won," she said. "Does that mean you'll be back again next year, or…?"

"Most likely. I don't really have anything else to do. What about you?"

"Well. Since nobody was all that interested in my demo song, and it certainly isn't going to pay the bills, I guess I'll keep riding for another couple of years." She shrugged. "It's okay. Wanting to get into the music industry is… It's very unlikely. I don't have any connections or anything like that. So… I don't see it as something that would be terribly easy. And definitely not something that's just going to happen."

"I've never even heard you sing."

She didn't want him to turn it around on her. Not just yet. "How come you're so good at hiding your emotions, Flint?"

"Practice?"

"But why? I guess what I don't get is… You don't really tell me that much. I mean, you're vague. You like to ask me questions, and you let me talk about myself, which is… It's nice. Sort of like therapy. But with a really good-looking man. But what about you?"

He lifted his wineglass and looked out at the ocean. It was strange to see him like this. The sun setting out on the sea, at a family home. They weren't in a cheesy motel or a bar. Or the cab of his truck. There was no one around. It was just different. And she felt different.

"What about me?"

"You never talk about yourself."

"There's not much to say," he said, and there was something in that smile that seemed false. It seemed very clear now, that the man she had met that first night, and the man she was looking at now, was a character. She had seen real pieces of Flint in the time since then. But this…this was a put-on.

The whole charming thing he did. The whole devil-may-care thing. She had seen moments of real emotion in him, but they weren't accompanied by revelations. The way that he gave her advice, that was real. The way that he listened to her, the way that he cared for her.

The care that he showed by respecting her boundaries, all of that was real.

But it also kept them protected and safe.

She wanted to find a way to get through those walls. But she was at a loss as to how.

Because here they were, theoretically temporary, so why should she be able to get through those walls? Why should he give her anything? She didn't know the answer to that.

And she didn't know if wanting to break them down was particularly fair.

She had plenty of her own defenses, so she understood that. She might not do such a great job of repressing her emotions, but the whole thing with him… Not sleeping with him… Holding herself back from him… Well, that definitely had to do with her dad.

With being afraid.

Because they'd said it was a fling, but now things felt different for her, and she wanted to be blasé and sophisticated and basically the most okay with the fact that this would have an end, but she didn't know if she could be.

It didn't make her want to leave, though.

She wanted to do something, give him something. To find a way to make him open up to her the way she had him. She wanted to know him. Know him like he knew her. But she didn't know what to do. So she just sat with him. There was a firepit out on the deck, and he started it up, and they sat on the couch there, and just sat together.

Not speaking.

They did that a few nights, things getting fairly hot and heavy in front of the fire more often than not.

It was harder and harder to not just join him in bed every night.

But she just wanted to be sure.

Do you? Or are you just scared?

Well. She didn't really have an answer for that. Because she was scared. She did know that. She just didn't know if that fear was smart, or if it was holding her back.

She got out her guitar that night when they sat by the fire, and started to pluck the strings.

"Play me a song."

And she knew exactly which one she wanted to play. The one she had never played for anyone.

"All right. This is some… This one's called 'Taillights.'"

The thing I remember most of all is the taillights
on your truck

When you drove away from me and Mom, you
said we weren't enough
I remember the taillights most of all
If you were ever there on birthdays, it doesn't
matter now
If you ever sang me to sleep, I really can't recall
It's the taillights, from when you drove away

Her heart ached as she sang the song. As she poured
everything of herself into the phrasing. Because when
she'd written those words, she'd bled for them.

It was the very end that flipped it.

Someday, I hope you're sitting in a crowded bar,
and you look out the window
And you'll see my taillights
In a car that's way fancier than anything you could
ever afford
And you'll think of all those times
Of those missed birthdays, and when you
should've said good night
Every time you see taillights, you'll think of me.
And I won't think of you at all

She stopped, and wiped a tear off of her cheek.

"You need to record that," he said.

"I don't have anything I'd…"

"No. Just like that. Just you and the guitar. Send that
to your manager. And have them share that. It's amazing, Tansey."

"I don't know about that…"

"No. It really is. You should do it while you're here. We've got another week."

"Okay. I'll do it."

She did that night, and uploaded the file for her manager to grab. It wasn't professional, there weren't other instruments, it wasn't as good production-wise as the other song they had sent out, so she really didn't expect anything to come of it. And it wasn't what she was focused on right now anyway.

The next day they went to the local coffee shop, and as they walked down the street, he held her hand. And that was when she knew. It was when she really knew. That it was right. That she was ready. Because it wasn't just kissing, or fraught moments in the cab of his truck. It was holding hands. On the street. For anyone to see, and yeah, neither of them lived here, and no one knew who they were, but it was the principle of the thing.

It was the gesture that was just about touching. Just about being linked. Not about anything else. And she loved it.

Because she loved him.

It terrified her to think that. It broke the rules to feel it.

And she was willing to throw every last bit of caution that she had held in her chest into that coastal wind, and let it fly out into the sea. Because the world could keep all that, as long as she could keep him.

They had dinner out on the deck like they had done every night, kissed by the fire, and then he excused himself to go to bed. And she sat there.

For one breath. Two. Three.

And then she went after him. She took a deep breath and opened the door to his room, crossed the space and got into bed beside him. He sat up, looking at her. And she curved her arm around his neck and leaned in, kissing him on the mouth.

"Tansey," he said. "I am all about not pushing you to do anything. I am very committed to not pressuring you… Getting into my bed is maybe a bridge too far."

"I'm actually here for sex, Ace," she said, pressure and need building in her chest until she thought she might die of it.

"Well, that's something," he said.

She kissed him, his mouth that was so familiar now, but it was like falling. Knowing that it wasn't going to stop here. Knowing that it was going to keep on. That every desire inside of her would be answered tonight. That he would be inside of her tonight. It made her shiver, shake. He was already wearing nothing but boxer shorts, and he drew her up against his body, taking her shirt and stripping it up over her head. He made quick work of her bra, and he had already touched her between her legs once, so she wasn't really embarrassed.

And…why should she be?

They cared about each other. They had built to this. This wasn't a one-night stand with a stranger; this man had sat and talked with her.

He knew her.

She couldn't feel embarrassment in front of him. Not when he was…he was the one.

It made her feel jittery and strung out to even think such a thing, to believe in something she had told herself she didn't. Except maybe the problem was, maybe the issue all along was that she had always imagined that she would be one and done. That when she felt comfortable enough with a man to be with him this way, it would be love.

And that losing it would be devastation.

Would be something she would never be able to recover from.

He moved his thumbs over her nipples, and she gasped, arching her back, pressing her bare breasts to his chest. Oh, his chest. And suddenly, a surge of excitement went through her, because she had been thinking about being naked in front of him, and processing whether or not she was going to be embarrassed. But she hadn't thought about seeing him naked.

And that…

She hooked her thumbs in the waistband of his boxer shorts, and pulled them down. Throwing the covers back, and exposing his body to her gaze.

"Well, holy shit," she said.

"That's not exactly a song lyric," he said, his voice gruff.

"You're really hot," she said.

"Glad you approve."

She reached out tentatively, and wrapped her fingers around his thick arousal. He was glorious. Beautiful.

She squeezed him.

"Fuck," he said.

"See, it is a song. Just one only we're ever going to listen to."

He chuckled, and pulled her against him. He kissed her neck, down her collarbone, taking one nipple into his mouth and sucking hard. And it was better than just putting her fingertips on his cheek so that she could feel his stubble; his whiskers burned all over the tender skin of her chest.

It was intimate. Real and intense in a way she had never imagined this could be.

She felt like all her desires were somewhat childish. Or something she didn't quite understand. She got it now. She didn't know why the Tansey before this moment had been afraid. That girl hadn't understood. How right it would feel. How perfect.

She hadn't known just how wonderful it could be. She hadn't understood.

How easy, how right it was, when it was the person. The one.

But he knew her. The dark and ugly things. Her petty little heart and how much she wanted revenge on her father, how profoundly she'd been hurt by him.

How afraid she was. He knew those things. He knew those things and he seemed to just like her anyway. The way that she was.

And when he took the rest of her clothes off, and put his hand between her thighs, she cried out, not just because of the pleasure, but because of the overwhelming sensation of the emotion that was flooding her body.

Because it was deeper than desire. More than arousal.

He pushed a finger inside of her and she flexed her hips, trying to acclimate to the unfamiliar sensation. She liked it; it was just not…not something she'd experienced before.

He put a second finger in and began to thrust in and out of her gently, allowing her body to get used to him.

And then, very suddenly, she felt pleasure break over her like a wave, her internal muscles pulsing around him. She cried out, and he withdrew from her, then put his fingers in his mouth, sucking on them, slow and leisurely, like he was savoring the taste of her. And she shivered. "I have been waiting for this," he said.

He moved down her body and grabbed hold of her thighs, then he pushed them out wide, lowering his head to her center and tasting her deep. Long. She clung to him, forking her fingers through his hair and holding him there. Arching her body against him as she writhed with need. He pushed his fingers back inside her again as he teased her with his lips, his tongue. She couldn't breathe. Couldn't think. Couldn't do a damn thing but submit to the onslaught of pleasure.

She lost herself. In the absolute wave of need. In the wildness of her desire. And as she lay there spent, he moved away from her, going into the adjoining bathroom for a moment and returning with a box of condoms.

She was torn between…indignation, a lot of questions and relief.

"I'm an optimist," he said, by way of explanation. "And anyway, it's better safe than sorry."

"Well. I guess that is true."

He chuckled, tearing the box open, and then taking a strip out, tearing an individual condom from the strip. And then opening it quickly. He took care of the necessities, and then joined her back on the bed. He pressed his forehead to hers, and kissed her, deep and long. "Ready?"

She nodded, words deserting her entirely. He pressed himself inside of her, inch by inch, filling her. And the emotion that swamped her was almost too much to bear. It was beautiful. Wonderful. And so much more. This wasn't just about pleasure. Not just about satisfaction. Flint was inside of her. And she felt like something more than she'd ever been before. Complete in a way. In touch with parts of herself that she had never given a whole lot of thought to.

She had been right to be afraid of this. It was too much. It was transformative. She had been right to be afraid of it, but now, she embraced it. Wholly. Completely. With all that she was.

He began to move, deep, decisive thrusts, and she clung to him, until she began to feel the rhythm, find it. Arching her hips against his each and every time he moved against her.

She surrendered to it. To him. And when her climax hit, she could scarcely breathe. It was too much. And not enough all at once. Overwhelming, leaving her storm-tossed and just right where she needed to be.

With him. She was wild, and fractured, but safe all at once, because she was in his arms, and she knew that she could trust him.

And when his own climax hit, when his control fractured, his movements becoming hard and erratic, a growl rising up inside of him, she thought it might almost be better than her own pleasure. This man's pleasure. This man coming apart because of her.

Because he might be her first, but he'd had any number of women. And that he could still fall apart over her mattered.

And she didn't think of her mother's dire warnings then. Because it was different. He was different.

And they were different together. Maybe different than anyone had ever been.

The euphoria of it all carried her off to sleep. And she just let him hold her.

And she felt...like she was home.

She was still in a euphoric haze the next day when her manager called and said that a major radio station had picked her song up for airplay as part of an indie artist showcase. She wasn't really going for being an indie artist, but if it got her radio airplay... Well, it was more than anything else had ever done.

It felt exposing, that song. And yet... It was what she wanted her dad to hear, wasn't it? What he had done to her.

"It's going to be on a radio station," she said to Flint.

"That's amazing," he said. "And fast."

"I guess... When they know, they know. I just kind of can't believe that... Something I just kind of threw together like that..."

"The song was from your heart. It didn't need anything other than your voice."

And she held that close. That confidence. That simple belief in her.

Her manager decided to distribute the song online, which she hadn't done before, mostly because she didn't see why anybody would want to hear the song if none of the radio stations wanted to play it, but he was adamant that they get it out there before it played so that people could look it up after. Which was a good idea.

So within two days, the song was published onto various streaming platforms. And then something very unexpected happened.

The song got picked up on a popular app when a

viral "daddy issues" challenge happened, and people played the song in the background while listing terrible things their fathers had done. Making light of it, and using dark humor, but it pushed the sound around, which pushed it up various streaming charts in a way that no one expected.

Least of all Tansey.

"It's number one on the country streaming chart now," she said, shaking as she walked down the stairs into the living room.

Flint stood up and picked her up and swung her in a circle. "Does that mean I get to buy you a truck now?"

"You can't buy me a truck."

"Well, you won *something*, surely."

"You did," she said. "You're the one that told me I had to record that song."

"I think you gotta go with your feelings."

That was when she got a call that a morning show wanted to interview her, because she had gone from unknown to number one streaming thanks to the viral nature of the hit.

And she really had no idea how to process the fact that all of this had happened in a couple of weeks. The nature of the internet, she guessed, but it was just so far outside her comfort zone, and she was dealing with the fact that she was in love for the first time in her life, and having sex.

The morning show bit was short, and they didn't fly her out or anything; she just did an on-camera interview over the computer.

And when she asked the local bar that night if she

could play, it was a resounding yes, and what she couldn't believe was how the place packed out. For her.

And Flint sat in the front row, watching her, the pride on his face doing something to her insides.

When they got back to the house, he kissed her. Rough and intense, and she let herself get caught up in it. Let him hold her close. Tear her clothes off of her. He lowered her down onto the bed, and their need for each other was a whole tornado. He was inside of her before she could think, and even though it was fast and furious, she came twice, dizzy in the aftermath.

He kissed her throat, her jaw. "You're amazing," he said.

And she just felt it. Welling up inside of her. The need to say it. The need to think it. To really get it out there. "I love you."

His withdrawal was immediate, and she felt horrified. How had she said that; how would she even let herself feel it? That wasn't what this was supposed to be. And she knew it.

It was a fling. It was supposed to be a fling. And yes, she had started to fantasize about it being more. Of course she had. But… But she wasn't going to tell him like this. She was going to… She was going to feel out how long he could see this going. She was going to do it differently. That was all.

"Forget I said anything," she said.

"Tansey, I'm not sure that I can."

He looked grave. He sounded even graver.

"You have to," she said. "I know… I know that's not what this is."

"Do you?" he asked seriously.

"Yes," she said. "Yes, I…"

"Because if you can't…"

"I'm not done yet," she said. "Are you?"

"No." He shook his head. "I'm not done."

"Good. Then we don't have to talk about this. You can forget I said it. It was… You know. Post-sex euphoria, or whatever."

"I need you to listen to me. I can't give you that. I can't give it to anybody. Don't take it personally."

"No, I know. I… I listened to you. I did."

But she couldn't ignore the fluttering of her heart. The vague hope there.

She just felt like… She felt like maybe there wouldn't be grand declarations or anything like that, but like they might settle into something that was a little bit more long-term. That was all she wanted. Just a little longer.

She didn't need for him to love her.

And she didn't need to say anything like that again. She didn't.

She just wasn't ready for it to end.

And she would do whatever she had to do to keep him with her. For now. She would do whatever she needed to for now.

A week later, she realized that her period hadn't started when it should have. And she had no idea what to do. She was usually pretty regular, and she knew full well that they'd had unprotected sex the night of the open mic.

She wasn't stupid. If you spent your whole life not having sex, and having regular periods, then you started having sex and the period didn't come…

She knew what that meant.

She was terrified. Trembling. But she couldn't risk going out and buying a pregnancy test. People were already starting to take pictures of them. There were weird rumors online, a lot of speculation about her personal life. People treated her like she was a fictional character. There were so many stories about who her dad was, and what he had done, and it was like what she shared about herself had taken on a life of its own.

And if anybody took a picture of her buying a pregnancy test… How did actually famous people handle that? She had one song, and was having some kind of a moment on the internet. She didn't know how anybody stood this for years on end.

But before she did any of that, she would tell him. Tell him what she suspected. Because she wanted to have a deeper conversation with him about…about the fact that this wasn't a fling anymore. That much was clear. It had become something so much deeper. So much more serious. They actually talked. They shared things. And really, it had always been wrong to call it a fling.

They had been friends first. And it mattered.

A baby.

She wasn't ready for this. And she was afraid. What if he rejected her? What if he rejected the baby?

This is why you can't depend on anyone else.

No. Because she was shaking. Because it felt like he held her life, her future in his hands.

It was horrible.

She walked downstairs, into the kitchen, where he

was preparing dinner. It felt domestic. They felt domestic. They felt like something special and perfect.

Except for… Except for all the walls. He had told her about those walls from the beginning.

To see what he says, you have to tell him. You can't keep it a secret.

"I need to talk to you."

"We talk all the time," he said. "Does it require an announcement."

"This might," she said. "I'm late."

She looked at him, full of meaning. And waited for him to get it. She watched as about ten emotions cycled over his face. More than she had maybe ever seen him express in their time together.

"Well… You need to find out."

"I'm just… I don't know how. I'm afraid of what will happen if I go to a store here. Because people know that we are here. You saw that stuff pop up online. It's… It's a little bit unnerving."

"You need to find out," he said, his voice hard.

"I know," she said. "I will, Flint. I promise… And…"

"I don't want a baby," he said.

She blinked. "Well… I don't know that I was really planning on…"

"No. We said this was a fling. That was it. I told you, I am not up for this."

"I…"

Everything in her started to shut down. She didn't know how to handle this. Because he looked like a stranger. His eyes had gone deadly flat, his body language so distant… So…

"Are you saying that you would want me to get rid of it?" she asked.

He shook his head, decisively. "No. I'm not gonna tell you what to do. I just…"

"So you would just not have anything to do with it?"

"I didn't say that either," he said, his voice hard. "I said I didn't want a kid. And I don't. But I would be responsible. I would make sure that you had everything you needed. I'd be there. Physically. But I don't have anything to give, Tansey. Not emotionally. This… This was nothing. We hung out, we ate, we talked. We fucked. It wasn't real life. It wasn't really me. It was… It was something different. It's not my life. It's not who I am."

"So you… What? You would be in your child's life, begrudgingly?"

"Like a kid is going to know the difference."

"I… I can't have this conversation. I can't…"

"This has to end," he said. "Whatever the outcome. It can't keep going on like this. It's already too much."

"What?"

She didn't know how she had gone from telling him that she might be pregnant, to him talking about how he didn't want a child but he would be there in the child's life, to him wanting to end things.

"We've been careless, and this was supposed to be short-term. If you're not pregnant…"

"Right," she said, everything inside of her dissolving, breaking apart. And she could see herself, the little girl that she'd once been, collapsed on the gravel driveway, watching her father drive away. And if he had looked at his rearview mirror even once, he would've seen how badly she was devastated.

She wouldn't let Flint see it. She pushed the rising dread, the awful pain down. She cut it off; she didn't let herself feel it. She didn't let herself show it. She couldn't. She couldn't give him that. Because she would be different this time. She would push it down.

She would handle it.

She would stand upright, because she knew who she was.

"I should go," she said.

"Right now?"

"Yes. If it's done, then it should be done. I… I'll let you know. I'll let you know what happens."

"I don't want you to leave until…"

"You said it was finished. And you're right. Of course you're right. It was getting to be too much. And this is just… It's proof. I promise I'll tell you."

She packed up her things, and everything was numb. It wasn't until she left, until she drove all the way to a roadside motel six hours away that she let her chest break open entirely. That she let everything dissolve within her.

She cried until she thought she would be sick with it.

Curled up in a ball in the middle of the bed, weeping.

She didn't find a pregnancy test. She didn't know whether or not to pray that she was or pray that she wasn't.

Five days later, she started bleeding. And she was angry at herself, because now she would never even know if it had been a fluke, or if she had one of those early miscarriages that were far too common. Maybe it was better. Except nothing felt better.

She texted him.

Not pregnant.

He didn't respond. And she tried to heal. She tried to write music. She tried to move on. But the only lyrics she could write were about him.

And finally, during one session, she gave in to that. All the anger, all the pain. All the brokenness. The most scathing, personal lyrics that had ever come from her.

She couldn't stop them.

"It's perfect," said her manager. "It's the best song you've written."

"I don't know if I can put it out," she said.

"It's your pain," he said. "You can do whatever you want with it."

She held on to that. It was her pain. He was the one that had said they needed to be finished, and she hadn't fought him, because what would the point have been? She didn't want to show him that she cared more than he did. She refused to show him that.

And it had to go somewhere. She had to put it somewhere. It was her pain; her manager was right. Didn't she deserve to get something from what they had?

"Yeah," she said. "You're right. Let's…let's make that the next single."

Chapter 9

After

He didn't know what had drawn him downstairs. And he didn't expect to see her sitting there, her face in her hands, and notebook in her lap, and her elbows resting there.

Her shoulders were shaking, and he found that no matter what, he wanted to walk to her. He wanted to go and pull her in his arms, even though he had no right to do that. Even though he had no right at all, because it would just be more promises he couldn't keep.

"Tansey?"

She looked up at him, her eyes wide, tears streaming down her cheeks.

"I didn't expect you down here, I'm sorry. I'm just…"

"What's wrong?"

"I was just remembering," she said, her voice watery.

She swallowed hard. "And maybe…maybe it's okay that I'm letting you see it. Because I didn't let you see it then. And I told myself that I didn't feel it anymore. And that's why it's been easier to snipe at you. But that's how it was in the beginning too, wasn't it? I was mean to you because I wanted to push you away."

"You were never all that mean," he said, something sore blooming at the center of his chest.

"Don't tell me that. That ruins my street cred. I was really trying to be mean."

"No, the thing was, I just liked it," he said, taking a step closer to her. It was dark, and he wanted to give her this. A little bit of honesty. Because the truth was, they hadn't spoken with honesty about what had been happening between them at the time. She had called it a fling, and he'd let her do it, because he needed to put those parameters around it in order to deal with it. He needed that border so that he could allow himself to do it.

And he hadn't given her or himself any honesty about that.

"Why did you like it?"

"Because you didn't act charmed by me. And I found that fascinating. You were not my type."

"I wasn't your type?"

"No. I didn't like squeaky-clean, fresh-faced virgins. I liked women who knew what they're doing."

"That is actually really insulting. I'm not sure why you thought that you would come in here while I was crying and…"

"Because you got to me. You got to me and I couldn't explain why." The words were rough and tortured. His voice didn't even sound like his own. "And I kept telling myself that it wasn't anything. That I wasn't attracted to you, because I couldn't be. Because you weren't a rodeo queen, and you didn't have a single rhinestone on. Because you were too young for me. Because even before you told me that you were a virgin, I knew that you were more innocent than anyone that I should be… talking to at all."

He took a breath, and his chest hurt. "But yeah, I loved that attitude. From the beginning. It was why I couldn't stay away from you. And I couldn't stay away from you, you remember that, right?"

"I try not to. And actually, most of the time I remember my version of events. I remember the breakup. But I forget… I forget that I stood there and hid everything that I felt, and that I told you that I agreed. I mean, I know I did, but I forget…that you couldn't see inside me to how I hurt."

"I knew," he said. "I knew because I hated it too. You don't… You don't know, Tansey. I had feelings for you. In a way that I never had for anybody else."

He swore he could hear the snowflakes falling outside it went so quiet between them. It was like his heart barely dared beat.

He had never admitted that out loud. He had barely admitted it to himself in coherently formed sentences in his own mind. He had allowed himself to act on feeling only, and call it nothing.

Making excuses about what he couldn't feel and what he couldn't do. But the problem was—and he knew it— that his feelings were there; they were just erratic. Uncontrolled. And he couldn't handle them.

He'd never wanted to inflict them on another human

being. He had trained himself in that brutal art a long time ago. Built a wall up around himself. Toughened himself up. Because he had never ever wanted to feel…

"You know, I feel too much. And sometimes I feel nothing at all. And sometimes when I feel too much, it turns into anger. And it's bullshit no matter what scenario it is. Believe me when I tell you that. I didn't want to admit to myself that I had feelings for you. I didn't want to admit that you telling me you might be pregnant scared the hell out of me. Really, the hell."

"It scared me too. It scared me too and then it… I felt like I was dying. When I started bleeding. Because I wanted it. I *wanted* it. Even though I didn't want it. And it was such a mess. It was a horrible mess. And you were the only person that I wanted to talk to about it, and I texted you and you never texted me back." She was breathing hard now, crying again, and he felt like this was what he deserved. This conversation.

"I didn't know what to say," he said. "I didn't know what to say, because part of me wanted you to be pregnant. So that I could keep you anyway, even though I knew it was a bad idea. I'm… I'm toxic, Tansey, and I tried my best not to be toxic with you. I did. But I froze you out instead, and it wasn't better."

"So you know that about yourself and, what, you just sit in it?"

"Yes," he said.

"Why?"

"Because I don't want to fix it. I didn't want to care about you. I didn't want it. I wanted to *possess* you. I wanted to keep you. And hell, the contortions I would've gone through to do that if the whole pregnancy scare hadn't happened… I would still be torturing you. I can't even imagine. Not letting you go, not really, and not giving you what you wanted. Because I can't let myself care that deeply about someone. But it doesn't mean I don't want you. With absolutely every part of myself. It doesn't mean you're not the only woman I dream about."

"You…you do?"

"How many women do you think I've been with since you?"

She looked away from him. "I don't want to have this conversation."

"None," he said. "I haven't been with anybody. I haven't even wanted to. It's just you. You're the reason that I wake up at night hard. You're the reason I wake up in a cold sweat. You are what I want. You are everything that I want."

"Please don't," she said. "Please don't. Because if you can't give me one more piece of you, if you can't give me one more piece of who you are and why you're this way, then why are we having the conversation at all?"

"Do you want to know why? Do you want to know why I'm like this?" He swallowed hard. "My sister died. When I was fourteen. And I was…fucking destroyed. And it just… Everybody around me fell apart. They were so sad. And I was just so angry. So angry. At the universe, at God, at my parents, at the doctors. And at everybody for just crying all the time. Because it killed me."

"Flint," she whispered. "I didn't… I'm so sorry."

"I didn't want you to know. I didn't want to have the conversation with you, because I didn't want you to look at me like that. Like I was an object of pity that you could fix, because you can't fucking fix it, Tansey. Nobody can. That's what death is. It ends something, and you can't fix it. You can't get it back. It broke something in me. And I had to... I had to find a way to get rid of that anger..."

"What did you do?"

"I put a wall up..."

"No," she said softly. "What did you do? Because you are not acting this way because of a feeling you had. You must've done something."

"Yeah," he said, shame burning over his skin. "I did. You know my brother Boone? One time... We shared a room all the time when we were on the road. Right? When we were on the road with the rodeo. And one night he was crying. He was twelve. And he was crying and crying and he wouldn't stop. He just said how much he missed her. I told him to stop. I told him he had to stop. Because it was like... Every time he cried, it was like I was being stabbed in the damn chest. I couldn't handle it. I couldn't listen to it. Because everything that came out as sadness for him stoked the fire of rage inside of me. Because what was tragic to him was just so desperately unfair to me. I told him to stop crying and he didn't. He couldn't. So I punched him in his face. I punched him in his face and I told him he'd better not cry like a little girl anymore. Because it wouldn't bring her back. Because it didn't do anything. It didn't mean anything."

He watched her face, watched to see if she was shocked, because it still shocked him. He still hated it. And he still hated himself for it. "I still remember what that felt like. That anger. It was so pure. It was probably the most real thing I've ever felt in my life. I hated him. And I hated his feelings and what they did to me…"

"That was grief," she said. "That was grief. And I know that I've never experienced grief like that, but I know what it's like to feel angry. I know what it's like to feel like you would rather just be a toxic awful person than the bigger person. Because everything is terrible so why should you have to be anything but terrible."

"You know, my brother still loves me. A lot. He still loves me, because that's what younger brothers have to do. And we're still family. But you… You're not stuck with me. My brother needed me and I failed him. And that's all I know how to do."

"And you don't want a relationship because of what you'll…"

"Because if something happens, that's who I'm going to be. Because in sickness, that's who I would be. Because for poorer, that's who I would be. Because the dark side of those vows would show the dark side in me. And I have never wanted to submit anyone to that. Or a child. I can't imagine that. I would be such a bad father."

"Why do you think that? Because of a reaction you had when you were fourteen? To something hideously traumatizing. Flint, you can't live your entire life based on…"

She faltered. And anger ignited in his gut.

Didn't she understand? He was protecting her. From him. She'd seen a little bit of what he could be like when he was cornered, when someone got too close.

Didn't she understand this was for her?

"Isn't that what you've done? Lived your whole life

in response to a few things that hurt you? Turned them into the biggest thing about you?"

"That's not fair. That's not fair at all."

"Why? Anyway, who said I had to be fair. You wanted to know. You wanted to know why. And that is why. So now you know."

"I'm sorry," she said again. "I'm sorry I… But I want to fix it. I want…"

He didn't know why it hurt so much to talk about, still. It just did. And it probably always would. And it was the pain that he hated so much. That pain that wouldn't go away.

That pain that felt like it defined him.

"And that's why I didn't want to tell you. Because I don't want you to try to fix me. You need to understand that I'm broken, and I know that. I know it. The mistake was getting involved with you at all. And maybe not explaining it then. But I didn't want it to be… I was pretending. I was pretending that I could be something I wasn't. I was pretending that it wouldn't matter. That it could just be for a little while, and I wouldn't hurt you. I really didn't want to hurt you."

He moved toward her, and he put his hand on her cheek. But that was a mistake.

Because he felt it right then. All the anger and pain rising up inside of him, mixing with a desperation that twined around them both.

"Flint," she whispered.

And that was when he leaned in and tasted her lips for the first time in two years.

Chapter 10

She was living in a riot of pain. Of grief. And she knew that she should turn away from him. She knew that she should stop this. She knew that it was insane. He had just told her…everything. He had bared his soul to her. He had told her what he was, who he was. And it was… It was so painful. It was still spinning around inside of her, and she was trying to grapple with it, and failing.

He had lost his sister.

He and his brother…

And he felt like somehow that made him wrong. Made him beyond redemption.

Made him broken.

But it didn't. She knew that it didn't. And she knew she shouldn't kiss him. But his mouth was on hers, and she couldn't deny it, not any more now than she had been able to back then. Because he tasted like everything she wanted. Everything she had always wanted. And there was a reason it had been him. Only him.

And there hadn't been anyone else for him, not since her.

She had been so certain that he had broken her. But maybe they had broken each other a little bit.

"Flint," she whispered. "I haven't… There hasn't been anyone else."

He growled, his large hand cupping the back of her head as he deepened the kiss.

She knew that this was a mistake, for a variety of reasons. They should probably keep talking. They should probably keep talking instead of this. Because this was always there. And it was too easy. And it was maybe going to cut her open. But she couldn't stop. Because it was everything she wanted. Because it was maybe the language he spoke.

Or maybe it was just pure, unsquashed hope inside of her; no matter how much she wanted to believe she was immune, no matter how much she wanted to believe she knew better, she just didn't, never did, never would. Not when it came to him.

And so she kissed him. And kissed him. And there they were in an empty hotel, and there was nobody to walk in on them. Nobody to see.

"I need you," she said. "Please. Please."

Except, he didn't keep her on the couch; he lifted her up into his arms, and began to walk her through the lobby, up the stairs. He carried her away from the direction of her room, down the hall to where she hadn't been to before. He pushed a door open, and her eyes went wide.

It was amazing. A larger, much more masculine bed was in the center of the room, the large windows open. And she knew where they faced. The mountains. So even with them open, even with the lights on, and the darkness outside, nobody would be able to see them.

He set her down at the center of the bed, and pulled his T-shirt up over his head. His body…

It was so perfect. As perfect as it had ever been. His muscles well-defined and cut, every movement making them ripple and shift.

She began to desperately tear at her own clothes. She didn't have a bra on, thankfully, so it was just a sweatshirt, and the pants. And she wasn't embarrassed. Not to be with him. But she never had been. It was right. It felt right. It always did, and it made her want to weep. Because whatever happened, whatever happened when the sun rose, whatever happened when this was all said and done, she was going to be with him again now. And she wanted it. She needed it. Was desperate for it.

"I'm on the pill," she said, her lips feeling numb as she got up on her knees and went to the edge of the bed, putting her hand on his bare chest, her breath hissing through her teeth as she touched him. "I… After I…"

He put his hand over hers, pressed it more deeply against him. "I get it," he said. "Because…because I hurt you. Because I changed things for you. Because I… Fuck," he said. "I'm sorry I said that to you. About being defined by those things. I just hate that I did it. I hate that I did that to you."

"Well, don't hate it right now. Because you probably don't have any condoms, do you?"

He shook his head, a rusty laugh escaping his mouth.

"I sure as hell don't. Because there hasn't been anyone. Not even a temptation, and I definitely didn't plan on meeting anyone up here. Least of all you." He touched her face, skimming the edge of his thumb over her cheekbone. "Least of all you. But then... I never counted on you. Not ever."

She laughed, the sound almost a sob as she wrapped her arms around his neck and kissed him, pressing her naked body against his bare chest.

He growled, moving his hands down her back, to her hips, to her thighs. Then he lifted her up, wrapping her legs around his waist as he carried them both to the center of the bed. He was still wearing his jeans, and she arched against him, his erection, covered in denim, hard still against her body. Rough.

She moaned, rolling her hips against him.

She was so desperate for him. So filled with need, but it wasn't just physical. She felt like she had been alone for two years. While this person, the one person that had ever got to her in this way, was just out there, away from her. Gone from her. And it had been hell.

Singing about it... All the time. Hearing it over and over again, her own pain, unfiltered and raw, playing in her ears all the time...

It was hell, and this wasn't heaven. Because it had a time limit on it, like it always did. Like it always would. And it made her want to hide from truth, from reality, from the intensity of what was rioting through her, but she wanted it too much to hide from it. And that, in the end, was the hardest thing. To know that you were running square into the thing that had mortally wounded you before, and to accept that you were making the choice anyway.

That's what she was doing. She would never know better when it was him. Or maybe she did. Maybe she did, and it would never matter as much as being touched by him.

Maybe it would always be worth the burn to play with his brand of fire. She would despair of it in the morning. Maybe. She would despair of it for years. She knew that already, because she already had.

But now… Now she had him. Now she was with him. And it was everything, and so was he. She skimmed her hands over his chest, down his back. Up to his face again. And she cupped his cheek, and whispered against his mouth, "I want you. I want you so much."

"Tell me," he growled, flexing his hips against her again, her internal muscles pulsing as his hardness hit her right where she needed him most, unerringly.

"I'm wet for you," she said. "Only for you. Only ever for you. I can have anyone. I'm rich and famous. I basically have groupies. Men, women, I could have anyone I want, but I just want you. I just want you. You fucking broke my heart. And look at me, I'm desperate for you. You, Flint Carson."

He growled, and undid the buckle on his belt. Stripped his jeans off, and her breath caught when she saw him, totally naked. Glorious. Beautiful. She needed him. Needed this. More than anything.

"Take me," she said. "Make me yours again. Please. Please." And maybe she said other things, but they were incoherent. Other things, but she didn't understand them. She didn't understand anything except him. He was like a map to herself. This desire a guiding star, bringing her home.

And maybe it would never, ever make sense to anyone else, but she didn't need it to.

She only needed him. Only ever him.

"Take me," she whispered, and he thrust home.

She gasped, tears forming in her eyes, because it felt so right. To have him in her. So deep, she couldn't tell where he ended and she began. And she didn't want to. She wanted this. This feeling of being one. This feeling of being his.

And he began to move, and it was like an ignited spark within her soul. She clung to his shoulders, and she kept her eyes open, because she didn't want to look away.

His name was her every heartbeat.

Flint.

Because whatever happened after this, he was here now. Whatever happened after this, he was hers now.

Whatever happened after this, she would be okay. She had to be okay. Because this had to be worth the risk. This had to be more than a sad country song about being drunk and lonely and missing the one you shouldn't.

Because they had to be more than that. More than a country song. More than a few verses, a chorus and a bridge.

More than her anger. More than her hurt. More than his grief.

Right then, she felt like it might be true. Like they weren't just Tansey and Flint, but all the stars and everything else. Like they weren't just the bad things, but a whole universe of possibility.

She didn't want the moment to pass, because once it did, there would be reality to contend with.

And she didn't want it.

She just wanted him.

That was the scariest thing. After all this time, after all of this.

Knowing better. Knowing he was the cowboy her mother had warned her about…

She just wanted him.

As orgasm crashed over her like a wave, she let herself get taken under.

His heart was still beating so hard he could barely breathe.

He was back in bed with her. With Tansey. And he could pretend that sex was all the same. That he had been the one with experience, so he was the one who was armed against this kind of thing. The one who knew what it was. Whatever that meant. Because there was no defining what this was. Not easily. It wasn't that simple, and it never could be.

It was something different, though. It was something he'd never experienced before, and it was why he hadn't been able to touch anyone since.

She shifted beside him, and he rolled onto his side and looked at her.

And there was something still about it. Something peaceful.

A feeling that he hadn't let himself feel in more years than he could count.

"I'm not really sad that I'm stuck up here anymore."

"Good to know."

"You haven't been with anybody... Why?" She frowned.

"Why haven't you?"

"Well. I could go into a whole monologue about broken trust. And another one about being famous. And how it affects the way that people see you. How it affects the way that you interact with people in all of that. But the simple truth is... I didn't want to be."

He shook his head. "Me either." He wasn't good with feelings; he wasn't good with words. And it wasn't just that he didn't like sharing his feelings; at this point, it was like a language that he had lost. He had feelings— he could acknowledge that. But he had done such a good job of pushing them behind a wall, of suppressing them, that the truth was, he didn't quite know how to translate them. Within his own self, to his own self.

"There was something different about being with you. The idea of letting somebody else put their hands where you'd put them... It was like cursing in a church. Walking on top of sacred ground, when you're supposed to leave it be. I don't know."

She rolled onto her back and looked up at the ceiling. "I don't think I can claim to have felt like it was sacred ground. I just couldn't imagine... I just couldn't imagine. And maybe we needed this. Maybe we needed something more finished. Something not quite so painful." She turned to her side again and put her hand on his chest. He closed his eyes. There was a goodbye in those words. He knew that. Goodbye had always been the only option. Because he couldn't do forever. Which meant goodbye was inevitable, which meant he couldn't rail against what she was saying. Not without changing everything, the entire landscape that he had built up inside of his chest.

The map to who he was.

He remembered vaguely thinking that she was a map to somewhere else, but… He wasn't sure he could follow it.

He wasn't sure he wanted to.

And that meant accepting the silent goodbye.

But for now, they were here. For now, there was no leaving here.

"You changed me," he said finally. "Everything that I'm doing… It's because of you."

"Well, because you were angry at me," she said.

"Does it matter? It was still a change."

"I guess not. Because I guess the same could be said for me."

"What are your plans for Christmas?" he asked. His own family would have their big rowdy get-together, and he would pretend he didn't hate it.

"I'm going to visit my mother. In Palm Springs. That's where her house is. She wanted to be warm. She wanted palm trees." He saw a tear slide down her cheek. "I'm always so afraid that I might lose this. You know, the money is a big deal. My mother raised me in a trailer, never knowing if we were going to have enough to make rent, to keep the lights from being shut off. I found that in the end, revenge wasn't the important piece so much as love. Giving back for the love my mother showed me. She's a tough woman. But she loves me. I know that having me made her life harder, but she never acted like I was a burden. She always said that I was a gift. I like giving her things. I like paying her back… I like…"

"You bought your mother a house," he said. "And on top of all of that, you're her daughter. I don't think you'd lose her if something happened with your career."

"Maybe not. But she's the only person that stayed in my life always. The only person who was there at every step, and I finally got to give back to her, and what if someday it isn't enough?"

Unspoken was the idea that she clearly felt like she hadn't been enough for her father.

"Do you think you weren't enough for me?"

The words scraping his throat raw, it was dancing close to things that he didn't want to talk about. Things that he didn't want to admit.

"What else is a woman supposed to think? If I had been enough…"

He reached out and put his hand on her cheek. "No. If you learn one thing from what I told you, if you take one thing away from it, then take this. If there was anything that could fix me, it would've been you. It was never fair for me to touch you. Because when I tell you my problems are mine, and when I tell you they are built into the deepest part of who I am, I need you to believe that."

She didn't say anything. "Like I said. I think we needed this. I think this is important."

He nodded slowly. Except he didn't really like that conclusion for some reason. He'd always been like this with her. He wanted it both ways. To have her. To stay safe. He already knew he couln't do both.

"I might not be able to fix all the things inside of me, but maybe I can fix what I did to you," he said.

"I don't need you to fix me, Flint. That's actually been part of the conclusion that I've come to. Yeah, I was angry at you. I was. But I was afraid too, because if I hadn't been, I wouldn't have saved all of that for a song. I would have said it to you. Yes, I was hurt by what happened. You know that. I was devastated. I let myself believe that what you said about yourself was wrong. I let myself believe that because things changed for me they would change for you too. But I wasn't trying to spare you by holding back, I was trying to spare myself."

"That's all any of us are trying to do," he said, the words coming from somewhere deep inside of him, and he hadn't realized how true they were until he'd said them.

But he made a concerted effort to shut off any realizations that might come as a result.

"My family always does a big Christmas thing," he said finally. "And I pretend that I like it. But I don't. I pretend that I like it, because you have to do that with your family. You have to do that for your family. Especially when… You know, I feel like they've all moved on without me. Like they've all reached some kind of healing that I just can't find. Some of my brothers have lagged behind a little bit. But now three of them are getting married." He laughed. "Well. Not all of them. My brother Buck… Something happened a long time ago, and he left. There was an accident and he… He wasn't the same after. I know that eats at my parents. Because even though he didn't die, they lost another child. He was never himself, and then he went away. He's the only one that didn't stay. The only one that didn't stay on the ranch, the only one that didn't stay in the rodeo. I'm angry at him, you know. I'm angry at him for leaving. For not doing what I do."

"And what's that?"

"I don't feel any of it either. I don't feel healed. I don't feel happy to be there. I can't handle the emotions of it. I can't handle the way my mom wants to talk about my sister and share memories. I can't handle sitting around and telling stories, like there could ever be happy memories of somebody that you'll just miss for the rest of your life. But I do it. And if I want to rage, I do it on the inside. Because I did what I had to do to deal with myself so that I could be there for my family. So honestly, fuck him."

He watched a series of complicated emotions flit across Tansey's face. And of course, he saw pity among them.

"I never wanted you to feel sorry for me," he said.

"Only a jerk wouldn't feel sorry for you. Are you sorry for me that my dad left?"

"Well, yeah…"

"I'm sorry for you. Because this is hard, and terrible. Because it's more than anyone should have had to deal with. Because it's difficult and sad. Because…"

"What?"

"Because it's not fair. All the things that happened to us that break our hearts before we can ever make choices. You don't choose your family. And I had a terrible father. You have a great family, but it still came with tragedy, and I… I just don't think it's fair."

"No. It's not." An idea turned over in his head. "But

you know, I was going to take the opportunity to decorate the hotel while it was empty."

"You were going to decorate."

He shrugged. "I told you. That's the thing I'm good at doing. And I figured I would do it myself. Get the Christmas decorations up before the guests start coming to spend their holidays here. There's a lot of people planning to spend Christmas Day right here. We got a big Christmas dinner and…there's a big tree out on the back porch that I haven't brought in yet, and decorations ready to go in one of the back offices."

"Let's do it," she said. "Let's decorate."

"You want to decorate?"

She nodded. "We had a tiny tinsel tree in the mobile home, and then… We don't really do Christmas every year. Because sometimes I'm busy, and we're not always in the same place. We always call. But if I'm by myself, there's no reason to put up decorations and…"

"Well. If you're interested."

And he didn't say what he knew. That they were both maybe trying to make the night last longer. Because who knew what would happen come morning. When trees could be moved and roads could be plowed, and the temperatures would get above freezing and everything would start melting.

Yeah, he didn't know what would happen after that.

Chapter 11

She waited, wrapped in just the robe again, while Flint went and got boxes of ornaments from where they'd been stored back in the manager's office.

He was shirtless, and in her mind, she knew this would always be Christmas. This man, wearing nothing but jeans low riding on his lean hips, carrying big boxes of decorations.

And it made her a little bit sad, because it was another thing that would belong to Flint Carson forever.

You have to figure that out.

She did. Because she hadn't slept with him again to break her own heart again. She had wanted to say good-bye.

Not because anything he'd told her about himself horrified her. No. He wasn't the monster that he thought he was, and she knew that. It was simply that she also knew who she was.

And they had tried this before.

And now she needed to listen when he told her who he was.

And what he wanted.

She pushed off the sadness, and watched as he went toward the back of the major lobby area, throwing open the doors at the back.

They had the whole place lit up, and she wondered if anyone could see that, at 2:00 a.m., this giant building was a beacon of light on the hill. If anyone could see the outline of his body as he stood there, backlit in the doorway. Snowflakes whipped in around him, and she just sat and stared.

"What are you doing?"

"Christmas tree," he said. "It is a huge ass tree."

He had already placed a stand at the center of the room, and he disappeared a moment later, and then came back. The tree was huge. It must weigh hundreds of pounds, and he had it hefted over his shoulders, like one of those guys at the gym that did all the major weight lifting like it was just a fun thing people did on a Saturday morning.

"You need help?"

"Oh come on," he said, a grin curving his lips.

So she just sat there, and watched as he positioned the tree in the stand. It was massive.

But she didn't really care about the tree. Mostly, she was watching him. How beautiful he was. How perfect.

There was just no other man that made her feel this way. No other man that captured every facet of her attention. But she didn't think there was a more beautiful man in the entire world. How could there be? And she sat there, living in the feeling she'd had when they had walked up from her truck. When she had let those broad shoulders—so perfectly defined and glorious, revealed to her now—shield her from the wind.

And she realized, it was the man he was.

Not the man he could be.

Because she listened to him talk about his family.

It wasn't that he didn't do that, all the time. Shoulder other people's burdens, protect them.

He used his strength all the time, every family gathering, every Christmas. He denied himself, and his own comfort, for the people he cared for.

The issue was, he just didn't have the capacity to extend it to her too.

It was a painful realization, but one she could accept. How could she not accept the fact that he gave everything to a family that loved him so much?

Family was supposed to be who you did that for.

Her father had never done it for her, and look at the way it had broken things.

His older brother was gone, and that, she knew, put more pressure on him. It was why he was angry.

Because he was already at capacity.

She couldn't ask him to do any more.

It would make her love a burden.

It wasn't a flaw in him. It was actually because he was just so...

"All right," he said. "Let's get some decorations on this thing. Well, let's start with a fire, because now I'm freezing."

"That's the hazard of going outside half naked in this weather." She grinned. "Not that I'm complaining." She didn't want to slide into morose thinking. She didn't want to think about when the sun would rise. She didn't want to think about anything but this moment.

Because this would be the moment that sustained her. The moment that moved her on. That moved her into a place of acceptance about what they'd had, and what was possible. Because that was the issue; that was why she was so hurt. It was believing they could have had more if only… If only he could change. And she realized that he couldn't. That he needed to be who he was to survive, and to be there for his family.

It wasn't a deficiency in him.

It was almost sadder than if he just wasn't good at all.

But only almost.

And this was their moment. So she was going to take it.

He built a fire, big and warm, almost enough to take her robe off. But she felt like maybe decorating the Christmas tree naked was a bridge too far.

They took strings of sparkling white lights out of boxes, and he put up a ladder so that the lights could get wrapped all the way around, all the way to the top.

There were large sparkling red globes, and gold stars, and when they were finished, she had never seen anything more beautiful.

A Christmas tree that was theirs. That had nothing to do with her mother's stress with the season, or her childhood guilt over making her mother put any extra effort into anything, because she already worked so hard, and she definitely didn't deserve to feel guilty over the presents that she couldn't buy Tansey.

Just something that belonged to them. And even in this moment it was absent the sadness that had been inside of her ever since…

Ever since she had met this man, and then had to figure out how to live a life that didn't have him anymore.

Ever since they'd lived one summer that had defined so much of who they were. Because even he had admitted that it had changed him.

And maybe that was the real thing that she needed to understand. That it had been fate, even if it had been a bruised and bloody fate, one that they'd had to fight to find the meaning of.

Maybe she had to accept that sometimes she had to go through hard things, terrible things, to become who she was supposed to be.

Wasn't that every highbrow Hollywood movie? The complicated happy ending, rather than the traditional one.

She had certainly never seen that sort of happy ending in real life.

In real life, her mother was having a happy ending by herself, in Palm Springs with other people her age, laughing and drinking and enjoying life by the pool. Reaping the benefits of having been a good mother, a hard worker, and not having to do it anymore.

She didn't have a man. She didn't need a man. The lesson of her heartbreak had been that she didn't need one to be happy.

Tansey had needed her heartbreak for her fame, and she needed this bittersweet moment to find the next phase.

Flint was important to her. But that didn't mean he was her forever, not in a way that meant he would be in her life always.

He was forever in terms of how he'd changed her, though.

And maybe that was the most real way for a relationship to last.

"Hang on just a second."

He went behind the reception desk, and bent down for a moment, and then music filled the room. Old-fashioned Christmas carols. And she looked around the glittering space, looked at the way his body was in the firelight and the way the tree sparkled.

It was the sweetest, sexiest moment of her whole life. And she didn't know how those two things combined to become one thing, but they had. Did.

He reached his hand out. "Want to dance?"

"I don't know how," she said.

"Me either. But I want to."

She took his hand, and he lifted her up off the couch, and twirled her in time with the music, her robe spinning out around her, exposing her legs, and maybe more, but there was no embarrassment with him. She laughed, and he brought her back to him, and they swayed back and forth, and whether or not it could be called dancing was up for debate.

But it was perfect. This moment, was perfect. Even if she couldn't see past it.

And with the music swirling around them, and the firelight glowing, she stretched up on her toes, and she kissed him.

* * *

His heart was pounding so hard he thought it might burst through his chest.

He had never liked Christmas. He had never liked any of the symbolism associated with it. But for him, he knew that this would always be Christmas. Every time he had to sit through an endless family present-opening session, every time they went down to the fanciest restaurant in Lone Rock for their annual Christmas Eve dinner, he would think of this. He would think of her.

The only person he'd ever wanted to do a romantic thing for. The only person who had ever made him wish that he was someone else.

He didn't waste time regretting the things that had happened. He didn't waste time railing against the universe anymore for taking his sister away from them. Because it didn't do any good. It only reopened old wounds.

But this made him want to do that. She had always made him want to do that, and maybe that was the biggest reason he had let her go. Because she made him wish that things could be different. And he knew that that was an endless trap that you could fall into and never get out of.

But right now, he just wanted the moment. He wanted to surrender to it. To her.

And so he did. He kissed her, with every ounce of desire in his soul. He held her against him, relishing the feel of her curves against his body as he did.

He kissed her. Kissed her like he might die if he didn't, and he wondered if part of him had. All these years when he'd been without her. All these years when he'd told himself that he didn't need her. That he had done the right thing. *How can anything but this be right?*

He cradled her face in his hands, kissed her deep, kissed down the elegant column of her throat, sliding his tongue over the line of her collarbone. At the same time, his hands found the belt on her robe, and undid it slowly, pushing it away from her body. Letting it fall to the ground. She was beautiful. And it was like unwrapping a Christmas present. The only one he'd ever cared about. The only one he could remember ever wanting.

She was famous now. A woman the whole world wanted a piece of.

But she was a woman that he had. A woman whose body he knew better than his own, even though before tonight it had been two years since he'd seen her. Two years since he'd touched her.

Mine.

The word welled up inside of him. He couldn't remember the last time he'd wanted anyone or anything this badly.

Maybe he never had. Because he hadn't let himself.

Because wanting… Wanting like this, it was almost a curse. But he couldn't turn away from it. Not now. Not when it was like this. So desperate. Her hands went to his belt buckle, undid it slowly, then to his jeans.

And he let himself feel what he hadn't that first time. The all of it. That she had never let anyone else inside of her, except for him. And he had done what with that?

Why had he taken it if he had known that he couldn't honor it? Why had he taken her if he had known he couldn't give her what she deserved?

Maybe because he wasn't as strong as he liked to

think. He was weak. For her. It had always been that way. From moment one.

And right now he just needed her. He hadn't needed sex in two years. It wasn't just about that. Wasn't just about a simple dry spell, because if so, he would have done something about it. If so, he would have found someone else. That was just sex. For him, it was about her.

And he wanted to show that to her.

He laid her down slowly on the thick rug in front of the fireplace, kissed her mouth, kissed her breasts.

Her body was a brilliant gift, something rich and lovely in the firelight. Something that nothing and no one would ever be able to overshadow.

She was his summer. And now she was his winter too.

Or maybe he'd made his own winter these past two years, but she was the reason why. The reason why it felt so dark. The reason why everything in him had changed.

Because it had been an eclipse on anything good when he let her walk out of his life.

He wanted to show her that.

He wanted to give her everything.

He kissed his way down the softness of her body, kissed her inner thigh, then licked a line to her center. She gasped. And he fed off of her. Off of her pleasure. Off of her arousal. Her need.

He let himself disappear into the moment. Into the glory of pleasuring her. The responsibility of it. The honor of it.

To be allowed to taste her like this. To be allowed to touch her like this. Who was he? He was just some dumbass. And she had always been special. Always been singular. And the men in her life, him included, had made her feel like she was second. Had made her feel like she wasn't good enough. Made her feel like she was a burden. How dare they? And how dare he?

He didn't deserve this moment. He didn't deserve her.

But he was taking her. Because he needed it. Because he needed her to know.

He licked her, took her essence as an offering, a gift. Even as it fed his soul.

The taste of her. The sound of her cries. Her desperate arousal, the way that she clawed at his shoulders, the way that she cried out her need when he pushed two fingers inside of her and took her to the heights.

He waited for her to come down, and then he kissed her hip bone, her stomach, back up to her mouth, where he let her taste the evidence of her own desire on his lips.

"You," he said, "are like no one else. You are like nothing else. You are air. And I hadn't realized that I'd been suffocating all this time."

"Flint…"

The way that she said his name, all sweet and tender and questioning, it did something to him.

The way that she looked at him, like he might be something amazing. Something great.

He wanted to be.

He wanted to be more than he'd been. He wanted to be something better. Something right for her.

He wanted that.

He kissed her, deep and long, lost himself in her.

But it was what she did next that he couldn't handle. It was what she did next that broke him.

She pushed against his chest, reversing their positions, and once he was stripped naked, she knelt down before him, and took him into her mouth. She looked up at him, her beautiful green eyes piercing him through the soul while she racked his body with torturous pleasure.

Fuck.

He pushed his hands into her hair, held her there, bucking his hips, desperate for release and desperate for it to go on forever.

He could remember when a blowjob had been entertainment. When it had meant nothing to him. When it had touched nothing but his cock. And now… It was like it was all of him. He couldn't take pleasure anymore unless it was her. He couldn't take pleasure with her without involving everything. His whole body. All that he was. His soul.

She sucked him deep, and he growled. "No. I need to be in you."

It was her turn to kiss him. Her turn to let him taste what she'd done to him.

And then she straddled his hips, angling herself so that the head of him was pressed against the slick entrance to her body. He gritted his teeth as she lowered herself onto him, allowing him in, inch by torturous inch.

She was so tight, so perfect.

And he had never done this before her. Taking a woman without a latex barrier. That was the kind of thing reserved for trust.

Trust.

She had trusted him so much back then and he had broken it.

He didn't deserve it now. But he needed it.

Needed her.

Needed all these things that he had no call to want. Dammit all, he did.

With his whole soul.

His heart was raging, as she began to move. She began to ride him like she was made for it. And hell, she had to be. Had to be made for this, for him. Because God knew he thought he might be made for her.

In another life maybe. One where he hadn't lost so much. One where he hadn't hurt so damn much.

That realization almost stopped him, but then, he was overcome, seeing her body as she rose over him like that, feeling the clasp of her around him, watching the pleasure on her face as she began to chase her own climax.

He wasn't a man who had the ability to do what she did. To take feelings and turn them into song lyrics. Hell, he couldn't even take feelings and turn them into words.

He couldn't take feelings and turn them into much of anything.

But he wanted to. For her.

He wanted to do more, to be more. To be better.

For her.

He wished that he could erase his past. His loss. His pain. Because it had broken him.

And he never wished that. He never wished it because there was no point. Just like there was no point in tears. No point in regret.

But she had come to him untouched, and not without pain, and he had come to her broken beyond repair.

He wished he could be different.

And he gave himself up to that. To the need to be more than he ever had been for her.

Because who had been there for her?

Here she was, worrying about what she could give her mother… Who worried about what they could give to her?

She thought she wasn't enough.

And he had been part of that.

"You're beautiful," he said, gripping her hips and guiding her up and down on his cock. "The most beautiful woman I've ever seen. You deserve everything. You deserve the world."

Hands braced on his chest, he could see her eyes begin to glitter. See tears welling there, and it just made him want to give her even more.

"You deserve everything you've got. You deserve all the money from that song. You are absolutely perfect. In every way."

She closed her eyes, and began to shake, and he could feel the tenuous grip he had on his control beginning to slip. "You're a star," he said. "And you're more than enough."

And then she dissolved, and he went right along with it, his climax like a vicious beast, grabbing him around the throat and shaking him hard.

"I love you," she said. "I love you."

And just like that, very deep inside of her, with her words echoing inside of him, it was like a sledgehammer had been taken to the walls all around his soul. The gates that held back his emotions demolished with three simple words.

And he felt like he had been dragged out into the middle of an open field, naked. Exposed and vulnerable to every attack.

It was as if blinders he had put up intentionally had dissolved. As if everything that he had put up between them had vanished.

Everything.

I love you.

And it was too much. Too much. It reminded him of the moment when he had hit Boone. Because it was like something sharp and vicious was cutting open his insides. Like his heart was going to explode. It wasn't that he felt nothing. It was that he felt everything, and he had no idea how to combat that. No idea what to do about it. There was nothing, he realized. Because the problem was knowing it was the truth. Knowing that what he had been protecting himself all along from was the intensity of it.

The desperation of it.

And he couldn't un-know it now.

He felt terrified. Utterly terrified. Because she loved him, and he felt more than any one person should. Because she loved him, and he felt like he might break apart. Because she loved him, and it truly felt like hell. Because she loved him, and he was faced with the realization that she was so fragile. So beautiful. And life had come along and taken that from him. It had already taken so much.

The more you cared, the more you could lose.

And he realized...

That was all this was. It was all it had ever been. All he had ever been truly afraid of. It was losing someone he loved again. It was caring so much he could be in that position where he felt too much. Where he wanted too much.

He had punched Boone, because Boone had felt all of the things that lived inside of him. All of the things he wanted to turn away from. All of the things he wanted to deny.

But he was still holding her, and he was still in her, and he couldn't help himself. "I love you too."

He lay back on the floor, feeling like he had just lost a war.

One he had been fighting for the better part of his life. One he hadn't even realized he'd been on the slow path to losing from the minute he had first seen her.

Every bit of his resolve. Every bit of everything, it was broken. Demolished. And so was he.

He knew why he had been fighting it all this time. Knew why he had been fighting her.

He damn well did.

Because this was terrifying. He was happy to throw himself on the back of an angry bull; he was happy to work until his body ached and his hands bled.

It was the feeling. That was what he didn't want to do. Not what he couldn't do. It was the thing that scared him. Believing so much in something, hoping so much. Loving someone so much, and losing them anyway. Losing everything anyway.

"You love me?"

He sat up, staring straight at the Christmas tree that they had just decorated together.

Staring straight at the Christmas that could be his if...

"Shit," he said.

"What?"

"I…"

He was suddenly choked. By the memories. The memories of that night that they had broken up. The memory of the night that he had lost her.

That he had let her walk away.

She had thought that she might be pregnant with his baby and he'd said he didn't want it. Of course he wanted it. He wanted everything with her. He wanted a whole life. A baby and everything, but facing down that possibility, that little bit of hope… It had been too much for him. He hadn't been able to claim it. He hadn't been able to admit it.

And now… He felt swamped with it. With the loss of it. The loss of that potential future. The baby, her.

All the things that he hadn't been able to say then. And he wanted to say them now.

So he looked up at her, and he tried. "I don't know if I'll be a good dad," he said. "I don't know if I'll be able to be a good husband. I have lived in absolute fear for so long, Tansey. For so long. Because when I was a kid, I knew my sister was sick. Of course I did. We spent all that time in hospitals, all that time around doctors, and it wasn't like my parents didn't try to prepare us. But you don't understand *dead* when you're fourteen years old. And you can't. It's just the most absurd thing. I had a sister. And she was wonderful. The cutest kid. The sweetest… And why? *Why?* It never made any sense. That I could never… I couldn't live with what it made me feel. I had to figure out some way to stop it. I couldn't help Boone with what he felt because it was killing me. As if my own pain wasn't enough, I had to watch it torture him too. I had to watch it torture everybody, and that was what broke me. It absolutely broke me into pieces. And that was the man that met you."

He sat there, his words so heavy. Everything so heavy. "I have told myself that I did not have it in me to give anybody the support they needed if they were going through a hard time. That I didn't have it in me, because of the way I reacted to Boone. But when you said that... When you said you loved me just now... It was like you shone a light on all those dark places inside of me, and I can't pretend I don't know what it really is."

"What is it?" she asked.

"Fear. I'm afraid. I'm a coward. Because you're a gift. A beautiful, lovely gift. Too perfect to be real almost. And more what I want than I ever wanted to admit. More than I ever wanted to want. And suddenly it terrifies me. Like the sky might cave in and take you away from me." He cleared his throat. "When you told me that you thought you might be pregnant... It was the ferocity of what I felt that shut me down. Because it was like...hope, with teeth. It's the best way I can describe it."

"I know all about that. About hope with teeth. Every time I've ever looked at you, Flint. And wanted to believe that we could be something that we were never meant to be. Because you were that cowboy, the one that I was supposed to stay away from. The one that I was never supposed to love. You were that cowboy. And I knew better. But something in me didn't want to know better. Because it just wanted you. What I really wanted was you."

"I don't know what to do with this. I don't know.

But I know that I can't walk away from you. Not again. Not ever again."

"I can't walk away from you either. I need you too much. I need us."

"I… I don't know if I can. I don't know… But I want it. I want to do whatever I have to do to figure this out. To fix myself. So that I can be what you need."

"Flint…"

"But you were always enough," he said. "It was me. It was always me. I was the one who couldn't cope. I was the one who flinched. You were always enough. What your father couldn't do was fix himself. I want to. For you. For us. For the future. I'm glad you wrote that song. I'm glad you told the truth about what I did to you. Because I needed to know. I needed to really know."

"But what about you?"

"It ruined me. Broke me. And now… You put me back together. I'm still not quite in perfect condition. But I'm trying. I want… I want forever. Please."

"Are you serious?"

"I am dead serious. I know that I don't deserve that level of trust. I know that I don't deserve for you to give that to me… But damn, I want you. More than I've ever wanted anyone or anything. And I want you more than I want to be the kind of safe I've been all these years. Because it was too late. The minute I caught you outside that gate, the minute that happened, it was too late. Too late for me to keep doing what I was doing. Too late for me to hang on to all the ugly stuff. All the broken stuff. I tried. And I nearly broke us both. So now I just want to surrender to it."

"I had accepted… I had accepted the idea that there

was no way for us to have a happy ending. That I was going to have to accept that it was going to be another kind of happy. You know, the kind when you walk away, but at least you learned something."

"It's the easy way," he said. "This… What I want with you… It's going to be the hard way. Because I'm not perfect. And I am certainly not perfectly healed all of a sudden just because I want to be. This might be hard. Deciding to be together instead of just deciding to walk away wounded. I know that. I get that. But I think it's worth it. You and me. I think it damn well will be. Those endings… Those endings where people are apart, it's not better. It's not deeper. It's just easier. Because it's easier to walk around with your own shit and never have to deal with it. It is so much harder to have to take someone else's on, and I got to ask you to take on mine."

Her face went soft. "Well, you're gonna have to take on mine too. I'm not exactly in perfect working order myself. I couldn't tell you what I wanted then."

"Tell me what you want now. I will do my damnedest to give it to you, because I love you. Because you are worth it to me. Because you are everything. You are everything and none of it matters. Because there is no protection worth having, there is no piece of my soul worth preserving, if you are out there in the world and I'm not with you."

Tears started to fall down her cheeks. "I want to spend the rest of my life with you. I don't want this to end. I want you to be the father of my children. I want you to be everything. I fell in love with you, Flint, even knowing that I shouldn't. I fell in love with you even though it wasn't what I wanted. I was afraid, but I knew that loving you was worth the risk. I just did somehow. These last two years I questioned it, and I tried so hard to call it something important. To call it something worthy. I tried to tell myself that I didn't need that fairy-tale happy ending. But I wanted it with you. It was never enough to not have you. When you sent me away, I was devastated." She wiped tears away from her cheek. "I waited until I got to a motel six hours down the road, and then I cried. For days. And then..."

"Do you think you were pregnant?"

She nodded slowly. "Probably. Even if we would've stayed together, I think I would have lost it."

"But I could've been there for you," he said. Everything in him felt wrong. Sad. Angry at himself for the choices that he'd made. For the ways in which he hadn't protected her. The ways in which he had protected himself instead. "I wish that I would've been there for you. Because if there's one thing I know, it's that I cannot promise you a life without pain. It's something I'm coming to accept. The fact that I can't escape it no matter how much I might want to. But I can promise to be there for you. And I can promise to help try to carry the burden if it's too heavy. And to carry you if I have to."

"Yes," she whispered, closing her eyes. "But I need you to do something." She put her hand on his chest. "I need you to forgive yourself. Because our relationship shouldn't be a penance that you're paying. Our love isn't you making up for the past. You did the best you could then. I just want you to do the best you can do now."

"I promise you that," he said, his heart about ready to pound through his chest. "I promise."

He felt raw, and exposed. He felt fundamentally changed. His whole world felt like it had been tilted a bit. Or maybe like it had been put right. It was a lot, to recognize that he was afraid, and had been all this time.

And he was going to take a long time to sort through it; he knew that. But he knew one thing now. And he knew it well.

"I love you."

Chapter 12

Of all the things Tansey had thought she would hear from him as the sun was just beginning to rise over the tops of the mountains…that was not it. The night had not turned out the way she had expected. Because she had been certain they would be parting from each other in the morning, again.

She had even been ready for it.

But she kept thinking about what he said. About how redemption, change, was the hardest thing.

She knew it was true.

Forgiveness, and the choice. The choice to just love.

To believe that it wasn't her that was broken, but her father. To believe that she was enough all on her own.

But that she really wanted to be with Flint all the same.

She had accepted that she might say she loved him, and not have a life with him.

She had never imagined this. The chance to have a life with him.

And suddenly, none of it mattered. If she ever wrote another song—but she was pretty sure she would. It just all felt like…there was more now. More than striving. More than trying to show people that she was worth something.

More than trying to be the best. It was the strangest thing, but loving him, being in this moment, it made her feel like she might be able to live for herself for the first time.

And living that way with him…

It was a happy ending that was somehow beyond anything she had ever fantasized about.

"I love you too," she said.

"Marry me. The whole thing. Everything. The forever thing."

"Just like that? Just like that you aren't scared anymore?"

"I'm terrified. Fucking shaking in my boots. It's just that now I know it doesn't matter. I would rather love you, and live every day with some kind of fear that I might lose you, than not have you in my life. I would rather feel everything. Be damn near overflowing with it, than live comfortable and empty without you."

"You make it sound awful."

"No." He smiled. "It's wonderful."

And she thought what she had concluded earlier. That they were some kind of fate. Even if it was a bloody, hard-won fate. And she knew that it was even more than that. Because they had the chance to be the kind of fate that she had imagined briefly earlier tonight. The kind that was bittersweet and sad.

But they were choosing to be more. The kind of fate that was more. The kind of fate that was everything. She realized that this kind of fate involved a whole lot of choosing. Because you could fall right into a man's arms, but unless you chose each other, you might not end up together. Unless you decided to let go, of all kinds of things, of hurt, of fear, and embrace hope...

Hope with teeth.

She knew exactly what he meant by that. And she would risk getting savaged by hope every time, if it meant getting to be with him.

But as she looked at him, as she went willingly into his arms, she realized, it wasn't hope with teeth. Not anymore.

This was hope with strong arms, with a steady smile and the truest heart she knew.

"This is a song," she said.

"I can't wait to hear it," he said.

She grinned at him. "I can't wait to live it."

Chapter 13

He decided to go home for Christmas with Tansey. She called her mother and invited her to come from Palm Springs, and she had agreed to make the trek, which had surprised Tansey, since her mom was pretty wedded to her warm weather and palm trees.

But it also pleased her.

He would've done whatever he had to do to make sure they could do Christmas in both places, or maybe he would've had to disappoint his family.

He was willing to do that.

Because he was done performing. Done trying to do things to make up for what he thought he lacked.

But there was one thing he needed to do. And it was the thing that made Christmas so special this year.

Not just because he was going to be introducing Tansey as his fiancée, but he was pretty excited about that.

First, he had to give her the ring.

Which he intended to do at midnight on Christmas Eve. Then on Christmas morning she could wear it and show his family.

Yeah. He was looking forward to that.

But first, during a family board game, he sneaked into the kitchen to find his mother. "Hi, Mom," he said.

She turned to him, smiling. "What is it, honey?"

He reached out and pulled her into his arms, hugging her. "I just wanted to tell you that I love you. And that I'm sorry. It's been hard for me to say things like this. But… Things are changing for me. I'm going to try to change. I'm going to try to be different."

His mother put her hand on his forearm, and patted it. "Flint, honey. You never needed to change."

"I did. I think… I think in time you'll see the difference."

"Well, I love you all the same."

He nodded, and walked out of the kitchen. The next person he needed to talk to was Boone. When he walked out into the hall, Tansey was there. "Are you okay?" she asked.

"Yeah. I'm just… You know. I'm doing what we talked about."

"Yeah. It's going to be fine."

"I know it will be. Because I have you."

"Good luck." She squeezed him, and he went outside, where he knew his brother was, down at the barn.

Boone was facing away from him, on the phone. "Yeah, well, if you're going to go on a bender on Christmas Eve, you might want to fucking call your wife and let her know where you're at…No idea…She texted me,

because she was looking for you. And I think you should
be ashamed that your wife has an easier time getting a
hold of me than she does you…Yeah. Well. Get over
yourself. You're drunk. And it's not even 5:00 p.m., and
your wife and your two kids are…Seriously. Whatever.
I'm not going to lie for you. I'm going to tell her that
you're drunk. It's your problem to sort out, Daniel." He
hung the phone up and turned around. "Oh. How long
have you been standing there?"

"That Daniel Stevens?"

"Yeah. Fucker." He rubbed his hand over his face.
"It's… You know, it's Christmas Eve and he's not home
and Wendy texted me looking for him and… I can't lie
for him. And I'm not going to. She's way too good for
him. He's such a dick."

The ferocity on Boone's face told a whole story. But
Flint had a feeling his brother wasn't in the space to
tell it. Daniel was another rodeo rider, and a friend of
Boone's, and he'd gotten married ten years ago. Flint
had met his wife on a few occasions. She was very
pretty. He had to wonder if his brother thought so too.

"Well. Sounds like you should do the opposite of
lying for him. You should probably tell on him."

"Yeah. I have half a mind to."

"Boone…" He cleared his throat. "This is going to
seem like it's coming out of the blue for you. But… You
know I brought Tansey home."

"Yeah. And the song was about you."

"The song was about me. And she and I had a lot
to work out. In regard to that. We had to address why
I broke up with her in the first place. And I told her
about…about the thing I am most ashamed of."

"What's that?"

He looked at his brother, and he could see that Boone genuinely didn't know.

"When you were crying about Sophia. And I hit you. And I told you not to cry anymore."

Boone looked away. "Hey. That's not a big deal. We were kids. You were a kid."

"Yeah. I was. But there was still… I was afraid. I was afraid of everything, and most of all, I was afraid of that pain never going away. Never ending. And your pain made mine worse. So I lashed out. And then… I have carried the guilt for that, and I use that guilt as an excuse. I used it to tell myself that I didn't deserve to have relationships because I wouldn't be able to be there for someone, because look at what I did to you when you needed me most." He shook his head. "But that wasn't it. I was just afraid of how much I felt. And I took it out on you. And I used it as an excuse my whole life."

"There's no guidebook on how to handle stuff like that," said Boone. "And I'm not gonna claim I'm any less messed up than you."

"Yeah. But some of the messed up you are might be my fault."

"No," said Boone. "Hell no. You were always there for me. And yeah, you're kind of a stoic bastard. But you're a good man, Flint, and you have been the whole time. Not saying you haven't made mistakes. I've heard the song."

"Well. She forgives me. I'm going to marry her."

"Good," said Boone. "You should. And hell, if she can forgive you, I certainly can. Even if I don't feel like there's much to forgive."

"Thank you," he said, and he meant it. Because whether Boone was willing to admit it or not, Flint knew that he needed that forgiveness.

And then he did something he knew his brother would be allergic to. He reached out and hugged him. Clapped him on the back. "I'm going to ask her to marry me," he said. "Well. I already did. But I'm going to get down on one knee and give her a ring and everything."

Boone looked at him long and hard. "Good for you."

"Do you think you're ever going to do that?"

He chuckled. And it sounded kind of bitter. "I have a barrier to that. It isn't the same thing you have. But it's…an issue."

And yet again, he wondered about the phone call he just overheard.

"Well. If you want to talk about it, I'm here. And newly in touch with my feelings."

"Wow. I'm going to pass on that."

"Okay. Love you."

And he'd said it. And he meant it. Boone flipped him off, and that felt about perfect.

At midnight, he and Tansey were in his room, and that was when he did it.

"I have something for you." He got down on one knee in front of her. "Tansey Martin…will you marry me? For real. Forever?"

Tears sparkled in her eyes as she nodded, and he took the ring out of the box and slid it onto her finger. "I know you can buy yourself any piece of jewelry that you want."

"But I want this one. Because it's from you." She smiled. "I have a song that I want to play for you."

"Well. Then I want to hear it."

She sat down on the edge of the bed, holding her guitar, and this one was different. A little more upbeat than the songs she usually played.

And this song was about love. Choosing it, hanging on to it.

Love is cactuses
Good-luck charms and bad-luck nights
Sunny days and colder weather
Letting go and holding on
And I've heard the best revenge is living well
But the best is letting go
So you can just love
In the end, it's all that matters
In the end, it's the greatest

And he knew it was true. The real story of them. Good and bad and the two years in between, when they didn't have each other at all. And he was grateful. So grateful, that she had decided to let go of all the anger she had every right to have, so that they could love each other instead.

She had apologized to him recently, for the song. For the fact that some people would never accept they were back together, because they were still holding on to that story she'd told so well.

"It's part of our story," he'd said. "And I wouldn't trade it. Because it had to happen for us to end up here."

It was true. He'd had to break again to know that he wanted to be whole.

"You know," he said. "I was wrong, about winning. I

said that you couldn't love anything. That you couldn't care about anything more. But loving you, that is winning. And everything else… Everything else is just noise."

She kissed him. "I love you. And it's winning for me too."

"It was the cactus."

She laughed. "You can't prove that."

And he smiled against her mouth. "You can't prove that it wasn't."

* * * * *

A TEXAN FOR CHRISTMAS

JULES BENNETT

One

Scarlett Patterson clutched the handle of her small suitcase and waited.

And waited.

She'd knocked twice on the door, but still no answer. She knew this was the address she'd been given—a small cabin nestled in the back of the sprawling, picturesque Pebblebrook Ranch. She'd been told exactly who she'd be working for and her belly did flips just thinking of Beau Elliott—deemed Hollywood's Bad Boy, the Maverick of Movies, Cowboy Casanova...the titles were endless.

One thing was certain, if the tabloids were correct— he made no apologies about his affection for women. Scarlett wasn't sure she'd ever seen an image of him with the same woman.

That is, until his lover turned up pregnant. Then the

two were spotted out together, but by then the rumors had begun—of drugs found in his lover's carry-on, of affairs started…or maybe they'd never stopped.

Why he'd come back home now, to this quiet town in Texas and his family's sprawling ranch, was none of her concern.

With a hand blocking her eyes from a rare glimpse of winter sun, Scarlett glanced around the open fields. Not a soul in sight. In the distance, a green field dotted with cattle stretched all the way to the horizon. This could easily be a postcard.

The Elliott land was vast. She'd heard there were several homes on the property and a portion of the place would soon become a dude ranch. In fact, this cabin would eventually be housing for guests of said dude ranch.

So why was Beau Elliott staying here instead of one of the main houses, with his brothers? Was he even planning to stick around?

So many mysteries…

But she wasn't here to inquire about his personal life and she certainly wouldn't be divulging any extra information about hers.

She was here to help his baby.

Even if that meant she had to come face-to-face with one of the sexiest men on the planet.

The snick of a lock had her turning her attention back around. When the door swung wide, it was all Scarlett could do to hold back her gasp.

Beau Elliott, Hollywood's baddest boy, stood before her sans shirt and wearing a pair of low-slung shorts. Scrolling ink went up one side of his waist, curling around well-defined pecs and disappearing over his shoulder.

Don't stare at the tattoos. Don't stare at the tattoos. And, whatever you do, don't reach out to touch one.

"Who are you?"

The gravelly voice startled her back into reality. Scarlett realized she'd been staring.

Beau's broad frame filled the doorway, his stubbled jaw and bedhead indicating he hadn't had the best night. Apparently, according to the information she'd received, his last nanny had left last evening because of a family emergency.

Well, Scarlett wasn't having the best of days, either, so they were at least on a level playing field—other than the whole billionaire-peasant thing.

But she could use the extra money, so caring for an adorable five-month-old baby girl shouldn't be a problem, right?

Tamping down past hurts that threatened to creep up at the thought of caring for a child, Scarlett squared her shoulders and smiled. "I'm Scarlett Patterson. Your new nanny."

Beau blinked and gave her body a visual lick. "You're not old or frumpy," he growled.

Great. He'd already had some visual image in his head of who she should be. Maggie, the original nanny, was sweet as peach pie, but she *could* be best described as old and frumpy. Obviously, that was what Hollywood's Golden Child had thought he would be getting this morning, as well.

Beau Elliott, raised a rancher and then turned star of the screen, was going to be high maintenance. She could already tell.

Why would she expect anything less from someone who appeared to thrive on stardom and power?

Unfortunately, she knew that type all too well. Knew the type and ran like hell to avoid it.

She'd grown up with a man obsessed with money and getting what he wanted. Just when she thought she'd eliminated him from her life, he went on and became the governor. Scarlett was so over the power trip. Her stepfather and her mother weren't happy with her choices in life and had practically shunned her when they realized they couldn't control her. Which was fine. She'd rather do life on her own than be controlled... by anybody.

"Not old and frumpy. Is that a compliment or an observation?" She waved her hand to dismiss his answer before he could give her one. "Forget it. My looks and age are irrelevant. I am Maggie's replacement for the next three weeks."

"I requested someone like Maggie."

He still didn't make any attempt to move or to invite her inside. Even though this was Texas, the morning air chilled her.

Scarlett wasn't in the mood to deal with whatever hang-ups he had about nannies. Coming here after a year away from nanny duties was difficult enough. If she'd had her way, she would've found someone else to take this assignment, but the agency was short staffed.

This job was only for three weeks. Which meant she'd spend Christmas here, but the day after, she'd be heading to her new life in Dallas.

After the New Year, she'd start over fresh.

She could do this.

So why did she already feel the stirrings of a headache?

Oh, right. Because the once-dubbed "Sexiest Man Alive" was clearly used to getting his own way.

A bundle of nerves curled tightly in her belly. He might be sexy, but that didn't mean she had to put up with his attitude. Maybe he needed to remember that he was in a bind. He'd hired a nanny and Scarlett was it.

"Maggie, and everyone else at Nanny Poppins, is unavailable during the time frame you need."

Scarlett tried like hell to keep her professional smile in place—she did need this money, and she'd never leave a child without care. Plus, she wouldn't do a thing to tarnish the reputation of the company she'd worked for over the past several years.

She tipped her head and quirked a brow. "You do still need help, correct?"

Maggie had told Scarlett that Beau was brooding, that he kept to himself and only really came out of his shell when he interacted with his baby girl. That was all fine and good. Scarlett wasn't here to make friends or ogle the superstar, no matter how delicious he looked early in the morning.

A baby's cry pierced the awkward silence. With a muttered curse, Beau spun around and disappeared. Scarlett slowly stepped through the open door and shut it behind her.

Clearly the invitation wasn't going to happen.

"I feel so welcome," she muttered.

Scarlett leaned her suitcase against the wall and propped her small purse on top of it. The sounds of a fussy baby and Beau's deep, calming voice came from the bedroom to the right of the entryway.

As she took in the open floor plan of the cabin, she noted several things at once. Beau was either neat and tidy or he didn't have a lot of stuff. A pair of shiny new cowboy boots sat by the door and a black hat hung on a hook above the boots. The small kitchen had a drying rack with bottles on the counter and on the tiny table was a pink-and-white polka-dot bib.

She glanced to the left and noted another bedroom, the one she assumed would be hers, but she wasn't going to put her stuff in there just yet. Across the way, at the back of the cabin, was a set of patio doors that led to another porch. The area was cozy and perfect for the soon-to-be dude ranch.

The lack of Christmas decorations disturbed her, though. No tree, no stockings over the little fireplace, not even a wreath on the door. Who didn't want to celebrate Christmas? The most giving, joyous time of the year?

Christmas was absolutely her favorite holiday. Over the years she'd shared many Christmases with various families…all of which had been more loving and fulfilling than those of her stuffy, controlled childhood.

Scarlett continued to wait in the entryway, all while judging the Grinch's home. She didn't want to venture too far from the front door since he hadn't invited her in. It was obvious she wasn't what he'd expected, and he might ask her to leave.

Hopefully he wouldn't because she needed to work these three weeks. Those extra funds would go a long way toward helping her afford housing when she left Stone River to start her new life.

Even so, the next twenty-one days couldn't pass by fast enough.

Beau came back down the hall and Scarlett's heart tightened as a lump formed in her throat. A full assault on her emotions took over as knots in her stomach formed.

She couldn't do this. No matter how short the time span, she couldn't stay with this man, in this confined space, caring for his daughter for three weeks and not come out unscathed.

She wasn't sure which sight hit her hardest—the well-sculpted shirtless man or the baby he was holding.

Being this close to the little girl nearly brought her to her knees. Scarlett knew coming back as a hands-on nanny would be difficult, but she hadn't fully prepared herself for just how hard a hit her heart would take.

She'd purposely given up working in homes only a year ago. She'd requested work in the office, even though the administrative side paid less than round-the-clock nanny services. She'd been Nanny Poppins's most sought-after employee for eight years, but after everything that had happened, her boss completely understood Scarlett's need to distance herself from babies and families.

Fate had been cruel, stealing her chance of having kids of her own. She wasn't sure she was ready to see another parent have what she wanted. Working for Beau Elliott would be difficult to say the least, but Scarlett would push through and then she could move on. One last job. She could do this…she hoped.

The sweet baby continued to fuss, rubbing her eyes and sniffling. No doubt she was tired. From the looks of both of them, they'd had a long night.

Instinct had Scarlett reaching out and taking the baby, careful not to brush her fingertips against the hard planes of Beau's bare chest.

Well, she had to assume they were hard because she'd stared at them for a solid two minutes.

The second that sweet baby smell hit Scarlett, she nearly lost it. Her eyes burned, her throat tightened. But the baby's needs had to come first. That's why Scarlett was here. Well, that and to get double the pay so she could finally move to Dallas.

She could've turned down this job, but Maggie was in a bind, the company was in a bind, and they'd been so good to Scarlett since she'd started working there.

Scarlett simply couldn't say no.

"Oh, sweetheart, it's okay."

She patted the little girl's back and swayed slowly. Maggie had told her the baby was a joy to be around.

"Madelyn."

Scarlett blinked. "Excuse me?"

"Her name is Madelyn."

Well, at least they were getting somewhere and he wasn't ready to push her out the door. Scarlett already knew Madelyn's name and had read all the pertinent information regarding this job, but it was nice that Beau wasn't growling at her anymore.

Still, she wished he'd go put a shirt on. She couldn't keep her eyes completely off him, not when he was on display like that. Damn man probably thought he could charm her or distract her by flexing all those glorious, delicious muscles. Muscles that would no doubt feel taut beneath her touch.

Scarlett swallowed and blinked away the erotic image before she could take it too far. At least she had something else to think of other than her own gut-clenching angst and baby fever. Hunky heartthrob to the rescue.

Scarlett turned away from the distracting view of

her temporary boss and walked toward the tiny living area. The room seemed a little larger thanks to the patio doors leading onto the covered porch, which was decorated with a cute table and chair set.

The whole cabin was rather small, but it wasn't her place to ask why a billionaire film star lived in this cramped space on his family's estate. None of her business. This would just be a quick three weeks in December—in and out—in the most un-festive place ever.

Maybe she could sneak in some Christmas here and there. Every child deserved some twinkle lights or a stocking, for heaven's sake. Definitely a tree. Without it, where would Santa put the presents?

"She's been cranky all night," Beau said behind her. "I've tried everything, but I can't make her happy. I've never had that happen before."

The frustration in his voice softened Scarlett a bit. Beau might be a womanizer and a party animal, if the tabloids were right—which would explain his comfort level with wearing no shirt—but he obviously cared for his daughter.

Scarlett couldn't help but wonder where the mother was, but again, it was none of her concern. She'd seen enough tabloid stories to figure the mother was likely in rehab or desperately needing to be there.

Madelyn let out a wail, complete with tears and everything. The poor baby was miserable, which now made three of them, all under the same roof.

Let the countdown to her move begin.

How the hell had his nanny situation gone from Mrs. Doubtfire to Miss December?

The sultry vixen with rich skin, deep brown eyes, and silky black hair was too striking. But it was those curves in all the right places that had definitely woken him up this morning. His entire body had been ready to stand at attention, so perhaps he'd come across a little gruff.

But, damn it, he had good reason.

He'd been assured a replacement nanny would arrive bright and early, but he'd expected the agency to send another grandmother type.

Where was the one with a thick middle, elastic pants, sensible shoes and a gray bun? Where the hell did he order up another one of those? Warts would help, too. False teeth, even.

Beau stood back as he watched Scarlett comfort his daughter.

Scarlett. Of course she'd have a sultry name to match everything else sultry about her.

Not too long ago she would've been exactly his type. He would've wasted no time in charming and seducing her. But now his entire life had changed and the only woman he had time for was the sweet five-month-old he'd saved from the clutches of her partying, strung-out mother.

Money wasn't something he cared about—perhaps because he'd always had it—but it sure as hell came in handy. Like when he needed to pay off his ex so he could have Madelyn. Jennifer had selfishly taken the money, signed over the rights, and had nearly skipped out of their lives and onto the next star she thought would catapult her career.

The fact that he'd been used by her wasn't even relevant. He could care less about how he'd been treated, but he would not have their baby act as a pawn for Jennifer's own vindictive nature.

Beau couldn't get Madelyn out of Hollywood fast enough. His daughter was not going to be brought up in the lifestyle that too many fell into—himself included.

He'd overcome his past and the ugliness that surrounded his life when he'd first gotten into LA. He'd worked damn hard and was proud of the life he had built, but now his focus had to shift and changes needed to be made.

Coming home hadn't been ideal because he knew exactly the type of welcome he'd get. But there was nowhere else he wanted to be right now. He needed his family, even if he took hell from Colt, Hayes and Nolan for showing up after years of being away…with a kid in tow.

Thankfully, his brothers and their women all doted over Madelyn. That's all he wanted. No matter how people treated him or ignored him, Beau wanted his daughter to be surrounded with love.

His life was a mess, his future unknown. Hell, he couldn't think past today. He had a movie premiere two days before Christmas and he'd have to go, but other than that, he had no clue.

All that mattered was Madelyn, making sure she had a solid foundation and family that loved her. The calls from his new agent didn't matter, the movie premiere didn't matter, all the press he was expected to do to promote the film sure as hell didn't matter. To say he was burned out would be a vast understatement.

Beau needed some space to think and the calming serenity of Pebblebrook Ranch provided just that.

Unfortunately, concentrating would be rather difficult with a centerfold look-alike staying under his roof. Well, not his roof exactly. He was only using one of the small cabins on the land until the dude ranch officially opened in a few months. His father's dream was finally coming to fruition.

Beau wondered how he'd come to this moment of needing someone. He prided himself on never needing anyone. He had homes around the globe, cars that would make any man weep with envy, even his own private island, but the one place he wanted and needed to be was right here with his family—whether they wanted him here or not.

Beau had turned his back on this land and his family years ago. That was the absolute last thing he'd intended to do, but he'd gotten swept away into the fortune and fame. Eventually days had rolled into months, then into years, and the time had passed too quickly.

But now he was back home, and as angry as his brothers were, they'd given him a place to stay. Temporary, but at least it was something. He knew it was only because he had Madelyn, but he'd take it.

"She's teething."

Beau pulled his thoughts from his family drama and focused on the nanny. "Teething? She's only five months old."

Scarlett continued to sway back and forth with Madelyn in her arms. His sweet girl sucked on her fist and alternated between sniffles and cries. At least the screaming wasn't so constant like last night. Having his daughter so upset and him feeling so helpless had absolutely gutted him. He would've done anything to help her, but he'd been clueless. He'd spent the night questioning just how good of a father he really was.

Madelyn's wide, dark eyes stared up at the new nanny as if trying to figure out where the stranger had come from.

He was having a difficult time not staring, as well, and he knew full well where she came from—every single one of his erotic fantasies.

"Her gums are swollen and she's drooling quite a bit," Scarlett stated. "All perfectly normal. Do you happen to have any cold teething rings in your fridge?"

Cold teething rings? What the hell was that? He was well stocked with formula and bottles, diapers and wipes, but rings in the fridge? Nope.

He had an app that told him what babies should be doing and what they needed at different stages, but the rings hadn't been mentioned yet.

"I'm guessing no from the look on your face." Scarlett went into the kitchen area and opened the freezer. "Can you get me a napkin or towel?"

Beau wasn't used to taking orders, but he'd do anything to bring his daughter some comfort. He grabbed a clean dishcloth from the counter and handed it to her. He watched as she held on to the ice through the cloth and rubbed it on his daughter's gums. After a few minutes the fussing grew quieter until she finally stopped.

"I'll get some teething rings today," Scarlett murmured as if talking to herself more than him. "They are wonderful for instant relief. If you have any children's pain reliever, we can also rub that on her gums, but I try natural approaches before I go to medicine."

Okay, so maybe Miss December was going to be an asset. He liked that she offered natural options for Madelyn's care. He also liked that she seemed to be completely unimpressed with his celebrity status. Something about that was so refreshing and even more attractive.

Watch it. You already got in trouble with one sexy woman. She's the nanny, not the next bedmate.

He told himself he didn't need the silent warning that rang in his head. Scarlett Patterson would only be here until the day after Christmas. Surely he could keep his libido in control for that long. It wasn't like he had the time anyway. He couldn't smooth the ruffled feathers of his family, care for his child and seduce a woman all before December 26.

No matter how sexy the new nanny was.

Besides, he thought, it couldn't get more clichéd than that—the movie star and the nanny. How many of those stories had he read in the tabloids of late?

No, there was no way he was going to make a move on the woman who was saving his sanity and calming his baby. Besides, he respected women; his mother had raised Southern gentlemen, after all. The media liked to report that he rolled out of one woman's bed and right into another, but he wasn't quite that popular. Not to mention, any woman he'd ever been with had known he wasn't looking for long-term—and agreed with it.

Beau had a feeling Scarlett would be a long-term type of girl. She likely had a family—or maybe she didn't. If this was her full-time job, she probably didn't have time to take care of a family.

Honestly, he shouldn't be letting his mind wander into the territory of Scarlett's personal life. She was his nanny, nothing more.

But damn it, did she have to look so good in her little pink capris and white sleeveless button-up? Didn't she have a uniform? Something up to her neck, down to her ankles and with sleeves? Even if she was completely covered up, she still had those expressive, doe-like eyes, a perfectly shaped mouth and adorable dimples.

Damn it. He should not be noticing each little detail of his new nanny.

"Why don't you go rest?" Scarlett suggested, breaking into his erotic thoughts. "I can take care of her. You look like hell."

Beau stared across the narrow space for a half second before he found his voice. Nobody talked to him like that except his brothers, and even that had been years ago.

"Are you always that blunt with your clients?"

"I try to be honest at all times," she replied sweetly. "I can't be much help to you if you just want me here to boost your ego and lie to your face."

Well, that was a rarity...if she was even telling the truth now. Beau hadn't met a woman who was honest and genuine. Nearly everyone he'd met was out for herself and to hell with anyone around them. And money. They always wanted money.

Another reason he needed the simplicity of Pebblebrook. He just wanted to come back to his roots, to decompress and figure out what the hell to do with his life now. He wanted the open spaces, wanted to see the blue skies without buildings blocking the view. And he needed to mend the relationships he'd left behind. What better time than Christmas?

"I'm Beau." When she drew her brows in, he went on. "I didn't introduce myself before."

"I'm aware of who you are."

He waited for her to say something else, but clearly she'd formed an opinion of him and didn't want to share.

Fine. So long as she kept his daughter comfortable and helped him until Maggie returned, he could care less what she thought.

But she'd have to get in line because his brothers had already dubbed him the prodigal son and were eager to put him in his place. Nothing less than he deserved, he reasoned.

As he watched Scarlett take over the care of Madelyn, Beau knew this was what he deserved, too. A sexy-as-hell woman as his nanny. This was his penance for the bastard he'd been over the past several years.

He'd do well to remember he was a new man now. He'd do well to remember she was here for his daughter, not for his personal pleasure. He'd also do well to remember he had more important things to do than drop Scarlett Patterson into each and every one of his fantasies…even if she would make the perfect lead.

Two

Madelyn had calmed down and was now settled in her crib napping. There was a crib in each of the two bedrooms, but Scarlett opted to put Madelyn in the room Maggie had vacated. This would be Scarlett's room now and she simply didn't think going into Beau's was a smart idea.

After she'd put her luggage and purse in her room, Beau had given her a very brief tour of the cabin, so she'd gotten a glimpse into his personal space. The crib in his room had been nestled next to the king-size bed. Scarlett tried not to, but the second she recalled those messed sheets, she procured an image of him lying there in a pair of snug boxer briefs…or nothing at all.

Scarlett groaned and gently shut the bedroom door, careful not to let the latch snick. She wasn't sure how light of a sleeper Madelyn was, so until she got to know the sweet bundle a little better—

But she couldn't get to know her too much, could she? There wasn't going to be time, and for Scarlett's sanity and heart, she had to keep an emotional distance. Giving herself that pep talk and actually doing it were two totally different things.

Before her surgery, she'd thrown herself into each and every job. Before her surgery, she'd always felt like one unit with the families she worked with.

Before her surgery, she'd had dreams.

The hard knot in her chest never eased. Whether she thought of what she'd lost or was just doing day-to-day things, the ache remained a constant reminder.

Scarlett stepped back into the living area and found Beau standing at the patio doors, his back to her. At least he'd put a T-shirt on. Even so, he filled it out, stretching the material over those chiseled muscles she'd seen firsthand. Clothes or no clothes, the image had been burned into her memory bank and there was no erasing it.

"Madelyn's asleep," she stated.

Beau threw her a glance over his shoulder, then turned his attention back to the view of the open field.

Okay. Clearly he wasn't chatty. Fine by her. He must be a lonely, miserable man. She'd always wondered if celebrities were happy. After all, money certainly couldn't buy everything. Her stepfather was proof of that. He'd been a state representative for years before moving up to governor. He'd wanted his children—he included her in that mix—to all enter the political arena so they would be seen as a powerhouse family.

Thanks, but no thanks. She preferred a simpler life—or at least one without lies, deceit, fake smiles and cheesy campaign slogans.

"If there's something you need to go do, I'll be here," she told Beau. Not surprisingly, he didn't answer. Maybe he gave a grunt, but she couldn't tell if that was a response or just indigestion.

Scarlett turned toward the kitchen to take stock of what type of formula and baby things Madelyn used. Being here a short time, she wanted to make sure the transitions between Maggie and her then back to Maggie went smoothly. Regardless of what Scarlett thought of Beau, Madelyn was the only one here who mattered.

Before Scarlett could step into the kitchen, a knock sounded on the front door.

Beau shifted, his gaze landing on the closed door. He looked like he'd rather run in the opposite direction than face whoever was on the other side. Given that they were on private property, likely the guest was just his family, so what was the issue? Wasn't that why he'd come home? To be with his family for the holidays?

When he made no attempt to move, Scarlett asked, "Should I get that?"

He gave a curt nod and Scarlett reached for the knob. The second she opened the door, she gasped.

Sweet mercy. There were two of them. Another Beau stood before her, only this one was clean shaven and didn't have the scowl. But those shoulders and dark eyes were dead on and just as potent to her heart rate.

"Ma'am," the Beau look-alike said with a drawl and a tip of his black cowboy hat. "I'm Colt Elliott, Beau's twin. You must be the replacement nanny."

Another Elliott and a *twin*. Mercy sakes, this job was not going to be a hardship whatsoever if she had to look at these men each day.

She knew there were four Elliott sons, but wow. Nobody warned her they were clones. Now she wondered if the other two would stop by soon. One could hope.

"Yes," she said when she realized he was waiting on her to respond to his question. "I'm Scarlett."

Colt's dark eyes went from her to Beau. "Is this a bad time?"

Scarlett stepped back. "Not at all. I just got the baby to sleep. I can wait outside while you two talk. It's a beautiful day."

She turned and caught Beau's gaze on her. Did he always have that dramatic, heavy-lidded, movie-star stare? Did he ever turn off the act or was that mysterious, sexy persona natural?

"If you'll excuse me." She turned to Colt. "It was a pleasure meeting you."

"Pleasure was mine, ma'am."

Somehow Scarlett managed to get out the front door without tripping over her own two feet, because that sexy, low Southern drawl those Elliott boys had was rather knee-weakening.

Once she made it to the porch, she walked to the wooden swing on the end in front of her bedroom window. She sank down onto the seat and let the gentle breeze cool off her heated body. December in Texas wasn't too hot, wasn't too cold. In this part of the state, the holiday weather was always perfect. Though the evenings and nights could get chilly.

Good thing there were fireplaces in this cabin. Fireplaces that could lead one to instantly think of romantic talks and shedding of clothes, being wrapped in a blanket in the arms of a strong man.

Scarlett shut her eyes as she rested her feet on the porch and stopped the swaying swing. There would be no romance and no fires…at least not the passionate kind.

Raised voices filtered from inside. Clearly the Elliott twins were not happy with each other. Two sexy-as-hell alphas going at it sounded like every woman's fantasy, but she couldn't exactly barge in and interrupt.

Then she heard it. The faint cry from her bedroom, right on the other side of the window from where she sat. Well, damn it.

Scarlett pushed off the swing and jerked open the front door. Hot men or not, powerful men or not, she didn't take kindly to anyone disturbing a sleeping baby.

As she marched toward her bedroom, she shot a warning glare in the direction of the guys, who were now practically chest to chest. She didn't have time to worry about their issues, not when Madelyn had barely been asleep twenty minutes.

Scarlett crossed to the crib and gently picked up the sweet girl. After grabbing her fuzzy yellow blanket, Scarlett sank into the nearby rocking chair and patted Madelyn's bottom to calm her.

Madelyn's little sniffles and heavy lids were Scarlett's main focus right now. She eased the chair into a gentle motion with her foot and started humming "You Are My Sunshine." Madelyn didn't take long to nestle back into sleep and Scarlett's heart clenched. She'd just hold her a tad longer… It had been so long since she'd rocked a little one.

She had no idea what happened with Beau and the baby's mother, but the tabloids and social media had been abuzz with a variety of rumors over the past few weeks.

Well, actually, the couple had been quite the fodder

for gossip a lot longer. It was over a year ago when they were first spotted half naked on a beach in Belize. Then the pregnancy seemed to send shock waves through the media. Of course, after the baby was born, there was all that speculation on the state of the mother and she was seen less and less.

Chatter swirled about her cheating, then her rehab, then the breakup.

Then there was talk of Beau. One online source stated he'd been passed over for a part in an epic upcoming blockbuster. One said he'd had a fight with his new agent. Another reported that he and his ex had been spotted arguing at a party and one or both had been inebriated.

Honestly, Beau Elliott was a complication she didn't want to get tangled with, so whatever happened to send him rushing home was his problem. That didn't mean, however, that a child should have to suffer for the sins of the parents.

Once Madelyn was good and asleep, Scarlett put her down in the crib. There was a light tap on the door moments before it eased open.

Scarlett turned from the sleeping baby to see Beau filling the doorway.

"Is she asleep again?" he whispered.

Stepping away from the crib, Scarlett nodded. "Next time you want to have a family fight, take it outside."

His eyes darkened. "This isn't your house," he stated, taking a step closer to her.

Scarlett stood at the edge of the bed and crossed her arms. "It isn't exactly your house, either," she retorted. "But Madelyn is my job now and I won't have her disturbed when she's been fussy and obviously needs sleep. Maybe if you put her needs first—"

In a second, Beau had closed the gap and was all but leaning over her, so close that she had to hold on to the bedpost to stay upright.

"Every single thing I do is putting her needs first," he growled through gritted teeth. "You've been here less than two hours, so don't even presume to know what's going on."

Scarlett placed her hand on his chest to get him to ease back, but the heat from his body warmed her in a way she couldn't explain…and shouldn't dwell on.

She jerked her hand back and glanced away, only to have her eyes land on the pile of lacy panties she'd thrown on her bed when she'd started unpacking earlier.

There went more of that warmth spreading through her. What were the odds Beau hadn't noticed?

She risked glancing back at him, but…nope. He'd noticed all right. His eyes were fixed on her unmentionables.

Beau cleared his throat and raked a hand over the back of his neck before glancing to where his baby slept peacefully in the crib on the other side of the room.

When his dark eyes darted back to her, they pinned her in place. "We need to talk." Then he turned and marched out, likely expecting her to follow.

Scarlett closed her eyes and pulled in a breath as she attempted to count backward from ten. This was only the first day. She knew there would be some bumps in the road, right?

She just didn't expect those bumps to be the chills rushing over her skin from the brief yet toe-curling contact she'd just had with her employer.

* * *

Beau ground his molars and clenched his fists at his sides. It had been quite a while since he'd been with a woman and the one currently staying under his roof was driving him absolutely insane…and it wasn't even lunchtime on her first day of employment.

Those damn panties. All that lace, satin…strings. Mercy, he couldn't get the image out of his head. Never once did he think his nanny's underwear would cause his brain to fry, but here he was with a silent seductress helping to take care of his daughter and he couldn't focus. Likely she didn't even have a clue how she was messing with his hormones.

Scarlett honestly did have Madelyn's best interest in mind. She was none too happy with him and Colt earlier and he wasn't too thrilled with the situation, either. Of all the people angry with him for his actions and for being away from home so long, Colt was by far the most furious. Ironic, he thought. He'd figure his own twin would try to have a little compassion.

Unfortunately, there was so much more contention between them than just the missing years. Coming home at Christmas and thinking things would be magical and easily patched up had been completely naive on his part. But damn it, he'd been hopeful. They'd been the best of friends once, with a twin bond that was stronger than anything he'd ever known.

Delicate footsteps slid across the hardwood floor, interrupting his thoughts. Beau shored up his mental strength and turned to face Scarlett. Why did she have to look like a walking dream? That curvy body, the dark eyes, her flawless dark skin and black hair that gave the illusion of silk sliding down her back.

Damn those panties. Now when he saw her he wondered what she wore underneath her clothes. Lace or satin? Pink or yellow?

"What do you want to talk about?" she asked, making no move to come farther into the living area.

Beau gestured toward the oversize sectional sofa. "Have a seat."

She eyed him for a moment before finally crossing the room and sitting down on the end of the couch. She crossed her ankles and clasped her hands as if she were in some business meeting with a CEO.

Beau stood next to her. "Relax."

"I'd relax more if you weren't looming over me."

Part of him wanted to laugh. Most women would love for him to "loom" over them. Hell, most women would love him under them, as well. Perhaps that's why he found Scarlett of the silky panties so intriguing. She truly didn't care that he was an A-list actor with more money than he could ever spend and the power to obtain nearly anything he ever wanted.

Beau didn't want to make her uncomfortable and it certainly wasn't his intention to be a jerk. It pained him to admit it, but he needed her. He was only a few weeks out on his own with Madelyn and he really didn't want to screw up this full-time parenting job. This would be the most important job he'd ever have.

"We probably need to set some rules here," he started.

Rules like keeping all underwear hidden in a drawer at all times. Oh, and maybe if she could get some long pants and high-neck shirts, that would certainly help. Wouldn't it?

Maggie sat straighter. "I work for you, Mr. Elliott. Just tell me the rules you had for Maggie."

Beau nearly snorted. Rules for Maggie were simple: help with Madelyn while Beau was out working on the ranch and trying to figure his life out. The rules for Scarlett? They'd go beyond not leaving your lingerie out. He mentally added a few more: stop looking so damn innocent and sexy at the same time, stop with the defiant chin that he wanted to nip at and work his way down.

But of course he couldn't voice those rules. He cleared his throat and instead of enumerating his expectations, he took a different approach.

"I'm a hands-on dad." He started with that because that was the most important. "Madelyn is my life. I'm only going to be at Pebblebrook for a short time, but while I'm here, I plan on getting back to my roots and helping to get this dude ranch up and running."

That is, if his brothers would let him in on realizing their father's dream. That was still a heated debate, especially since Beau hadn't been to see Grant Elliott yet.

His father had been residing in an assisted-living facility for the past few years. The bad blood between them couldn't be erased just because Beau had made a deathbed promise to the one man who had been more like a father to him than his real one.

Still, Beau was man enough to admit that he was afraid to see his dad. What if his dad didn't recognize him? Grant had been diagnosed with dementia and lately, more often than not, he didn't know his own children. Even the sons who'd been around the past few years. Beau wasn't sure he was strong enough to face that reality just yet.

"Beau?"

Scarlett's soft tone pulled him out of his thoughts. Where was he? Right, the rules.

"Yeah, um. I can get up with Madelyn during the night. I didn't hire a nanny so I could be lazy and just pass her care off. I prefer a live-in nanny more because I'm still…"

"Nervous?" she finished with raised brows. "It's understandable. Most first-time parents are. Babies are pretty easy, though. They'll pretty much tell you what's wrong, you know, just not with actual words."

No, he actually didn't know. He just knew when Madelyn cried he wanted her to stop because he didn't want her unhappy.

Beau had spent the past five months fighting with his ex, but she'd only wanted Madelyn as a bargaining chip. He'd finally gotten his lawyer to really tighten the screws and ultimately, Jennifer James—wannabe actress and worthless mother—signed away her parental rights.

As much as he hated the idea of Madelyn not having a mother around, his daughter was better off.

Beau studied his new, refreshing nanny. "I assume you don't have children since you're a nanny full-time."

Some emotion slid right over her, taking away that sweet, calm look she'd had since she'd arrived. He could swear an invisible shield slid right between them. Her lips thinned, her head tipped up a notch and her eyes were completely unblinking.

"No children," she said succinctly.

There was backstory behind that simple statement. He knew that for sure. And he was curious.

"Yet you know so much about them," he went on. "Do you want a family of your own one day?"

"My personal life is none of your concern. That's my number-one rule that you can add to your list."

Why the hell had he even asked? He didn't need to know her on a deeper level, but now that she'd flat-out refused to go there, he wanted to find out every last secret she kept hidden. He hadn't asked Maggie personal questions, but then Maggie hadn't pulled up emotions in him like this, either.

Even though he'd just vowed to stay out of Scarlett's personal business, well, he couldn't help himself. If she was just standoffish, that would be one thing, but hurt and vulnerability had laced her tone. He was a sucker for a woman in need.

Scarlett, though, clearly didn't want to be the topic of conversation, something he not only understood but respected. He told himself he should focus on his purpose for being back home and not worry about what his temporary nanny did in her off time.

Beau nodded in affirmation at her demand. "Very well. These three weeks shouldn't be a problem, then."

He came to his feet, most likely to get away from the lie he'd just settled between them. Truthfully, everything about having her here was a problem, but that was on him. Apparently she didn't care that his hormones had chosen now to stand up and pay attention to her. She also didn't seem to care who he was. He was just another client and his celebrity status didn't do a damn thing for her.

While he appreciated her not throwing herself at him, his ego wasn't so quick to accept the hit. This was all new territory for him where a beautiful woman was concerned.

"I'm going to change and head to the main stable

for a bit." He pulled his cell from his pocket. "Give me your cell number and I'll text you so you have my number. If you need anything at all, message me and I'll be right back."

Once the numbers were exchanged, Beau picked up his boots by the front door and went to his room to change. He slipped on a pair of comfortable old jeans, but the boots were new and needed to be broken in. He'd had to buy another pair when he came back. The moment he'd left Pebblebrook years ago, he'd ditched any semblance of home.

Odd how he couldn't wait to dig right back in. The moment he'd turned into the long white-fence-lined drive, he'd gotten that kick of nostalgia as memories of working side by side with his brothers and his father came flooding back.

Right now he needed to muck some stalls to clear his head and take his mind off the most appealing woman he'd encountered in a long time…maybe ever.

But he doubted even grunt work would help. Because at the end of the day, he'd still come back here where she would be wearing her lacy lingerie…and where they would be spending their nights all alone with only an infant as their chaperone.

Three

"You're going to get your pretty new boots scuffed."

Beau turned toward the open end of the stable. His older brother Hayes stood with his arms crossed over his chest, his tattoos peeking from beneath the hems of the sleeves on his biceps.

"I need to break them in," Beau replied, instinctively glancing down to the shiny steel across the point on the toe.

If anyone knew about coming home, it was Hayes. Beau's ex-soldier brother had been overseas fighting in Afghanistan and had seen some serious action that had turned Hayes into an entirely different man than the one Beau remembered.

Whatever had happened to his brother had hardened him, but he was back at the ranch with the love of his life and raising a little boy that he'd taken in as his own. He'd found a happy ending. Beau wasn't so sure that would ever happen for him—or even if he wanted it to.

"So, what? You're going to try to get back into the ranching life?" Hayes asked as he moved to grab a pitch-fork hanging on the inside of the tack room. "Or are we just a stepping stone?"

Beau didn't know what the hell he was going to do. He knew in less than three weeks he had a movie debut he had to attend, but beyond that, he'd been dodging his new agent's calls because there was no way Beau was ready to look at another script just yet. His focus was needed elsewhere.

Like on his daughter.

On his future.

"Right now I'm just trying to figure out where the hell to go." Beau gripped his own pitchfork and glanced to the stall with Doc inside. "Nolan ever come and help?"

Hayes headed toward the other end of the row. "When he can. He stays busy at the hospital, but he's cut his hours since marrying and having a kid of his own. His priorities have shifted."

Not just Nolan's priorities, but also Colt's and Hayes's. All three of his brothers had fallen in love and were enjoying their ready-made families.

Beau had been shocked when he'd pulled into the drive and seen his brothers standing on Colt's sprawl-ing front porch with three ladies he didn't know and four children. The ranch had apparently exploded into the next generation while he'd been gone.

Beau worked around Nolan's stallion and put fresh straw in the stall before moving to the next one. For the next hour he and Hayes worked together just like when they'd been kids. Teamwork on the ranch had been important to their father. He'd instilled a set of ethics in his boys that no formal education could match.

Of course they had ranch hands, but there was something about getting back to your roots, Beau knew, that did some sort of reset to your mental health. At this point he needed to try anything to help him figure out what his next move should be.

He actually enjoyed manual labor. Even as a kid and a teen, he'd liked working alongside his father and brothers. But over time, Beau had gotten the urge to see the world, to find out if there was more to life than ranching, and learning how to turn one of the toughest professions into a billion-dollar lifestyle. The idea of being in charge of Pebblebrook once his father retired held no shred of interest to Beau. He knew Colt had always wanted that position so why would Beau even attempt to share it?

"So you all live here on the estate?" Beau asked when he and Hayes had completed their stalls and met in the middle of the barn.

Hayes rested his hand on the top of the pitchfork handle and swiped his other forearm across his damp forehead. "Yeah. I renovated Granddad's old house back by the fork in the river and the creek. I've always loved that place and it just seemed logical when I came back."

The original farmhouse for Pebblebrook would be the perfect home for Hayes and his family, providing privacy, but still remaining on Elliott land.

When they'd all been boys they'd ventured to the back of the property on their horses or ATVs and used it as a giant getaway or a man cave. They'd had the ultimate fort and pretended to be soldiers or cowboys in the Old West.

Once upon a time the Elliott brothers were all close, inseparable. But now...

Beau was virtually starting over with his own family. That deathbed promise to his former agent was so much more difficult to execute than he'd originally thought. But Hector had made Beau vow he'd go home and mend fences. At the time Beau had agreed, but now he knew saying the words had been the easy part.

He leaned back against Doc's stall and stared blankly.

"Hey." Hayes studied Beau before slapping a large hand over his shoulder. "It's going to take some time. Nolan is hurt, but he's not pissed. Me? I'm just glad you're here, though I wonder if you'll stay. So I guess that makes me cautious. But Colt, well, he's pissed and hurt, so that's the one you need to be careful with."

Beau snorted and shook his head. "Yeah, we've already had words."

Like when Colt swung by earlier to talk, but ended up going off because of the new nanny. Colt claimed Beau was still a wild child and a player, hiring a nanny looking like that. Beau had prayed Scarlett hadn't heard Colt's accusations. She was a professional and he didn't want her disrespected or made to feel unwelcome. Not that his brother was disrespecting Scarlett. No, he was aiming that all at Beau.

Even if the choice had been his, Beau sure as hell wouldn't have chosen a woman who looked like Scarlett to spend twenty-four hours a day with inside that small cabin. Even he wasn't that much of a masochist.

Beau had no idea what had originally brought Colt

over to see him, but he had a feeling their morning talk wasn't the last of their heated debates.

"You'd think my twin would be the most understanding," Beau muttered.

"Not when he's the one who held this place together once Dad couldn't," Hayes retorted. "I was overseas, Nolan was married to his surgery schedule and you were gone. Colt's always wanted this life. Ranching was it for him, so I guess the fact you wanted nothing to do with it only made the hurt worse. Especially when you rarely called or came back to visit."

Beau knew coming back would rip his heart open, but he'd had no clue his brother would just continually pour salt into the wound. But he had nobody to blame but himself. He was man enough to take it, though. He would push through the hard times and reconnect with his family. If losing Hector had taught him anything, it was that time was fleeting.

"I can't make up for the past," Beau started. "And I can't guarantee I'll stay forever. I just needed somewhere to bring Madelyn, and home seemed like the most logical place. I don't care how I'm treated, just as long as she's loved. I can work on Colt and hopefully mend that relationship."

"Maybe you should start with seeing Dad if you want to try to make amends with anyone."

The heavy dose of guilt he'd been carrying around for some time grew weightier at Hayes's statement. His older brother was absolutely right, yet fear had kept Beau from reaching out to his father since he'd been home.

"Will he even know me?" Beau asked, almost afraid of the answer.

Hayes shrugged. "Maybe not, but what matters is that you're there."

Beau swallowed the lump of emotions. Everything he'd heard over the past year was that their father barely knew anything anymore. The Alzheimer's had trapped him inside his mind. He and Beau may have had major differences in the past, but Grant Elliott was still his father and Beau respected the hell out of that man... though he hadn't done a great job of showing it over the years.

His father had been a second-generation rancher and took pride in his work. He'd wanted his sons to follow in that same path of devotion. Beau, though, had been a rebellious teen with wandering feet and a chip on his shoulder. Pebblebrook hadn't been enough to contain him and he'd moved away. On his own for the first time, he'd wanted to experience everything that had been denied him back home, and ended up in trouble. Then he was discovered and dubbed "a natural" after a ridiculous commercial he wanted to forget.

Beau threw himself into the acting scene hard. His career had seemed to skyrocket overnight.

At first he'd been on a path to destruction, then a path to stardom. And through it all, he hadn't even thought of coming home. He'd been too wrapped up in himself. No excuses.

Then one day he'd realized how much time had passed. He had come home but the cold welcome he'd received had sent him straight back to LA.

But this time was different. This time he was going to stay, at least through the holidays, no matter how difficult it might be.

"I'll go see him," Beau promised, finally meeting Hayes's eyes. "I'm just not ready."

"Always making excuses."

Beau and Hayes turned to the sound of Colt's angry voice. Just what he needed, another round with his pissed brother.

Colt glanced to the pitchfork in Beau's hand. "Are you practicing for a part or actually attempting to help?"

"Colt—"

"No." Beau held out his hand, cutting Hayes off. "It's not your fight."

Hayes nodded and took Beau's pitchfork and his own back to the tack room, giving Beau and Colt some privacy.

"I came home because I needed somewhere safe to bring my daughter," Beau stated, that chip on his shoulder more evident than ever. "I came home because it was time and I'd hoped we could put aside our differences for Christmas."

Did he think he could just waltz back onto the ranch and sing carols around the Christmas tree and all would be well? Had he been gone so long that he could just ignore the tension and the hurt that resided here?

"You won't find a red-carpet welcome here," Colt grunted. "We've gotten along just fine without you for years. So if you're just going to turn around and leave again, don't bother with all this show now. Christmas is a busy time for Annabelle at the B and B. I don't have time to figure out what the hell you're doing or not doing."

Seeing his twin back here where they'd shared so many memories…

Every part of Colt wished this was a warm family reunion, but the reality was quite different.

Beau had chosen to stay away, to make a new family, a new life amidst all the Hollywood hoopla, the parties, the women, the money and jet-setting.

Bitterness had settled into Colt long ago and showed no sign of leaving.

"What did you want when you came by this morning?" Beau asked. "Other than to berate me."

Hayes carried a blanket and saddle down the stable and passed them, obviously trying to get the hell out of here and not intervene.

Colt hooked his thumbs through his belt loops. "I was going to give you a chance to explain. Annabelle told me I should hear your side, but then I saw your replacement nanny and realized nothing about you has changed."

Of course Beau would have a stunning woman living under his roof with the guise of being a nanny. Was his brother ever going to mature and just own up to his responsibilities?

"Replacement nanny?" Hayes chimed up.

Beau's eyes narrowed—apparently Colt had hit a nerve. But they both ignored Hayes's question.

The resentment and turmoil that had been bubbling and brewing over the years was best left between him and his twin. Colt didn't want to drag anybody else into this mix.

Though his wife had already wedged herself into the drama. He knew she meant well, he knew she wanted one big happy family, especially considering she lost her only sibling too early in life. But still, there was so much pain in the past that had only grown like a tumor over the years. Some things simply couldn't be fixed.

Beau kept his gaze straight ahead to Colt. "Who I have helping with Madelyn is none of your concern and I didn't decide who the agency sent to replace Maggie. Her husband fell and broke his hip so she had to go care for him for a few weeks until their daughter can come help. If you have a problem, maybe you'd like to apply for the job."

"Maybe you could worry more about your daughter and less about your dick—"

Beau didn't think before his fist planted in the side of Colt's jaw. He simply reacted. But before he could land a second shot, a restraining hand stopped him. Hayes stood between the brothers, his hands on each of their chests.

"All right, we're not doing this," Hayes told them both.

"Looks like I missed the official work reunion."

At the sound of the new voice, Beau turned to see Nolan come striding in. No fancy doctor clothes for his oldest brother. Nolan looked like the rest of them with his jeans and Western shirt and boots and black hat.

There was no mistaking they were brothers. Years and lifestyles may have kept them apart, but the Elliott genetics were strong. Just the sight of his three brothers had something shifting in Beau's chest. Perhaps he was supposed to be here now, for more than Madelyn.

"Throwing punches took longer than I thought," Nolan growled, closing the distance. "You've been here a whole week."

Beau ignored the comment and glared back at Colt. "You know nothing about me anymore, so don't presume you know what type of man I am."

"Whose fault is that?" Colt shouted. "You didn't let us get to know the man you grew into. We had to watch it on the damn movie screen."

Guilt…such a bitter pill to swallow.

"Why don't we just calm down?" Hayes suggested as he stepped back. "Beau is home now and Dad wouldn't want us going at each other. This is all he ever wanted, us together, working on the ranch."

"You haven't even been to see him," Colt shot at Beau, his dark eyes still judgmental.

"I will."

Colt shook his head in disgust, but Beau didn't owe him an explanation. Beau didn't owe him anything. They may be twins, but the physical appearance was where their similarities ended. They were different men, with different goals. Why should Beau be sorry for the life he'd created for himself?

Nolan reached them then and diverted his attention. "Pepper wanted me to invite you and Madelyn for dinner," he stated in that calm voice of his. "Are you free this evening?"

Beau blew out the stress he'd been feeling and raked a hand along the back of his neck. "Yeah. I'm free. Madelyn's been a little cranky. Scarlett thinks she's cutting teeth, but we should be able to make it."

"Scarlett?" Nolan asked.

"His new nanny," Colt interjected. "She's petite, curvy, stunning. Just Beau's type."

Beau wasn't going to take the bait, not again. Besides, already he knew that Scarlett was so much more than that simple description. She was vibrant and strong and determined...and she'd had his fantasies working overtime.

"You're married," he said instead to his twin. "So my nanny is none of your concern."

"Just stating the facts." Colt held his hands out and took a step back. "I'm happily married with two babies of my own, so don't worry about me trying to lay claim. I'm loyal to my wife."

"Scarlett can come, too, if you want," Nolan added, clearly ignoring his brother's argument. "Pepper won't mind."

Scarlett joining him? Hell no. That would be too familial and definitely not the approach he wanted to take on day one with his temporary help. Not the approach he'd want to take on any day with her, actually.

Not that long ago he would've jumped at the excuse to spend more time with a gorgeous woman, but his hormones were just going to have to take a back seat because he had to face reality. The good times that he was used to were in the past. His good times now consisted of a peaceful night's sleep and a happy baby.

Damn, he was either getting old or finally acting like an adult.

He'd always tried to keep himself grounded over the years, but now that he was home, he realized just how shallow Hollywood had made him. Shallow and jaded. Yet another reason he needed to keep himself and his daughter away from that lifestyle.

"It will just be Madelyn and me," he informed his brother. Then he shifted his attention back to Colt. "Do you want my help around here or not?"

"From the prodigal son?" Colt's jaw clenched, and Beau could see a bruise was already forming there. Colt finally nodded. "I've got most of the guys on the west side of the property mending fences. I'll take your free labor here."

Well, that was something. Maybe there was hope for them after all. Beau decided since they weren't yelling or throwing more punches, now would be as good a time as any to pitch his thoughts out there.

"I want in on the dude ranch, too."

Beau didn't realize he'd wanted that until they all stood here together. But there was no denying his wishes now. Whether he stayed on the ranch or not, he wanted to be part of his father's legacy with his brothers.

Colt's brows shot up, but before he could refuse, Beau went on. "I'm part of this family whether you like it or not and Dad's wish was to see this through. Now, I know you plan to open in just a few months and a good bit of the hard work is done, but that doesn't mean you couldn't use me."

Hayes shrugged. "Wouldn't be a bad idea to have him do some marketing. He'd have some great connections."

Colt's gaze darted to Hayes. "Are you serious?"

"Hayes is right," Nolan added. "I know none of us needs the extra income, but we want Dad's dream to be a success."

Colt took off his hat, raked a hand over his hair and settled the hat back in place. "Well, hell. Whatever. We'll use you until you take off again, because we all know you won't stick."

Beau didn't say a word. What could he say? He knew full well he likely wasn't staying here long-term. He'd returned because of a deathbed promise and to figure out where to take his daughter. Pebblebrook was likely a stepping stone…nothing more. Just like Hayes had said.

Four

Scarlett swiped another stroke of Cherry Cherry Bang Bang on her toes. Beau had taken Madelyn to dinner at his brother's house and told her she didn't need to come.

So she'd finished unpacking—getting all of her panties put away properly. Then she'd caught up on social media, and now she was giving herself an overdue pedicure with her new polish. She wasn't a red type of girl, but she figured with the new move coming and another chapter in her life starting, why not go all in and have some fun? Now that she was admiring it against her dark skin, she actually loved the festive shade.

And that's about as wild as she got. Red polish.

Could she be any more boring?

She never dreamed she'd be in this position at nearly thirty-five years of age: no husband, no children and a changing career.

She was fine without the husband—she could get by on her own, thank you very much. But the lack of children would always be a tender spot and the career change hurt just as much. Not that her career or lack of a family of her own defined her, but there were still dreams she'd had, dreams she'd had to let go of. These days she tried to focus on finding a new goal, but she still scrambled for something obtainable.

Scarlett adored being a nanny, but she simply couldn't continue in that job. Seeing all that she could've had but never would was just too painful.

Ultimately, she knew she had no choice but to walk away from that career. And because she had no family, no ties to this town of Stone River, she'd decided to move away, as well. In a large city like Dallas, surely there would be opportunities she didn't even realize she wanted.

As she stretched her legs out in front of her on the bed, Scarlett admired her toes. If Christmas wasn't the perfect time to paint her toes bright red, she didn't know when would be.

She settled back against her thick, propped pillows and reached for her laptop. In three weeks she'd be starting her new job as assistant director of activities at a nursing home in Dallas. While she was thrilled about the job and the prospect of meeting new people, she had yet to find proper housing. The one condo she'd hoped to rent had fallen through, so now she was back to the drawing board. Her Realtor in the area kept sending listings, but most were too expensive even with her pay raise.

While her toes dried, she scrolled through page after page of listings. She preferred to be closer to the city so she could have some social life, but then the costs just kept going up. She also preferred a small home instead of a condo or apartment, since privacy was important to her. But there was no way her paycheck would stretch enough to make a mortgage payment on a house. The condo she'd wanted to rent had an elderly lady living on the other side, so Scarlett had been comfortable with that setup.

She was switching to a new website when she heard the cabin door open and close. She eased her laptop aside and, after checking that her toes were nice and dry, she padded barefoot toward the living room.

As soon as she stepped through the door, Beau held his finger up to his lips and Scarlett noticed the sleeping baby cradled in his arm…against one very flexed, very taut biceps.

Down, girl.

She'd seen him on-screen plenty of times, but seeing him in person was quite a different image. She didn't know how he managed it, but the infuriating man was even sexier.

Wasn't there some crazy rule that the camera added ten pounds? Because from her vantage point, she thought maybe he'd bulked up since being on-screen because those arms and shoulders were quite something.

Scarlett clenched her hands, rubbing her fingertips against her palms at the thought of how those shoulders would feel beneath her touch.

She seriously needed to get control of her thoughts and focus. The only person she needed to be gripping, touching or even thinking about was Madelyn.

Scarlett motioned toward her room and whispered, "Let her sleep in here tonight since you didn't sleep last night."

He looked like he wanted to argue, but Scarlett quirked a brow, silently daring him to say one word. He may be the big, bad billionaire, but she wasn't backing down. Part of being a good nanny was to not only look after the child, but also take note of the parent's needs.

When Beau took a step toward her room, Scarlett ushered ahead and pulled the blinds to darken the space over the crib. The moon shone bright and beautiful tonight, but she wanted Madelyn to rest peacefully.

Scarlett took her laptop and tiptoed out of the room while Beau settled Madelyn in her crib. After taking a seat on the leather sofa in the living room, Scarlett pulled up those listings again. The sleeping baby didn't need her right now and she figured Beau had things to do. So, until he told her differently, she wouldn't get in the way.

Moments later, he eased from her room and closed the door behind him.

"I have food for you."

His comment caught her off guard. "Excuse me?"

Beau came around the couch and stood in front of her. That black T-shirt and those well-worn jeans may look casual, but the way they fit him made all her girly parts stand up and take note of just how perfectly built he truly was. Not that she hadn't noticed every other time she'd ever looked at him.

"Pepper, Nolan's wife, insisted I bring you food and she was angry I didn't invite you."

Scarlett smiled, but waved a hand. "No reason to be angry. You didn't need me."

Something flared bright and hot in his eyes, but before she could identify what she'd seen, he asked, "Have you eaten?"

"I had a granola bar, but I'm not really that hungry." She was too concerned with being homeless when she moved to Dallas.

Beau muttered something about needing more meat on her bones before he headed back out the front door. An instant later he came back in with containers and headed toward the open kitchen.

Scarlett set her laptop on the raw-edged coffee table and figured it would be rude if she didn't acknowledge the gesture.

"I could eat a little more," she commented just as her belly let out a low grumble. "What do you have?"

He gestured to the stool opposite the island where he stood. "Have a seat and I'll get you a plate before your stomach wakes my daughter."

As Scarlett eased onto the wooden stool, she couldn't believe her eyes. Hollywood heartthrob Beau Elliott was essentially making her dinner. There wasn't a woman alive who wouldn't want to be in her shoes right now.

Beau pried lids off the plastic storage containers and Scarlett's mouth watered at the sight of mashed potatoes with gravy, green beans, and meatloaf he heaped onto a plate. Mercy sakes, a real home-cooked meal. There was no way she could eat all of that and still button her pants.

"Don't tell me you're one of those women who count every carb," he growled as he spooned a hearty dose of potatoes onto a plate.

"Not every carb, but I can't exactly afford to buy bigger clothes."

He shook his head as he once he filled the plate he placed it in front of her. He pulled open a drawer and grabbed a fork, passing it across, too.

"What would you like to drink? I haven't been the best at keeping food in here for me," he stated as he walked to the fridge. "I have formula, cereal, organic baby juice or water."

Wasn't it adorable that everything in the kitchen was for a five-month-old? But, seriously, what on earth was the man going to live on? Because someone as broad and strong as Beau needed to keep up his stamina… er, energy.

Do not think about his stamina—or his broad shoulders. Or tracing those tattoos with your tongue.

"Water is fine, thanks."

She decided the best thing to do was just shovel the food in. She may regret overeating later, but at least her mouth would be occupied and she couldn't speak her lascivious thoughts.

"I'll take Madelyn and make a grocery run tomorrow," she offered as she scooped up another bite of whipped potatoes.

Beau opened one cabinet after another, clearly looking for something. "I don't expect you to do the work of a maid."

"Then who will do it?" she countered before she thought better of it. But then she opened her mouth again and charged forward. "Either you have to go or I have to, unless you want the media to chase you through aisle seven and see what type of toilet paper you buy."

Beau stopped his search and turned to face her. He flattened his palms on the island and leaned in.

Maybe she'd gone too far, but seriously, who would do the shopping? Surely not his brothers, who were obviously not taking Beau's homecoming very well, for reasons that were none of her concern but still inspired her curiosity. Still, she probably should've left that last part off, but she'd never had a proper filter.

"Are you always this bold and honest?" he asked.

Oh, he didn't want her complete honesty. Was this a bad time to tell him she'd been holding back?

Scarlett set her fork down and scooted her plate back. Resting her arms on the counter, she cocked her head.

"I believe in honesty at all times, especially in this line of work. But I really am just trying to make things easier for you."

He stared at her another minute and she worried that she had a glob of gravy in the corner of her mouth or something, but he finally shook his head and pushed off the counter.

"You don't have to go," he told her. "I can ask one of my sister-in-laws to pick some things up for me."

As much as she wanted to call him out on his bull-headedness, she opted to see a different side. She may not know the dynamics of his family or the stormy past they'd obviously had, but she recognized a hurt soul when she saw one.

"I'm perfectly capable of grocery shopping," she stated, softening her tone. "I've lived on my own for some time now and besides, you wouldn't be the first client I've shopped for."

Beau folded his arms across his broad chest and leaned back against the opposite counter. "And where do you live?"

Her appetite vanished, pushed out by nerves as she pondered her upcoming move.

"Currently here."

"Obviously." His dry tone left no room for humor. "When you're not taking care of children, where do you call home?"

Between his intense stare and the simple question that set her on edge, Scarlett slid off the bar stool and came to her feet.

"I have no home at the moment," she explained, sliding her hands in the pockets of her jeans. "I'm still looking for a place."

Beau's dark brows drew in, a familiar look she'd seen on-screen, but in person... Wow. That sultry gaze made her stomach do flips and her mouth water. She didn't care if that sounded cliché, there was no other way to describe what happened when he looked at her that way.

"You're only here three weeks," he stated, as if she'd forgotten the countdown.

Scarlett picked up her plate and circled the island. She covered the dish up and put it inside the fridge. She needed to do something to try to ignore the fact that she wasn't only under the same roof as Beau Elliott, she was literally standing within touching distance and he was staring at her as if he could see into her soul.

No, that wasn't accurate at all. He was staring at her as if she stood before him with no clothes.

Maybe she should've kept that island between them.

"I'm moving to Dallas," she explained, trying to stay on topic. "This is my final job with the Nanny Poppins agency."

The harsh reality that this was it for her never got any easier to say. But, hey, if she had to leave, at least she was going out on the highest note of her nanny career. Staying with Hollywood Bad Boy Beau Elliott and taking care of his precious baby girl.

"Why the change?" he asked. "You seem to love your job."

The burn started in her throat and she quickly swallowed the emotions back. This was the way things had to be, so getting upset over it would change absolutely nothing. She might as well enjoy her time here, with the baby and the hunk, and move on to the new chapter in her life.

New year, new start, and all that mumbo jumbo. This was the second time in her life she'd started over on her own. If she did it when she was younger, she could certainly do it now.

"Why don't you get me a grocery list and I'll take Madelyn when she wakes in the morning," she said.

Scarlett started to turn, but a warm, strong hand curled around her bare biceps. She stilled, her entire body going on high alert and responding to the simplest of touches.

But this wasn't a simple touch. This was Beau Elliott, actor, playboy, rancher, father. Could he be more complex?

When he tugged her to turn her around, Scarlett came face-to-face with a sexy, stubbled jawline, firm mouth, hard eyes.

No, not hard, more like…intense. That was by far the best adjective to describe her boss. There was an intensity that seemed to radiate from him at all times, and that powerful stare, that strong, arousing grip, had her heart pounding.

"Women don't walk away from me."

No, she'd bet not. Most likely he gave them one heavy-lidded stare or a flash of that cocky grin and their panties melted off as they begged him for anything he was willing to give.

"I'm not walking away from you," she defended. "I'm walking away from this conversation."

"That's not fair." He still held on to her arm and took a half step closer until his torso brushed against hers. "I guarantee you know more about me than I know about you."

Scarlett laughed, more out of nerves than humor. "That's not my fault you parade your life in front of the camera. You know all you need in order for me to do my job."

The hold he had on her eased, but he still didn't let go. No, now he started running that thumb along the inside of her elbow.

What the hell?

She'd say the words aloud, but then he might stop and she wanted to take this thrill and save it deep inside her memory. So what if this was all wrong and warning flags were waving in her head?

"You don't look like a nanny," he murmured, studying her face. "Maggie looked like a nanny. You…"

Her entire body heated. With each stroke of that thumb she felt the zings down to her toes.

"What do I look like?" she asked. Why did that come out as a whisper?

"Like trouble."

Scarlett wanted to laugh. Truly she did. Of all the words used to describe her, *trouble* certainly had never been a contender.

This had to stop before she crossed the professional boundary. She'd never had an issue like this before, and by issue she meant a client as potent and as sexy as Beau Elliott. No wonder women flocked to him and wanted to be draped over his arm. If she were shallower and had no ambitions, she'd probably beg to be his next piece of arm candy.

But she wasn't shallow and she most definitely had goals…goals that did not include sleeping with a client.

"Make me that grocery list and text it to me," she told him as she took a step back. "Madelyn and I will head out in the morning."

She didn't wait on him to reply. Scarlett turned and fled to her room. She didn't exactly run, but she didn't walk, either. There was no way he wasn't watching her. She could practically feel that heavy gaze of his on her backside.

No doubt Beau knew just how powerful one of his long looks were. He'd gotten two big awards for his convincing performances and she couldn't help but wonder just how sincere he was with his affection or if he was just trying to find another bedmate.

Scarlett gently closed the door behind her and leaned against it. Over in the corner Madelyn slept. That little girl was the only reason Scarlett was here. There was no room for tingles or touching or…well, arousal.

There, she'd admitted it. She was so turned on by that featherlight touch of Beau's she didn't know how she'd get any sleep. Surely if she so much as closed her eyes, she'd dream of him doing delicious things to her body. That was the last image she needed on this final nanny assignment.

Scarlett moved away from the door and started changing for bed.

One day down, she told herself. Only twenty more to go.

Five

What the hell had he been thinking touching her like that?

Beau slid his cowboy boot into the stirrup and swung his other leg over the back of Starlight, the newest mare to Pebblebrook.

He'd gotten up and out of that house this morning before seeing Scarlett. A niggle of guilt had hit him when he'd slunk out like he was doing some walk of shame, but damn it. He couldn't see her this morning, especially not all snuggly with Madelyn.

He hated not kissing his daughter good morning, but one day would be all right. Perhaps when he got back to the cabin he'd have a little more control over his hormones and unwelcome desires.

Damn it. He'd been up half the night, restless and aching. Likely Scarlett had been sleeping and not giving him another thought. This was all new territory for him, wanting a woman and not being able to have her.

With a clack of his mouth and a gentle heel to the side, Beau set Starlight off toward the back of the property.

Last night, his thoughts volleyed all around. He couldn't help wondering what Scarlett planned on doing when she left the agency, or why she was even leaving in the first place, but what kept him up all night was wondering what the hell she slept in.

Maybe she had a little pair of pajamas that matched that bright red polish she'd put on her toes. Mercy, that had been sexy as hell. He was a sucker for red.

Beau gripped the reins and guided the beautiful chestnut mare toward Hayes and Alexa's house. Beau hadn't been to the old, original farmhouse nestled in the back of the ranch since coming home. It was time he ventured out there and started making amends with his brothers. So what if he was starting with the one least pissed at him?

When Hector had been diagnosed with the inoperable brain tumor, Beau had known things weren't going to end well for them. Hector had been so much more than an agent. He'd been like a father figure, pulling Beau from the mess he'd gotten himself into when he'd first hit LA. For years they'd been like one unit, and then Beau's foundation was taken away.

But Hector had made Beau promise to go home and work on the relationships with his brothers and father. So, here he was. Having a sexy woman beneath his roof was just added penance. It was like fate was mocking him by parading Scarlett around like some sweet dream that would never become reality.

Which was why he'd been scolding himself all morning.

He couldn't touch her again. First of all, he'd put her in an uncomfortable position. That wasn't professional and he probably owed her an apology…but he wasn't sorry. He wasn't sorry that he'd finally gotten to touch her, to inhale that sweet, floral scent and see the pulse at the base of her neck kick up a notch.

Second of all, he couldn't touch her again because last night he'd been about a half second from jerking that curvy body against his to see exactly how well they'd fit.

He felt his body react to that thought, and forced his mind onto something else. The weather. That was innocuous enough. He looked around. The morning sun was warming up and already burning off the fog over the ranch.

He hoped the ice around Colt's heart would burn off just as easily. Granted, the cold welcome Beau had received was his own fault. Still, Colt acted like he didn't even want to try to forgive. Maybe that was just years of anger and resentment that had all built up and now that Beau was home Colt felt justified to unload.

But Christmas was only a few weeks away, and Beau wondered if he'd even be welcome at the table with the rest of the family. Hopefully by then, the angry words would be out of the way and they could start moving forward to a more positive future.

Beau had a movie premiere just two days before Christmas, but he planned on being gone only two days and returning. There was nothing he wanted more than to have his daughter at the ranch during the holiday and with the rest of the family.

Beau's cell vibrated in his pocket, but he ignored it. Instead, he kept Starlight at a steady pace and let himself relax as they headed to the back of the estate. He'd ridden horses for movie roles, but nothing was like this. No set could compare to being on his own land, without worrying about what direction to look or how to tip his hat at just the right angle for the camera, but not to block his eyes.

Being out here all alone, breathing in the fresh air and hoping to sew up the busted seams of his relationships kept Beau hopeful.

And really, his future depended on how things went over the next few weeks. Apologizing and crawling home with his proverbial tail between his legs wasn't easy. Beau had his pride, damn it, but he also had a family that he missed and loved.

If Christmas came and there was still no further progress made with Colt, Beau would go. He'd take Madelyn and they would go...somewhere. Hell, he had enough homes to choose from: a mansion in the Hollywood Hills, a cabin in Montana, a villa in France, his private island off the coast of Italy. Or he could just buy his own spread and build a house if that's what he chose. Maybe he'd start his own ranch and show Madelyn the way he was brought up.

But he wanted Pebblebrook.

The cell continued to vibrate. Likely his new agent, worried Beau had officially gone off-grid. Maybe he had. Maybe he wouldn't emerge until the premiere in a few weeks—maybe not even then. He didn't necessarily want to go to the premiere, but this was the most anticipated holiday movie and the buzz around it had been bigger than anything he'd ever seen.

Apparently *Holly Jolly Howards* struck a chord with people. The whole family falling apart and finding their way back together after a Christmas miracle saved one of their lives was said to be the next holiday classic. Move over *White Christmas* and *It's a Wonderful Life*.

Getting his on-screen family back together had been easy. All he'd had to do was act out the words in the script. But in real life, he was on his own.

Beau had only been back in Pebblebrook a short time, but already there was a peacefulness that calmed him at times like this. Just being out in the open on horseback helped to clear his mind of all the chaos of the job, the demands of being a celebrity, and the battle he waged with himself.

These past several months since becoming a parent had changed his entire outlook on life. He wanted the best for Madelyn, and not just the best material things. Beneath the tailor-made suits, the flashy cars and extravagant parties, he was still a simple man from a Texas ranch. He'd always had money, so that wasn't anything overly important to him.

He wanted stability. He knew it was vital in shaping the future of a child. The simplicity of routine may sound ridiculous, but he'd found out that having a schedule made his life and Madelyn's so much easier. She needed to have a life that wasn't rushing from one movie set, photo shoot, television interview or extravagant party to another. That whirlwind lifestyle exhausted him; he couldn't imagine a baby living like that.

Beau may have a nanny now, but that's not how he wanted to live his entire life. He wasn't kidding when he said he wanted to be a hands-on father. He wouldn't be jetting off to various locales just to have someone else raise his daughter.

As Hayes's white farmhouse came into view, guilt reacquainted itself with Beau. His parents had done a remarkable job of providing security and a solid foundation for the four Elliott boys.

Once their mother passed, that foundation was shaken and everyone had to figure out their purpose. Beau had started getting that itch to see if there was something else out there for him. Since money hadn't been an issue, he'd taken a chunk out of his college fund and headed to Hollywood, despite his father's demands to stay.

The cell in Beau's pocket vibrated once again as he pulled his horse up to Hayes's stable. He dismounted and hooked the rein around the post. When he turned toward the house, Alexa stepped out the back door and her son, Mason, came barreling out past her.

Beau smiled, loving how his brother had found this happiness. They'd even decorated the house for the holidays. Sprigs of evergreen seemed to be bursting from the old wagon in the yard, a festive wreath hung on the back door, and red ribbons were tied on the white posts of the back porch.

"Hope you don't mind me stopping by," Beau said as he approached the steps. "I figured I should get to know my new family members a little better."

Alexa crossed her arms and offered a welcoming grin. "Never in my life did I think I'd meet a movie star, let alone have one for a soon-to-be brother-in-law."

Mason stopped right in front of Beau and stared up at him. "Hi."

Beau tipped his hat back and squatted down to the little guy. "Hey, buddy," he greeted. "How old are you?"

Mason held up one finger and smiled. Beau had already been educated on the ages of his nieces and nephews. This was just another reason he wanted Madelyn here. This new generation of Elliotts should be close, because when your life went to hell and got flipped upside down, family was invaluable.

Beau thought of his brother Colt's reaction yesterday. Part of him knew that if Colt didn't care, he wouldn't be acting like a wounded animal right now. The ones you loved most had the ability to cause the most pain.

"Why don't you come on in," Alexa invited. "Mason and I were just about to make some muffins to take to Annabelle this afternoon. She's got her hands full at the B and B, so I offered to help. I'm not a great baker, but I can make muffins."

"I don't want to interrupt."

Alexa raised her brows. "Yet you rode out here without calling or texting?"

She offered a wide smile and waved her hand. "Get in here. Family doesn't interrupt."

Beau could see how Hayes hadn't stood a chance with this one. She was sassy and headstrong…pretty much like the sultry seductress down in his cabin.

Granted, Scarlett didn't have a clue how his stomach knotted up just thinking of her, how he'd been in a tangle of sheets all night because…well, the fantasies wouldn't let him sleep.

Mason lifted his arms toward Beau. Without hesitation, Beau picked up his…well, this would be his nephew. He hadn't been around children until he'd had his own. Oh, there were a few on some sets that he worked with, but they weren't his responsibility or they were a little older and so professional, they didn't act like regular kids.

But this little guy didn't care that Beau had two shiny acting awards back at his Hollywood Hills mansion. He didn't even know who Beau was or why he was here. Mason wanted affection and he was open and trusting and ready to accept the comfort of a stranger.

If only the rest of the family could be as welcoming as a child.

"Hayes actually just ran into town to get more supplies at the store," Alexa stated as she stepped into the house and held the door open for him. "I offered, but he keeps saying he needs to get out more."

Which was a huge accomplishment in itself. Suffering from PTSD had kept Hayes hidden away and everyone shut out for too long. Alexa had pulled him out of the rubble he'd buried himself in. The love of a good woman, Beau reckoned, was clearly invaluable. All of his brothers had found their perfect soul mate and secured a happy future.

There was clearly something in the water on Pebblebrook Ranch. No way in hell was he drinking from the well. The last thing he needed was more commitment or a relationship to worry about. Maybe one day—maybe—but not now.

Beau stepped into the kitchen and stilled. "Wow."

Alexa smiled. "I know. Hayes did an amazing job of renovating this place, though he did take my advice on the kitchen and use some of my Latino heritage as inspiration."

Judging by the bold colors from the blue backsplash to the yellow and orange details in random tiles on the floor, there was no doubt Hayes had made his fiancée feel part of this renovation.

"I haven't been back," he murmured as he held on to Mason and stepped farther into the room. "I'm going to need a tour."

Alexa reached for an apron on the hook by the pantry doors. "I'm going to let Hayes do that," she stated. "I'd say you two need some time alone."

The back door opened and Beau spun around to see his brother step in carrying bags of groceries.

"That place was pure hell," he growled as he set everything on the raw-edge kitchen table. "Remind me never to go in the morning again. Every senior citizen from town was there, all wanting to talk or shake my hand."

Beau knew his brother was grateful for the people who appreciated his service to their country, but Hayes had never been one for accolades.

"That's because they're thankful for your service." Alexa laughed and crossed to Beau. She lifted Mason from his hands. "Your brother wants a tour of the house. Now, go do that and let me work on these muffins so Annabelle doesn't have to do everything for her guests."

Annabelle, Colt's wife and owner of the bed-and-breakfast next door, was not only the mother of nearly two-year-old twin girls, rumor had it she was also a phenomenal chef. Beau had the utmost respect for her because he could barely make a bowl of cereal and care for Madelyn at the same time.

Hayes eyed his brother and Beau slid off his cowboy hat and hooked it on the top of a kitchen chair. "Care to show me what you did to the place?"

"Are we rebuilding the brotherly bond?" Hayes asked.

"Something like that."

Hayes stared another minute before giving a curt nod. "Let's go, then."

Beau followed Hayes out of the kitchen and caught Alexa's warm smile and wink as he left.

They stepped into the living room, and Beau noticed the old carpet had been replaced with wide-plank wood flooring. The fireplace and mantel had been given a facelift. The room glowed with new paint, new furniture.

The fireplace had garland and lights draped across it, as well as three knitted stockings. A festively decorated Christmas tree sat in the front window. Presents were spread all beneath and Beau figured Hayes may have gone a bit overboard with the gifts for Mason.

Everything before him, from the renovations to the holiday decor, was the sign of a new chapter in his brother's life.

Beau wanted to start a new chapter, but he couldn't even find the right book for his life.

"We'll start upstairs," Hayes said over his shoulder. "That way I can grill you without Alexa overhearing."

Beau mounted the steps. "Why do you think I came here instead of Colt's? I'm easing into this re-bonding process."

Hayes reached the landing before making the turn to the second story. "Heard you went to Nolan's last night. Does that mean Colt is tomorrow?"

Beau shrugged. "We'll see."

"And Dad?"

Beau stood on the narrow strip with his brother and stared into familiar dark eyes. "I'll get there," he promised.

Hayes seemed as if he wanted to say more, but he

turned and continued on upstairs. "Then we can discuss your nanny while I show you what I did with the place."

Great. As if she hadn't been on his mind already. She actually hadn't gotten *off* his mind since she'd showed up at his door looking like she'd just stepped off a calendar for every male fantasy. The fake women in LA didn't even compare to the natural beauty of Scarlett Patterson.

"There's nothing to know about her," Beau stated, hoping that would end the conversation, but knowing better.

"Here's the guest bath." Hayes motioned toward the open doorway, but remained in the hall. "We gutted it and started from scratch. So, Scarlett replaced Maggie. That was quite a change."

"That wasn't a very smooth transition from the bath to the nanny."

Hayes merely shrugged and leaned against the door frame, clearly waiting for an answer.

Returning his attention to the renovated bath, Beau glanced around at the classy white and brushed nickel decor. He was impressed with all the work that went into the restoration, but he couldn't focus. Just hearing Scarlett's name had his body stirring. It had simply been too long since he'd been with a woman, that's all. It wasn't like he had some horny hang-up over his nanny. For pity's sake, he was Beau Elliott. He could have any woman he wanted.

Yet he wanted the one with a killer body, doe-like eyes, a layer of kickass barely covering a heavy dose of vulnerability. The fact that she cared for his daughter above all else and wasn't throwing herself at him was just another piece in the puzzle that made up this mystery of emotions.

His cell buzzed again and this time Beau pulled his phone out, grateful for the interruption so he could stop the interrogation.

The second he glanced at the screen, though, he barely suppressed a groan at the sight of four voice mails and three texts. The texts, all from his new agent, were frantic, if the wording in all caps was any indicator.

"Problem?" Hayes asked.

Beau read the messages, but ignored the voice mails. "The movie I have coming out is getting in the way of my sabbatical."

Hayes crossed his arms and leaned against the wall. "Is that what this is? You're just passing through until something or someone better comes along?"

Beau muttered a curse and raked his hand through his hair. "Hell, that didn't come out right. I just… I have no clue what I'm doing and it's making me grouchy. My agent and publicist have scheduled so many media slots for me to promote this movie, but I've told them I need to cancel. I'll do call-ins, but I'm not going to LA or New York right now to appear on talk shows."

He simply couldn't handle it. First, he wasn't dragging Madelyn to every event because they lasted from early morning until late at night. Second, well, he needed a damn break.

"You're a good dad."

Beau jerked his attention to Hayes, surprised by his brother's statement. "Thanks. My agent, he tried to get me to take Madelyn and basically use her for more publicity. I won't do that. Jennifer tried and I won't have it. I want Madelyn as far away from the limelight as possible."

Hayes nodded, whether in understanding or approval Beau didn't know. Perhaps a little of both.

"Maybe now you can see a little where Dad was coming from."

Hayes muttered the statement before moving on down the hall like he hadn't just delivered a jab straight to the heart of the entire matter.

Beau respected the hell out of his brothers and his father. Perhaps because they all had chosen one path and been happy with their lives. Beau had thought he'd been happy and on the right path, until he became a father and his ex had decided drugs and wild parties and a future as a star were much more important.

"Show me what else you've done with the house," Beau said, shoving his cell back in his pocket.

"Don't you need to call someone?"

"This is more important."

Hayes offered a half grin, which was saying something for his quiet, reserved brother. "There's hope for you yet. But we're still going to circle back to Scarlett."

Of course they were, because why not? He'd left the house to dodge her for a bit, but now he was forced to discuss her. There was no end in sight with that woman.

Well, in less than three weeks there would be an end.

But he had a feeling she'd haunt his thoughts for some time.

Six

Scarlett handed Madelyn another fruit puff while she sat in her high chair. She wasn't surprised Beau wasn't here when she'd gotten home from the store.

Home. No. Pebblebrook wasn't her home by any means.

Yet she'd gone a tad overboard purchasing Christmas items to decorate the place. But she couldn't pass them by. She only hoped Beau didn't mind.

She busied herself putting together one of her favorite dishes. She'd come here in such a hurry and at the last minute, she had no clue if Beau had food allergies or what he liked.

Madelyn smacked her hands against the high chair tray and made little noises then squeals. Her little feet kicked and Scarlett smiled.

As much as being with a baby hurt her heart, Scarlett couldn't deny it was something she'd missed. Madelyn was such a sweetheart and so easy to care for. The few times she'd fussed with her swollen gums had passed quickly, thanks to cold teething rings.

Once the casserole was assembled and put into the oven, Scarlett unfastened Madelyn from the high chair. Madelyn let out high-pitched happy squeals and Scarlett's heart completely melted. Babies had their own language, no doubt about it.

"You need a bath," Scarlett crooned. "Yes, you do. You have sticky fingers and crazy hair."

The click of the front door had Scarlett shifting her focus from the baby to the sexy man who filled the doorway. The second he stepped inside, his dark eyes met hers. Even from across this space, she felt that intense stare all through her body. Those eyes were just as potent as his touch.

For a moment, Beau didn't move and she wondered what he was thinking. She really wished he'd say something to ease the invisible charge that crackled between them.

Scarlett finally broke eye contact, needing to get beyond this sexual tension because suddenly she was getting the idea that it wasn't one-sided anymore. And that could be trouble.

Big trouble.

"I just put dinner in the oven," she stated as she held on to Madelyn and circled the island. "I'm about to give Madelyn a bath."

The front door closed, then the lock clicked into place. Beau slid his black hat off his head and hung it on a peg by the door. Finally, his gaze shifted from her and roamed around the open cabin.

"What's all that?" he asked, nodding toward the sacks lining the sofa and dotting the area rug.

Madelyn reached for Scarlett's hair and tugged. "Just some Christmas decorations," she said, pulling her hair from the baby's sticky grasp.

Beau propped his hands on his hips and shook his head. "Give her to me. I'll give her a bath."

"Are you sure? I don't mind at all."

Beau stepped toward her, that long stride closing the distance between them pretty quickly. "I'll do it."

He slid Madelyn from Scarlett's arms and once he had his daughter, he lifted her in the air and a complete transformation came over him. He smiled, he made silly noises and had the craziest baby-talk voice she'd ever heard.

Well, Maggie had been right on this. Beau was completely different with Madelyn. He may be dealing with his own personal battles, but he wasn't letting that get in the way of his relationship with his baby.

When he went into his room and closed the door, Scarlett figured she might as well tidy up the kitchen. She'd put groceries away, then fed Madelyn when he brought her out, and laid her down for a nap. With time on her hands, she knew she should continue the house hunt. Each day that passed took her closer to her move and it was looking more and more like she'd be in a hotel for longer than she'd anticipated.

But she pushed those worries aside for now, eschewing the laptop for the bags of decorations. She got to work taking the holiday items out of the sacks and figuring where to put them. Considering she was watching every penny, she hadn't bought too much, but now that she was looking at everything in this small space, maybe it was a good thing she'd limited her impromptu spree. But there had been sales and, well, she was a savvy woman who couldn't turn down a bargain—or those little rustic cowboy boot ornaments.

Live garland nestled perfectly on the thick wood mantel. Once the two plaid stockings were in place, Scarlett stood back and smiled. This was already starting to look like home. Not for her, but for the little family in the other room.

She tried to take into consideration Beau's tastes, though she didn't know him well. At least she'd kept the decor more toward the masculine side. Though it had been difficult to leave behind the clearance garland with kissing reindeer and red sparkly snowflakes.

For reasons she couldn't explain, there wasn't a tacky Christmas decoration she didn't love.

Before Scarlett could go through the other bags, the oven timer went off.

She'd just set the steaming casserole dish on the stovetop when Beau stepped from his bedroom. He had Madelyn in a red sleeper with little reindeer heads on the feet. The baby looked so cute, but it was the man who drew her eyes like a magnet. Beau looked so sexy, his chest bare and his jeans indecently low on his narrow hips.

She licked her lips, then realized that wasn't the smartest move when his eyes dropped to her mouth. There went that tug on the invisible string pulling them together.

Why did he have to put those tattoos on display? The image of wild horses obviously paid homage to his roots, but she couldn't help it they also encompassed his true spirit of wanting to be wild and free...or maybe he used to be.

Either way, the ink was a distraction she didn't need, yet she desperately wanted to explore. Along with the lean muscles and six-pack abs.

Scarlett cleared her throat. "Dinner is ready."

Beau moved closer, his eyes locked on hers as if he could read her thoughts. "Is that why you're staring at my chest?"

Scarlett blinked and snapped her eyes to meet his. "I was not."

"You're a liar, but I won't report that to your employer." As he handed Madelyn over, he leaned in close and inhaled right by her neck. "Dinner smells good."

That low, gravelly tone sent shivers throughout her body and she nearly gave in to the temptation to close the two-inch gap and touch that gorgeous chest that beckoned her. But before she could move, he turned away and went back into his bedroom. Scarlett just stood there, stock still, wondering what the hell had just happened. What was he doing and why had she almost let herself get caught up in it? Damn it. That behavior was not at all professional.

Done berating herself, she took Madelyn to the portable swing in the living area and fastened her in. Once the music and swing were on, Scarlett went back to the kitchen and started dishing up the casserole. There was no way she was knocking on Beau's door to see if he was coming out to eat. She'd simply make a plate and he could eat when he wanted.

Scarlett had just poured two glasses of sweet tea when Beau stepped from his room. With his wet hair glistening even darker than she'd seen and a fresh T-shirt stretched across his broad shoulders, it was all she could do to force her eyes away.

He eyed the two plates sitting on the island, then he glanced to her. "You don't have to cook for me."

"You're welcome." The snarky reply just came out, so she added, "I had to cook for myself anyway. Hope you like cabbage."

He didn't say a word, but came over and sank onto one of the stools on the bar side of the island. As he dug in, she watched for a moment and figured he must not hate it. Part of her was relieved, though she didn't know why. What did it matter if he liked her cooking? She wasn't here to impress him with her homey skills.

Scarlett remained on the kitchen side of the island and started eating. The cabbage, bacon and rice casserole was one of her favorites. It was simple, filling, and rather healthy.

"You can have a seat," he told her without looking up from his plate. "I only bite upon request."

Why did she have to shiver at that? Just the idea of his mouth on her heated skin was enough to have her keeping this island between them. She may only "know" Beau from what she'd read online over the years, but she knew enough to realize he was a ladies' man and an endless flirt. And she was just another female in what she was sure was a long line of forgettable ladies.

So the fact that she lit up on the inside and had those giddy nerves dancing in her belly was absolutely ridiculous. She was leaving soon and he'd go on to more women and probably more children.

"I'm fine," she told him. "I'm used to eating standing up anyway."

That wasn't a lie. In fact, when she'd worked in other homes with small children, she'd been happy simply to get her meal hot. Besides, there was no way she'd get close to him. It wasn't so much him she was afraid of but her growing attraction, and she worried if she didn't keep some distance...

Well, she'd keep her distance so they didn't find out.

"I can keep an eye on Madelyn this way," she went on.

Beau glanced over his shoulder to where his daughter continued to swing. Then he jerked around, his fork clattering to the plate.

"What the hell is all that?" he barked.

Scarlett nearly choked on her bite. She took a drink of her sweet tea and cleared her throat. "Christmas decorations. I told you earlier."

His dark eyes shifted straight to her. "I know what you said earlier, but I didn't realize you were taking over the entire cabin. I thought you were putting stuff in your room. Why the hell is it all over my living room?"

"Because it's Christmas."

Why did he keep asking the most ridiculous questions?

"I didn't ask you to do that," he grumbled.

"Well, you didn't ask me to cook for you, either, but you're clearly enjoying it."

He muttered something else before going back to his plate, but she couldn't make it out. And she didn't ask him to repeat it. Instead, they finished eating in awkward silence. Only the sound of the nursery rhyme chiming from the swing broke through the space.

"There's no reason to get cozy here."

His words sliced right through her and she pulled in a deep breath before addressing him.

Scarlett propped her hands on her hips. "Are you talking to me or yourself?"

His dark eyes darted to hers once more. "Both."

"Well, I don't know what's going on in your personal life, but this is Madelyn's first Christmas. She deserves to have a festive place, whether it's temporary or not."

Madelyn started to fuss and Scarlett ignored her plate and went to the baby.

"Eat," Beau stated as he came to stand beside her. "I can give her a bottle and get her ready for bed."

Scarlett unfastened Madelyn and turned off the swing. "I've got her. You worked all day, so finish your dinner."

She didn't wait for his reply or give him an opportunity to argue. She started to make a bottle, but Beau beat her to it.

"Lay her in my room." He kissed Madelyn's head and glanced up to Scarlett. "I'll keep her tonight."

He stood so close, too close. His arm brushed hers, those eyes held her in place. She'd thought they were dark brown, but now she could see almost golden flecks. They were nearly hypnotic, pulling her in as if in a trance she couldn't resist.

But you have to.

The silent warning broke the spell and she cleared her throat.

"You're paying me to watch her," Scarlett told him, pleased when her voice sounded strong. "If you're going to the stables early, then you need your rest."

She should take a step back, but she didn't want to. He smelled too good and looked even better.

"I also said I'm a hands-on dad." He handed over the bottle. "So leave her in my room after she eats."

Scarlett wasn't going to argue with him. She worked for him and this was his child. If he wanted to be woken up during the night, that was his call.

She clutched the bottle in one hand and held the baby in the other as she headed toward his room, leaving him in the kitchen to finish his dinner. The second she stepped into his bedroom, a full-on assault hit her senses. If she thought he smelled good a moment ago, that was nothing compared to the masculine, fresh-from-the-shower scent that filled his space.

The sheets were rumpled and she found herself transfixed by the sight. Just the thought of Beau Elliott in a tangle of dark navy sheets would fuel her nighttime fantasies for years. He was a beautiful man, all sculpted and tan, with just a little roughness about him.

Was it any wonder Hollywood had pulled him into its grasp and cast him in that first film set in the Wild West? He'd been perfect. Captivating and sexy, riding shirtless on his horse. A handsome cowboy straight from a Texas ranch. He didn't just play the part; he was the part.

Scarlett hated to admit how many times she'd watched that exact movie.

She closed her eyes and willed herself to stop the madness of these mind games. Hadn't she vowed not to focus on the man and remain dedicated to the child?

She fed Madelyn and soothed her until she was ready to be laid down. Once she had the baby in her crib, Scarlett turned to leave, but once again her eyes went to that messy king-size bed.

How many days did she have left?

Scarlett closed her eyes and pulled in a deep breath.

She would get through this and keep her lustful desires out of the picture.

She tiptoed from the room and gently shut the door behind her. When she came back into the open area, she noted the kitchen had been cleaned up and the dishes were all washed.

She was stunned. Not only at the idea of a celebrity getting dishpan hands, but a billionaire who had employees who likely did everything from his laundry to making his reservations with arm candy dates.

Scarlett nearly laughed at herself. She wasn't going to date Beau; she wasn't even going to be friends with the man. This relationship, if it could be called such, was strictly professional.

She turned from the kitchen and spotted Beau standing in front of the fireplace. With his back to her, Scarlett had a chance to study him…as if she needed another opportunity or reason to ogle. But that shirt stretched so tightly across his shoulders and that denim hugged his backside in all the perfect places.

"I used to want this."

His low words cut through her thoughts and she realized she'd been caught once again staring. He'd known she was back here.

Scarlett took a few cautious steps forward and waited for him to continue. Clearly he was working through some thoughts.

"Christmas as a kid was always a big deal," he went on as he continued to stare at the stockings. "My mom would bake and I remember coming in from the barns and smelling bread or cookies. There was always something in the oven or on the counter."

She continued to listen without interrupting. Whatever he was working through right now had nothing to do with her. But the fact she was getting a glimpse into his personal life only intrigued her more. Scarlett had a feeling not many people saw this side of Beau.

"Mom would pretend that she didn't see Colt and me sneak out a dozen cookies before dinner." He let out a low rumble of laughter. "That poor woman had a time raising four boys and being a loving wife to my dad. She never worried about anything and was so relaxed. I guess she had to be, considering she was in a house full of men."

Beau paused for a moment before he went on. "Christmas was her time to shine. She had every inch of that house covered in garland and lights. I always knew when I married and settled down I wanted my house to be all decked out. I wanted my kids to feel like I did."

Scarlett's heart did a flip and she realized she'd closed the distance and stood so close, close enough to reach out and touch him. She fisted her hands at her sides.

Beau turned to face her. The torment on his face was something she hadn't seen yet. The man standing before her wasn't an actor. Wasn't a billionaire playboy. The man before her was just a guy who felt pain and loss like anyone else.

"I appreciate what you did here for Madelyn," he told her.

Scarlett smiled. "I did it for both of you."

His lips thinned and he glanced down as if to compose himself. "You didn't have to," he said, his gaze coming back up to hers.

"I wanted to."

Before she thought twice, Scarlett reached out, her

hand cupping his cheek. She meant to console, to offer support, but his eyes went from sad to hungry in a second.

Scarlett started to pull away, but he covered her hand with his and stepped into her. Her breath caught in her throat at the brush of his torso on hers.

If she thought his stare had been intense before, it was nothing compared to what she saw now. Raw lust and pure desire.

"Beau."

He dipped his head and she knew exactly what was coming. She also knew she should move away and stop this before they crossed a line neither of them could come back from.

But she couldn't ignore the way her body tingled at his touch, at the passion in his eyes. She desperately wanted him to put that tempting mouth on hers. She didn't care if she was just another woman to him. She wasn't a virgin and she knew exactly what this was and what this wasn't.

It was just a kiss, right?

Beau feathered his lips over hers. The instant jolt of ache and need shot through every part of her body. But then he covered her mouth, coaxing her lips apart as he teased her with his tongue.

He brought their joined hands between their bodies and the back of his hand brushed her breast.

She'd been wrong. So, so wrong.

This was so much more than a kiss.

Seven

Beau had lost his damn mind, yet there was no way he could release Scarlett now. He'd wanted to taste her since she showed up at his doorstep looking like some exotic fantasy come to life.

Alarm bells went off in his head—the ones that usually went off when he was about to make a mistake. He ignored them.

Scarlett's curvy body leaned in, her nipple pebbled against the back of his hand. The way she groaned and melted into him had Beau ready to rip off this barrier of clothing and take exactly what they both wanted.

Beau took his free hand and settled it on the dip in her waist, curling his fingers and pulling her in tighter. She reached up and gripped his biceps as she angled her head just enough to take more of the kiss.

Kiss. What a simple word for a full-body experience.

Beau eased his fingertips beneath the hem of her shirt and nearly groaned when he came in contact with silky skin.

Scarlett tore her lips away and stepped back. Coolness instantly replaced the heat where her body had been. Beau had to force himself to remain still and not reach for her.

She covered her lips with her shaky hand and closed her eyes. "We can't do that."

"We just did." Like hell he'd let her regret this. They were adults with basic needs. "Did you not want me to kiss you?"

She pulled in a breath and squared her shoulders before she pinned him with that stunning stare. "I wanted it. No use in pretending I didn't, considering I nearly climbed up your body."

Beau couldn't help the twitch of a smile. "Then what's the problem?"

"The problem is that I'm your nanny," she volleyed back. "The problem is I won't be another woman in your long line of panty-droppers."

Panty-droppers? Beau laughed. Full from the belly laughter. Well, at least now he knew exactly what she thought.

Scarlett narrowed her dark eyes. "I don't see what's so funny."

"You can't believe the tabloids," he told her. Because he really wanted her to understand, he explained further. "I know everyone thinks I'm a major player, but that perception is fueled by the tabloids. They like to come to their own conclusions and then print assumptions. Just because a woman was on my arm or in my car doesn't mean she was in my bed."

"I won't be in your bed, either."

That smart mouth of hers kept him smiling. "Well, no, because Madelyn is in there. We should use your bed."

Scarlett let out an unladylike growl and turned away. "We are not discussing this."

"What? Sex? Why not?"

Beau started after her, but stopped when she spun back around. "Other than the obvious reason of me being your daughter's nanny, and I really hate clichés, I'll repeat that I won't be another girl in your bed."

Now she was just pissing him off. "You're really hung up on who's in my bed."

"Or maybe I'm just reminding myself not to get caught up in your charm." She propped her hands on her hips and tipped her head. "I realize I may be a challenge and you're not used to people saying no, but we kissed, it's over. Can we move on?"

She had to be kidding. That heat wasn't just one-sided. She'd damn well melted against him. She claimed to always be honest, but she wasn't just lying to him, she was lying to herself.

"Move on?" he asked. "Not likely."

Her dark eyes flared wide. The pulse at the base of her throat continued to beat faster than normal.

Yeah, that's right. He wasn't one to hide the truth, either. There was no way he could just move on now that he'd tasted her and felt that lithe body against his.

"I have no interest in a fling or to be bullied by someone just because they have money and power," she sneered. "I'm going to bed. I'll keep the monitor on in case you need me."

Money and power? What the hell did that have to do

with anything? Clearly she had other issues that went well beyond him, this moment and her attraction.

The second Scarlett turned from him, Beau closed the gap between them and curled his arm around her waist, pulling her side against his chest.

"I never make a woman do anything," he corrected. Above all, she had to know he wasn't like that. "We were both very involved in that kiss. If I thought for a second you weren't attracted to me, I never would've touched you, Scarlett."

She shivered beneath him when he murmured her name in her ear. His thumb eased beneath the hem of her shirt and slid over that dip in her waist.

"Tell me who hurt you," he demanded, his tone firm, yet low.

He didn't like the idea of any woman being hurt by a man, but something about Scarlett made him want to protect her, to prevent any more pain in her life.

Scarlett stiffened and turned those dark eyes up to his. There was a weakness looking back at him that he recognized. He'd seen that underlying emotion every single day in the mirror for the past year. Whatever she was battling, she was desperately trying to hide it. Damn it, he knew how difficult it was to keep everything bottled up with no one to talk to, to lean on.

Circumstances as of late had led him to that exact vulnerable point in his life.

Beau hadn't expected a layer of admiration to join the physical attraction, but slowly his take on Scarlett was evolving into something he couldn't quite figure out.

"I won't be here long enough for my personal life to matter to you," she whispered.

"So I can't care about your feelings while you're here?"

Her eyes darted away, looking in the direction of the fireplace. Maybe the holidays were difficult for her, as well. Did she have family? She hadn't mentioned being with them or buying presents or anything that came with sharing Christmas with someone special.

Everything in him screamed that he was walking a fine line with her. He had a sinking feeling she was alone or she'd lost someone. Whatever the reason, the holiday was difficult on her.

Something twitched in his chest, but Beau refused to believe his heart was getting involved here. There was nothing wrong with caring or worrying about someone, even if that person was a virtual stranger. He'd been raised to be compassionate, that's all. Just because he was concerned didn't mean he wanted a relationship.

He stroked his thumb along her bare skin again, reminding himself anything between them should and would stay physical.

Finally, her eyes darted back to his. "I don't think this is a good idea."

The goose bumps beneath his touch told a different story. He feathered another swipe across her waist.

"What part isn't a good idea?"

"The kiss, the touches." She shook her head and stepped away from him. "I'm going to my room. I still need to find housing before my move so I'm not stuck in a hotel forever...and I need some space from you."

"I'll give you space," he vowed. "That still won't make the ache go away. You know ignoring this will only make the pull even stronger."

She took another step away, as if she could escape what was happening here.

"Then we both better hope we can control ourselves until my time here is up."

Well, so far she'd managed to find eight places to rent, all over her budget, she'd done some yoga trying to calm her nerves, and she was now browsing through social media but not really focusing on the posts.

And it was one in the morning.

Scarlett kept telling herself to go to sleep because the baby would need her undivided attention tomorrow and she may even wake during the night.

Honestly, though, there was just no way she could crawl between the sheets when her body was still so revved up. She didn't even have to concentrate to feel his warm breath tickling the sensitive spot just below her ear or the way he kept that firm yet gentle touch just beneath the hem of her shirt. He tempted, teased…left her aching for more of the forbidden.

How dare Beau put her in this position?

Granted, she hadn't exactly resisted that toe-curling kiss. She'd thoroughly enjoyed Beau. She knew he would never force himself on her. No, he'd kissed her because she hadn't been able to hide her desire and that made her just as easy as all the other women he'd charmed. Damn it, she'd told herself to hold it together. It was only three weeks, for pity's sake.

The last thing she needed was a temporary, heated fling with her movie star boss. Other than the obvious working relationship that should keep them apart, she valued herself as more than someone forgettable—because she knew once she was gone, Beau wouldn't remember her.

Scarlett's heart clenched. Her family had forgotten her, as well. When she didn't bow to their wishes or aim to fulfill any political aspirations to round out the powerhouse family, they'd dismissed her as easily as a disloyal employee.

She slid off her bed and stretched until her back popped. She'd like to grab a bottle of water, but if he was out in the living room, then she really should stay put. She hadn't heard him on the monitor, so either he was incredibly stealthy or he hadn't gone to bed yet.

Scarlett eased over to her closed door and slowly turned the knob to peek out. There was a soft glow from the Christmas lights she'd strung on the mantel, but other than that, nothing. She didn't see him anywhere.

Tiptoeing barefoot, she crossed the living area and went into the kitchen. She tried her best to keep quiet as she opened the fridge and pulled out a bottle of water. When she turned, she spotted the bags of Christmas decor she hadn't done anything with yet.

She wasn't sure if she should mention a tree to Beau or just have one appear. Even if it was a small one, everyone needed a little Christmas cheer. She'd seen a tree farm in town earlier and had heard good things about the family-owned business. Maybe she'd check it out tomorrow just to see if they had something that would work in this small space.

Growing up she'd never been allowed to decorate. Her stepfather always had that professionally done. After all, what would their guests say when they showed up for parties and the tree had been thrown together with love by the children who lived there?

Not that Scarlett got along with his kids. They were just as stuffy and uptight as he was. The one time Scarlett tried to have a little fun and slide down the banister from the second floor to the entryway, her step-siblings were all too eager to tattle.

Scarlett crossed the small area and sank down onto the rug. Glancing from one shopping bag to the next, she resisted the urge to look inside. The rattling of bags would definitely make too much noise—besides, she knew exactly what she had left. Little nutcracker ornaments, a few horses, some stars. Nothing really went together, but she'd loved each item she'd seen so she'd dumped them into her cart.

Scarlett uncapped her water and took a sip.

"Can't sleep?"

She nearly choked on her drink, but managed to swallow before setting her bottle on the coffee table beside her.

Beau's footsteps brushed over the hardwood floors as he drew closer. Scarlett didn't turn. She was afraid he'd be in something like boxer briefs and all on display. Not that she was much better. She had on her shorts and a tank, sans bra and panties because that was just how she slept. At least she'd thrown on her short robe, so she was covered. Still, her body tingled all over again at the awareness of him.

She didn't answer him. The fact that she sat on the floor of the living room at one in the morning was proof enough that she couldn't sleep.

When Beau eased down beside her, Scarlett held her breath. Were they going back for round two? Because she wasn't so sure she could keep resisting him if he didn't back off a little.

Or perhaps that was his plan. To keep wearing her down until he could seduce her. Honestly, it wouldn't take much. One more tingling touch and she feared she'd strip off her own clothes and start begging for more.

There really was only so much a woman could handle.

"I still won't apologize for that kiss."

And here they went. Back at it again.

"But I also won't make this more difficult for you," he quickly added. "I need you and Madelyn needs you."

She exhaled that breath she'd been holding. That was what she'd wanted him to say, yet now that she knew he was easing off, she almost felt cheated.

Good grief. Could she be any more passive-aggressive? She just... Well, she just wanted him, but that wasn't the issue. The issue was, she *shouldn't* want him.

"I'm not sorry we kissed," she admitted. Might as well go for honesty at this point. "But I need this job, so we have to keep this professional."

Now she did risk turning to look at him. He had on running shorts, not boxers, thank God. But then she raised her eyes and saw that he wore shorts and nothing else.

Why could men get away with wearing so little? It simply wasn't fair. It sure as hell wasn't fair, either, that he looked so perfectly...well, perfect.

"You have somewhere to put all of this?" he asked, nodding toward the bags.

Scarlett nodded, pulling her attention from that bare chest to the sacks. "On the tree."

"I don't have a tree."

"I plan on fixing that very soon."

When he continued to stare at her, she didn't look

away. Scarlett stretched her legs out in front of her and rested her hands behind her, daring him to say something negative about Christmas or decorations.

"I assume you saw the Christmas tree farm down the road?" he asked.

Scarlett nodded. "I believe Madelyn and I will go back into town tomorrow and check it out. I'll just get something small to put in front of the patio doors."

"Were you going to ask?"

"Like you asked about kissing me?"

Damn it. She hadn't meant to let that slip, but the snark just came out naturally. The last thing she could afford was for him to know she was thinking of him, of that damn kiss that still had her so restless and heated.

"Forget I said that." She shook her head and looked down at her lap. "I'm—"

"Right," he finished. "I didn't ask. That's because when I see what I want, I just take it. Especially since I saw passion staring back at me."

He didn't need to say he wanted her—she'd gotten that quite clearly. Most likely she appealed to him because she hadn't thrown herself at him or because she was the only woman around, other than his brothers' women.

Beau slid his finger beneath her chin and forced her to look at him. Oh, that simple touch shouldn't affect her so, but it did. She was human, after all.

"What makes you so different?" he muttered beneath his breath, but she heard him.

Scarlett shifted fully to face him. "What?"

Beau shook his head, almost as if he'd been talking to himself. That fingertip beneath her chin slid along her jawline, gentle, featherlight, but she felt the touch in every part of her body. The stillness of the night, the soft glow of the twinkling lights just above Beau's head had her getting wrapped up in this moment. She told herself she'd move away in a second. Really, she would.

Beau didn't utter a word, but his eyes captivated her, held her right in this spot. He feathered his fingertips down the column of her neck and lower to the V of her robe. She pulled in a deep breath and tried not to stare at those tattoos on his chest that slid up and disappeared over his shoulder. If she looked at his body, then she'd want to touch his body.

Scarlett clenched her fists in her lap. The robe parted slightly, and her nipples puckered in anticipation.

"Beau," she whispered.

His eyes dropped to where his hand traveled and explored, then he glanced back up to her. "I want you to feel."

The raw statement packed a punch and Scarlett wasn't sure what he wanted to happen, but she definitely felt. Just that soft touch had her body tingling and burning up.

He dropped that same hand to the top of her bare thigh and she stilled. Those dark eyes remained locked on hers as he slid his palm up her leg and beneath the hem of her robe.

Scarlett's breath caught in her throat as she glanced down to watch his hand disappear. Beau leaned in closer, his lips grazed her jaw.

"You promised no more kissing," she whispered.

"I'm not kissing you." His warm breath across her skin wasn't helping. "Relax."

Relax? He had to be kidding. Her body was so revved up, there was no relaxing. She trembled and ached and it took every bit of her willpower not to strip her clothes off, lie down on this rug and beg him for every single thing she'd been denying them both.

His fingertips slid beneath her loose sleep shorts. If he was shocked at her lack of panties, he didn't say so and his fingers didn't even hesitate as they continued their journey to the spot where she ached most.

She shifted, easing her legs apart to grant him access...all while alarms sounded and red flags waved trying in vain to get her attention. All that mattered right now was his touch. Who they were didn't matter. They were beyond that worry and clearly didn't give a damn.

There was only so long a woman could hold out and Beau wasn't an easy man to ignore. Damn it, she'd tried.

Scarlett spread her legs wider, then before she knew it, she was lying back on that rug with Beau propped on his elbow beside her. He slid one finger over her before sliding into her. She shut her eyes and tipped her hips to get more. Did he have to move so agonizingly slow? Didn't he realize she was burning up with need?

"Look at me," he demanded.

He slid another finger into her and Scarlett opened her eyes and caught his intense gaze. The pale glow from the Christmas lights illuminated his face. This wasn't the movie star or the rancher beside her. Right at this moment, Beau Elliott was just a man with basic needs, a man who looked like he wanted to tear off her clothes, a man who was currently priming her body for release.

"Don't hold back." It was half whisper, half command.

Considering she'd had no control over her body up

until this point, let alone this moment, holding back wasn't an option.

The way he continued to watch her as he stroked her was both arousing and intimidating. What did he see when he looked at her? Was he expecting more? Would they carry this back into her room?

Scarlett's thoughts vanished as her body spiraled into release. She couldn't help but shut her eyes and arch further into his touch. He murmured something, perhaps another demand, but she couldn't make out the words.

Wave after wave rushed over her and Scarlett reached up to clutch his thick biceps. He stayed with her until the tremors ceased, and even then, he continued to stroke her with the softest touch.

How could she still be aroused when she'd just been pleasured?

After a moment, Beau eased his hand away and smoothed her shorts and robe back into place. Scarlett risked opening her eyes and found him still staring down at her.

"You're one sexy woman," he told her in that low, sultry tone that seemed to match the mood and the dark of night.

Scarlett reached for the waistband of his shorts, but he covered her hand with his. "No. Go on to bed."

Confused, she drew back and slowly sat up. "You're not—"

Beau shook his head. "I wanted to touch you. I *needed* to touch you. I'm not looking for anything in return."

What? He didn't want more? Did men like that truly exist? Never would she have guessed Beau to be so giving, so selfless.

Scarlett studied his face and realized he was completely serious.

"Why?" The question slipped through her lips before she could stop herself.

Beau answered her with a crooked grin that had her stomach doing flips. "It's not important. Go on, now. Madelyn will be ready to go early and I need you rested."

When she didn't move, Beau came to his feet and extended his hand. She slid her fingers into his palm and he helped her up, but didn't release her.

"I'll be busy all day," he told her. "I look forward to seeing that Christmas tree when you're done with it."

He let her go, but only to reach up and smooth her hair behind her ears. His eyes held hers a moment before he turned and headed back to his room and silently closed the door.

Scarlett remained in place, her body still humming, and more confused than ever.

Just who was Beau Elliott? Because he wasn't the demanding playboy she'd originally thought. He was kind and passionate, giving and self-sacrificing. There was so much to him that she never would've considered, but she wanted to explore further.

Which would only prove to be a problem in the long run. Because a man who was noble, passionate and sexy would be damn difficult to leave in a few weeks.

Eight

Colt eased back onto the patio sofa and wrapped his arm around Annabelle. Lucy and Emily were happily playing on the foam outdoor play yard he'd just put together. With the padded sides and colorful toys in the middle, the two seemed to be perfectly content.

"You're home earlier than usual," Annabelle stated, snuggling into his side. "Not that I'm complaining."

"I knew you would be in between cleaning the rooms and checking new guests in."

She rested her delicate hand on his thigh. Those gold bands on her finger glinted in the late-afternoon sunshine.

"We are actually free for the night," she replied. "The next several days are crazy, but I love it."

He knew she did. Annabelle's goal had always been to have her own B and B where she could cater to guests and showcase her amazing cooking skills.

Colt never could've imagined how much his life would change when this beauty came crashing onto his ranch...literally. She took out the fence in her haste to leave after their first meeting and he had been smitten since.

"You've not talked much about Beau."

Her statement brought him back to the moment and the obvious situation that needed to be discussed...even though he'd rather not.

"What do you want me to say?"

Lucy patted the bright yellow balls dangling on an arch on one side of the play yard. Annabelle shifted in her seat and eased up to look him directly in the eye.

He knew that look...the one of a determined woman.

"I can't imagine how difficult this is for you," she started, then patted his leg. "But think about Beau. Can you imagine how worried he was coming back, not knowing if he'd be accepted or not and having a baby?"

Colt doubted Beau had ever been worried or afraid in his life. He'd likely come home because... Hell, Colt had no idea the real reason. He hadn't actually asked.

"I can see your mind working."

Colt covered Annabelle's hand with his and gave her a slight squeeze. Lucy let out a shriek, but he glanced to see that she was laughing and nothing was actually wrong.

"This is tough," he admitted, hating the vulnerability, but he was always honest with his wife. "Having him back is all I'd ever wanted for so long. I guess that's why I'm so angry now."

"Then maybe you should talk to him about your feelings."

Colt wanted to. He played various forms of the conversation over and over in his mind, but each time he approached Beau, something snapped and the hurt that had been building inside Colt seemed to snap.

"Do you trust me?"

Colt eased forward and kissed Annabelle's forehead. "With everything."

"Then let me take care of this," she told him with that grin of hers that should scare the hell out of him. She was plotting.

Colt wasn't so far gone in his hurt that he wouldn't accept help and he trusted his wife more than anyone.

"I love you," he told her, then glanced to their twin girls. "And this life we've made."

Annabelle settled back against his side and laid her head on his shoulder.

"Let's see if we can make it just a bit better," she murmured.

If anyone could help repair the relationship between him and Beau, he knew it was Annabelle.

Maybe there was hope, because all he'd ever wanted was a close family. That was the ultimate way to honor their father.

Beau glanced over the blueprints of the dude ranch. The cabins, one of which he was using, were in perfect proportion to the river, the creek, the stables. His brothers couldn't have chosen a better spot for the guests to stay.

The mini-prints hung in raw wood frames on the wall of the office in the main stable closest to Colt's house. Beau's eyes traveled from one print to the next. The four original surveys of the land from when their grandfather purchased the ranch were drawn out in quarters.

So much was the same, yet so different since he was home last.

A lump of guilt formed in Beau's throat. His brothers had designed this and started construction while he'd been in LA living his own life and dealing with Jennifer and her pregnancy. His father's main goal for his life was to see a dude ranch one day on the Elliott Estate. Now the dream was coming to fruition, but Grant couldn't even enjoy it because he was a prisoner in his own mind. Even if Beau or his brothers managed to bring their father here to see the progress, he'd likely never realize the sight before him, or the impact he had on his boys.

"I was hoping to find you here."

Beau glanced over his shoulder at the female voice. Annabelle, Colt's wife, stood in the doorway with a sweet smile on her face. Her long, red hair fell over both shoulders and she had a little girl on her hip.

"Which one is this?" he asked, smiling toward the toddler.

"This is Emily. Lucy is back at the house for a nap because she didn't sleep well last night."

Emily reached for him and Beau glanced to Annabelle. "May I?"

"Of course."

Beau took the child in his arms, surprised how much different she felt than his own. Granted, there was nearly a year between the two.

"I imagine having twins is quite a chore," he stated. "Do you ever get sleep?"

Annabelle laughed. "Not at first, but they're pretty good now. Lucy is getting another tooth, so she was a bit fussy during the night."

Apparently teeth were a huge deal in disrupting kids' sleep habits.

Emily smacked her hands against his cheeks and giggled. Such a sweet sound. "What brings you to the stables?" he asked Annabelle. "If you're looking for Colt, I haven't seen him today."

Likely because his brother was dodging him, but Beau wouldn't let that deter him. He was here to try to repair relationships and he couldn't give up.

"I'm actually looking for you," Annabelle stated. "I'd like you to come to dinner this evening. Well, you, Madelyn and Scarlett."

Beau stilled. Dinner with his disgruntled twin brother? Dinner with his baby and his nanny? Why the hell would he want to torture himself?

When he and Colt got a chance to speak about their past, Beau sure as hell didn't want an audience.

There was so much wrong with this dinner invitation. First of all, he wasn't quite ready to settle around a table with his brother and second, he couldn't bring Scarlett. Having her there would make things seem too familial and that would only give her the wrong impression.

Damn it. Beau could still feel her against him, still hear her soft pants and cries of passion. Last night had been a turning point, though what they'd turned to he had no idea. All he knew was they were far beyond nanny and boss—which was the reason she couldn't come to dinner.

"I can tell by your silence you're not thrilled." Annabelle smiled. "Let me rephrase. You will come to dinner and bring your daughter and your nanny."

"Why are you so determined to get me to dinner?" he asked.

Emily reached for her mother and Annabelle took the little girl back. "Because you and Colt need to keep working on this relationship. My husband is agitated and he's keeping his feelings bottled up. The more time you two can spend together, the better off you both will be."

He nodded, not necessarily in agreement, but in acknowledgment of what his sister-in-law had just said.

Beau tipped back his hat. "Why does Scarlett need to join us?"

Annabelle rolled her eyes. "Because it's rude to leave her at the cabin and I imagine she wants some female companionship."

Did she? He'd never asked. Granted, it was difficult to talk about her needs when he'd only been worried about his own—which basically involved touching her, tasting her.

Annabelle's intense stare held him in place and he wrangled in his errant thoughts and let out a deep sigh.

"Does Colt ever win an argument with you?"

A wide smile spread across her face. "Never. We'll see you all at six." Then she turned and headed out of the office.

Beau stared after her until he realized he was still staring at the open doorway. That was one strong-willed woman, which was exactly what Colt needed in his life.

The Elliott men were headstrong, always had been. A trait they'd all inherited, right along with their dark eyes and black hair. Beau figured there would never be a woman who matched him, but that was all right. He had Madelyn and she was more than enough.

He turned back to the blueprints on the opposite wall and continued to admire what would become of this property. Beau didn't know if his father would ever be able to come see this, but he couldn't help but wonder if he should take a copy of these blueprints to show him. Maybe seeing something that meant so much to him his entire life would trigger some memory.

Beau just wanted to do something, to make it possible for his dad to have some semblance of his past to hopefully trigger the present.

In all honesty, Beau wondered if his dad would even recognize him.

He did know one thing. He couldn't keep putting that visit off. He pulled his cell from his pocket and figured it was time to set up a time to see his father.

Scarlett adjusted the tree once again, but no matter how much she shifted and tilted it, the stubborn thing still leaned...and by leaned she meant appeared as if it was about to fall.

She let out the most unladylike growl, then startled when she heard chuckling behind her.

"Problem?"

Turning toward the doorway, Scarlett tried to keep her heart rate normal at the sight of Beau. First of all, she'd thought she was alone, save for Madelyn. Second, she hadn't seen him since he'd sent her to her room last night, though she'd thought of him all day.

Okay, she'd actually replayed their erotic encounter over and over, which was quite a leap ahead of just thinking of her hunky roommate. Had Beau thought about what happened? Did the intimacy mean anything to him at all or was this just one-sided?

"The damn tree is crooked," she grumbled.

Beau tilted his head to the side and narrowed his eyes. "Not if I stand like this."

She threw up her hands. "This doesn't happen in the movies. Everything looks perfect and everyone is happy. Christmas is magical and everyone has matching outfits and they go sleigh riding in some gorgeously decorated sled pulled by horses."

Beau laughed as he slid his hat off his head and hung it on the peg by the door. "That's quite a jump from worrying about a tree. Besides, everything is perfect in the movies because decorators are paid a hefty sum to make that happen. Real life isn't staged."

Scarlett turned to stare back at the tree. "It was the only one they had that would fit in this space. I thought I could make it work. Now what am I going to do?"

Beau's boots tapped across the hardwood, then silenced when he hit the rug...the very rug where she'd lain last night and on which she'd been pleasured by this man. She'd tried not to look at it today. Tried and failed.

"Decorate it."

She glanced over her shoulder at his simple, ridiculous answer, but he wasn't looking at her. He only had eyes for his little girl who sat in her swing, mesmerized by the spinning bumblebee above her head.

"How's she been today?"

"Pretty happy." Scarlett stepped around the bags of ornaments and lights she had yet to unpack. "I made some organic food for her so you have little containers in the fridge we can just grab whenever. It's better than buying jars."

Beau jerked his dark eyes to her. "You made her food?"

"I know you want to keep things simple and healthy for her." Now she felt silly with the way he seemed so stunned. "I mean, if you don't want to use it, that's fine, I just—"

"No."

He reached for her arm and Scarlett tried not to let the warmth from his touch thrust her into memories of the night before. But considering they were standing right where they'd made the memory, it was rather difficult not to think of every single detail.

"I'm glad you did that for her," he added, sliding his hand away. "I just didn't expect you to go above and beyond."

Scarlett smiled. "Taking care of children is my passion. There's nothing I wouldn't do for them."

Beau tipped his head. "Yet you're not going to be a nanny anymore when you leave here."

There was no use trying to fake a smile, so she let her face fall. In the short time she would be here, Scarlett really didn't want to spend their days rehashing her past year and the decisions that led to her leaving her most beloved job.

Scarlett stepped around him and turned the swing off. She unfastened Madelyn and lifted her up into her arms. When she spun around, Beau faced her and still wore that same worried, questioning gaze. Not what she wanted to see because he clearly was waiting on her to reply.

Also not what she wanted to see because she didn't want to think about him with those caring feelings. Things were much simpler when she assumed him to be the Playboy Prince of Hollywood.

"Let me get Madelyn settled into her high chair and

I'll start dinner." Maybe if she completely dodged the topic, then maybe he wouldn't bring it up again. "Do you like apricots? I found some at the farmer's market earlier and I want to try a new dessert."

Before she could turn toward the kitchen, Beau took a step and came to stand right before her.

"Actually, Annabelle is making dinner tonight," he told her. "She came to the stables earlier and invited me."

"Oh, well. No worries. I'll make everything tomorrow." She brushed her hand along the top of Madelyn's baby curls. "Should I put Madelyn to bed while you're gone or are you taking her?"

Beau cleared his throat and rocked back on his boot heels. "We're all going."

"Okay, then I'll just clean her up and—" Realization hit her. "Wait. We're all going. As in *all* of us?"

Beau nodded and Scarlett's heart started that double-time beat again.

Why on earth would she go to Colt and Annabelle's house? She wasn't part of this family and she wasn't going to be around long enough to form a friendship with anyone at Pebblebrook Ranch. She was trying to cut ties and move on, not create relationships.

"There's really no need," Scarlett stated, shaking her head. "I can make myself something here."

"Annabelle didn't exactly ask," he told her. "Besides, why wouldn't you want to come? The only person Colt will be grouchy with is me."

"It's not that."

Silence nestled between them. She couldn't pinpoint the exact reason she didn't want to go. There wasn't just one; there were countless.

"One meal. That's all this is."

Scarlett stared up at him as she held on to Madelyn. Beau's dark eyes showed nothing. No emotion, no insight into what he may be thinking, but his words were clear. Just dinner. Meaning there was no need to read any more into it.

Was that a blanket statement for what happened between them right here last night? Was he making sure she knew there was nothing else that could happen? Because she was pretty sure she'd already received that message. A message she needed to keep repeating to herself.

"We should discuss last night." As much as she didn't want to, she also didn't want this chunk of tension growing between them, either. "I don't know what you expect of me."

"Expect?" His dark brows drew together.

Why did he have to make this difficult? He had to know what she was talking about.

"Yes," she said through clenched teeth. "You don't think I believe you don't want…something in return."

Beau's eyes darkened as he took a half step closer, his chest brushing her arm that held his daughter. "Did I ask you for anything in return? Did I lay out ground rules?"

Scarlett shook her head and patted Madelyn when the baby let out a fuss. She swayed back and forth in a calming motion.

"Then I expect you to listen to your body," he went on in that low, whisky-smooth tone. "I expect you to take what you want and not deny the pleasure I know you crave. I expect you to come to me when you're ready for more, because we both know it will happen."

Scarlett licked her lips and attempted to keep her breathing steady. He painted an erotic, honest image. She did want him, but would she act on that need?

"You sent me away last night," she reminded him. "If you know what I want, then why did you do that?"

He reached up and slid a fingertip down Scarlett's cheek, over her jaw and around to just beneath her chin. He tipped her head up and leaned in so close his lips nearly met hers.

"Because I want you to ache just as much as I do," he murmured in a way that had her stomach tightening with need. "Because I knew if we had sex last night, you'd blame it on getting caught up in the moment. But now, when you come to me, you'll have had time to think about what you want. There will be no excuses, no regrets."

Her entire body shivered. "You're so sure I'll come to you. What if I don't?"

Beau's eyes locked onto hers and he smiled. "If you weren't holding my daughter right now, I'd have you begging for me in a matter of seconds. Don't try to lie to me or yourself. You will come to me."

"And if I don't?"

She fully expected him to say he'd eventually come to her, but Beau eased back and pulled Madelyn from her arms. He flashed that high-voltage smile and winked. That man had the audacity to wink and just walk away.

That arrogant bastard. He thought he could just turn her on, give her a satisfying sample, then rev her up all over again and she'd just…what? Jump into his bed and beg him to do all the naughty things she'd imagined?

Scarlett blew out a sigh. That's exactly what she

wanted to do and he knew it. So now what? They'd go to this family dinner and come back to the cabin, put Madelyn down and...

Yeah. It was the rest of that sentence that had nerves spiraling through her.

Beau Elliott was a potent man and she had a feeling she'd barely scratched the surface.

Nine

Beau was having a difficult time focusing on the dinner set before him. Between his brother's glare at the opposite end of the table, the noise from the three kids, and Scarlett sitting right across from him, Beau wondered how much longer he'd have to stay at Colt's.

He'd left Scarlett with something to think about back at the cabin, but he hadn't counted on getting himself worked up and on edge. That flare of desire in her eyes had given him pause for a moment, but he had to be smart. Wanting a woman wasn't a new experience, but wanting a woman so unattainable was.

The temporary factor of her presence didn't bother him. After all, he wasn't looking for anything long-term. He actually hadn't been looking for anything at all...but then she showed up on his doorstep.

What bothered him was how fragile she seemed beneath her steely surface. He should leave her alone. He should, but he couldn't.

Scarlett wasn't playing hard to get or playing any other games to get his attention. No, she was guarded and cautious—traits he needed to wrap his mind around before he got swept up into another round of lust.

"Scarlett, what are you going to be doing in Dallas?"

Annabelle's question broke into Beau's thoughts. He glanced across the table as Scarlett set her fork down on the edge of her plate.

"I'll be an assistant director of recreational activities at a senior center."

She delivered the answer with a smile, one that some may find convincing. Even if Beau hadn't been an actor, he knew Scarlett enough to know the gesture was fake.

"I'm sad to leave Stone River," she went on. "But Dallas holds many opportunities, which is what I'm looking for. I'm excited. More excited as my time to leave gets closer."

"What made you decide on Dallas? Do you have family there?"

Beau was surprised Colt chimed in with his questions. But considering Beau was curious about more of her life, he turned his focus to her as well, eager to hear her answers.

Her eyes darted across the table to him, that forced smile frozen in place. "I have no family. That's one of the reasons being a nanny was so great for me. But circumstances have changed my plans and I'm looking for a fresh start."

Colt leaned back in his seat and smiled. "Well, good for you. I wondered if my brother would convince you to stick with him."

Beau clenched his teeth. Was Colt seriously going to get into this now? Did every conversation have to turn into an argument or a jab?

"There's no convincing," Scarlett said with a slight laugh. "I've already committed to the new job. Housing has turned into a bit of a chore, though. I didn't realize how expensive city living was."

"Small towns do have perks." Annabelle came to her feet and went to one of the three high chairs they'd set up. She lifted one of her twins—he still couldn't tell the difference—and wiped the child's hands. "Miss Emily is messy and I need to clean her up and get her changed. I'll be right back."

Scarlett took a drink of her tea and then scooted her chair back. "I can start taking these dishes to the kitchen. Dinner was amazing."

"Sit down." Colt motioned to her. "Annabelle wanted to make a good impression so she made everything herself, but our cook will clean up."

Scarlett didn't sit, but she went to Madelyn who played in her high chair, patting the top of the tray, then swiping her hands in the water puddles she'd made by shaking her bottle.

"Let me get her," Beau said as he rose and circled the antique farm-style table to extract her from the high chair. "I haven't seen her much today and when we get back she'll need to go to bed."

Which would leave them alone again. Night after night he struggled. Last night had barely taken the edge off. No, that was a lie. Last night only made him want her even more. She'd come to him tonight, that much he was sure of.

"Never thought I'd see you back at the ranch," Colt stated. "Let alone with a child."

Beau patted Madelyn's back as she sucked on her little fist. "I knew I'd come back sometime, but I never had intentions of having children."

When Lucy started fussing, Colt immediately jumped to get her.

"You plan on settling down anytime soon?" he asked as he picked up his daughter. "Maybe have more kids?"

Beau wasn't sure what his next move was, let alone if there was a woman somewhere in his future. "I have no idea," he answered honestly. "Believe it or not, I did love growing up here and having a large family. I'm not opposed to having more kids one day. Being a parent changes you somehow."

Scarlett cleared her throat and turned away. "Excuse me."

She fled the room and Beau glanced over his shoulder to see her heading toward the front of the house. What was wrong with her? Was it something he'd said? Was she that uncomfortable being at this family dinner?

She didn't owe him any explanations, but that wouldn't stop him from finding out what he could do to make her stay here a little easier. The pain that she kept bottled up gnawed at his gut in a way he couldn't explain, because he'd never experienced such emotions before.

"She okay?" Colt asked.

Beau stared at the empty doorway another minute before turning to his twin and lying to his face. "She's fine. We can head on out if you'd rather. I know Annabelle probably forced your hand into this dinner."

Lucy plucked at one of the buttons on Colt's shirt.

"She didn't, actually. I wanted you here and she offered to cook."

Shocked, Beau shifted Madelyn in his arms and swayed slowly back and forth as she rubbed her eyes. "So she jumped at the chance when she saw an opening?"

Colt shrugged. "Something like that. Listen, I don't want—"

"Sorry about that." Scarlett whisked back into the room and Beau didn't miss the way her eyes were red-rimmed. "Let me take Madelyn back home and put her to bed. You two can talk and maybe Colt can bring you back to the cabin later."

"I'll come with you," he offered.

She eased a very tired baby from his arms and shook her head. "I'll be fine," Scarlett said, then turned to Colt. "Please tell Annabelle everything was wonderful."

"I will, though I'm sure she'll have you over again before you leave town," Colt assured her. "I'll make sure Beau has a ride back."

Scarlett nodded and then turned to go, catching Beau's eyes before she did so. Her sad smile and that mist in her eyes undid him. She took Madelyn and left, leaving Beau torn over whether he should stay or go.

"You're really just going to let her go?" Colt asked. "She's clearly upset."

Shoving his hands in his pockets, Beau weighed his options. "She wants to be alone. I can talk to her once I'm back and Madelyn is asleep. Besides, you and I need to talk, don't we?"

Staring at his brother had Colt really taking in the moment. He loved Beau—that was never in question.

He loved him in a completely different way than Hayes or Nolan. Not more, just different. Perhaps because of the special bond from twins; he wasn't sure.

Colt knew no matter how much anger and resentment tried to push them apart, their connection could never be completely severed.

"I'm surprised you don't have plans set in place to leave the ranch," Colt stated after a moment.

Or if Beau did, Colt didn't know. And he wanted to… no, he needed to know. He had to steel his heart if his brother was just going to hightail it out of town again and not be heard from for years.

"I came back for Madelyn," Beau replied.

"You came back for you," Colt tossed back, unable to stop himself. "You may have had a change of heart from whatever you were doing in LA, but you needed to be here because something or someone has made you face us again. You didn't come back because you actually wanted to."

Beau stared at him for a minute. Silence settled heavy between them and Colt waited for his brother to deny the accusation. He didn't.

"I've wanted you home for so long." Colt softened his tone. He didn't want to be a complete prick, but he also had to be honest. "When you left, I was upset, but I understood needing to do your own thing. But then you didn't come back and… I resented you. I felt betrayed."

Beau muttered a curse and glanced down to his still-shiny boots before looking back to Colt. "I wanted to see just how far I could get," he admitted. "I knew I was good at acting. So once I did that commercial, then my agent landed that first movie, things exploded. I admit I got wrapped up in my new lifestyle. But I never forgot where I came from. Not once. It just wasn't me anymore."

Colt gritted his teeth and forced the lump of emotions down. "And now? Is this ranch life still not you?"

Beau's lips thinned as he hooked his thumbs through his belt loops. "I want a simpler life for my daughter. I don't want her growing up around pretentious people and worrying if she fits in and all the hustle and bustle. Becoming a parent changed everything I thought about life."

On that, Colt could agree one hundred percent. "Being a father does change you."

But Beau still hadn't answered the question completely.

Before Colt could dig in deeper, Annabelle came back into the room without Emily. "Well, Little Miss was happy lying in her crib in her diaper, so I left her there chatting with her stuffed elephant."

His wife stopped her chatter as she came to stand next to Colt. "What's going on?" she asked as she slid Emily from Colt's arms.

"Just talking with my brother," Colt stated.

"I'm glad to hear it." She rocked Emily back and forth and patted her back. "Where is Scarlett?"

"She took Madelyn back to the cabin for bed," Beau told her. "She wanted me to tell you thanks for everything."

Annabelle shot a glance to her husband. "And did she leave because you guys were bickering or to give you space to actually talk?"

"She really was putting Madelyn to bed," Beau added. "I'm sure she wanted to give us space, too."

"And how has the talking gone?" Annabelle asked, her gaze darting between them. "I lost my sister in a car accident not long ago. We had our differences, we said things we thought we meant at the time, but I'd give anything to have her back. I just don't want you guys to have regrets."

Colt's heart clenched as Annabelle's eyes misted. When he stepped toward her, she eased back and shook her head. Such a strong woman, his Annabelle. He admired her strength and her determination to repair this relationship between brothers.

"You're getting another chance, so work on it," she added. "It's Christmas, guys. Just start a new chapter. Isn't that what your parents would've wanted?"

Beau stepped forward and wrapped an arm around her shoulders. "They would've," Beau agreed before releasing her.

Annabelle sniffed and swiped a hand beneath her eye.

"Babe, don't cry." Colt placed his hand on her shoulder and looked to his twin. "We're making progress. It's slow, but it's coming. Right, Beau?"

He nodded. "We're better than we were, but we're working on years of animosity, so it might take a bit."

Something settled deep within Colt—something akin to hope. For the first time in, well, years, Colt had a hope for the future with his brother.

Did Beau ultimately want that? Colt truly believed fatherhood had changed him, but they'd have to see because words were easy…it was the actions that were difficult to execute.

"I'll let you guys finish your chat," Annabelle said with a soft smile and left the room.

Colt nodded toward the hallway and Beau followed him to the living room. They truly had taken a giant leap in their relationship.

Once they were in the spacious room with a high-beamed ceiling and a stone fireplace that stretched up to those vaulted beams, Beau took a seat on the dark leather sofa.

They had a full, tall Christmas tree in this room, as well. He couldn't help but laugh. As beautiful as the perfectly decorated tree was, he suddenly found himself longing for the tiny cabin with the crooked, naked tree.

If he were honest with himself, he longed more for the woman in the cabin who was determined to give his daughter a nice first Christmas.

How could he not feel a pull toward Scarlett? Sexual, yes, but there was more. He couldn't put his finger on it…or maybe he didn't want to. Either way, Scarlett was more than Madelyn's nanny.

"Are you planning on leaving Hollywood?" Colt asked as he stood next to the fireplace.

Beau eyed the four stockings and shrugged. "No idea, honestly. I know I don't want that lifestyle for Madelyn. There's too much in my world there that could harm her. I couldn't even take her to a park without the paparazzi attacking us. I just want a normal life for her."

"You gave up the normal life when you chose to pursue acting," Colt sneered. "You had a life here, on the ranch."

Beau shook his head and rested his elbows on his knees. "I'm not rehashing the past or defending myself again. I'm moving on. I won't stay at Pebblebrook, though. There's clearly no room and I'm still not sure what my place is."

"What the hell does that mean?" Colt demanded.

"Your place is as an Elliott. You're still a rancher whether you want to be or not. It's in our roots."

Yes, it was. Being back here had been like a balm on his tattered heart and soul. But even with coming home and diving right back into the life he'd dodged for years, something was still missing. His world still seemed as if there was a void, a huge hole he'd never fully be able to close.

Perhaps it was Hector's death. Losing his best friend, his father figure, his agent, was hell. But Beau wondered if being home and not seeing his actual father riding the perimeters or herding cattle was the main reason he felt so empty.

"I'm just trying to figure things out," Beau admitted. "I have a movie premiere a few days before Christmas. I'll have to attend that, and then I'd like to be here for the holidays. I'll go after that."

"And when will you fit a visit to Dad in there?" Colt propped his hands on his hips.

"I'm hoping to go see him tomorrow."

That shut Colt up. Beau knew his brother hadn't expected that comeback and Beau would be lying if he didn't admit he was scared as hell to see his dad. He didn't know how he would feel if he walked into the room and Grant Elliott had no clue who he was.

Ironic, really. He was an award-winning movie star, but the one person in the world he wanted to recognize him was his own father.

"Do you want me to come with you?"

Colt's question shocked him. Beau never expected his twin to offer. Maybe this was the olive branch that Beau wondered if he'd ever see.

He swallowed the lump of emotions clogging his throat and nodded. "Yeah, sure."

Colt gave a curt nod, as well. They may not be hugging it out and proclaiming their brotherly love, but this was a huge step in what Beau hoped was just the first phase in repairing their relationship. Because this process wouldn't be quick and it wouldn't be easy. But it was a start.

Ten

Scarlett continued to stare at the tree mocking her in the corner. The one in Colt and Annabelle's house had looked just like the perfect ones she'd described to Beau. There had even been ornaments on the tree of twin babies with a gold ribbon across that said "Babies' First Christmas."

Scarlett hadn't been able to handle another moment. As much as she wanted to be the woman for Beau, she also knew she could never fully be the woman he wanted...not if he wanted more children and a family.

And this little cabin may not be her home, but Scarlett was determined to give Beau and Madelyn a nice Christmas. Too bad she felt she was failing miserably.

Madelyn had taken a bottle and gone right to sleep, leaving Scarlett alone with her thoughts...thoughts that drifted toward the man who would walk through that door any minute.

So she'd opted to try to decorate this tree. Once the lights went on and she plugged them in, she decided to stop. Maybe this was the best this poor thing would look. The crooked trunk didn't look so bad on the tree lot, but now that it was in the small cabin the imperfection was quite noticeable.

Maybe if she turned it slightly so the leaning part faced the patio doors?

Scarlett groaned. Perhaps she should bake some cookies instead. That would help liven up her holiday spirit, plus the house would smell better than any potpourri or candle she could've bought.

But it was late, so she decided to postpone that until tomorrow. Now she headed to her room to change her clothes, figuring on making some tea with honey to help her relax. She really should make it quickly and get back to her room before Beau came home.

Beau…

He'd tempted her in ways that she'd never been tempted before. Never had a man had her so torn up and achy and…damn it, confused.

She shouldn't want him. There was no good ending to this entire ordeal. They clearly led different lives and he was so used to getting what he wanted, yet another reason why they couldn't work. If she stayed and tried at a relationship, even if he was ready for that, she couldn't ultimately give him what he wanted.

But there were so many turn-ons—so, so many.

Scarlett pulled on a tank and a pair of cotton shorts as she mentally argued with herself. She could either continue to dodge the pull toward Beau or she could just give in to this promised fling. After all, she was leaving in a few weeks. She could have the fling and then move, start her new life and not look back.

He'd already pleasured her, so she knew what awaited her if she surrendered to him. And she knew it would be even better when they actually made love, when his body was taking her to those heights instead of just his hand.

Just thinking about that orgasm caused her cheeks to flush. Yes, that was an even bigger reason to want to agree to everything he'd been ready to give. If that had been part of his master plan the entire time, well then, he'd won this battle.

Fanning her heated cheeks, Scarlett opened her bedroom door...and froze. Beau stood just on the other side, his raised fist poised to knock.

She gripped the doorknob in one hand and tried to catch her breath. Between the surprise of seeing him here and the intense look in his eyes, Scarlett couldn't find a reason to ignore her needs any longer.

Not that she could ignore them even if she wanted to. Not with this gorgeous, sexy, intense man looking at her like he was.

She did the only thing she could do at that moment. She took a step toward him and closed the gap between them.

She kept her eyes locked onto his as she framed his face with her hands. That dark stubble along his jaw tickled her palms, the simple touch sending waves of arousal and anticipation through her, fanning the flames her fantasies had ignited.

"Scarlett—"

She slid her thumb along his bottom lip, cutting off his words. "Do you still want me?"

She had to take charge. She had to know the power belonged to her or he wouldn't just win the battle between them...he'd win the war.

Beau's tongue darted out and slid across her skin as he gripped her hips and pulled her to him, aligning their bodies. There was no mistake how much he wanted her, no mistake in what was about to happen.

She needed this distraction, needed to forget how much she'd hurt earlier seeing all those babies and the happy family. Maybe she shouldn't use him for her need to escape, but she'd wanted him all along and why shouldn't she take what she wanted?

"Why now?" he asked, studying her face. "What changed?"

Scarlett's heart thumped against her chest as she swallowed and went for total honesty...well, as much as she was willing to share about her pain.

"Sometimes I want to forget," she murmured. "Make me forget, Beau."

The muscle clenched in his jaw and for a moment she wondered if he'd turn her down and leave this room. But then he covered her mouth with his and walked her backward until her back came in contact with the post of the bed.

His denim rubbed her bare thighs, only adding to the build of the anticipation. As much as she loved how he looked in his cowboy wardrobe, she desperately wanted to see him wearing nothing but her.

Beau's hands were instantly all over her, stripping her of her shorts, then her tank. He only broke the kiss long enough to peel away the unwanted material and then he wrapped her back in his strong arms and made love to her mouth.

That was the only way to describe his kisses. He didn't just meet her lips with his; he caressed them, stroked them, laved them, plundered them. And she felt every one of those touches not only on her mouth but in the very core of her femininity.

Needing to touch him the same way, Scarlett reached between them for the hem of his T-shirt. She'd lifted it slightly when his hands covered hers and he eased back.

"In a hurry?" he asked.

She nodded. "I'm the only one ready for this."

"Baby, I've been ready since you walked in my door."

She shivered at his husky tone and glanced down to their joined hands. Her dark skin beneath his rough, tanned hands had her wondering why this looked so... right. Was it just because she hadn't been with someone in so long? Was it because this was *the* Beau Elliott?

She didn't think so, but now wasn't the time to get into why she had these unexplainable stirrings at just the sight of them coming together.

"Someone is thinking too hard. Maybe this will keep your thoughts at bay."

Beau stepped back and pulled off his shirt, tossing it aside. He was playing dirty and he damn well knew it.

As if to drive the point home, he quirked his dark brows as a menacing, sexy smile spread across his face.

"What did you want when you came to my room?" she asked, surprised she even had the wherewithal to speak.

He went to the snap of his pants and shoved them off as he continued to stare at her. He stood before her in only his black boxer briefs and she couldn't keep her eyes from roaming every inch of muscle and sinew on display before her. His body was pure perfection. The sprinkling of dark chest hair and the dark tattoos over his side, pec and shoulder were so sexy. Who knew she was a tattoo girl?

"I wanted to talk," he replied.

"That look in your eye doesn't look like you wanted to talk."

His lips thinned. "Maybe I needed to forget, too."

She crossed her arms and glanced down, suddenly feeling too vulnerable standing before him completely naked as he let a crack open so she could glimpse into his soul.

Beau reached out, unhooking her arms. "Don't hide from me. I've been waiting to see you."

Scarlett swallowed and looked up at him. "You saw me last night."

"Not enough."

His fingertips grazed down the slope of her breasts and around to her sides. She shivered when his hands slid down the dip in her waist, then over the flare of her hips.

"Not nearly enough."

He lifted her by her waist and wrapped his arms around her. Scarlett wrapped her legs around his waist as he carried her to the bed. She slid her mouth along his as she tipped back, then found herself pressed firmly into the thick comforter, Beau's weight on her. She welcomed the heaviness of this man.

The frantic way his hands and mouth roamed over her made her wonder if he was chasing away some demon in his own mind.

Maybe for tonight, they were just using each other. But right now she didn't care. She wanted him. She needed him. Right now.

When Beau sat up, Scarlett instinctively reached for him to pull him back to her.

"I need to get protection," he told her as he grasped his jeans.

Scarlett hadn't even thought of that. Of course pregnancy wasn't an issue for her, but she didn't know his history and he didn't know hers. Safety had to override hormones right now. She was just glad one of them was thinking straight.

She watched as he removed his boxer briefs and sheathed himself, relishing the sight of his arousal. Nothing could make her turn away or deny this need that burned through her. Well...if Madelyn started crying, but other than that, nothing.

Beau eased his knee down onto the bed next to her thigh. Scarlett rose up to her elbows, her heart beating so fast as desire curled all through her.

He trailed his fingertips up her thigh, teasing her as he went right past the spot she ached most, and on up her abdomen.

"You're one sexy woman," he growled. "It was all I could do to hold back last night."

Which only made him even more remarkable. He wasn't demanding and selfish. Even now, he was taking his time and touching, kissing, enjoying...all while driving her out of her mind.

Those fingertips circled her nipples and Scarlett nearly came off the bed.

"Beau."

"Right here," he murmured as he leaned down and captured her lips.

She opened to him and shifted her legs restlessly. Beau settled between her thighs and she lifted her knees to accommodate him. He hooked one hand behind her thigh and lifted her leg at the same time he joined their bodies.

Scarlett cried out against his mouth as she tilted her hips to meet his. He seemed to move so slow in comparison to the frantic need she felt. The man was maddeningly arousing.

She clutched at his shoulders and arched against him, pulling her mouth from his as she tipped her head back. Beau's lips traveled a path down her neck to her breast and Scarlett wrapped her legs around his waist, locking her ankles behind his back.

Beau never once removed his lips from her skin. He moved all over her, around her, in her, and in minutes that familiar coiling sensation built up within her and Scarlett bit her lip to keep from crying out again.

But Beau gripped her backside, his large powerful hand pulling her to him as he quickened the pace and Scarlett couldn't stop the release from taking over, nor could she stop the cry.

Beau's body tightened against hers as he surged inside her, taking his own pleasure. After a moment, that grip loosened and he eased down onto the bed, shifting his weight so he wasn't completely on top of her.

When the pulsing stopped and her heartbeat slowed, and she was able to think once again, Scarlett realized she was in new territory. She wasn't sure what she was supposed to say or do here. Anyone she'd ever slept with had been someone she was committed to. What did she do now, naked, sated and plastered against a man who was nothing more—could be nothing more—than a fling?

"Someone is thinking too hard again," he said, trail-

ing his finger over her stomach and up the valley between her breasts. "Maybe I didn't do my job well
enough."

Scarlett laughed. "You more than did your job. I'm
just confused what to do now."

Beau sat up and rested his head in his hand as he
stared down at her. The entire moment seemed so intimate, more than the act of sex itself.

"This doesn't have to be anything more than what it
was," he told her. "You needed to escape something and
so did I. Besides, this was bound to happen."

His words seemed so straightforward and matter-of-
fact. They were all true, but she wished he'd...

What? What did she wish? That they'd start a relationship and see where things went? She knew full well
where they'd go. She'd be in Dallas and he'd be back
in LA. There was nothing for them other than a brief
physical connection.

Scarlett shifted from the bed and came to her feet.
Being completely naked now made her feel too vulnerable, too exposed emotionally.

She started putting her sleep clothes back on, trying
to ignore the confident cowboy stretched out on her bed.

"Care to tell me what had you running from Colt's
house?"

Scarlett pushed her hair away from her face and
turned to face him. "I told you. Madelyn was tired and
I was letting you guys talk."

He lifted one dark brow and stared, silently calling
her out on her lie.

"Could you cover up?" she asked. "I can't concentrate with you on display like that."

Beau laughed and slowly came to his feet...which

maybe was worse because now he was closing in on her with that naughty grin. "I like the idea of you not concentrating."

Scarlett put her hands up and shook her head. "Don't touch me. We're done for the night."

He nodded. "Fine, but I still want to know what had you scared or upset."

From his soft tone, she knew he truly meant every word. He didn't care that they weren't diving back in for round two and he genuinely wanted to know what had bothered her.

Scarlett didn't want to get into her emotional issues. Dredging them all up wouldn't change anything, and the last thing she wanted was pity from Beau. Besides, he'd said he was dealing with his own issues.

"I think it's best if we don't get too personal," she told him and nearly laughed. This was Beau Elliott and women all around the world would give anything to trade places with Scarlett right now.

"We're already personal," he countered, reaching for her. When she tried to back away, he cupped her elbow. "You're taking care of my daughter, living with me and we just had sex. Not to mention my sisters-in-law have all taken to you. We're temporarily bonded, so stop trying to push me away. I can listen and be a friend right now."

Scarlett raked her eyes over him. "With no clothes on?"

He cursed beneath his breath as he spun around and grabbed those black boxer briefs. As if putting on that hip-hugging underwear helped.

The second he turned his focus back to her, she

crossed her arms and decided to give the interrogation right back at him.

"Do you want to tell me what's got you so torn up here?" she asked. "Other than your brothers?"

He stared at her for a moment before he shrugged. "I'm not sure what future I have to offer my daughter because I have no clue what I want to do. I'm mending relationships with my brothers, hopefully my father, and figuring out if I even want to go back to LA."

Scarlett couldn't believe he'd said anything, let alone all of that.

"My life is a mess," he went on. "My former agent was more like a father figure and best friend. He recently passed away."

Scarlett put her hand over her heart. "Oh, Beau, I'm sorry."

"Thank you. It's been difficult without him, but each day is a little easier than the last. But the next step is so unclear." He pursed his lips for a moment before continuing. "I have a feeling someone with her new life laid out before her isn't so worried about the future."

"Not when I'm constantly haunted by my past," she murmured.

She rubbed her arms, hating how he was somehow managing to break down her walls. He'd easily opened and didn't seem to care that she saw his vulnerability. Could she do the same?

"I could guess and I bet I'd be right."

She shook her head. "You don't know me."

Beau stepped into her and reached up, smoothing her hair from her face. "You love Christmas and more decorations than anyone needs. You chose the most hideous tree I've ever seen, yet you're determined to make this a good holiday. You're passionate in bed and let yourself lose all control, which is the sexiest thing I've ever seen, by the way."

She stared at him, listening as he dissected her from the nuggets of information he'd gathered over the past few days. Beau was much more perceptive than she gave him credit for. No selfish man would've taken every moment into consideration and parsed each portion of their time together to understand her better.

"I also know that my daughter and I are lucky you're here," he went on, inching even closer until she had to tip her head to look up at him. "And I know too much discussion on babies or families makes you shut down and get all misty-eyed, yet you're a nanny."

Scarlett tightened her lips together and tried to ignore that burn in her throat and eyes.

Beau slid his finger beneath her chin and tipped her head up. "Shall I keep going?" he asked. "Or maybe you could just tell me what you're running from."

Scarlett pulled in a shaky breath and closed her eyes. "I can't have children."

Eleven

Beau's suspicions were right. He wished like hell he'd been wrong because he could see the pain in her eyes, hear it in her voice.

Just as he started to reach for her again, she opened her eyes and held up one hand. "No. I don't need to be consoled and please, don't look at me like that."

He didn't know what she saw in his eyes, but how could he not comfort her? He may have the reputation of a playboy, and perhaps he didn't do anything to rectify that with the media, but he did care.

Even though he'd only known Scarlett a short time, it was impossible to ignore the way he felt. Attraction was one thing, but there was more to this complex relationship.

Unfortunately, he had to ignore the pull and remain closed off from tapping into those unwanted, untimely feelings. He had a future to figure out and he'd already screwed up with one woman.

"I love being a nanny," she went on, her voice still laced with sadness and remorse. "But my life changed about a year ago, and I just can't do this job anymore."

"That's why you're leaving."

Beau crossed to the bed and sat down. Maybe she'd feel more apt to talk if he wasn't looming over her in only his underwear. He never wanted her to feel intimidated or insecure. He doubted she really had anyone she could talk to and the fact that she chose him—after he'd somewhat forced her hand—proved she was more vulnerable than he'd first thought.

But he actually wanted to listen and he wanted to know how he could help...even if that only came in the form of making her forget.

"I can't be in Stone River." Scarlett's words cut through his thoughts. "There are too many memories here of my life, my hopes and dreams. Starting over somewhere fresh will be the best healer for me."

He understood all too well about needing to start over. The need to find a place that would be comforting and not pull you down further. Her reasons for leaving Stone River were the exact reasons he'd left LA. They both needed something new, something that promised hope for an unknown future.

"I'm sure that wasn't an easy decision to make," he stated.

She turned to face him and shrugged one slender shoulder. "There wasn't much else I could do. After my surgery, I took a position out of the field, in the office. I love the people I work with. I just couldn't be a nanny anymore. I thought working in the office would be easier, but it wasn't. I was still dealing with families and listening to the stories of my coworkers. Then Maggie asked me to fill in for these few weeks before I leave and I couldn't tell her no."

"I'm glad you didn't."

Scarlett stared at him for a minute. The lamp on her bedside table set a soft glow on her mocha skin. Skin he ached to touch again. Scarlett was one of the sexiest, most passionate women he'd ever known, and after hearing a bit of her story, he knew she was also one of the strongest.

"Me, too," she whispered.

He did reach for her now and when her hand closed in his, he pulled her toward him. Scarlett came to stand between his legs and she rested her hands on his shoulders.

"What surgery did you have to have?" he asked.

When she pulled in a shaky breath, he placed his hands on her waist and offered a comforting squeeze.

"I had a hysterectomy," she explained. "The short version of my story is I had a routine checkup. The test results came back showing I had some abnormal cells and the surgery was necessary. Unfortunately, that took away any chance I had at my own family, but in the end, the threat of uterine cancer was gone."

He couldn't imagine wanting something, dreaming of having it your whole life and then not obtaining it. There was nothing Beau didn't covet that he couldn't get through money or power. That's how he'd been raised. Yes, his parents had instilled in him a strong work ethic, but he also knew that at any given time he could reach for anything and make it his.

Yet with all his money, power and fame, he couldn't

make his own future stable when he was so confused where he should land. And if he had the ability, he'd sure as hell do something to make Scarlett's life easier.

With a gentle tug, Beau had Scarlett tumbling onto his chest. He gripped her thighs and helped her straddle his lap. As he looked up into her eyes, he realized that if there was any woman who could make him lose his heart, it could be her.

Which was absolutely crazy. Why was he even having such thoughts? He'd screwed things up before when he'd let his heart get involved. Wanting a woman physically and thinking of deeper emotions were two totally different things and he needed to refocus before he found himself even further from where he needed to be.

Between all of this with his family and now his mixed feelings for Scarlett, he needed to remain in control before he completely lost himself.

"Let's keep our painful pasts out of this room, out of this bed," he suggested as he nipped at her chin. "For as long as you're here, stay with me."

Her eyes widened as she eased slightly away. "You want to continue this fling?"

"'Fling'? That's such a crass word." He let his hands cover her backside and pull her tighter where he needed her most. "We don't need a title for this. Just know I want you, for however long you're here."

Scarlett laced her hands behind his neck and touched her forehead to his. "I swore I wouldn't do this with you," she murmured.

"Yet here we are."

She laughed, just as he'd hoped. "I guess I'm wearing too many clothes."

He stripped her shirt off, sliding his hands and eyes over her bare torso, her breasts. "Let's make each other forget."

Scarlett pushed Madelyn in the child swing that had been hung on the back patio. Even though winter had settled in and they were closing in on Christmas, the sun was shining bright in the cloudless sky and with a light jacket and pants, the day was absolutely beautiful.

Madelyn cooed and grinned as the swing went back and forth. Scarlett couldn't help but return the smile. It was impossible to be unhappy around Madelyn. Even when she'd fussed about her sore gums, Scarlett cherished the time. Madelyn was such a special little girl and having a father who cared so deeply made her very fortunate.

Beau had made a difficult decision to leave his Hollywood home and find out what life he and his daughter should lead.

Maybe he'd go back to his home in LA, but for now he seemed to be in no hurry. After spending the past several nights in his bed—well, hers—Scarlett wasn't in too big of a hurry to leave, either.

But she had to. She couldn't stay here forever playing house. There was no happily-ever-after for them, no little family. No, Scarlett wasn't going to get that family…at least not with Beau.

Maybe one day she'd meet a man and he might have kids already or maybe they'd adopt. She still couldn't let go of that dream. A new dream had replaced the old one and Scarlett had a blossom of hope.

Strong arms wrapped around her from behind, pulling her out of her thoughts, and Scarlett squealed.

"It's just me," Beau growled in her ear. "Unless you were expecting someone else."

Scarlett eyed him over her shoulder. "My other lover was supposed to come by because I thought you were out."

He smacked her butt. "There are no other lovers as long as I'm in your bed," he said with a smile.

Which would only be for another two weeks.

Scarlett didn't want to think of the end coming so soon. Only a few days ago she was counting down until she could hightail it out of town, but now...

Well, falling into bed with Beau had changed everything.

"I thought you were with Colt and Hayes looking over résumés for guides for the dude ranch."

The new business venture of the Elliott brothers was due to start in early spring. Scarlett had heard Beau discussing how much still needed to be done, she was only sorry she wouldn't be around to see how magnificent all of this would be. Pebblebrook was a gorgeous, picturesque spread and no doubt they would draw in thousands of people a year.

Scarlett wondered if Beau and Colt had told their dad about the ranch, about the way they were closing in on making his dream a full reality, when they'd gone to see him yesterday morning. But Beau had been closed off when he'd returned. Scarlett hadn't wanted to press him on a topic that was obviously so sensitive. She couldn't imagine that bond father and son had shared growing up and how much this must be hurting Beau.

Growing up, she did everything to avoid her stepfather and mom. They'd been so caught up in their own worlds anyway, so she went unnoticed.

"We finished early," Beau told her. "I told my brothers I needed to get back home to see Madelyn."

Scarlett gave the swing another gentle push and turned to face Beau. Those dark eyes, framed by thick lashes, all beneath a black brim only made him seem all the more mysterious. Over the last week she'd found out that there were several sides to him, and she had to admit she liked this Beau.

The man before her wasn't the actor she'd seen on-screen or the playboy the media portrayed. This Beau Elliott was a small-town rancher.

Albeit a billionaire.

She glanced over at Madelyn. "She woke from a nap about twenty minutes ago, so you're just in time."

Beau slid his hands up her arms, over the slope of her shoulders, and framed her face. "I may have wanted to see you, too."

Scarlett couldn't help the flutter in her chest. The more time she spent with him and his daughter, the more she realized how difficult leaving would be. But she'd be fine. She had to be.

"I also left because I have a surprise planned for you."

"A surprise?" she repeated, shocked he'd think to do anything for her. "What is it?"

Beau slid his lips softly over hers, then stroked her cheeks with the pad of his thumbs. "If I tell you then it won't be a surprise."

"Oh, come on," she begged. "You can't tease me like that."

He thrust his pelvis toward hers and smiled. "You weren't complaining about being teased last night, or the night before, or the night before that."

Scarlett slapped him on the chest. "Fine. But you'll pay for that."

Beau grazed his mouth along her jaw and up to the sensitive area just behind her ear. "I'm counting on it."

Madelyn let out a fuss, which quickly turned into a cry. Before Scarlett could get the baby from the swing, Beau had moved around her and was unbuckling her.

Scarlett stepped away and watched as he cooed and offered sweet words and patted her back. Something stirred inside her. An unfamiliar feeling. An undeniable feeling.

She was falling for Beau.

How ridiculous that sounded even inside her own mind. But there was no denying the fact. Beau Elliott had worked his way past her defenses and into her personal space, quite possibly her heart. There was no future here and she was a fool for allowing this to happen.

Of course she didn't *allow* anything. There had been no stopping these feelings. From the second Beau showed her just how selfless he was, how caring, Scarlett couldn't help but fall for him.

Beau lifted Madelyn over his head and spun in a circle. With the sun off in the distance and the soft rolling hills of the ranch as the backdrop, Scarlett had to tamp down her emotions. The father/daughter duo was picture perfect and maybe neither of them realized how lucky they were to have each other.

Scarlett let them have their moment as she slipped inside the tiny cabin. As silly as it was, she'd come to think of this little place like home. This was nothing like the massive home she'd grown up in. The place might as well have been a museum with the expensive furniture, priceless art and cold atmosphere.

Maybe that's why this cozy cabin touched her so much. There was life here, fun, a family. All the things she'd craved as a child and all the things she wanted as an adult.

But they weren't hers…and she needed to remember that.

Instead of dwelling on those thoughts, Scarlett moved to the kitchen where she'd baked sugar cookies earlier. They were ready to be iced and taken to Annabelle, Alexa and Pepper.

Scarlett didn't proclaim to be the best baker, but she did love her sugar cookie recipe. In fact, she'd made extra just for Beau. Maybe part of her wanted to impress him still, which was silly, but she hadn't been able to help herself. She cared for him, so much. Much more than she should be allowed.

The man came through the doorway just as her thoughts turned to him once again. Of course, he was never far from her thoughts, just as he was never far from her in this tiny space.

"I thought I smelled cookies when I came in earlier." He held Madelyn with one strong arm as he came to stand on the other side of the island. "But it looks as if you have enough to feed a small army. Are we expecting company?"

Scarlett started separating the icing she'd made into smaller bowls so she could dye it in different colors. "I'm taking a dozen each to your brothers' houses later. I just… I don't know. I thought I should do something and I love to bake. I think Christmas just demands the house smell like warm sugar and comfort."

She applied two drops of yellow food coloring into the icing for the star cookies, then she put green drops into another bowl for the tree cookies. The silence had her unsettled so she glanced up to find Beau staring at her with a look on his face she'd never seen before.

"What?" she asked, screwing the lids back on the small bottles of food coloring.

"You watch my baby all day, you cook, you decorate—"

"Don't call that tree in the corner decorating," she grumbled. "Maybe I baked because I need a chance to redeem myself."

He chuckled and shifted Madelyn around to sit on the bar and lean back against his chest. He kept one firm hand on her belly.

"The mantel is beautiful and way more than I'd ever think of doing, and the front porch looks like a real home with the wreath and whatever you did to that planter by the steps." He slid his hat off and dropped it onto a bar stool. "I don't know how you do it all. Maybe women are just born with that gene that makes them superhuman."

"We are."

His smile widened. "And a modesty gene, too, I see."

"Of course," she said without hesitation.

"Regardless of how you get everything done, I'm grateful."

The sincerity of his statement just pulled back another layer of defense she'd tried to wrap herself in. Unfortunately, every time the man opened his mouth, he stripped away more and more. She was losing this fight with herself and before these next couple of weeks were up, she had serious concerns about her heart.

"How long until the cookies are ready to deliver?" he asked.

"I just need to ice three dozen." She glanced behind her to the trays lining the small counter space. "I can ice the dozen for us after I get back."

"You made cookies for us, too?"

Scarlett laughed. "You think I'm baking and not thinking of myself?"

Madelyn let out a jumble of noises as she patted her father's hand. Was there anything sexier than a hunky rancher caring for his baby? Because she was having a difficult time thinking of anything.

"Well, as soon as you get those iced, you'll get your surprise," he told her. "This will all work out quite well."

"What will?"

"The deliveries, your surprise." He leaned in just a bit as his eyes darted to her mouth. "Coming back here later and pleasuring you."

Her body heated, not that she needed his promise for such a reaction. Simply thinking of him incited her arousal. But all of the emotions swirling around inside her were so much more than sexual. Her heart had gotten involved in this short span of time. She hadn't seen that coming. She'd been so worried about not falling for his seduction, she hadn't thought of falling for the man himself.

Damn it. She was sinking fast and not even trying to stop herself. Why bother? Why not just enjoy the ride as long as this lasted?

She deserved to go after what she wanted, no matter how temporary, and she wanted Beau Elliott. Considering he wanted her just as much, there was no reason to let worry in now.

For the time they had left, she planned on enjoying every single moment of her last job as a nanny.

As for her heart, well, it had been broken before. But she hadn't experienced anything like Beau Elliott. Would she ever be able to recover?

Twelve

Scarlett put the final lid on the gold Christmas tin. She stacked the festive containers in a tote and went to get Madelyn from her swing in the living room. Thankfully, she wasn't so fussy with her swollen gums now. The teething ring had helped.

"All ready?"

She turned to see Beau. "I'm ready." Giddiness and anxiousness spiraled through her. "Just what is this surprise?"

That familiar, naughty smile spread across his face. Beau could make her giddy like a teenager with her first crush and arouse her like a woman who knew exactly what she was getting into. She'd never met a man who could elicit such emotions from her.

"You're about to find out," he promised with a wink. "Let me take the cookies out and I'll be right back."

"I can carry them," she argued.

Beau put his hand up. "No. Stay right there with Madelyn. Actually, she'll need a jacket and hat. It's cool this evening and we'll be outside for a bit."

Scarlett narrowed her eyes. "We're not driving to your brothers' houses?"

The estate had a ridiculous amount of acreage—she thought she'd heard the number of five thousand thrown out—so the only way around the place was on tractors, four-wheelers, horses or cars.

With only a smile for her answer, Beau adjusted the wide brim of his black hat before he grabbed the bag stuffed with cookie tins and headed out the front door.

Scarlett glanced to Madelyn and tapped the tip of her nose.

"Your daddy is driving me crazy."

By the time Scarlett grabbed the jacket and hat for Madelyn from the peg by the door, Beau swept back inside.

"I'll finish getting her ready," he said, taking his daughter. "Take a jacket and hat for yourself, too. I can't have you shivering or you won't appreciate the surprise."

Scarlett laughed. "You're making me nervous, Beau."

He reached up and stroked one finger down the side of her face. "Trust me."

How could she not? She trusted him with her body… and he was closing in on her heart.

Scarlett smiled, mentally running from the unfamiliar emotions curling through her. "You know I do."

She went to her room to get her things. Whatever Beau had planned, he seemed pretty excited about what he'd come up with.

Warmth spread through her at the thought of him thinking of a way to surprise her. Was this a Christmas present or just because? Or did this surprise involve something he liked, as well? The questions and the unknowns were driving her crazy.

It was difficult not to read more into this situation because they'd agreed to have just these last couple of weeks of intimacy before she left. So why was he going that extra mile? Why was he treating this like…well, like a relationship?

Scarlett groaned as she tugged on her red knit hat. Her thoughts were trying to rob her happy time here. She had one of the sexiest men in the world waiting to give her something he'd planned just for her. And she'd simply enjoy it.

She slid on her matching red jacket, perfect for the holiday season and delivering Christmas cookies. For another added bit of flair, she grabbed her black-and-white snowflake scarf and knotted it around her neck.

When she stepped back into the living room, Beau held Madelyn in one hand and extended his other toward her. He kept that sneaky grin on his face and she just knew he was loving every minute of torturing her.

Giddy with anticipation, Scarlett slid her hand in his. She had to admit, she liked the look of her darker skin against his. Her bright red nails were quite the contrast with his rough fingertips from working on the ranch.

Beau tugged her forward until she fell against his side and he covered her mouth with his. The short yet heated kiss had her blinking up at him and wondering how he kept knocking her off her feet. She never knew what he'd do next, but he continued to have her wanting more.

"Everything's ready," he told her. "Go on outside."

She couldn't wait another second. Scarlett reached around him and opened the door. The moment her eyes focused on the sight before her, she blinked, wondering if this was a dream.

"Beau," she gasped. "What did you do?"

Directly in front of the porch were two chocolate-brown horses in front of a wide wooden sled. A sled decorated with garland and lights. On the seat she saw plaid blankets. There was evergreen garland wrapped around the reins, and the horses stood stoic and stared straight ahead as they waited for their orders.

Scarlett spun back around and threw her arms around Beau, careful of how she sandwiched Madelyn in the middle.

"I can't believe you did this," she squealed. "How on earth did you manage it?"

Beau took her hand in his and led her to the sled. "I have my ways and that's all you need to know."

Scarlett didn't hesitate as she carefully climbed into the sled. Once she nestled against the cushioned seat, she reached down for Madelyn.

The sled jostled slightly as Beau stepped up into it and folded his long, lean frame next to her. He gripped the reins in hand as Scarlett pulled the cozy blanket up over their laps. She laced her hands around Madelyn and glanced to Beau as he snapped the reins to set the sled in motion.

"Why did you do all of this?" she asked.

"Why not?" he countered, shooting her that toe-curling grin and dark gaze. "You mentioned loving Christmas and sleigh rides. I'm just giving you a bit of extra cheer."

Scarlett wasn't quite sure what to say. Beau had put so much thought into this, even though he tried to brush the sweet gesture aside. This full-on reality was so much better than anything she'd ever seen in the movies.

"I'm glad I made you a dozen cookies, then," she joked as he headed in the direction of Nolan's house. "You may even get extra icing."

"Is that a euphemism?"

Scarlett's body heated, but she laughed because she didn't want to get all hot and bothered when she was in the midst of this festive family moment.

The breath in her throat caught and was instantly replaced with thick emotions. Family. This fantasy moment she was living in had thrust her deeper into her job than she'd ever been.

Feeling like part of the family was often just a perk of being a nanny. But nothing had ever prepared her for falling for the man she worked for, or for his daughter. And how could she not fall for him? He'd been attentive since day one...which really wasn't all that long ago.

Still, Beau actually listened to her. He met her needs in the bedroom and out, and she was an absolute fool if she thought she'd walk away at the end of this without a broken heart.

"So you'll be leaving at the end of next week for your movie premiere," she stated, more reminding herself and making sure this stayed out in the open. "Are you sure you'll be home Christmas Eve?"

"Positive," he assured her. "Nobody else is playing Santa to my girl but me."

"I wondered if you'd bought presents."

He shot her a side glance. "Of course I have. You

think I'd let my baby's first Christmas come and go and not have presents?"

"Well, you didn't have a tree or a stocking," she reminded him with an elbow to his side.

Beau guided the horses as Nolan's home came into view. The large log resort-type home looked like something from a magazine. Not surprising, though, since the Elliotts had the lifestyle of billionaire ranchers and Nolan was a surgeon. He and Pepper lived here with their little one and their home was beautifully decorated, with wreaths adorning every window and a larger one with a red bow on the front door.

"Maybe I didn't have a tree or stockings," Beau added. "But I'm not a complete Scrooge."

Scarlett shifted in the seat and glanced down at the baby. "I think we're putting her to sleep," she stated. "Next time her gums are bothering her, just hitch up the sled and take her for a ride."

"Sure." He snorted. "No problem."

Within another minute, Madelyn was fast asleep. There were so many questions Scarlett had for Beau regarding his future, but she wasn't sure if she had a right to ask…or if she even truly wanted to know the answers.

She decided to wait until they left Nolan's house to bring up her thoughts. Nolan and Pepper weren't home, so Beau left the tin on the porch swing and sent his brother a text.

As they took off again, this time toward Hayes and Alexa's house, Scarlett figured this was the perfect time. If he didn't want to answer, then he didn't have to, but she couldn't just keep guessing.

"When you go back for the movie premiere, do you think you'll want to stay?"

"No. I'll definitely be back here for Christmas."

Scarlett pulled the plaid blanket up a little further. "I mean, will being back there make you miss that life?"

He said nothing. Only the clomping of the horses through the lane broke the silence. Scarlett wondered if she'd gone too far, simply because he hadn't talked much about the movie and she got the impression that topic was off the table.

"Forget it," she said after waiting too long for his reply. "None of my concern. It's not like I'll be here or part of your life."

"It's okay." He shifted in his seat, his thigh rubbing against hers. "Honestly, I doubt it. I'm not looking forward to going back."

"Do you hate that world so much?"

Beau's brows dipped as he seemed to be weighing his words. "I hate how people can get so swept up in their own lives they forget there's a world around them. The selfishness runs rampant out there. Everyone is out for themselves, but they're never happy because when they get what they want, they still want more."

He pulled in a deep breath and shook his head. "I can say that because I'm that person."

Scarlett slid her left hand over Beau's denim-clad thigh. "You're not that person at all."

The muscles in his jaw clenched. "I am," he volleyed back. "I left here because I wanted more. I made it in Hollywood, had a career people would kill for and still wanted more. Then I won two big acting awards, and that wasn't enough, either. I met Jennifer and thought we might have had a future together, but that went to hell. I have a gorgeous baby, yet I'm still looking for more."

Scarlett didn't like the defeated tone in his voice. "You're not looking for more," she scolded. "You're looking for the right place to raise your daughter and trying to reconnect with your family. That's not selfish. And it sure as hell wasn't selfish that you surprised me with a horse-drawn sleigh ride."

"Oh, the sleigh ride was just so I'd get laid."

Scarlett squeezed his thigh until he yelped.

"I'm joking," he laughed. "Well, not really. I still want in your bed tonight."

"You didn't have to do this to get there," she reminded him. "I haven't been complaining, have I?"

He pulled back on the reins until the horses and sleigh came to a stop. When Beau shifted in his seat to face her, Scarlett's heart kicked up.

"I've been thinking…" He gripped the reins in one hand and slid his other beneath the blanket to cover hers. "I don't want to cheapen this to just sex or for you to ever think I'll forget you when you leave."

A burst of light filled the cracks in her heart. What exactly was he trying to say?

"I know you're moving and I have no idea where I'll be," he went on. "But I don't want to just hide in the cabin and keep you naked."

Scarlett rolled her eyes and glared. "Really?"

His lips quirked into a half grin. "Okay, that's exactly what I'd like, but I want you to know you're more important to me than Madelyn's nanny or my temporary lover."

Scarlett pulled in a breath and held his dark gaze. "So what are you saying?"

"I want to take you on a date."

"A…a date?"

Not what she thought he'd say, but she wasn't exactly opposed to the idea.

"I didn't think you wanted to be seen in town or anywhere because of privacy."

He squeezed her hand and leaned forward to graze his lips across hers. There was no chill in the December air at all when she had Beau next to her. Just one simple touch, just one promised kiss had her entire body heating up.

When Beau eased back, he stroked the back of her hand with his fingertip. "Some things are worth the risk."

Well, that sealed the deal. There was no coming back from this because her heart tumbled, flipped, flopped, did all the amazing things that had her wanting to squeal and yell that she'd fallen completely in love with Beau Elliott.

Unfortunately, there was no room in this temporary relationship for such emotions. There would be no love, no family Christmas cards and definitely no happy-ever-after.

She only had a week left with Beau and then she'd bc out of his life for good.

Thirteen

Beau wasn't sure what had made Scarlett shut down after he'd asked her on a date. Honestly, he hadn't planned on that impromptu invitation, but he'd needed her to know that she wasn't just some woman he'd seduced and conquered. He'd never thought of any woman in that manner, and he sure as hell had more respect for Scarlett than that.

She was special. Not because of how she cared for Madelyn and not because she was so easy to talk to. Scarlett presented the entire package of an honest woman, one who genuinely cared.

Part of him wanted to give her the world, but what part of his world could he actually give? He couldn't even figure out his own plan. Though after being at Pebblebrook for a few weeks, he knew he wanted a ranch of his own. The hands-on approach he'd taken each day had turned something inside of him. The fact that he wasn't interested in looking at scripts now was rather telling.

Maybe one day he'd look to the screen again, but for now, Beau truly felt this was his destiny. He'd gone and explored like he'd wanted. He'd made himself one of the biggest names in Hollywood, but like he'd told Scarlett, something had still been missing.

Beau nearly laughed at himself for his *Wizard of Oz* epiphany. Everything he'd ever wanted was right here in his own backyard…literally.

He stood in front of the crazy Christmas tree in the corner of the cabin. Scarlett's soft singing voice filtered in from his bedroom as she got Madelyn to sleep for the night.

They'd delivered cookies and both Annabelle and Alexa were thrilled with the surprise. Beau loved the praise they gave Scarlett, and the fact that they treated her like family had him wanting to explore more with her. He'd never wanted someone like this before. Not just for sex, but to see if they could grow together.

But she was moving to Dallas.

Beau's mind raced in too many directions to try to keep up with, but he figured he didn't have a set place he wanted to be. He was quite literally free to do anything.

Was he even ready for something like this? He'd come back home to mend relationships, not to try to build a new one. Added to that, he hadn't known Scarlett very long. Was he honestly considering this? He'd made such a terrible judgment call with Jennifer, but Scarlett was so different than his ex. Scarlett wasn't out to gain anything for herself or trying to use him for anything other than a job before she left.

As one idea formed into another, Beau found him-

self smiling while still staring at the undecorated tree—
save for the lights.

"She's out."

Scarlett's words had him turning to face her. When
he met her gaze across the room, she stopped and set
the bottle on the kitchen island.

"What?" she asked, tipping her head. "You're smiling and you've been staring at my tree. You're plotting
something, aren't you? Are we burning it and roasting
marshmallows?"

Beau shook his head and circled the couch to head
toward the kitchen. She never glanced away and he
figured he looked like a complete moron because he
couldn't wipe the smile off his face.

If she thought the sleigh ride was nice, she'd be utterly speechless when he presented her with the next
surprise.

"We aren't burning it," he told her as he drew closer.
"But in continuing your festive holiday cheer, I say we
break out our cookies and get them iced."

She narrowed her dark eyes. "Why do I have a feeling this will end with my clothes on the kitchen floor?"

Beau shrugged. "Because you're realistic."

Scarlett shook her head as she laughed. "You don't
have to talk me into getting naked, you know?"

Beau slid his hands over the dip in her waist. "Maybe
not, but I'm in the mood for dessert."

He backed her up until they circled the island. Scarlett gripped his biceps when she stumbled.

"What are you doing?" she asked, smiling up at him.

Beau planted a kiss on the tip of her nose. Her frea-
kin' nose. Now he knew he'd gone and lost his mind.
He'd never done such an endearing action before, but

he couldn't help himself. For as sexy as Scarlett was, she was also quite adorable.

"We're going to ice those cookies," he told her. "You did promise."

She jerked back, her brows shooting up. "You seriously want to ice cookies? Does this mean I'm melting Scrooge's heart?"

He smacked her on the butt before releasing her. "I'm hardly Scrooge, but I'll admit I've never iced cookies. My mom did all of that. Baking and cookie decorating was serious business at Christmastime in my house and she wanted it to be perfect."

Beau grabbed the icing from the counter next to the stove and set it on the island. Then he reached back around for the tin of cookies.

"I guess Christmas baking was the one time she wasn't about to let a bunch of boys ruin her creations." Beau glanced at the spread before him and laughed as he turned to Scarlett. "So I guess your work is cut out for you."

Scarlett went to pull off all of the lids, revealing the yellow, green and red food coloring. The instant smell of sugar hit him and he couldn't wait to take a bite.

Beau picked up a bare cookie and dipped it in the yellow icing before taking a bite. "You're right. These are good."

"Beau," she exclaimed, smacking his chest. "The icing isn't a dip."

He chewed his bite and went back in for more icing—red this time. "I think I'm onto something here."

"You're impossible." She reached into a drawer and pulled out a plastic spatula. "Let me show you how you should ice cookies."

As he continued to dip, Beau watched her expertly smooth the frosting over the tree cookie. When she was finished, she laid it aside on the wax paper and grabbed another.

"Want to try?" she asked.

"Sure."

He took the cookie and the utensil, then dipped the spatula into the red icing. With a quick move, he streaked a stripe across her shirt.

"Oops." He smiled and shrugged. "That didn't work. You might want to take your shirt off before that stains."

Scarlett propped a hand on her hip and narrowed her eyes. "That's not very original."

He gave another swipe. "Maybe not, but I bet you take that shirt off."

She kept her eyes on his as her fingers went to the top button. One slow release at a time, she revealed her dark skin and festive red bra.

Once she dropped her shirt to the floor, she reached around him and picked up another cookie. She grabbed the spatula from his hand and proceeded to decorate.

"Just because you act childish doesn't mean the lesson is over," she informed him. "Do you see how I'm using nice, even strokes?"

"I can use even strokes, too."

Scarlett rolled her eyes and laughed. "I'm talking about icing."

Beau leaned in and nipped at her ear. "Maybe I was, too."

Scarlett leaned slightly into him. "I can't concentrate when you're doing that."

Good. He slid his hand along the small of her back, around the dip in her waist, and covered her flat abdomen. She shivered beneath his touch, just as he'd expected.

"I can't concentrate when you're not wearing a shirt," he whispered in her ear.

She tipped her head back to meet his gaze. "And whose fault is that?"

"You're the one who took it off."

Beau spun her slightly and gripped her hips. He lifted her onto the counter, away from the mess. "Let's see what else we can do with this icing."

Her eyes darkened as she raised a brow. "You didn't really want to learn how to decorate cookies, did you?"

He flashed her a smile. "Not at all."

But he did make use of all of the icing and by the end of the night, Scarlett wasn't complaining.

Scarlett lifted Madelyn out of the car seat and adjusted the red knit cap. Downtown Stone River may be small, but people bustled about and businesses thrived like in a major city.

The sun was high in the sky, shining down on this picturesque square. The large tower clock in the middle struck twelve. Benches in a circle around the clock were filled with couples eating lunch. Every single lamppost had garland and lights wrapped around it. Oversize pots sat on each corner and overflowed with evergreens and bright red poinsettias.

Scarlett would miss this place.

"Hey. You okay?"

Beau came to stand beside her, his hand resting on her back. She offered him a smile and nodded.

"I'm fine," she told him. "And ready to eat. I used too much energy last night."

"We could've had more cookies for breakfast," he offered with a naughty grin and a wink.

"Considering you ate every cookie and, um…we finished the icing, that wasn't an option."

Mercy, her body still tingled just thinking about what they had done with those colors. The extra-long shower to cleanse their bodies of the sticky mess had only led to even more intimacy. And more intimacy led to Scarlett wishing she didn't have to leave.

"I think we should try that café on the corner," he said, pointing over her shoulder. "It looks like you."

"I've eaten there before," she told him, without looking to see which place he referred to. "And what do you mean it looks like me?"

Beau shrugged and looked back down at her. His wide-brim hat shielded a portion of his face from the sun. She didn't know if he wore the hat because he'd gotten used to it since he'd been back or if he'd brought it to be a little discreet. Either way, he looked like the sexy cowboy she'd come to know and love.

Fine. There it was. The big L word she'd been dancing around and not fully coming to terms with. She knew she was falling, but she could admit now that she was there.

"It's all festive with the gold-and-red Christmas signs out front," he told her, oblivious to her thoughts. "The big wreath on the doorway, the candles in the windows. It just looks like you."

She figured that was a compliment, but she wasn't quite sure.

Madelyn let out a yawn and rubbed her eyes. Scarlett patted her back and eased her head down onto her shoulder.

"We should eat so we can get this one to take a nap on the car ride home," she told him.

Beau's cell went off and he groaned. "I'm not answering that."

"You should," she retorted. "It could be about your dad."

Which he'd still never talked about. She wanted to know his feelings and help him if she could. Maybe when they got back home she'd address the topic.

Beau pulled his cell from his pocket and stared at the screen, then a wide smile spread across his face.

"I take it that's not your agent?" she asked.

He pocketed the cell and leaned in, covering her mouth with his. The kiss ended as quickly as it started, leaving her a bit unbalanced.

"What was that for?" she asked.

"I have a surprise for you."

Her heart warmed. "Another one?"

"I promise, this one is much better than the last."

Scarlett's face lit up. "Tell me."

He kissed her once again, lingering a bit longer this time. "When we get home."

"Then we're getting our food to go."

Beau laughed as he steered her toward the café. "No, we're not. I promised you a date and that's what we're doing."

Fourteen

Scarlett wasn't sure whether to be nervous or not with Beau's mysterious surprise. They stepped into the cabin and Madelyn was wide-awake now after a brief nap in the car.

Beau had only been asked about twenty times at the café for his autograph, and with each person who approached him, he took the time to talk and sign. He might be a star, but he was also humble and so far removed from the celebrity she'd originally thought him to be.

Christmas was coming quickly and he'd be leaving in just a few days for his premiere. Their time together had been rocky at first, but then it had become an absolute fantasy. She'd never, ever gotten involved with someone she worked for. Beau had made that personal ethic impossible, though, and she wasn't the least bit sorry.

"Wait right there," he told her.

Scarlett stood in the living area and obeyed. She couldn't imagine what could top the horse-drawn sleigh, but she couldn't wait.

She took Madelyn to the little play mat on the floor. Carefully, Scarlett eased down to her knees and laid Madelyn beneath the arch where random plush animals swung back and forth. At the sight of them, she started kicking her feet and making adorable cooing noises.

Scarlett stood back up and smiled. She was seriously going to miss this sweet little nugget.

"Are you ready?"

She spun around and her smile widened as Beau came back in with his laptop. "I don't know what I'm ready for, but bring it."

He took a seat on a bar stool and patted the other one for her. Once his computer was up, he clicked through several screens before pulling up a page with several images of a beautiful old white farmhouse. There was a stone path leading up to the door, four gables on each side of the house, a pond in the back. The landscaping had to have been professional and there was even a white porch swing with colorful pillows. The entire place looked straight out of a magazine.

"If you like the outside, I can move on and show you the inside," he told her.

Scarlett gasped. "Beau, did you buy this?"

He clicked on the next screen and pulled up the entryway photo. "I knew it was the one the second my real estate agent sent options."

Joy consumed her and she reached for his hand. "Beau, I'm so happy for you. I didn't know you were that close to finding a permanent home."

She glanced back to the screen and looked at the thumbnail photos. "Click on that one," she said, pointing. "I think that will make a perfect room for Madelyn. Does it overlook the pond?"

"Wait." He squeezed her hand until she shifted her focus to him. "I bought this house for you."

Scarlett jerked back. "What? For me?"

He released her hand and clicked on another tab. "See? It's just outside of Dallas and only a twenty-minute commute to your new job."

Shock and denial replaced happiness. She stared at him for a moment before looking back to the image of the route from the new house to her new job. She didn't even know where to start with the questions because there were so many swirling around in her head.

"If you don't like it, I can put this on the market and find another," he went on.

She snapped her attention back to him. "Do you hear yourself? When people give gifts they usually give a scarf or a candle, sometimes jewelry. Who buys gift houses on a whim?"

Those dark brows drew in as if he were confused. "It wasn't necessarily a whim. I mean, I knew you were having trouble finding a place to live and I wanted to help you out. Besides, you've done so much for Madelyn and me, plus it's Christmas. I thought you'd like this."

Scarlett shook her head and slid off the stool. How in the world had this last job run the gamut of every single emotion she'd ever had? Worry, anxiety, stress, giddiness, love, anger...betrayal.

"You can't do this," she snapped as she turned back around. "You can't just send me on my way with a parting gift, as if that will replace what has happened here."

Damn it. She hadn't meant to let that sliver of her feelings out. She didn't want him to know how much she'd valued and cherished every second of their time together. When it was time for her to go, she'd have to make a clean break in an attempt to keep her heart intact...if that was even possible.

"You think that's what I'm doing?" he asked. "I bought this for you to make your transition easier, because you deserve a damn break. Why are you angry?"

Maybe her anger stemmed from confusion and hurt and the loss of a hope that maybe they could've been more. Which was ridiculous considering who he was, how they met and how little they'd known each other.

But still, how could she just ignore all that had transpired up until this moment? They'd shared a bed almost every night, he took her on a sleigh ride, he asked her on a date...they'd crammed a lifetime of memories into a few short weeks.

"I can't accept this gift," she told him. "I can't live in a house that you bought when you were thinking of me. When I leave here, I need to be done with what we had, and living there would only remind me of you. Besides, I couldn't accept something so extravagant. It's just not normal, Beau."

"It's not normal to want to help?" he tossed back. "Who's to say I wouldn't come visit?"

Oh, now that was just being cruel. "For what? To extend the affair? What happens if you meet someone else or I do? What happens when one of us decides to get married? We can't drag this affair on forever."

No, because that would be a relationship and they'd

both agreed this fling was temporary. Besides, after she left, she didn't want to know who he was seeing or what was going on in his personal life. No doubt she'd see another piece of arm candy at his side. She certainly wouldn't follow him on social media, but his face would be on every tabloid at the supermarket checkout line. It would be difficult to dodge him completely.

Beau opened his mouth, but a pounding on the cabin door stopped him. Scarlett propped her hands on her hips and stared at him across the room. More pounding on the door had Beau cursing.

He went to the door and jerked it open. "What?" he barked.

Colt stood on the other side holding his cell up for Beau to see a photo. Scarlett couldn't make out exactly what it was, but Beau's shoulders went rigid and he let out a string of curses.

"Want to explain what the hell this is?" Colt demanded. "I believed you when you said she was only your nanny."

Scarlett went nearer to see the image on the phone Colt held out. An image of Beau, Madelyn and Scarlett on the street earlier when he'd leaned in to kiss her. Above it was the headline: "A New Leading Lady for Hollywood's Favorite Cowboy."

Scarlett stilled. Was nothing sacred anymore? It just took one person to snap a picture on their phone and send it to the masses.

Colt's eyes went to her, then back to Beau.

"I am his nanny," Scarlett started. "We just—"

"It's not like that," Beau said, cutting her off. He kept his back to her and his focus on his brother. "She is my nanny and when I leave for the premiere, she'll stay here and care for Madelyn. Scarlett is moving next week and we went out for lunch. I leaned in and kissed her, so what? It's nobody's business."

"Nobody's business?" Colt roared as he pushed his way inside. "You do realize we are trying to honor our father and work on the opening of this dude ranch. Now you're back in town and making headlines like this. What about two weeks from now when it's another woman, or another? We're a close family, with strong core values Dad taught us. Those are the values we want to promote in this new business."

"Calm down," Beau demanded. "Scarlett and I kissed. Don't read anything more into that. It was an innocent kiss. I didn't think anything of it. The only person who will make a big deal about this is you."

Innocent kiss? He didn't think anything of it?

The air whooshed from her lungs and her throat clogged with emotions. She turned from the dueling brothers and went to Madelyn. Blinking against the tears gathering in her eyes, Scarlett bent down and lifted Madelyn in her arms. Then she headed toward her room.

"I'll let you two talk," she said without glancing their way.

She couldn't let Beau see her hurt. She couldn't let him see just how his words had cut her down. What happened to the man she'd come to know? To pretend their kisses meant nothing was flat out a bastard move.

So she'd hide out in her room and gather her strength. Because there was going to be a showdown and there was no way in hell she'd confront him with tears in her eyes.

Fifteen

"You better get your head on straight," Colt commanded through gritted teeth. "Scarlett isn't one of your random women."

Beau glanced to the closed bedroom door and wanted to punch something. He fisted his hands at his sides to prevent decking his own twin.

"I never said she was." Beau faced Colt and pulled in a deep breath. "I said this was nobody's business. And the dude ranch won't suffer because I kissed someone in public. Don't be so dramatic."

Colt adjusted his hat and pocketed his phone. "That's not what I'm saying. You claimed you've changed, but all of the media wrapped their claws around you and what woman you'd be with on any given day. I don't want that carried over here."

"It's not."

Damn it. He didn't want to have this conversation with Colt. He wanted to be in that bedroom because he knew he'd hurt Scarlett with his careless attitude. In his defense, he hadn't wanted to let Colt in on the relationship. He'd been trying to save her reputation. Instead, he'd left her thinking what they had wasn't special.

Only a jerk would purposely hurt a woman.

"If you're done berating me like a disappointed parent, you are free to go."

Colt clenched his jaw and nodded. "If you want to prove you've changed, then start by doing right with Scarlett."

His brother turned and left the cabin, closing the door with a hard click that echoed through the tiny space. Beau muttered a string of curses and raked his hand over the back of his neck. He should've seen this coming. One of the reasons he'd been staying in the cabin was because he'd wanted to dodge the press and any outsiders while he tried to find some semblance of normalcy.

Of course then Scarlett landed on his doorstep and everything snowballed from there. Somehow he needed to fix this—all of it. Her anger toward the home he'd purchased for her, hurting her and having Colt witness everything.

This morning he'd been full of hope and the possibility of exploring a future with her. Now…hell, he didn't have a clue what lay on the other side of that door.

Beau made his way across the cabin and tapped his knuckles on Scarlett's bedroom door. Without waiting for an answer, he tried the knob, surprised she hadn't locked him out.

Easing the door open, he peeked his head through.

Scarlett sat cross-legged on her bed reading a book to Madelyn, who lay in front of her on the plaid quilt.

"What you heard out there—"

"Was the truth," Scarlett said as she closed the book and laid it on the bedside table. "You didn't say anything but the truth. There's nothing more to us than a few weeks of passion and a good time. We've made memories, but that's where it ends."

Beau slipped into her room, but remained by the open door. Her words shocked him. Her steely demeanor seemed so out of character, and he wasn't sure what to say.

Scarlett swung her legs off the side of her bed and came to her feet. She made sure to keep distance between them.

"Since we are so close to the end of our time together," she said, "it's probably best to end the intimate side of things. I'm sure you understand why. And I'm sure you can see why I cannot accept the house. I appreciate the gesture, but you should have your agent put it back on the market."

Well, wasn't her speech all neat and tidy and delivered with an iciness he never expected from someone so warm and caring.

Beau had never experienced this before. Rejection. But it wasn't the rejection that stung. No, what really sliced him deep was the fact that he had caused Scarlett so much suffering that she'd resorted to this as her defensive mechanism.

"Maybe I'm not ready to end things," he stated, folding his arms over his chest.

She stared at him across the room and finally took a step toward him. "There's no reason to prolong this,

Beau. I will continue to care for Madelyn and watch her while you're gone to your premiere. But Maggie will be back next week and I'll be gone. This had to come to an end sometime."

Beau couldn't penetrate this wall she'd put up so quickly around herself. She'd need time and he needed to respect her enough to give it to her. Unfortunately, time wasn't on their side. He could give her today, but that's all he could afford.

"Scarlett, I never want you to believe that kiss, and everything before that, meant nothing." He needed her to know this above all else. "Anything I said to Colt was to protect you. Maybe I didn't go about it the right way, but don't think that I don't care for you."

Scarlett crossed her arms over her chest and nodded. "I'm going to feed Madelyn and take her for a walk to the stables. Then I'll come back and fix dinner."

She didn't extend the invite to the stables. Beau would stay behind, to give her time to think. Because there was no way she could just turn off this switch. If she felt half of what he felt for her, she couldn't ignore such strong emotions.

"I'll make dinner," he volunteered.

"Fine." She reached down and lifted Madelyn in her arms. "If you'll take her for a minute, I need to change my clothes."

"Scarlett—"

"Please."

Her plea came out on a cracked voice and he finally saw a sheen of tears in her eyes. She was struggling to hold everything together.

Beau reached for his baby and held her tight against

his chest. Scarlett continued to stare at him, blinking against her unshed tears.

Without another word, he turned and left her alone in her room. After he shut the door firmly behind him, Beau went to his own room to contact his agent.

Not his real estate agent about the house. No, Beau had every intention on keeping that.

He laid Madelyn down in her crib and handed her a plush toy to chew on. With a deep sigh and heavy dose of guilt, he pulled his cell from his pocket and dialed his agent.

"Beau," he answered. "You're one hell of a hard man to get ahold of."

There wasn't much to say and this conversation was long, long overdue. But it was time for some changes and they were going to start right now.

Beau gripped the phone as he watched his daughter play.

"We need to talk."

Scarlett didn't know what was more difficult, having Beau in the cabin or knowing he was miles away and gearing up for a fancy movie premiere tomorrow.

The past few days had been strained, to say the least. They'd been cordial to each other, like strangers who were stranded together and forced to cohabitate.

Scarlett had just put Madelyn down for her morning nap and was heading to the sink to wash bottles when a knock sounded on the front door.

She wore only leggings and an oversize sweatshirt, and her hair was in a ponytail—compliments of insomnia, anxiety, and a broken heart. But she ignored her state of dress and went to see who the unexpected visitor was.

After glancing through the peephole, Scarlett pulled in a long, slow breath and blew it out before flicking the dead bolt and opening the door.

"Annabelle," she greeted. "What brings you by?"

His beautiful sister-in-law offered a sweet smile and held up a basket. "I brought fresh cranberry apple muffins. Can I come in?"

"I would've let you in without the bribe, but I won't turn it down." Scarlett laughed as she stepped aside to let Colt's wife in.

Annabelle set the basket down on the island. "The muffins were just an excuse," she said as she turned back to face Scarlett. "Can we talk for a minute?"

Scarlett didn't know why Annabelle wanted to talk, but she wasn't stupid. Likely this had to do with Colt and Beau, but if the woman thought Scarlett had any hold over Beau or could sway him to work on the relationship with his brother, well, that couldn't be further from the truth.

"Sure," Scarlett replied. "Have a seat."

She hadn't seen or talked to any of Beau's family since Beau had left a couple of days ago. Scarlett didn't think Beau counted their kisses as nothing, but hearing the words had hurt just the same. And hearing those words only gave her the smack of reality that she'd needed in order to see that this wasn't normal. What normal, everyday woman fell in love with a movie star and had him reciprocate those feelings? The idea was simply absurd.

Annabelle took a seat on the leather sofa and Scarlett sat on the other end. "What's up?" Scarlett asked.

"I'm going to cut out the small talk because it's point-less." Annabelle crossed her legs and leveled her gaze at Scarlett. "I know you have feelings for Beau. Don't deny it. I saw the two of you together. And I can also tell you that he has feelings, too."

Scarlett wanted to deny both statements, but she simply didn't have the energy. Maybe if she let Annabelle talk, she'd get this off her chest and then leave. Scarlett preferred to sulk in private.

"I also know my stubborn husband came down pretty hard on Beau and you, by default," Annabelle went on. "This ranch is absolutely everything to him and he sometimes speaks before he thinks."

Scarlett smiled. "You didn't have to come down here to apologize for him."

"I'm not," Annabelle corrected. "He needs to apologize on his own. I'm here to tell you that you need to ignore what Colt says, what the media speculate and what you're afraid of."

She let out a soft sigh as she scooted over a bit farther. "What I'm trying to say is, your time here is almost up and I'd hate for you to go when you have so much unresolved."

Scarlett glanced down to her clasped hands and swallowed. "How do you know what's unresolved?"

Annabelle reached over and offered a gentle squeeze of her hand. "Because Colt and Hayes commented on Beau's broodiness before he left for LA and he was so happy before that. You make him happy. When he came back here he was broken and scared. He'd never admit that, so don't tell him I said it. But he was so worried for Madelyn and how his relationships with his brothers would pan out...or even if they would."

Scarlett glanced back up. "Beau and I aren't anything. I mean, I won't lie and say things didn't progress beyond a working relationship, but that's over."

"Is it?"

Nodding, Scarlett chewed the inside of her cheek before continuing. "He hasn't fully let me in. I know about the reasons he left here when he was eighteen. I know the issues with his brothers and his dad. But when he and Colt went to see their dad the other day, Beau shut down and wouldn't let me help. I don't even know what happened."

Annabelle leaned back on the couch and released Scarlett's hands. "Grant didn't remember his sons," she stated. "Colt said Beau took it pretty hard and wouldn't even talk to him on the ride home."

Oh, Beau.

"He has let you in," Annabelle went on. "And I'm here to tell you that if you want to give it a try with him, I'm going to help. Alexa and Pepper are ready to join in, too."

Stunned, Scarlett eased back and laughed. "Excuse me?"

Annabelle's smile spread wide across her face. "We all three figured if you want to make a statement, it's going to have to be bold."

"The three of you discussed this?" Scarlett asked, still shocked. "What do you all think I should be doing?"

That smile turned positively mischievous and the gleam in her eye was a bit disconcerting. Annabelle reached for her hand once again.

"What do you say about going to your first movie premiere?"

Sixteen

This entire thing was absurd. The fact that she'd let Annabelle, Alexa and Pepper not only talk her into using the Elliotts' private jet to fly to LA, but they'd given her a makeover on top of that. Somehow, in a whirlwind of deciding she couldn't let Beau go without a fight and getting her hair curled and lips painted, she'd ended up at a Hollywood movie premiere.

Scarlett sat in the back of a limo—somehow the dynamic trio managed to get her that as well—and looked over at Madelyn in the carrier car seat. She'd guarantee this was the only limo arriving tonight with a car seat in the back.

Somehow the ladies had not only procured a dress for Scarlett, along with shoes and a fashionable bag, they'd found a red sparkly dress and matching headband for Madelyn.

As the limo slowed, Scarlett turned her attention to the tinted window. Bright lights flooded the night, cameras flashed, the roar of the crowd filtered in and nerves swirled through her belly at the sight and sound.

What was she thinking coming here? She was so far out of her element. She didn't do crowds or glam or dressing up in a fitted, sequined emerald green gown with her hair curled and in bright red lipstick. She was more of a relaxed kind of girl who made homemade baby food and decorated with clearance Christmas decor.

"Ma'am, I'm going to pull closer to the red carpet entrance," the driver informed her. "Please wait until a guard opens your door and escorts you out."

Oh, mercy. She was really going through with this. Scarlett didn't know how the incredible Elliott women managed the jet, the wardrobe, the limo and a last-minute invite to the red carpet to arrive just after Beau's car. No doubt money talked and they had tapped into some powerful resources to make all of this happen in less than twenty-four hours.

The car came to a stop and Scarlett unfastened a sleepy baby from her car seat. She cradled Madelyn against her chest and adjusted the headband, which had slipped down over one eye like a pirate's patch.

"You'll just be around the block?" she asked the driver. "I'm leaving the rest of Madelyn's things in here."

"Yes, ma'am. You call me and I'll be right back. I'm only driving for you tonight."

Scarlett's stylish clutch was just large enough for a couple of diapers, a travel pack of wipes, her cell and her wallet. She'd just fed the baby before Madelyn fell asleep so they should be good for a few hours. Besides, who's to say Beau wouldn't publicly reject her and she'd be right back in this car in just a few moments?

But what if he asked her to stay? What if he wanted to take her and Madelyn into the premiere and whatever party after?

She'd worry about that when the time came. Right now, her car had eased up and came to another stop. The lights and the screams intensified and Scarlett had to concentrate on the sweet child in her arms, still sleeping and oblivious to this milestone moment.

The door opened and the warm California air hit her. She already missed Texas and the laid-back life with cool evenings. Maybe city life wasn't for her. Maybe she hadn't only found the man—she'd found a piece of herself that clicked right into place. Perhaps the next chapter she was going to start was the wrong one. She had so many questions…and they were all about to be answered.

Scarlett laid a protective hand over Madelyn's ears to protect her from the thundering noise, but she stirred and her eyes popped open.

Questions and microphones were shot in her direction, but Scarlett looked ahead, beyond the men in black suits with mics attached to their lapels. She ignored the questions of who she was, what part she had in the film, who was the cute baby.

Scarlett spotted a flash of the wide, familiar grin then broad shoulders eased away from one set of reporters to another. Beau was flanked by those men in suits who were unsmiling and whose eyes were always scanning the area.

A hand slid over her elbow and Scarlett jerked to see who was beside her.

"Right this way, ma'am." One of the suited men clearly recognized the newbie on the red carpet and tried to usher her along. "There is extra security tonight with all the hype. I'll make sure you and your little one get to the entrance of the theater."

She had to strain to hear him over the white noise of the crowd and she didn't even bother to tell him this child wasn't hers, but rather belonged to the star of the premiere. Had she made a mistake bringing Madelyn? Would Beau be upset? She wanted to show him they could all be a family—they could be one unit and build something solid together.

One thing she knew for certain: she wasn't about to stop and talk to the different media outlets. For one thing, she had nothing to say that she'd want printed or quoted. For another, she was here for only one reason and it wasn't to be interviewed.

Scarlett shifted Madelyn in her arms, still shielding the baby's ears from the chaos. She leaned toward the security guard as she tried to keep up with the pace he'd set.

"I don't need to talk to any reporters. I'm here with Mr. Elliott," she informed him. Then she realized how stalker-like that sounded, so she quickly added, "And this is his baby."

The guard looked at her then down to Madelyn, but Scarlett smiled, hoping he'd move this process along. She had a right to be here—she assumed since Annabelle assured her this was okay—and she couldn't wait.

The man finally nodded and gripped his lapel as he talked out the side of his mouth and ordered the guards up ahead to stop Beau from moving to the next set of reporters.

Scarlett pushed through, ignoring the yells from either side of the roped-off area. If she tried to take in all the lights, all of the questions, all of the chaos around her, she would give in to the fear and the anxiety that had accompanied her all the way from Texas.

She never should have let Beau walk out of that cabin thinking he didn't mean more to her. Their time together since she'd shut down had been so strained and she'd ached for him in ways she'd never imagined possible.

In her defense, she'd been hurt and thought it best if they made a clean break since their temporary arrangement was coming to an end anyway. Unfortunately, that clean break didn't work.

Because she loved him.

There was no way to ignore such strong emotions and if she had to make a fool of herself and take the biggest risk of her life, then she was willing to try for the man she'd fallen for so helplessly.

One of the escorts next to Beau tapped on his shoulder and intervened, pulling him from a current interview. Then the man leaned in and told Beau something that had Beau darting his gaze straight in her direction and their eyes instantly locked.

Scarlett wasn't sure if it was the shock in his eyes or the wide smile on his face that had her nerves kicking in even more. She watched as he raked that sultry dark gaze over her body. Even at this distance and despite the chaos around them, the visual lick Beau gave her had her body instantly responding.

His eyes snapped back to hers and then he was taking long strides to come back down the red carpet. Scarlett didn't think she'd ever seen him smile this much.

"Scarlett."

Beau reached her and shook his head, as if still processing what she was doing here. That went for her, too. She felt as if this whole night was surreal.

"How did you… What… Annabelle texted me and asked if I could get a couple of passes and a limo. My agent pulled everything together, but I just assumed she and Colt were coming."

Well, that explained how the quick red carpet treatment happened.

"Mr. Elliott, who's the lady?"

"Beau, is that your little girl?"

"Is Jennifer James no longer part of your life?"

Reporters shot off so many questions, so prying and so demanding. Part of Scarlett wished she would've waited until he got home, but the other part was glad she'd allowed herself to be talked into coming. Standing here, supporting him, was the only way she knew to truly show him how sorry she was and how much he meant to her.

"I wanted to surprise you," Scarlett told him. "This wasn't my idea, but I needed to tell you—"

He slid his hands up her bare arms and stepped farther into her, with Madelyn nestled between them.

"Say it," he demanded. "I need to hear it."

Scarlett stared up into those dark eyes. "What do you need to hear?"

"That you love me." A corner of his mouth quirked into a grin. "That's why you're here, isn't it?"

She shifted Madelyn, but Beau ended up easing his

daughter up into his arms. He palmed her back with one large hand and held her secure against his chest.

Questions roared even louder, but his eyes never left Scarlett's. The media might as well not even exist; all his attention was on her.

How did she ever think that his words weren't genuine? That he didn't think they were something special? He'd shown her over and over again just how much she meant to him and she'd shied away in fear. She firmly believed that everything he told Colt was to save her reputation, which only added another layer of respect and love.

"Scarlett."

She smoothed her hand down her emerald beaded gown and tucked the clutch beneath her arm.

"I wanted to be the one to tell you." Scarlett smiled, though her nerves were at an all-time high. "But you stole the words from my mouth."

Beau's hand went to her hip and he leaned down. If she thought the crowd was loud before, that was nothing compared to the roar now. They were yelling so much. She couldn't make out full questions, but she did pick up on "romance" and "love." Yes, they had all of that and so much more.

"Say it," he told her again.

Her eyes darted away, but he raised his hand to cup her face, drawing her attention back to him.

"I'm right here," he stated. "They don't exist. It's just the three of us."

His sweet girl was a package deal and she absolutely loved how he always put Madelyn first. And she wanted them as a package because she couldn't think of a better present.

"I love you," she told him as she reached up to lay her hand over his. "I'm sorry I didn't have the courage to say it before, but I got scared the other day. All of this happened so fast, but everything I feel is so, so real."

He closed the distance between them and touched his lips to hers. And that set the media into a tizzy.

"Beau, is this your new leading lady from the picture?"

"Does she have a name?"

"Is this the rumored nanny?"

"Are you planning a Christmas proposal?"

Beau pressed his forehead to hers. "Are you sure you're ready for all of this tonight?"

Scarlett wasn't sure, but if this was what Beau's life consisted of, she'd find a way to make things work.

"If you love me, then I'm ready for anything," she said, easing back to glance up at him.

"I love you, Scarlett. As crazy as it is, as little time as we've known each other, I love you more than I ever thought I could love any woman."

Her heart swelled and she knew the risk she'd taken had paid off.

"I know I could've waited for you to get back to Texas, but Annabelle thought I should make a statement."

Beau chuckled as he slid an arm around her waist. "Baby, that dress is quite the statement and I plan on showing you when we get back to my place tonight."

She hadn't thought that far, but the idea of ending the night at his house in the Hollywood Hills, of seeing even more into his world had her giddy with anticipation.

Scarlett smoothed a hand over Madelyn's dark curls.

"You mentioned wanting a big family and you know that I can't give you that."

"Adoption," he said, using one simple word to put her worries at ease and further prove just how amazing he was. "We'll have that large family when the time is right."

She chewed on her bottom lip and then smiled. "Is it too late to tell you that the farmhouse you bought is perfect for us?"

Beau tapped her forehead with a quick kiss. "That place was always for us," he explained. "I just didn't get a chance to tell you before Colt showed up and then you kicked me out of your room."

He'd planned that house to be for the three of them all this time? Scarlett's eyes welled with tears, but she couldn't cry. It had taken a small army to get this makeup so perfect.

"I think we need to give the reporters something to chew on before they break the barriers."

Scarlett nodded. "Whatever you think."

Beau cradled Madelyn in one arm and kept his other firmly around Scarlett's waist. He angled them toward the front of the red carpet so both sides of the aisle could see them. As soon as they were facing forward, the crowd seemed to hush, waiting for that next golden kernel of a story.

"I'm happy to announce that Scarlett Patterson is in fact my next leading lady," Beau declared. "And my future wife."

Wife? Scarlett jerked her gaze to his, which warranted her a toe-curling wink that set butterflies fluttering in her stomach.

"Is that a proposal?" she asked, shocked her voice was strong.

Beau kept that wide grin on his face. "What do you say? Be my leading lady for life, Scarlett."

"Yes." As if any other answer was an option. "There's nobody else I'd ever want for the star in my life."

Flashes went off, one after another, causing a strobe light effect. As people started yelling more questions, Beau waved and smiled. Scarlett wasn't sure what world she'd stepped into, but the strong man at her side would help her through.

She never thought she'd have the title of leading lady, but as Beau escorted her into the venue, Scarlett realized there was no greater role she could think of—besides wife and mother, of course.

Once inside, Beau ushered her down a hallway to find some privacy.

"I'm taking a break from Hollywood," he told her when they stopped in a quiet place. "I decided that before you came, but now that I see a better future, I'm not sure I'll want to come back here at all."

She didn't know how to respond, but she didn't get a chance. Beau backed her up a step until she came in contact with the wall. He held Madelyn in one arm and reached up with his free hand to stroke the side of her face, then sifted his fingers through her hair.

"You take my breath away, Scarlett. I want you forever, so if we need to take things slow before we marry, I'll do whatever you want."

He kissed her, pouring out his promise and love. When he eased back, he kept his lips barely a whisper away.

"This is the greatest Christmas present I could have ever asked for," he told her.

Scarlett rested her hand over his on Madelyn's back. "Me, too, but I don't know what to wrap up and put beneath our crooked tree."

He nipped at her bottom lip. "How about more of that cookie dip?"

She wrapped her arm around his waist and smiled. "I think I can manage that, but first we have a movie premiere to get to."

"And then we have the rest of our lives to plan."

Epilogue

"What the hell is that?" Colt demanded.

Scarlett smiled and held up her hands in an exaggerated fashion toward the tree. "It's our Christmas tree," she exclaimed.

"Why is it crooked?"

Beau stepped into the room after putting Madelyn down for the night. "Don't ask. Just go with it."

Scarlett rolled her eyes. "He loves it, don't let him fool you."

Colt's brows drew in before he shook his head and shrugged. "Whatever makes you two happy."

Oh, she was most definitely happy. Christmas Eve was magical here at the ranch and tomorrow was Christmas where all of the Elliotts—spouses, fiancées, and children—would gather and start a new chapter.

"I just wanted to come by and let you guys know that

I spoke with the nursing home and they're okay with us bringing Dad home for the day tomorrow."

Beau's eyes went from his brother to Scarlett, then back again. "Seriously?"

Colt nodded. "They said as long as he's having a good day. They offered to send a nurse, but I truly think once he's home, he might see something that triggers some memories, and we can care for him well enough. Even if he's only there an hour. I think we all need it."

Scarlett's heart swelled as tears pricked her eyes. She crossed the room to Beau and wrapped an arm around him.

"This is great news for you guys," she stated. "I think it's exactly what this family needs for a fresh start."

"I just hope he remembers," Beau added.

Colt nodded. "I have a feeling he will. I think this is definitely a Christmas for miracles."

He drifted his gaze toward the leaning tree. "I mean, if you can call that a Christmas tree, I think anything is possible."

Beau laughed as he hugged Scarlett tighter against him. "That tree embodies our lives. We're not perfect, but we're sure as hell trying."

Scarlett smiled as she watched the twins share an unspoken message with their eyes and their matching grins.

Yes, this was a season for miracles.

* * * * *

COWBOY
UNWRAPPED

VICKI LEWIS THOMPSON

For Isabeau the cat, 1994–2016. What a serene,
happy soul. You will be missed.

1

When Jake Ramsey pulled into the circular gravel drive in front of Thunder Mountain Ranch at sundown, he thought he'd stumbled onto the set of *National Lampoon's Christmas Vacation*. His foster brothers Cade Gallagher and Finn O'Roarke stood in the freezing cold struggling to untangle a string of Christmas lights while wearing thick gloves. Why they needed more lights was a mystery because the low-slung ranch house already looked as if Clark Griswold had been there.

Happy as Jake was to see those two cowboys after all this time away, his firefighter training took precedence over a sentimental reunion. He'd bet a month's pay neither of them had bothered to check the UL ratings to see if the fuse box could take another strand of what looked like incandescent bulbs. Hadn't they heard of LEDs? And was that an *indoor* extension cord connected to the net lights on a bush by the porch? Jesus.

He wondered if Damon Harrison had approved this setup. Damon, Cade and Finn had been the original three taken in by Rosie and Herb Padgett years ago when they'd decided to make the ranch a foster home for teenage boys. Cade had become a horse trainer who worked at the ranch, now a residential equine education center for older teens, called Thunder Mountain Academy. Finn had moved to Seattle and opened his own microbrewery. Those jobs didn't qualify either of them to handle electrical installations.

But Damon and Philomena, who'd married this past summer, renovated houses here in Sheridan. Jake doubted they'd been involved in this fustercluck. It had Cade written all over it. The guy was great with horses but not so great with a toolbox.

Cade and Finn glanced up as he pulled up next to them in his F-250. They wouldn't recognize the truck because he'd bought it since his last visit home in early March. Plus he hadn't seen Finn in years. Finn and his fiancée Chelsea were spending Christmas at the ranch, which had added to Jake's excitement about his first Christmas home since getting hired by the Jackson Hole Fire Department.

From the looks of things, they needed him here. Cade and Finn were fixing to burn down the house. He shut off the engine and climbed out, making sure his boots didn't slip on the ice he knew would be under the thin layer of snow covering the driveway.

Then he buttoned his sheepskin coat against the wind and crammed his Stetson a little tighter on his head before walking around the front of the truck. He could see his breath. That was another stupid thing—putting up Christmas lights when the temperature was near zero.

"Hey, bozos," he called out to Cade and Finn, who'd stopped what they were doing while they waited to see who'd driven up. "Why don't you let someone who knows what he's doing handle that job?"

"Jake?" Cade dropped his end of the lights into the snow and hurried toward him. "You got a new truck, man!"

"That I did." He exchanged a hug with Cade.

"Jake Ramsey?" Finn tossed his end away and came over. "I haven't seen your ugly mug since I left for Seattle! How the hell are you?"

Jake returned his hug. "I'm good, real good. Hated that I had to miss Damon's wedding, but a couple of guys got sick and I couldn't leave."

"You would've loved it," Cade said. "It rained like hell, the wind destroyed most of the decorations and we had to delay the ceremony until the storm passed. Then we had to stand in the mud while Damon and Phil said their vows. It was epic."

"Sounds awesome. Wish I'd been there. Speaking of the happy couple, where are they?"

"Wimping out in Florida with the in-laws," Finn said. "They'll be back tomorrow, looking all tanned and smug while the rest of us are the color of grubworms."

"Real Wyoming cowboys don't go to Florida for a winter vacation." Cade tucked his gloved hands into his armpits and stomped his feet in the snow. "They tough it out like manly men."

"Damn straight," Finn said. "But I'm thinking we should tough it out inside by the fire for a while and finish this project in the morning. We don't want to keep poor Jake standing out here shivering. He needs to head in and see the folks."

"I want to see them, too," Jake said, "but I have a question before we go in. Did you guys put up all these lights?"

Cade grinned at him. "You're impressed, right? You

didn't think we could do it without Damon around to help, but there's the evidence." Cade swept an arm to encompass the glittering front of the house. "Damon's gonna shit a brick when he sees this."

"That's for sure." Jake walked over and fingered the indoor extension cord. "I take it you ran out of outdoor cords."

"Yeah, but those work fine." Finn shrugged. "We bought a bunch of extra lights and forgot about getting more cords, but we found those in the barn. They're a little worn but we wound electrical tape around the parts where wires were sticking out."

Jake did his best to control himself. "How many of these are you using?"

"I don't know," Cade said. "Six, maybe seven. We're almost done, but I agree with Finn. We can quit now and finish up tomorrow. We have time before Damon and Phil get back."

"You know what?" Jake was proud of himself. He didn't yell and he didn't cuss, although he desperately wanted to do both. "Before I go in, let me take a quick run into town. With tomorrow being the last shopping day, the hardware store should be open. I'll just pick up a few outdoor extension cords."

"Ah, don't bother." Cade fished one end of the light strand out of the snow and began winding it around his arm. "Extra trouble, extra expense and for what?"

"Oh, I don't know." Jake kept his tone casual. "Maybe to keep those frayed extension cords from setting the house on fire."

Cade blinked. "We put electrical tape around them. That should do it."

"Hey, he's a firefighter." Finn clapped Cade on the

shoulder. "We should probably let him do his thing. I admit those cords are a little dicey."

Jake shuddered to think what they looked like. They'd probably been moldering in the barn for years. No doubt varmints had chewed on them. "I've seen the result of using frayed cords," he said. "I'd sleep better knowing I've replaced them. They're not designed for outdoor use, anyway, although the UL rating label is probably gone by now."

Finn exchanged a glance with Cade.

"Don't worry," Cade said in a low voice. "They're fine."

"What?" Jake didn't like the sound of that. "What's fine?"

Cade finished winding the strand around his arm. "Some of the lights were on sale. The labels said for indoor use only, but they were really reasonable so I thought if we put them on the porch—"

"Holy hell, Cade!" Jake finally lost it. "Are you telling me even the lights aren't rated for outdoor use?"

"A few, but—"

"Okay, here's what we're going to do. I'll drive into town and pick up a whole bunch of outdoor extension cords and more lights with the proper rating. In the morning I'll help you and Finn replace those extension cords and indoor lights. In the meantime, I want you to turn off everything."

Cade looked as if he wanted to argue.

"I know you think I'm an anal safety nut, but last week I hauled a single mom and her two little kids out of a house fire caused by frayed extension cords."

Finn sighed. "I hate to say it, but he's right, bro." He

dug in his pocket. "Let me donate some cash toward that purchase, Jake."

"Nah, my treat." Jake waved off the money. "I didn't know what to give the folks for Christmas so I was going to buy something after I got here. I'll just make this my gift."

Cade nodded. "Okay, I bow to your superior knowledge regarding decorative lighting. But can I make a small request?"

"Sure."

"Could you not mention any of this to Damon and Phil? The folks will have to know since this'll be your Christmas present, but Damon would never let me hear the end of it."

"I'll be silent as the tomb."

"Good. Oh, and that goes for Lexi, too. She's attending an indoor riding clinic and won't be back in town until tomorrow, either. My goal was to surprise all three of them with an awesome display."

"We'll do that, I promise." Jake knew how much Cade wanted to please Lexi, the love of his life. "It'll look just as fantastic as it does now, only it'll be safe."

Cade's gusty exhale created a cloud of vapor. "Thanks." He glanced back at the house. "I'm guessing nobody heard you drive up since they didn't come out, so you can probably just go and they won't be the wiser."

"Perfect. I'll make this quick."

"Dinner's at six-thirty," Finn said. "Tuna casserole."

"Hot damn. I'll be back in time." He left them, rounded the truck and climbed in behind the wheel, but he didn't pull away until the Christmas lights had winked out. Only then did the muscles in his neck and shoulders relax. Disaster averted.

The road into Sheridan had been recently plowed so he made good time, accompanied by the sultry voice of Amethyst Ferguson on his truck stereo. In his opinion she sounded way better than Katy Perry or Taylor Swift, but then again, he could be prejudiced. And he still hadn't decided what to do about her. Initially he'd planned to send her a text saying he'd be in town for a few days, but then he'd reconsidered.

He'd be busy with his foster family and she'd probably be busy with her folks, too, assuming she wasn't performing somewhere. If she happened to be out of town that would settle his dilemma, but he couldn't find that out without contacting her. He'd hate knowing she was here only to discover that family obligations would prevent them from having any private time.

And that's what he was hoping for. Last summer she'd had a gig at a resort in Jackson Hole and he'd caught her final show. Because he hadn't seen her since their PG-rated dates in high school, he'd invited her for drinks afterward. Sure enough, they'd reignited the spark and had spent the rest of the night in her hotel room.

The sex had been super hot, but they'd agreed that her budding career, his demanding schedule and the miles between Sheridan and Jackson Hole would keep them from meeting on a regular basis. They'd made no definite plans. If she had another gig in Jackson Hole she'd let him know, and if he paid a visit to his foster parents he'd give her a shout.

But this was a special holiday, not some random long weekend. He hadn't spent Christmas at the Last Chance in years due to his rookie status at the fire station. Finally he could look forward to celebrating with his foster parents and any foster brothers who showed up.

That could turn into a crowd. Because of the holidays, the Thunder Mountain Academy students had cleared out of the log cabins down in the meadow. Finn and Chelsea had likely claimed one and Jake had figured on taking another one but that left two more plus guest rooms in the ranch house.

Although his foster mom used to make a big pot of vegetable soup on Christmas Eve, she'd told him on the phone that she'd decided to have a buffet this year. But the tradition of opening presents after the meal would continue as always. Christmas Day was filled with card games, basketball on TV, snowball fights in the yard and a turkey dinner. He didn't want to miss any of that.

On the other hand, he'd thought about Amethyst fairly often during these past few months. He'd downloaded all of her music and played it quite a bit. The prospect of seeing her again affected his pulse rate. Imagining another night like they'd spent last summer sent all his blood south.

Yeah, he had a little fixation going on when it came to Amethyst Ferguson, whereas she might have put him right out of her mind. Besides, she'd mentioned sharing a house with her sister and he'd be at the ranch with a whole lot of people around. The cabins were set up with bunk beds, so even if he invited Amethyst to spend the night with him, it wouldn't be the luxurious and intimate setup they'd had in Jackson Hole.

He should probably forget trying to connect with her and concentrate on enjoying his first Christmas home in years. While Jackson looked great for the holidays, Sheridan had its own small-town charm. He'd always loved how the old-fashioned lampposts looked when they were decorated. As he'd predicted, the hardware store was still open. The extension cords should be in stock but he wondered if the lights would be picked over. If so, they'd just make do with fewer lights.

He found a parking spot and pulled in. Last-minute shoppers with colorful Christmas bags hurried along the sidewalk. He was glad for an excuse to come into town and be part of the bustling scene. Thanks to his foster parents and his years at Thunder Mountain, he'd learned to love the season.

Displays of gift ideas dominated the front of the store and he paused to look at a selection of smoke alarms. Last time he'd visited the ranch he'd worried that the ones in the house weren't top of the line. If he bought these for the folks, then he wouldn't have to announce that the extension cords were his gift and Cade could save face. Matter of fact, he could buy smoke alarms for everyone on his list. An extra one was always help-ful and then he wouldn't have to come back into town tomorrow to Christmas shop.

"Typical fireman, mesmerized by the beauty of smoke alarms."

He turned around and there stood Amethyst with a smile on her face and a sparkle of laughter in her blue eyes. She wore a red knit cap pulled over her dark hair and a red coat with a furry collar. His heart kicked into high gear and he couldn't think of a single thing to say.

"Thought you could sneak into town, did you?" There was a teasing note in her voice.

He remembered how she liked to tease, especially in bed. "No! I was going to contact you, but then I thought about your family and how you probably wouldn't have time, so—"

"I understand." Her gaze gentled. "I was kidding you. It's not like we had an ironclad agreement. Christmas *is* busy."

"But I'd love to spend time with you." He couldn't help saying it. She looked more beautiful than ever and he had vivid memories of how she felt in his arms. He wanted her there again.

"I'd love to spend time with you, too." The flicker of awareness in her eyes sent an unmistakable message.

It went straight to his groin. "But I don't know when. Tonight's out. I just got here."

"I couldn't anyway. Family dinner."

"And tomorrow night's Christmas Eve. That's a big deal at the ranch. Maybe you'd like to come out there?"

"That's a possibility. Our big celebration is on Christmas Day. But I'd need to check with my folks and see what's planned. You know how it is."

"Absolutely. That's why I didn't contact you. I knew it could be dicey."

"True, but there has to be some free time." She brightened. "Maybe tomorrow during the day?"

He was encouraged by her eagerness to see him. "I have some stuff to do with the guys in the morning, but how about tomorrow afternoon? If you'd be willing to drive out to the ranch in the early afternoon, we could—" He thought fast. "Go for a sleigh ride. How about that?"

"Sounds like fun! What time?"

"Let's say around two. That'll give me time to get the sleigh hitched up." And find one somewhere. Thunder Mountain didn't have one, but surely someone in the area would. A sleigh ride down the snowy Forest Service road sounded like a terrific holiday idea—lots of blankets and maybe some privacy.

"Great. I'll be there. Listen, I have to go. I saw you walk in here and followed you so I could say hi, but my sister's coming into town tonight and—"

"Coming into town? I thought she was living with you."

"Not anymore. I have another woman sharing the house."

"Oh." That didn't help.

"But she's gone for the holidays."

That perked him up fast. "Is that right?"

Amethyst laughed. "You should see your face."

"Sorry. It's just that—"

"I know." Merriment danced in her blue eyes. "We'll talk tomorrow. Maybe we can work something out." Grabbing his arm for balance, she stood on tiptoe and pressed a quick kiss to his mouth. "See you then." She turned and left the store.

He wasn't sure how long he stood there gazing after her while his fevered brain processed her brief but potent kiss and the information about her absent roommate. Okay, so she had to be with her family during the bulk of the holiday, but at some point she'd go home to bed. He'd be with his peeps at Thunder Mountain, but once everyone was sleeping, it wouldn't matter whether he was there or not.

"Sir, can I help you with something?"

He snapped out of his daze and turned toward the hardware store clerk. "Yes, you sure can. For starters I'll take…let me see…seven of these smoke alarms and if you have holiday bags to put them in that would be great." Now that he'd be seeing Amethyst he might as well get her one.

The clerk stacked them into the crook of his arm. "I'll take these up to the counter. Our store bags have a little holly on them."

"That'll do. I also need several outdoor extension cords and whatever LED Christmas lights you have left."

"We moved all the cords and lights to the Christmas decoration section against the far wall."

"Thanks."

"Is there anything else I can help you with?"

"Do you know anyone with a sleigh for rent?"

"You mean like a business that provides sleigh rides? I think one of the guest ranches is offering—"

"No, not the whole ride. I have access to a horse. I just need the sleigh."

"Then I'm afraid I don't know anybody. Sorry."

"No problem. Just thought I'd ask." He wasn't worried. Somebody would have a sleigh he could use. Amethyst was in town and eager to spend time with him. Christmas had just become a whole lot more festive.

2

AMETHYST DROVE TO her parents' house singing at the top of her lungs. She couldn't wait to tell Sapphire that Jake Ramsey was in town. Her sister was the only person on the planet besides Jake who knew about that hot night in Jackson Hole. Talking about it, when it might never happen again, seemed like a mistake. Sapphire had promised to keep it to herself.

Ah, but Amethyst had so hoped it would happen again. She had a gig in Jackson Hole for New Year's Eve and she'd planned to contact him. She'd decided to wait until the last minute, though, in case he was off duty and had a date for New Year's. What they'd shared didn't fit in the category of dating and that made it twenty times more exciting.

But she'd been aware that he could meet someone in Jackson Hole who didn't have big dreams of a recording contract and was willing to work around his shifts at the fire station. Amethyst didn't want to stand in the way of him getting his happily-ever-after even though she wasn't in the market.

He hadn't found anyone, though, or he wouldn't have

asked her to come out to the ranch for a sleigh ride. The boy she'd known in high school and the man she'd enjoyed one scorching night with wasn't a cheater. Far from it. With his sun-bleached hair, green eyes and firefighter physique he was the all-American good guy.

She was a little surprised that some woman in Jackson Hole hadn't snapped him up, but since no one had, she hoped to make use of whatever stolen moments were available while he was here. A sleigh ride into a snowy landscape dotted with pine trees and devoid of people was a good start.

Grady Magee's truck in her parents' driveway told her that he and Sapphire had arrived from Cody. Amethyst was thrilled for her sister, a talented ceramic artist who'd vowed never to become involved with a creative guy again after several debacles. But Grady, whose recycled metal sculptures had taken the art world by storm, had changed her mind.

Coincidentally, Grady and his older brother Liam had also lived at Thunder Mountain for a couple of years while their mom had recovered from a debilitating car accident. Grady had been at the ranch when Jake had lived there, so as she parked behind Grady's truck she decided to immediately mention seeing Jake instead of waiting for a private chat with Sapphire. Come to think of it, Grady and Sapphire might be going to Thunder Mountain for Christmas Eve. Maybe she could tag along.

Dinner with five imaginative people at the table was lively. Clearly, Amethyst's mom, Sheridan High School's art teacher, and her dad, who'd had his own jazz band for years, had welcomed Grady into the fold. Amethyst could see why.

Unlike the other artists Sapphire had dated, he obviously fed her creativity instead of stifling it. Tonight she was 100 percent herself. Her clothes were vibrantly colored and a hand-carved comb held back her auburn hair to show off beaded earrings that dangled to her shoulders. Best of all, every time she looked at Grady her face glowed, so moving to Cody and working in Grady's renovated barn must agree with her.

Conversation flowed so fast that Amethyst didn't have a chance to mention Jake until they were having dessert, chocolate lava cake that was a family favorite.

Grady heaped praise on the dessert. "I could live on this."

"Me, too." Amethyst scooped up another spoonful of cake and syrup. "Before I fall into a sugar-induced coma, though, I wanted to tell you that I met Jake Ramsey in town just before I drove here."

Sapphire's eyes widened. "Oh, really?"

"Yep." Amethyst sent her a warning glance. "We bumped into each other in the hardware store."

"Jake's home for Christmas?" Grady's happy smile was one of his many endearing traits. "I didn't know he was coming back. That's terrific."

"I remember Jake from when you dated him," her mother said. "Nice boy, although he always seemed a little quiet for you."

"He was sort of shy back then. Not as much now." She didn't dare look at Sapphire, who had barely managed to cover a snort of laughter with a cough.

"I haven't seen him in forever," Grady said. "By the time I came back from working that pipeline job in Alaska he'd hired on with the fire department over in Jackson Hole. Did he say if he was still at that job?"

"I believe he is."

"I'll bet firefighting's a good fit for him. We used to tease him about his overdeveloped sense of responsibility. He didn't pull pranks like the rest of us. Anyway, it'll be great to see him. Always liked the guy."

Amethyst could feel her mother's assessing gaze. No doubt she was remembering the gig in Jackson Hole and wondering if there was more to the story than met the eye, especially after Sapphire's "Oh, really?" comment. Jane Ferguson was no fool and when it came to her daughters she seemed to know when a romance was in the making.

But this time her radar was off because there was no romance. Lust, definitely. But romance suggested a soft-focus ending to the story and Amethyst had no interest in that. She was hoping that a talent scout or someone with connections in the music industry would show up at one of her gigs. With luck, that could lead to a recording contract and a move to LA. Marriage and a family didn't fit in with that dream.

After the meal Sapphire offered to clean up the kitchen and recruited Amethyst to help for old times' sake. The minute they were alone she lowered her voice. "So? Did you know about this visit?"

"I didn't, and when I saw him in town I thought that meant he wasn't interested anymore. But you know how I am—can't just let something go. So I followed him into the store to find out for sure if he was deliberately ignoring me."

"And?"

"He's still interested." As she remembered the gleam in his eyes when he'd learned her roommate was gone, she couldn't hold back a grin.

"Then why didn't he contact you?"

"It's Christmas. He has family stuff. I have family stuff."

Sapphire nodded. "Makes sense. But surely you can work something out." She peered at her. "You want to, right?"

"You bet I do. You should have seen him standing there looking all rugged in his sheepskin coat and Stetson. Those green eyes are killer. I was ready to attack him on the spot."

"So what's the plan?"

"For starters he invited me out to the ranch for a sleigh ride tomorrow afternoon."

"You mean a sleigh ride or a *sleigh ride*?" Sapphire wiggled her fingers to make air quotes.

"That's tough to say with so many people around. Besides, it doesn't matter. I let it drop that Arlene is out of town for the holidays."

"She *is*?" Sapphire clapped her hand over her mouth and glanced at the kitchen doorway. "Sorry."

"It's okay. I think Mom already knows something's going on."

"Probably. It's my fault. I didn't expect you to suddenly announce that your red-hot lover boy was in town."

"I wasn't going to. Then I remembered that he and Grady lived at Thunder Mountain at the same time, so I felt obligated to mention it."

"Absolutely. Grady's always thrilled when he gets a chance to connect with some of his foster brothers. Anyway, that's fabulous news about Arlene being gone."

"She's a good roommate. Not as good as you, but we get along and she pays her share of the rent on time."

"I worried that she'd talk you to death. When I worked

with her at the Art Barn co-op she was quite the chatterbox. Sweet, but extremely verbal."

Amethyst smiled. "She is, but I love her work and she's given me a gorgeous watercolor of the Bighorns that I put in my bedroom. Whenever she carries on too long, I suddenly have to record another track for my next album and I scoot upstairs to my studio. Like I said, we get along."

"I'm glad. And she had the good sense to be out of town at a critical moment in your personal life."

"No kidding. Anyway, I need to go home tonight and put clean sheets on the bed and spruce up the place a little."

"Like he'll care. Hey, listen, I know hanging out in a crowd with your studmuffin isn't optimal, but Grady and I are going over to Thunder Mountain tomorrow night for their Christmas Eve celebration if you want to come along. We could—oh, wait, I just remembered something. There's a cat. His name's Ringo. I'll bet Jake's forgotten about your allergies."

"Is Ringo indoor or outdoor?"

"Both. He has a bed in the kitchen. I don't think he gets on the furniture in the house, but still, you don't want to go out there and start sneezing your head off."

"Thanks for the warning. I'll pick up some over-the-counter meds at the drugstore in the morning." She was headed there anyway. If Jake would be spending some late-night quality time at her house, she would be prepared with condoms. "It's one day and one evening with minimal exposure and I don't want to miss out on the fun. I'd love to go, but what about Mom and Dad? I hate to leave them in the lurch."

"They were invited, too, but they think Herb and

Rosie deserve to have Grady and me all to themselves. Mom and Dad claimed us for Christmas Day so it seemed fair to them if we went to the ranch tomorrow night. If you come with us, then they can do their love-bird thing."

"It's cute, isn't it? After all these years they're still nuts about each other."

"Mom pointed that out when I told her I couldn't be with Grady because he was an artist." Sapphire mimicked their mother's voice. "'Your father and I are both artists and we've managed to stumble through twenty-nine years without killing each other.'"

"And so will you and Grady." Amethyst gave her a hug. "You two have something special. The ring he gave you is gorgeous."

"I'm rather fond of it, myself." Sapphire held her hand out in front of her to admire it. "We've tried to set a date but we're both so busy we haven't figured out when."

"Whenever it is, I'll be there, and I want to sing."

"I would love for you to sing but you'll be the maid of honor. Can you do both things? I've never seen that done but if anyone can pull it off you can."

"I've never seen it done, either, but I'll be happy to set a precedent as the first singing maid of honor. I might even sing as I walk down the aisle." She looked at Sapphire. "What do you think?"

"I think it's a fabulous idea. In fact, when you get married, you should be the singing bride. You could sing your vows and turn the whole thing into a musical. Just make sure the groom can sing, too, or it'll be weird."

"Yeah, because having both the bride and groom sing their vows wouldn't be the least bit weird."

Sapphire laughed. "You should do it."

"I definitely would if I planned to get married. But I don't."

"Ever?"

"Probably not. I've watched how it goes with the big names and I'm hoping to be up there with them someday. It's not easy to maintain a high-profile career and a solid marriage."

Sapphire gazed at her as if evaluating the truth of that statement. Finally she nodded. "I guess you're right. You're smart to think that through, because you're going to make it big."

"That's my goal." She crossed her fingers. "But there are no guarantees, either. Even if I get a contract it could be a bumpy ride. It wouldn't be fair to drag some unsuspecting guy along."

"Nope. But I see why you're so excited about hanging out with Jake since he's not looking to settle down, either. You might as well soak up all that yumminess while he's in town."

"My thoughts, exactly."

SIX PEOPLE GATHERED around the kitchen table at the ranch house that night and, fortunately, Rosie, the woman he'd called *Mom* ever since she'd asked him to the first day, had made plenty of tuna casserole. Jake was on his third helping. Cade had mentioned that several times.

"Leave him alone." Chelsea came to his defense. "He's a growing boy."

"Thanks, Chelsea." Jake hadn't met her until tonight but she was easy to get to know. Her multicolored hair and funky clothes made him smile and he could tell she liked him, too. She worked in marketing and Finn gave her full credit for making his microbrewery a success and for mellowing out his workaholic tendencies. The two of them seemed to have a good thing going.

"He's definitely grown since I last saw him," Finn said. "You put on any more muscle and you'll rip the seams of that shirt, bro. I advise cutting back on the workouts or you'll be shelling out for a new wardrobe."

Cade grinned. "Hey, Finn, you're just jealous because Jake and I are manly men with jobs that increase the diameter of our biceps, while you only have to expend enough energy to put a head on a mug of beer."

"Are you saying I'm out of shape?" Finn propped his elbow on the table and lifted his hand in a challenge. "Arm-wrestle this, pony boy."

Cade left his chair. "My pleasure, suds stud."

"Suds stud?" Chelsea snorted. "I need to remember that one."

Jake wondered if they'd actually arm-wrestle. He wouldn't mind seeing that because he suspected Finn could take Cade. Finn had an air of steely determination, almost an edgy quality, whereas Cade was more easygoing.

"No arm wrestling at the dinner table." Rosie gave them a warning glance. "You know the rules."

"Yeah," Jake said. "Some of us are still eating, here."

"Oh, sorry." Cade sat again. "Wouldn't want to get in the way of that."

Jake smiled before he took another bite. Now that his hunger was mostly satisfied he could savor the taste. "I need to make this at the firehouse. I keep meaning to get the recipe from you." He glanced at Rosie. Short and blonde, with a little extra padding here and there, she was the most beautiful woman he knew. And talk about steely determination. She had it in spades.

"She doesn't use a recipe anymore, son." Herb, the person Jake considered his dad for all intents and purposes, was a wiry guy who could do the work of men half his age.

"Herb's right," she said. "I could make tuna casserole in my sleep. Probably have a time or two. But I'll try to come up with some directions for you. It would be a great firehouse meal. I hadn't thought of that."

"Most of the stuff you made for us would go over great at the firehouse. We look for good food that's not too expensive."

"Which is especially important if they all eat as much as you," Cade said.

"Some eat more." It wasn't true but he'd said it to get a reaction out of Cade.

"They do?"

"Oh, yeah. Once a week a semi backs up to the firehouse to unload our groceries. We make our salad in a wheelbarrow and our spaghetti sauce in a sterilized oil drum. In order to cook the pasta we build a fire under an antique bathtub."

Cade stared at him. "That's amazing."

Jake kept a straight face as long as he could but finally burst out laughing, which set off everybody else.

Cade blew out a breath. "Well, it *could* be true. After watching Jake put away food I was willing to believe it."

"I've always loved seeing my boys eat." Rosie beamed at them. "Who's ready for German chocolate cake?"

Jake left his chair and went over to kiss her cheek. "You made my favorite."

"Of course I did. You haven't been home for Christmas in years. We need to celebrate."

Everybody else seemed happy with the prospect of cake, too, but Jake was touched that she'd remembered how much he loved it. He'd never known his own mother but whenever he imagined what she might have been like, he pictured Rosie. A guy couldn't do any better than having a mom like her.

He helped her dish it and, as they were passing out plates, Herb looked over at Cade. "How come the Christmas lights are out? They were on at dusk but I noticed they're out now. Do we need to check the connections?"

"Nah, the connections are fine." Cade flicked a glance at Jake. "We decided to make a few changes in the morning and since no one will be driving up tonight, Finn and I wanted to save the electricity for now. Everything will be operational for Christmas Eve."

"Okay." Herb seemed unconcerned. "I leave that to you boys. I'm sure it'll look great."

"It will." Cade tucked into his cake.

Jake was glad he'd bought the smoke alarms as gifts and the cords and lights could be slipped into the mix without making a big deal of it. But he had more than Christmas lights on his mind. Before they'd all finished their dessert, he brought up the subject that had been nagging him since making the plan with Amethyst. "I'm looking for a sleigh to rent or borrow. Do any of you know of one?"

Cade paused, his fork halfway to his mouth. "What, now you're Santa Claus? Although if you keep eating like that you'll eventually fit the part."

"I invited a woman for a sleigh ride tomorrow afternoon."

Silence descended on the table as all attention swiveled in his direction.

He hadn't worked through this very well. He'd blame the shock of seeing Amethyst in the hardware store, but now he realized that he couldn't ask for a sleigh without offering more of an explanation.

He cleared his throat. "I made a quick run into town before dinner so I could pick up a few...things."

"It's Christmas." Rosie waved a hand as if to relieve him of giving the details. "We all have secrets. But who's the woman?"

"I ran into her when I was in town. Amethyst Ferguson."

Rosie's gaze sharpened. "You dated her in high school."

"For a while."

"You know she's a professional singer now."

"Yes, I know. Now, about this sleigh, I remember we used to hitch Navarre up to a wagon."

"And a couple of times to a toboggan." Finn exchanged a grin with Cade.

Jake ignored him. "I thought he could probably pull a sleigh."

"He could," Herb said, "but there's the slight problem of not having a sleigh for him to pull."

Cade put down his fork. "You know, that takes cojones, bro, inviting a woman on a sleigh ride when you're not in possession of one. I'm impressed."

"Do you know of anybody who has one?"

"Nope, can't say as I do, but I'm still impressed."

Jake figured there was no point in asking Finn and Chelsea. They didn't live here anymore. In desperation, he turned to Rosie. "Mom, do you know of anyone around here who has a sleigh?"

"Not at the moment, but if you need a sleigh, I'll find you one."

3

Luck blessed Jake with a clear sky the next morning. If a snowstorm had blown in, which was always possible in December, reconfiguring the lights would have been impossible. As it was the task wasn't simple, especially wearing gloves. Cade and Finn had woven a complex tapestry of dangerous cords and substandard lights.

Cade had apologized for his screw-up and had tried to take the blame, but Finn had insisted on sharing it. He, Cade and Damon were the triumvirate who'd called themselves the Thunder Mountain Brotherhood in the early days of the foster program. Their loyalty to each other ran deep.

Jake respected that. He'd arrived at the ranch later and, although every guy was now considered part of the brotherhood, the bond wasn't the same as the one shared by the first three. When those boys had come to the ranch there had been no tradition, no sense of belonging to something greater. They'd had to create that for themselves.

His buddies at the fire department had a unique connection because they faced life-and-death situations every day, but again, it wasn't the same. Firefighters could choose to quit and sever that connection. The kids who'd been brought to the ranch after the Thunder Mountain Brotherhood had been established could thank Cade, Finn and Damon for creating a positive and lasting identity for all of them. Once a Thunder Mountain brother, always a Thunder Mountain brother.

They'd nearly finished reconfiguring the lights when Rosie walked out onto the porch. She'd pulled a knit cap down over her ears and held her coat closed instead of zipping it, which meant she was making a brief visit. "I think you boys can quit, now. It's not as if the Pope is coming for a visit."

Jake had to laugh. She still called them boys, probably always would.

"But Lexi will be here." Cade arranged the net lights more evenly on a bush. "That's enough motivation for me."

"I'm sure she'll be very impressed. That's more lights than we've ever had on this house. But you need to finish up. I've found Jake a sleigh."

Jake glanced up, a three-pronged plug dangling from his gloved hand. "That's awesome! Where is it?"

"The Emersons have one, but it's too wide to fit in the back of a pickup. Their ranch isn't that far as the crow flies, so it makes more sense to ride over and get it, anyway. It may not be in the best of shape, so I suggest you take Cade or Finn with you."

"We'll all go," Cade said. "It'll be fun."

Jake gazed at her. "What do you mean, not in the best of shape?"

"It hasn't been used in years. They offered to sell it

to me for fifty bucks, so I said fine. I've always wanted a sleigh."

"Um, if it's only fifty bucks it could be falling apart." Jake didn't want to sound ungrateful but he also didn't plan to take Amethyst out in a sleigh that could collapse any minute.

"I asked them and they said it's functional."

"But if they haven't used it in years, how do they know?"

"That's an excellent point." She shivered and stomped her feet. "But I called everyone I could think of and this is the only one I found. If you'd rather not take a chance on it, I'll call them back and say never mind."

"Don't do that," Cade said. "We'll make it work. I've always wanted a sleigh, too."

"Then you'd better finish the lights and get over there. At the very least it'll need to be cleaned up and Amethyst will be here before you know it."

Jake glanced at the angle of the sun. "You're right. Thanks, Mom."

"You're welcome. If the sleigh doesn't work there's a toboggan in the barn. I seem to remember some people hitching a horse to that once upon a time." She winked and went back into the house.

"Nix on the toboggan idea," Cade said. "You can't make out with a woman on a toboggan."

Finn brushed snow off his gloves. "Might be a safer bet than a fifty-buck sleigh."

"That's what I'm thinking." Jake blew out a breath. "It's liable to be a piece of junk."

"Maybe not." Cade came over and clapped him on the shoulder. "Think positive, bro. Maybe it's a gem that's taking up space they want for something else."

"Or maybe the wood's rotted out and the mice have made a nest in the upholstery."

"One way to find out. I have a feeling we can rehabilitate this sleigh." Cade glanced up at the Christmas lights strung everywhere. "Are we done here?"

"You tell me. You're the one trying to impress your ladylove."

Cade nodded. "I think it'll do. If you two put the ladders away I'll start saddling the horses. I'm betting you're both out of practice."

"I can saddle a horse just fine," Jake said. "How about you, O'Roarke?"

"Never lost my touch. But if Gallagher wants to show off his horse whisperer technique, that's fine with me. Saves me the effort."

"Then I'll get started on that." Cade adjusted the fit of his Stetson and headed down to the barn, his boots crunching through the snow.

Finn collapsed one of the extension ladders with a loud clang before turning to Jake. "You know why he's putting so much emphasis on the decorations this year, right?"

"Haven't a clue other than he wants Lexi to think he's a holiday illumination genius."

"It's more than that. Christmas would be the perfect time for Lexi to propose and the more magical the setting, at least in Cade's mind, the more likely she'll pop the question."

"I see. Makes some kind of crazy sense." Jake was well aware of the interesting dynamic between those two. Cade had asked Lexi to marry him a year and a half ago and she'd gently turned him down. So Cade had put her in charge of proposing. "I hope she does it." He collapsed the other ladder and picked it up. "I've never seen a guy so eager to get married."

"I don't know about that. I'm pretty damned excited about marrying Chelsea. Can't wait for April." He picked up his ladder and they both started toward the barn.

"You don't mind the monkey suit and all the fuss?"

"Not really. Chelsea's family is pretty casual, so it won't be stuffy and formal." He looked over at Jake. "Any chance you can come?"

"You know I'd love to. I have to figure out the finances and then see if I can wrangle time off."

"I understand. I don't expect a lot of the guys will make it up to Seattle, but I'm hoping some do."

"At least now I've met Chelsea. She's terrific."

Finn laughed. "You don't have to tell me. Like I said, can't wait for April."

Jake pondered his two brothers and their anticipated marriages as he and Finn put away the ladders and helped Cade finish saddling up the horses. Both guys clearly wanted that kind of permanence. Jake had no such long-range plans.

He was eager for some private time with Amethyst, but he wasn't thinking beyond that. She was perfect for this stage of his life. Before their hot night in Jackson Hole, he'd dated a few women who had been nice but needy.

His job asked a lot of him. He loved the sense of accomplishment it gave him, but he didn't want to be emotionally responsible for someone on top of the demands at work. With Amethyst he didn't have to worry about that. She was focused on her career and didn't need anyone to take care of her,

That included her approach to sex. She asked for what

she wanted more frankly than anyone he'd been with. He loved that about her. This sleigh deal might or might not work out, but tonight after the festivities, he'd—

"Hey, Fireman Jake, you gonna get on that horse or not?"

Cade's voice cut into his libido-driven thoughts. Damn. Caught daydreaming about Amethyst for the second time in two days. He glanced up at Cade, who was mounted on Hematite, the black horse he'd trailered to the ranch summer before last. Finn was already up on Isabeau, Rosie's mare.

Jake, however, stood beside Navarre, Herb's gelding, while staring into space like an idiot. "Yep. Sorry. Just thinking about something." He swung into the saddle.

"More likely some*one*." Cade chuckled as he led the way to the Forest Service road. From there they'd cut across snow-covered open range to the Emerson place. "From what I remember about Amethyst Ferguson, I don't blame you. I wasn't at the high school Christmas concert where she sang 'Santa Baby' but I heard about it."

Finn laughed. "Didn't we all. Were you there, Jake?"

"I was." The road was deserted so they were able to ride three abreast with Cade in the middle. It felt great to be back on a horse again, especially with two of his brothers along. "We'd stopped dating two weeks before that concert. Bad decision on my part."

"*You* broke it off?" Cade glanced at him in disbelief. "I gave you credit for more brains than that."

"Nope. I was young and stupid. I thought she'd looked at another guy in a provocative way. She denied it, but I had that idea stuck in my head and refused to let the whole thing slide. The truth is, she was too hot for me back then."

"But not now, apparently," Finn said.

"No." Jake smiled. "Not now."

Once they hit open country, they picked up the pace a little, but not much since obstacles could be hidden under the snow and the air was still pretty damned cold. Jake wouldn't want to race through this landscape and create a wind chill effect, but a trot was invigorating. He'd picked up a second job at a stable in Jackson Hole because they were willing to work around his shifts, but he wasn't there to ride. Mostly he mucked out stalls and groomed the horses.

As they approached the Emerson ranch, he could see the sleigh sitting out in front of the barn. From here it didn't look too bad. The red paint job had faded and the runners were dull and rusted in spots, but the sleigh might be salvageable.

He glanced at Cade. "What's that luggage rack thing hanging off the back?"

"I guess that's where you put your picnic basket. If you're going for a sleigh ride you might take along hot cocoa, some cookies, maybe."

"I would do that," Finn said. "Sounds cozy."

Jake didn't think the rack looked sturdy enough to hold anything. "So what do you think of the sleigh itself?"

"A new coat of paint and some rust remover and it'll be a beauty," Cade said.

"I wouldn't know," Finn said. "Sleighs are not my area of expertise."

"Not mine, either," Cade said, "but—"

"Hold it." Jake brought Navarre to a halt. "I thought you knew something about sleighs."

Cade shrugged. "What's to know? It's a wagon on skis."

"Yeah, well, that would be the critical difference, wouldn't it? What if those runners are all messed up? What if they somehow malfunction and throw Amethyst into a ditch where she breaks something important like her neck?"

"Settle down, Fireman Jake. I would hope you're not planning to charge down the Forest Service road like you're running the Iditarod."

"Well, no, but—"

"Then we don't have a problem. All you need is a sleigh that will take you at a sedate pace from the ranch to the Forest Service road and from there to a little side lane where you can drink hot cocoa and make out. Am I right?"

Jake sighed. "Yeah."

"Then no worries. That fifty-buck sleigh will fulfill that mission. Let's find Emerson and close the deal."

Twenty minutes later Jake sat on the hard bench seat with the reins in his hands and Navarre hitched to the sleigh. He suspected there was no upholstery because the mice had actually made a nest in it and Emerson had ripped it out before they arrived. The red paint on the seat hadn't faded at all.

The rest was more pink than red. The sleigh looked a lot shabbier up close and he heartily wished he'd suggested a different entertainment to Amethyst, but it was too late, now. Cade had paid the rancher fifty dollars and the sleigh now belonged to Thunder Mountain.

Cade lifted his hand like the leader of a wagon train. "Move 'em out!"

"Oh, for God's sake." But Jake slapped the reins against Navarre's rump and the sleigh went forward, creaking in protest. "Hey, wagon master, this thing is wobbling."

"Of course it's wobbling." Cade seemed unconcerned. "It hasn't had an outing in ten years."

"Ten?" Jake bid goodbye to his fantasy of a romantic sleigh ride. "I didn't hear that part."

"I pinned him down before I gave him the money and he admitted it hadn't been used in ten years, maybe twelve. Actually, I'm guessing it's more like twenty."

The sleigh shuddered as Jake drove it away from the barn. "Why didn't you cancel the sale?"

"Because I really want a sleigh and this one has good bones."

Finn snorted at that. "You know zip about sleighs and you're able to tell this one has good bones?"

"I predict it has broken bones," Jake said. "We'll be lucky to get it back to the ranch in one piece. We might have to leave it by the side of the road like the pioneers had to dump their pianos."

"We can't do that," Finn said. "Littering is against the law in Wyoming. Which means we'd have to figure out how to haul the carcass back to the ranch so we could use it for firewood."

Cade shook his head. "Boys, boys, boys. Where's your faith in the goodness of the universe? Once we get this sleigh back to Thunder Mountain, and we will, then all it needs is a little TLC and it'll shine like a new penny."

"Or disintegrate like an old newspaper," Jake said.

"We're going over this thing with a fine-tooth comb before I put Amethyst in it. It either passes muster or..." He couldn't come up with an alternative.

"Or the toboggan?" Finn asked.

"No, not that." Jake balked at the idea of leading Amethyst down to the barn where she'd find Navarre hitched to a toboggan. "It was one thing when we were kids goofing around but I'd feel dumb using it now."

"See, the sleigh has to work," Cade said. "It'll provide a romantic touch for you and then later on for me and Lexi. This baby could be the final touch, the gesture that puts Lexi over the top."

Jake exchanged a glance with Finn. No doubt they were both thinking the same thing—Lexi needed to put this poor cowboy out of his misery. But Jake could see Lexi's side. Six years ago Cade had left town, apparently spooked by Lexi's urge to get married. When he'd finally showed up ready to tie the knot, Lexi had become her own woman and wasn't so sure she wanted that arrangement anymore.

Jake didn't understand why Cade couldn't simply enjoy the loving relationship and good sex without insisting on a document legalizing the whole thing. But Cade and Finn were both turning thirty next year, so maybe their itch to get hitched made sense. At twenty-seven, Jake hadn't felt it.

Once they were off the ranch property and moving over uneven hillocks of snow, the sleigh rattled and creaked so much that the guys gave up on conversation. They'd made it nearly halfway back when the runners hit something under the snow and the sleigh lurched to one side. It righted itself, but one of the rattles was now a lot worse.

Jake figured it was the luggage rack. "Hey, Cade," he called out. "Can you drop back and see if we're about to lose a piece of this contraption?"

"Sure." He pulled Hematite to a stop and waited while Jake passed him. Then he dropped in behind the sleigh. "Yeah, I see a few screws missing on the rack. Matter of fact, the whole thing could go, now that I look at the way it's leaning. You'd better hold up so we can evaluate the situation."

"But it's got good bones, right, Gallagher?" Finn wheeled Isabeau around and rode to the back of the sleigh. "Crap, that doesn't look good."

Jake climbed down and trudged through the snow to where his brothers had dismounted to assess the damage. The metal rack dangled, held in place by a couple of screws. The rest were AWOL. "We need to take it off before it falls off."

"With what?" Cade looked at him. "You packing a screwdriver?"

"No. Anybody got a penny? I don't like carrying change so I don't."

"I'm the same about change in my pockets," Finn said. "Bugs me."

Cade shrugged. "I don't have any, either. Maybe we should just keep going and let it fall. It's not like we won't hear it."

"You don't want to do that." Finn pointed to a crack in the wood next to one of the screws. "There's a lot of stress being put on the section where the remaining screws are. Once it goes, it could take a chunk of this back section with it. Then this thing will look like hell."

"Then I have a suggestion." Jake thought the sleigh already looked like hell but saying it wouldn't change anything. "If one of you gets in the sleigh with me, you can lean over the back and hold on to it. The other one can lead the extra horse."

"I'll hold the rack," Cade said. "But, Finn, you need to switch horses. Hematite isn't fond of being behind another horse."

"Then I'll hold the rack and you lead Isabeau," Finn said. "She's a sweetheart who doesn't mind being last." He handed the mare's reins to Cade.

"No, *I'll* hold the rack while Finn drives," Jake said. "If I hadn't invited a woman for a sleigh ride before I had the damn sleigh, we wouldn't be doing any of this."

"But where's the fun in that?" Cade grinned at him. "We're making us some memories right here."

"I guarantee I won't be forgetting this anytime soon." Jake climbed into the bench seat and leaned over to grasp the metal rack. "Better take it slow, O'Roarke. This isn't a real stable position I have, here."

Cade chuckled. "No, but it sure is a photo op. Wish I'd brought my phone so I could take a picture of you riding in that sleigh ass backward."

"Thank God for small favors. Knowing you, you'd put it on the internet."

"Yeah, I would."

Jake listened to the sleigh rattle along. It wasn't as noisy now because he was holding the rack and they were going slower. "Say, Cade, when are Damon and Phil due at the ranch?"

"They were hoping to hit town late this morning and stop by around lunchtime. They could be there now."

"That would be great."

"They'll be tired," Finn said. "And Phil's less than a month away from her due date, which is why they drove to Florida. Just in case you were hoping they could do a quick fix."

"I don't expect that, but they could give me their opinion on whether this thing is roadworthy before Amethyst arrives. How are we doing on time?"

"I'd estimate it's about one fifteen," Cade said. "Give or take."

"Yikes. I hope Amethyst's not early."

But of course she was. As Finn drove the sleigh into the open area in front of the barn, Amethyst climbed out of her yellow SUV. She took one look at Jake's position in the sleigh and started laughing. Terrific. His rep was ruined. Might as well hitch up the toboggan.

4

AMETHYST WOULD RECOGNIZE those buns anywhere. She'd admired them when Jake was seventeen and they'd become even more worthy of a good ogle since then. But the sleigh...oh, my God. She'd assumed when he'd invited her that Thunder Mountain Ranch had a sleigh, probably painted hunter green and brown, the colors of Thunder Mountain Academy.

Apparently, Jake had issued his invitation prematurely. His cheeks were tinged pink as he walked toward her and she doubted the cold was to blame. But, damn, he was gorgeous. Who cared what the sleigh looked like when she could feast her eyes on a muscled cowboy with soulful green eyes and a sculpted mouth that could kiss like nobody's business?

"I have to apologize," he said.

"No, you don't. That entrance was worth the trip out here."

"Yeah, I'll bet. I'm surprised you didn't whip out your phone."

"Wish I had." She wouldn't have minded a permanent

record of Jake's sexy butt. But she'd been too mesmerized to think of it.

"Look, obviously we don't have a working sleigh, so I'm afraid—"

"Don't be hasty, Fireman Jake!" Cade hurried over. "Hey, Amethyst. Good to see you." He touched the brim of his hat.

"Good to see you, too, Cade. I don't think we've run into each other since the last time I saw you at Rangeland Roasters having coffee with Lexi."

"I know. Sheridan's a small town, but you can go months without meeting up with folks who live here."

"And I'm on the road a lot."

"Yeah, I know! Love your music. Lexi and I listen to you all the time. Anyway, I don't want you two to give up on the sleigh ride just yet. Finn's unhitching Navarre so we can get to work on the chassis."

Jake shook his head. "It's no use, Gallagher. It might be salvageable but it'll take days."

"I'm not promising it'll look brand new in five minutes, but Damon and Phil are here and they never go anywhere without tools. It's possible with their help we can clean this baby up, tighten a few screws and she'll be good enough for a little ride down the Forest Service road. Have you had lunch, Amethyst? Rosie always has plenty to eat and you could relax inside while we work our magic."

"Yes, I've had lunch. And, really, we can skip the sleigh ride. I don't want anyone to go to a lot of trouble on Christmas Eve day."

"Me, either," Jake said. "Maybe Amethyst and I could just—"

"Jake, I'm telling you, it won't take much. I'm sure

Mom filled in Damon and Phil over lunch. They'd probably be insulted if we *didn't* ask them."

"I doubt it," Jake said. "They just got back from Florida, dude. And Phil's not in any shape to help."

"All the more reason not to bother them," Amethyst said. "Jake can give me a tour of the place. I've heard so much about it over the years but I've never visited."

"Hey, Jake Ramsey!" Damon's deep voice carried through the crisp air as he strode toward them. "What's this I hear about a fixer-upper sleigh?"

"Hey, Damon." Jake went to meet him. "Just my latest idiotic move."

Amethyst was touched by their warm embrace. She'd always had a soft spot in her heart for the Thunder Mountain boys. Most of them had some tragedy in their background and Jake was no exception. When they were dating she'd learned that his mom had died when he was a toddler and his father had turned into an abusive alcoholic. Jake used to spend his nights wherever he could get away from the beatings, sometimes at the home of a friend and sometimes hidden in the storeroom of Scruffy's Bar.

Jake didn't trust easily. She'd learned that when he'd broken up with her over a stupid misunderstanding. He'd never quite believed that she cared about him and he still might not. But at least they had a sexual connection that made them both happy.

She watched as Jake and Damon walked over to the sleigh. They were both laughing as Damon examined it from all angles. She turned to Cade. "I love your can-do attitude but, seriously, let's forget about the sleigh ride, okay? It was a cute idea but I can live without it."

"But that would mean giving up," Cade said. "Besides, Damon likes to show off his manly carpentry skills."

"That may be true but—"

"In these situations, it's best to sit back and let the Thunder Mountain Brotherhood do its thing."

She let out a breath. "Okay, I'll try."

Damon and Jake continued to joke around as they walked back over to where she stood with Cade.

"Damon's convinced me we need to give this sleigh a chance," Jake said. "So I'm prepared to work with him on it if you're willing to allow us a little time."

"Sure, why not? What do you want me to do?"

"I'm not going to put you to work, if that's what you're thinking. While Damon's assessing the job, let's go inside and see Rosie. I know you've had lunch but she'll have a pot of coffee going and I happen to know there's some German chocolate cake left over from last night."

"That sounds great." Amethyst hadn't known what to expect from this afternoon but she hadn't planned on much alone time with Jake, anyway. She'd popped an antihistamine before driving out here in case she ended up in the same space with Ringo the cat.

"I'll go in with you," Cade said. "I'm starving and I can only imagine your hunger pangs, Fireman Jake. From what I've seen, you need fuel and plenty of it. I'd hate to see you grow weak from lack of food."

"So you all missed lunch?" Amethyst was overwhelmed by the group effort to provide her with a sleigh ride.

"Yeah, but Finn's probably in there wolfing down a sandwich by now," Cade said. "Sad to say, Jake and I haven't taken any sustenance since breakfast."

"Then, by all means, let's all go in so you guys can get fed."

Shortly thereafter Amethyst was seated at Rosie's kitchen table with a mug of coffee and a slice of cake. Jake and Cade each had hefty sandwiches to go with their coffee. Finn had already left to help Damon, but his fiancée Chelsea was there along with Philomena, Damon's redheaded and exceedingly pregnant wife. Ringo, a gray tabby, was curled up in a bed in the corner, but the antihistamine was working so Amethyst was fine.

Jake paused between bites to address his foster mom, who'd joined them with coffee and cake. "Where's Dad?"

"In town, Christmas shopping."

"He still waits until the last minute?"

Rosie laughed. "He claims that's when he feels the Christmas spirit, when everyone in town is racing the clock."

"What he feels is frantic desperation," Cade said. "You couldn't pay me to be in town today."

Jake laughed. "How does two grand sound?"

"Okay, I'd do it for that."

"Case closed." Jake finished his sandwich and pushed back his chair. "Mom, that was wonderful." He glanced over at Amethyst. "Will you be okay for a little while? This shouldn't take long."

"Are you kidding? You're leaving me with interesting women and German chocolate cake. I'll be more than fine." Amethyst discovered she liked seeing him in this setting, surrounded by his foster family. He seemed emotionally stronger and more confident here. She wished he'd brought her to the ranch when they'd been dating but there'd been no reason.

Cade went with him, which left Rosie, Chelsea and Phil at the table with Amethyst.

She knew a little about Phil, who'd worked as a contractor in Sheridan for several years before meeting and falling in love with Damon. But Chelsea was a complete stranger so Amethyst started the conversation by asking about her work and how she'd happened to meet Finn. Turned out they'd been in line for coffee and had started up a conversation that had led to a business relationship and eventually love.

"Chelsea's been so good for him," Rosie said. "He's still very focused on his work, but he's not as driven as he used to be."

"The more I'm around the Thunder Mountain guys," Phil said, "the more I've noticed that most of them have a strong urge to succeed. Considering the crummy background they had, it's not surprising. Damon's mellowing out, finally, which is good. I want him to be able to relax enough to enjoy his kid."

Amethyst had abandoned the idea of having children when she'd decided on her career path, but she was curious all the same. "How's motherhood so far?"

"Disconcerting." Phil laid a hand over her big belly. "Normally, I work side by side with Damon on our renovation jobs, but in the last month that's been increasingly difficult. Life should be easier when she's born. I plan to pack her along on jobs, at least until she's mobile. Then I might need day care."

"So you're having a girl?" Amethyst asked.

"Oh, yeah, and I'm thrilled about that."

"So am I." Rosie sipped her coffee. "This ranch is loaded with testosterone, in case you hadn't noticed."

Amethyst smiled. "I've noticed, but I'm not complaining. I grew up with a sister."

Rosie's gaze warmed. "How's Sapphire doing? From a sister's perspective, I mean. Grady says everything's going well, but I had a little something to do with her decision to move to Cody and I dearly hope it's working out."

"It definitely is. You'll see for yourself tonight when they come to your Christmas Eve party."

"Are you coming?" Chelsea asked.

"Or more to the point," Phil said, "are you staying? You're here for this major-deal sleigh ride, so unless you have plans you might as well stay for the rest of the evening."

Amethyst was struck by the logic of it. She'd considered coming over later with Grady and Sapphire but that might not make any sense. She glanced at the kitchen clock. If the sleigh was cleaned up and ready before three, she'd be amazed. And dusk came early in December.

Then she looked down at her simple top and jeans. "I'm not dressed for a Christmas Eve gala."

Rosie laughed. "Honey, you're at Thunder Mountain Ranch. Around here we pay more attention to the people than the clothes they're wearing. Besides, you look very nice."

"All righty, then. I'd love to stay."

"Great!" Chelsea smiled at her. "Now that we have that settled, I'm dying to ask about your career. I understand you're a professional singer."

"I'm working at it. So far my gigs have all been in Wyoming and that's where I get the bulk of my music sales, too."

Chelsea's expression was animated. "Have you sent out demos?"

"I have, but no takers yet from the studios. I hoping for a big break eventually, but in the meantime I'm giving private voice lessons, mostly to kids. That's fun."

"I'll bet it would be," Phil said. "I love hearing little kids sing. Warms my heart."

"Mine, too." Amethyst smiled as she thought about Jenny, her favorite. "I have one little eight-year-old who has real promise. Cute as a button and that girl can sing. I can't wait to see what happens with her. Then there's a little guy who's only five but he really belts out those tunes. It's adorable. He could go places."

"I wonder if singing is like acting," Chelsea said. "You have to actually be in LA or New York in order to make something happen. Or Nashville if you're doing country."

"Maybe. I'm pop, not country, so it would be New York or LA for me." Amethyst always grew uneasy when this subject came up. "And I would go if I had some interest from one of the major studios. You know, a serious nibble. Moving to the city without that seems pretty darned risky. Sure, I could wait tables, but those are pricey places to live. I'd go through my savings in no time. At least here the cost of living is lower so I can support myself between the gigs I pick up and the private lessons."

"It *is* risky." Rosie got up to bring them all more coffee. "I was worried sick about Finn when he took off for Seattle to open a microbrewery. He didn't know a soul, but he'd researched the market and was convinced that was the best place to be." She gave Chelsea a fond look. "Then he met the right woman and it all worked out."

"He was really lucky," Amethyst said.

"So was I." Chelsea leaned back in her chair. "I'm grateful that he took that risk. I can't imagine my life without him."

"Finn's not the only one who's done that kind of thing," Rosie said. "One of my boys is out in LA right this minute trying to make it as an actor."

"Oh, yeah?" Phil looked over at her. "Who's that?"

"Matt Forrest."

"I remember him from high school!" Amethyst put down her mug and stared at Rosie. "He was a skinny kid one year behind me."

"Well, he's not skinny anymore," Rosie said. "Got a growth spurt, filled out, took some acting classes at the community college. Then he headed to LA. He's been there almost three years now. Like you'd expect, he's had to wait tables and take jobs making commercials. He had one bit part in a small-budget movie and I guess somebody from a major studio liked what they saw. The other day he called to say he was up for something much bigger."

"Wow, I hope he gets it. He seemed like a nice guy the few times I was around him." Amethyst cradled her mug in both hands as she imagined buying a one-way plane ticket to LA or New York and toughing it out for three years. She just didn't like the odds. "What I'm hoping is that I'll have some talent scouts in the audience one of these times. Entertainment folks often vacation in Wyoming."

"They do," Phil said. "They even buy homes here. Damon and I have done some renovations for some Hollywood types. Behind-the-camera people, not anyone you'd recognize."

"I've had some celebrity spottings in Seattle," Chelsea said. "It's always a thrill."

After that the conversation turned to actors, movies and which ones might win an Oscar, but Amethyst kept thinking about Matt Forrest. Maybe she was making a big mistake by not relocating to LA and hiring an agent. New York seemed like a different country to her, but LA wasn't *that* far from Wyoming.

"Sleigh's ready!" Cade came into the kitchen grinning. "Come on down!"

Amethyst glanced at him. "So where's Jake?"

"He's still fiddling with it, but Damon has declared it operational and Finn's hitching up Navarre."

"Then let's go take a look." Phil groaned as she rose from her chair. "At times like this I wish the stork brought the kid, after all."

Cade helped her on with her coat. "Aw, Phil, last I heard you loved being pregnant."

"That was last month. I've revised my opinion."

Once they were all bundled up, they walked down to the barn. Finn was hitching a brown horse to a sleigh that Amethyst thought didn't look half-bad. The rack Jake had been holding in place when they'd pulled in was gone and the dust and grime had been wiped away. If the sleigh didn't exactly sparkle, at least it looked clean.

Blankets had been piled onto the seat and allowed to spill over the edges, which covered some of the more faded parts of the chassis. Damon and Jake crouched near the back, each with a screwdriver as they tightened the struts attached to the runners.

Damon stood as they approached. "Your chariot awaits, milady."

"It's a huge improvement." She smiled at him. "Thank you for all the hard work."

"It didn't take much to make it serviceable. Making it pretty will require a lot longer."

"But we'll do it," Cade said. "Before we're finished you won't recognize this sleigh."

"We could put the Academy students to work on it," Rosie said. "That's if Damon or Phil would be willing to supervise."

"What a brilliant idea!" Phil beamed at her. "I volunteer to supervise. I'm going crazy sitting at home while Damon does all the fun stuff."

Damon rolled his eyes. "Yeah, she is. Great suggestion, Rosie." Then he turned back to the sleigh. "Your passenger has arrived, Ramsey. The runners are fine for now."

"Just making sure of that. Don't want us taking a header into a snowbank."

"You won't if you drive slow and easy."

Cade laughed. "You don't have to worry about it. Enter the word *cautious* into your browser and Fireman Jake will be staring back at you."

"Okay, okay. I get the point." Jake stood and walked over to Damon. "Here's your screwdriver, bro. Thanks for stepping in." Then he turned to Amethyst. "Ready?"

"You bet." She let him hand her into the sleigh while everyone stood around watching. She had the oddest feeling, as if they were a newly married couple leaving on their honeymoon. To her great surprise, she wasn't horrified by the image.

When he walked around the sleigh, climbed in next to her and took the reins, the feeling grew stronger. This was only a sleigh ride, she reminded herself. They'd be back in an hour or so.

"Have fun!" Rosie called out as Jake slapped the reins against the horse's rump and the sleigh began to move.

"We will!" Amethyst turned and waved, and they all waved back. She waited until they'd gone through the pasture gate and were far enough away that no one could hear before she spoke. Even then she kept her voice down. "Just so you know, we can't have sex on this sleigh ride."

He chuckled. "Is that so?" He kept his eyes on the path ahead. "Why not?"

She forced herself to resist that sexy chuckle. And the way his gloved hands on the reins reminded her of how he'd touched her last summer. "I'm not going right home afterward. Phil suggested I stay for the Christmas Eve celebration."

"That's great, but what does it have to do with anything?"

"If we have sex, I'll get all rumpled and kissed-looking. I'll have no way to repair the damage. When I walk back into the ranch house, everyone in your family will know what we've been doing."

"And you'd be embarrassed. I get that."

She sighed in relief. "Good. Because otherwise I'd want to."

"That's nice to hear."

"But I like the sleigh ride. I've never had one before. Cozy."

"Mmm."

"Thank you for going to so much trouble."

"You're welcome." He drove the sleigh in silence for a little while. "What if I told you we could have sex and you wouldn't end up all 'rumpled and kissed-looking'? Would you want to?"

"How could you manage that?" Her body began to hum.

"Trust me when I say I could. I learned early how to cover my tracks."

Her heartbeat accelerated. "I see."

"Kissing is fantastic, especially with you, but it's not a requirement for what I have in mind."

"I suppose not." Moisture dampened her panties.

"Well?" He glanced at her. Although his hat cast a shadow over his green eyes, the heat shimmering there was unmistakable.

She swallowed. "I think I'd be a fool to say no."

5

JAKE HAD BEEN hard as an ax handle ever since they'd gone through the pasture gate and escaped the watchful eyes of his family. He hadn't expected Amethyst to lay down a no-sex rule, but once she'd explained her reasons, he'd understood. Then he'd set to work figuring a way around the issue.

Not kissing her as a warm-up would seem strange, but he'd forgo that if it meant he'd be able to make the connection his body had ached for since she'd driven away from Jackson Hole. He'd considered asking someone else out. After all, he hadn't known whether he'd ever have that experience again with Amethyst, which made celibacy ridiculous.

But that red-hot memory had seared itself into his brain and he couldn't imagine taking another woman to bed until he knew for sure Amethyst was lost to him. Turned out she wasn't the least bit lost. She was right beside him and as eager for him as he was for her.

Fortunately smoke alarms hadn't been the only thing he'd picked up during his quick trip to town. After discovering that she was willing to make time for him, he'd added a quick trip to the drugstore. He'd tucked a condom in his jeans' pocket this morning to make sure he didn't forget.

As the sleigh's runners whispered over the ice and snow on the Forest Service road, he listened for any signs that the struts weren't holding. So far, so good.

But one question nagged him and he finally had to ask it. "Have you dated anybody since Jackson Hole? If you have, that's fine. It's been six months and I can't expect you to—"

"Nobody, Jake."

Music to his ears. "Me, either. Please don't think I'm trying to turn this into a commitment because we were both clear on that."

"There's no commitment," she said softly. "But, face it, that night was crazy. I couldn't imagine duplicating that with anyone else. So I didn't bother looking around."

"Neither did I."

"But you're gorgeous and you must have women who—"

"First of all, thanks, and second of all, none of them interested me. I know we're not making any promises, but compared to you, everyone else is boring."

She laughed. "Every woman wants to hear that at least once in her life! I appreciate the sentiment more than you know. But, Jake, what if even we can't duplicate what we had in Jackson Hole? What if that was a special time that will never happen again?"

"I don't believe that."

"And I certainly don't want to, but think back to August."

"I do. All the time."

"We hadn't seen each other in years and suddenly

we're fulfilling all of these fantasies. Maybe that's the best it'll ever be."

"You're depressing the hell out of me, Amethyst. No wonder some of your love songs are so sad."

She laughed again. "I just wonder if we should be realistic about this."

"You go ahead and be realistic. At the moment my cock aches so much that I don't care whether the sex is good or bad. I just want to have it."

"Wow, okay. I'm fairly desperate myself."

"You are?" He took heart from that. "Then help me look for a road that goes off to the right. It goes down a ways and then there's a wide spot where I can turn the sleigh around. We don't want to get stuck."

"You're taking me to one of your old make-out spots, aren't you?"

"Yes."

"You never brought me out here." She sounded miffed about it.

"It was too far from your house. Besides, you always made me nuts. I was afraid if I brought you to some secluded place like this I'd lose control."

"But I wanted you to! Jake, you were my choice, the one I wanted to give my virginity to."

That stunned him. "I was?" His deeply imbedded cautious streak had drawbacks, and this would be one of them. "So who…"

"Not Eddie, the one you thought I was making eyes at. I never dated him, never wanted to. We were joking around. I heard from him a few months ago. He's come out."

"He's gay?"

"A lot of us suspected it."

"Not me." And he'd caused her grief because he'd been a bonehead. "I'm sorry, Amethyst."

"It worked out for the best. If we'd kept dating that could have changed—hey, is that your turnoff?" She pointed to a narrow road leading into the woods.

"That's it." He pulled Navarre to a stop and gazed at the snowbank blocking the road. Looked like a plow had come through recently. "Damn."

She turned to him, her blue eyes sparkling. Today she'd worn a blue knit cap that matched her eyes. "What's wrong with right here?"

"On the main road?"

Reaching over, she cupped his face in her gloved hands. "I love it when you get that shocked look in your eyes. Makes me want to do outrageous things with you."

"Oh." His breathing rate picked up and his cock pressed painfully against his fly. He remembered her seductive gaze and how effectively it could erase all his misgivings.

"No one is out here but us." She stroked her thumbs over his cheeks as her eyes glowed with excitement. "Tell me what to do."

He barely had enough air to speak. "Take off everything from the waist down."

"Okay."

The air was perfectly still, not a breeze or a bird chirping or the rumble of an approaching vehicle. The only sound was the soft rustle of Amethyst removing her clothes. Golden light filtering through the trees told him sunset was approaching.

Before he could stop himself he'd pulled off his gloves and reached beneath the blankets. When he encountered warm, silky skin, he groaned. "Hold still. Let me…"

Her breath caught. "Oh, Jake."

"It's been so long." He slipped his hand between her thighs, his gaze locked with hers. "So long since I've touched you."

"I know."

"So long since I've made you come." Sliding his fingers deep, he began stroking her in the sensuous rhythm he'd learned that she needed.

With a soft moan she lifted her hips, inviting him deeper as heat blazed in her eyes. "I've...missed you."

"I'm here." He coaxed her higher and gloried in the flush on her cheeks and the way her lips parted in anticipation of...yes!

She surrendered with a soft cry of release, her body trembling and her breath coming in short gasps.

He wanted to kiss her more than he wanted to breathe, but he'd promised not to muss her, so he slowly eased away. Desire rushed through him with such force that his next movements were clumsy. Somehow he retrieved the condom from his jeans before letting them fall to the floor of the sleigh. Once his cock was free he had trouble tearing the foil on the condom.

A soft murmur sounded next to his ear. "Can I help?"

"No." He felt her body heat. Then her fingers brushed his thigh. *"Don't."*

"But I want—"

"Don't touch me, Amethyst. I'll go up in flames."

"I love hearing you come, Jake."

"And I'm really close." He wondered if he'd ever tell her she was the only woman who made him react with such intensity. He rolled on the condom. "I should..." He paused to gulp in air. "I should sit in the middle."

"Good idea." She moved to the far edge of the bench seat to make room for him.

He slid over. "Now."

"Can I touch you?"

His laughter was strained. "Gonna have to."

"We'll never forget this." She turned to face him and put one hand on his shoulder.

"I wouldn't want to."

Her eyes simmered with passion as she slid one bare leg over his thigh. "Me, either."

He shuddered. "I would love to kiss you."

"I would love to kiss you, too." She gripped his shoulders and balanced on her knees. "But I like knowing this will be our secret."

"Yeah."

"Grab hold of my hips."

He closed his eyes and savored the curved perfection of her body. "My fingertips remember you."

"My body remembers your fingertips." Her voice was husky. "Now show me the way to my favorite place."

He opened his eyes so he could see the response in hers. Carefully he guided her until she was poised above his waiting cock. Then he urged her downward until the tip made contact. Her pupils widened and a murmur of pleasure escaped her lips.

His heart beat like a wild thing. "You're in charge."

Looking into his eyes, she began a slow descent. She swallowed. "We need to do this more often."

He nodded. Forming words at a moment like this was beyond him. He concentrated on holding back when all he wanted to do was thrust upward and claim his release. That wouldn't be fair. She'd agreed to this crazy stunt and she deserved all the enjoyment he could give her.

By the time they were locked together she was panting. Then he felt a ripple over his cock. Thank God. She wasn't far behind him.

"This won't take long." Her breathy words were followed by a groan. "Not long at all." And she began to ride him, slowly at first and then faster.

Because he had his hands full of Amethyst, he couldn't control the blankets. They slid to the floor of the sleigh. He didn't care. The friction she was creating between them was generating enough heat that he wouldn't be surprised if the snow surrounding them melted away.

"I'm coming. I'm coming, Jake." She gasped for breath.

"I know." He felt her tremors and abandoned himself to the needs pounding through his body. "Amethyst... *Amethyst*." His spasms blended with hers. Oh, yes, he remembered this, too, the incredible feeling of sharing a climax with her. Something magical happened in that moment, something he'd never had with another woman. For a short space of time, they became one.

At least he thought they did. He'd never asked her about it because they'd agreed on the parameters. They'd enjoy a fun sexual relationship whenever it was convenient. Magic didn't figure into it. A meeting of souls didn't figure into it, either. She'd probably laugh if he started talking that kind of nonsense.

Eventually they both caught their breath and could focus well enough to look at each other. They both smiled.

"So good," he murmured.

Her gaze was soft. "Better than I remember."

"And that's saying something." He sighed. "Normally

I'd kiss you right now," he said. "But there's nothing normal about this situation."

"No, but it was fun."

"And satisfying."

"Very." She moved away from him with considerate delicacy. "Over to you. The next part is your department."

"I thought of that. All I need is my jeans, if you'd be willing to find them on the floor."

"Sure." She reached down and picked them up. "Better get dressed quick and wrap up in a blanket before the heat wears off."

"Yes, do that." He located the bandanna in his back pocket and used it to take care of the condom. "I don't want you getting chilled on Christmas Eve."

"And thanks to you I won't be frustrated." She wiggled into her jeans. "I wondered if I'd spend the evening in a constant state of arousal. But I should be okay."

"I'm not sure I will be. This might have only whetted my appetite for you."

She paused to gaze at him. "Are you saying we'll be worse off than we were before?"

"That might not be possible." He put on his jeans. "I was a desperate man."

"In a sleigh with a desperate woman."

"Who announced we couldn't have sex!"

She laughed. "Obviously, I wasn't thinking creatively. In my experience a great round of sex leaves the participants looking pretty ragged."

He finished putting on his boots and glanced over at her. "For the record, you look fantastic."

"Yes, but can you tell I've had sex?"

"I can, but I have inside intel."

"Pretend you didn't. Do you think you'd know?"

"Your cheeks are very pink."

"It's cold outside."

"And your eyes sparkle."

"It's Christmas Eve. My eyes always sparkle on Christmas Eve. I love this time of year."

"Me, too." He arranged the blankets over them, put on his gloves and repositioned his hat, which had stayed on through the entire incident. "I'm loving it more every minute."

"So what if I hadn't followed you into the hardware store? Would you have called or texted?"

Taking hold of the reins, he executed a maneuver that wasn't particularly elegant but got them headed back to the ranch. "Honestly, no. On the drive into town I'd made up my mind not to contact you. Then I turned around and there you were."

"Then let's make a bargain. If either of us is going to be in the other person's area, we'll send a text even if we're worried about interrupting something. If so, the one being contacted can always say it's a bad time."

"You're right. But we need complete honesty. If you've lost interest or found someone else, I want to know that. I don't want to hear that it's a bad time if it'll never be a good time again."

Reaching under the blanket, she squeezed his thigh. "I can't imagine losing interest."

"I can't, either, especially when you put your hands on me."

"That bothers you?"

"You have no idea. But I only brought one condom." She sighed. "Which is fine because they'll be expecting us back. But after the party's over, are you coming to my place?"

"I'd like that."

"You're invited. Maybe then we can finally have noisy sex."

That made him laugh. "You've been craving more noise?"

"Sort of. In the hotel room we had to be considerate of the people in the adjoining rooms. Out here we couldn't be yelling because sound carries and someone might call the sheriff."

"That can happen when you're making out in the boonies." He could think of one embarrassing incident when he'd been attending community college and had brought a woman out here. She'd been vocal and he'd almost been arrested.

"Yes, I know."

"Mmm." He didn't want to think of her having sex in the woods with someone else. Yet he'd had sex in the woods with someone else. They were both adults with a history, so what was his problem?

"That was an interesting sound."

"Was it?"

"If I didn't know better, I'd say it was the sound a man makes when he's jealous."

He had to chew on that for a moment. "Being jealous of someone you're not seeing anymore would be dumb, but I…" Gazing at her, he felt a tug at his heart that had nothing to do with excellent sex and everything to do with stronger, deeper emotions he wasn't prepared to discuss.

But that didn't mean he couldn't ask for what he needed to see if she'd go along with it. "Last summer we agreed that we'd meet up when we could, no obligations, which left us free to date—or, more accurately, have sex with…someone else in the meantime."

"True."

"Turns out I'm not happy with that idea. I actually hate it. But I didn't realize that until now." He took a deep breath. "So I propose a new arrangement. If it doesn't suit you, I need to know."

She nodded, although she seemed wary. "Fair enough."

"My plan is to see each other more often and agree not to have sex with anyone else unless we're ready to end the relationship, loose though it may be."

"Then we'd make definite plans to be together?"

"Would that bother you?"

"If you're asking if the prospect of more time with you and more regular sex would bother me, the answer is no. If you're asking if a more formal arrangement bothers me, the answer is yes. I realize I'm contradicting myself."

He completely understood her reluctance. "I'm not working up to marriage, Amethyst. I know your plans don't lead in that direction. But going six months without holding you in my arms is too damned long."

"I've missed you, too." She smiled. "FYI, I have a gig in Jackson Hole for New Year's."

"You do? That's great! Why didn't you let me know when you booked it?"

"I didn't want to interfere if you'd found someone special you wanted to take out for New Year's Eve."

"I have and she's you. I'll be there for that show and afterward we'll celebrate."

"But no strings."

"Absolutely no strings except one. No getting naked with someone else for now."

"I don't want to, anyway."

He let out a sigh of relief. "Good." Spending more time with her would strengthen those feelings that he couldn't talk about. Logically only a fool would want to be with someone who would ultimately leave, but when it came to Amethyst, logic went out the window.

6

AMETHYST HELPED JAKE carry the blankets into the tack room and while he unhitched Navarre she folded and stacked them on an empty shelf. Her body still hummed from her amazing orgasms and she looked forward to many more in the future.

Although Jake would have to leave after Christmas, she'd see him again on New Year's. Getting together on Valentine's Day seemed like a fine idea and she'd be sure to suggest it. Life had suddenly become a lot more interesting.

Being with Jake had always seemed right, even at seventeen. But if she'd been granted her wish and he'd been her first, life could have turned out very differently for both of them. At that age she hadn't been sure a professional career was for her. A college music professor she'd idolized had told her she had the talent to make it, but if she'd been madly in love with Jake at the time, she might not have listened.

The barn door opened, letting in a blast of cold air. "I'll give him a quick rubdown in his stall," Jake called out as he came into the barn leading Navarre.

"Go on down there. Let me get the door." She hurried past him and pulled it closed.

"Thanks. Could you please grab the grooming caddy? It's that plastic thing with all brushes and currycombs in it."

"Will do." She wasn't an expert on horses, but she recognized what he was talking about and took it down from a shelf. She'd always liked the earthy smell of barns and the sounds of horses moving around in their stalls. She and Sapphire had done some riding as kids but they hadn't kept it up as adults.

Jake had left Navarre's stall door open so she walked right in. As the horse munched on a flake of hay, Jake stroked his glossy brown neck and murmured to him.

"I hope you're telling him how much we appreciate him pulling the sleigh," Amethyst said.

"I am." Jake glanced up and smiled. "Navarre was my favorite when I lived here."

"He's been around that long?"

"Sure has. He and Isabeau were about eight when I came to the ranch, so they must be twenty-five or six by now."

"Wow, should we have hitched him to the sleigh at his age?"

"Absolutely. Some horses live to be forty. He's still in his prime."

"Now that you mention it, he doesn't look old at all. I love that he and Isabeau are named after the characters in *Ladyhawke*. Do you know who came up with that?"

"I'm pretty sure Mom and Dad named them. They're both romantics at heart."

"That's not hard to believe." She held up the tote. "Where do you want the caddy?"

"You can put it down right there. I'll come get what I need." He placed his hand on Navarre's rump as he walked around him and came toward her.

She loved Jake's hands—so strong and yet so tender. Having exclusive access to him and his talented hands in her hotel room last summer had been a dream come true. He'd had a knack for caressing a woman when he was seventeen, which had been one of many reasons she'd wanted him to be her first lover. Since then he'd turned his natural talent into an art form.

When she looked up at him, she had a feeling his thoughts weren't far from hers. The brim of his hat shadowed his eyes, but that didn't diminish the force of his gaze.

He shoved his hands into his coat pockets and swallowed. "It's taking all the self-control I have not to haul you into my arms and kiss you. Which would be stupid after what we just went through."

She mirrored him and tucked her hands into her pockets, too. "Maybe I should wait in the tack room until you're finished."

His attention drifted to her mouth and his breathing quickened. "Don't you have lipstick stashed somewhere?"

"In my purse, which I left in the house. Bad move."

"Very bad move. But don't go away." His voice roughened. "I'd rather have you here."

"Okay."

"This won't take long." He stepped back and reached into the tote for a cloth. "I just want to give him a little rubdown. He deserves it."

"That's for sure." As she imagined him doing the same to her, the atmosphere in the barn became too warm for comfort. She tucked her knit cap in her coat pocket and unwound the matching scarf from around her neck.

She shouldn't watch while Jake rubbed the supple cloth over Navarre's coat. It would only remind her of the time he'd gently used a washcloth on her body while they'd stood together in the shower during their memorable night together. Thinking of that, she unbuttoned her coat and took a deep breath.

He moved the cloth over the horse with the same circular motion he'd used when he'd massaged her slick skin. He'd teased her until she'd been wild for him. Then he'd lifted her out of the tub and onto a thick bath mat.

She hadn't quite fit but it hadn't mattered. Slippery as seals, they'd made love on the bathroom floor. They'd laughed like children until they'd been caught in the grip of passion. She'd never come as hard for any man as she did for Jake. Every time.

"What are you thinking about?"

Startled, she opened her eyes. She hadn't realized she'd closed them.

Jake's hands rested on the horse's back as if he'd paused in midmotion when he'd glanced over at her. "Never mind," he said softly. "I have a pretty good idea."

Desire tightened her core. "I—"

"The last time I saw that expression, you were standing in the shower." He wadded up the cloth. "I'm done here." Giving Navarre a final pat, he walked over and dropped the cloth in the caddy. His voice was low as he stood looking at her, his hands shoved firmly in his pockets. "How you tempt me, Amethyst Ferguson."

"I didn't mean to."

"I know. You don't even have to try." He took a shaky

breath. "Would you please put that stuff in the tack room? I'll meet you up there."

"Sure." She grabbed the caddy and walked out of the stall on rubbery legs.

Considering the level of heat they generated, she wondered if they'd be able to lock it down long enough to enjoy the Christmas Eve celebration. He needed to be there but she didn't, so maybe she could feign a headache and go home. Then he could drive to her place once he could get away.

She put the caddy back where she'd found it and took several calming breaths. Much as she'd love to experience Christmas Eve at the ranch house, driving home would be a safer option. She just had to retrieve her purse or ask Jake to bring it to her.

Water started running at the opposite end of the barn, which probably meant Jake was washing his hands prior to going in to the party. No doubt he looked forward to celebrating with his family. She'd been looking forward to it, too, especially because watching him in that setting warmed her heart. She wondered if he'd be disappointed or relieved if she backed out.

The sound of his boots on the wooden barn floor made her heart beat faster. If he affected her that way simply by walking toward her when she couldn't even see his handsome self, how could she expect to behave normally during the party? Instead of satisfying her hunger, the brief episode in the sleigh had whetted her appetite for more.

She stepped out of the tack room. Like her, he'd unbuttoned his coat and he looked determined, like a man on a mission. "Before we leave, we need to discuss something."

"Sure." He stopped a couple of feet away. "Shoot."

That's when she noticed he had a wet bandanna in one hand. Apparently he'd rinsed it out and disposed of the condom. She was glad men had to think of such things and she didn't. "Jake, I have a problem."

"What's that?"

"I can't look at you without fantasizing that we're having sex."

He smiled. "I don't consider that a problem."

"It is when we're hanging out with your family! So I think maybe I should pretend to have a headache and go home. Then you can come to my house when—"

"Whoa, whoa. You want to skip the party?"

"No, I'd love to go, but I'm worried that my thoughts will be written all over my face like they were a while ago."

"You know what? I doubt anyone but me would be able to tell what you were thinking. Don't worry about it."

"They might, and I do worry about it. At least I've figured out why I'm so obsessed. That's some comfort."

His smile widened. "I can't help it if I'm sexy as hell."

"That's not it."

"It's not? Now that's disappointing."

"Well, it sort of is the problem, but the bigger issue is that in August we went straight from having drinks to having an entire night of sex. We didn't interact with anyone."

His eyes darkened and he stepped closer. "Yeah, it was pretty damn hot having all that uninterrupted time to get reacquainted."

"But don't you see? That's what plays in my head when I look at you. I don't know how to be with you in a crowd of people. I just want you alone and naked!" She was alone with him right now but she didn't have any hope that he'd get naked. That didn't mean she wasn't thinking about it.

"Always alone?" His eyebrows lifted. "That could be tricky."

She considered that. "Unrealistic, huh?"

"I guess it could be arranged, but it limits what we can do together." He reached over and fingered a strand of her hair. "I have a different theory."

"What?" Even though he was only touching her hair, she shivered. He also had a telltale gleam in his eyes that she remembered very well.

"We had one amazing night of sex and then didn't see each other for five months. No wonder we're both obsessed with being naked again. We wouldn't be so desperate if we hadn't let so much time go by."

"That makes sense, I guess."

"But that's a future fix, and this is now. I'd like you to be there tonight. We went through a lot of trouble not to muss you up so you could take part in the celebration without being embarrassed."

"True." She swallowed. "But the thing is, I still want you."

"I know." He touched her cheek. "It's written all over your face."

"See?"

"I do, although I still say nobody else would. But we don't have to go inside yet. Let's step into the tack room."

Her breath caught. "Why? You said you didn't have any more—"

"I don't. I left the box in my truck, which is down by the cabin I'm staying in. But that doesn't mean we can't enjoy ourselves." Taking her lightly by the shoulders, he gently backed her through the door. Then he closed and locked it before turning to her. "That's why I washed up." He took off his coat and tossed it aside. Then he helped her out of hers. "I felt a little cheated this afternoon."

Her heart raced and she had trouble getting her breath. "Because you couldn't touch my breasts?"

"Yes, ma'am." He laid her coat across a nearby saddle and hung his hat on the horn. "You have your fantasies and I have mine. Your beautiful breasts are a big part of my memories of that night." He pulled her knit shirt over her head.

Of course she let him do it. Now that he'd begun, she wanted his hands on her, even if that didn't lead to anything. "How will this help?"

"Trust me, it will." After unhooking her bra, he took that off, too. Then he stepped back and sighed. "Even prettier than I remembered." He swallowed. "I never saw you like this." Closing the gap between them, he wrapped one arm around her waist and cradled her breast in his other hand as his hot gaze found hers. "We stripped down so fast and then didn't put on clothes until morning."

She slipped her arms around his neck. "I couldn't get enough of you."

"We couldn't get enough of each other." As he caressed her, he leaned down, his lips nearly making contact. "And this would be the moment when normally I'd kiss you and thrust my tongue deep into your inviting wet mouth. But I can't."

Desire poured like lava through her veins. "There are other places you can kiss me."

"I know." His voice was thick with anticipation. "That

was my plan." Releasing her breast, he hoisted her up and carried her to the shelf where she'd stacked the blankets. "Pull those down."

"I just—"

"I know. Pull them down."

She grabbed the bottom one and jerked so the entire pile tumbled to the floor.

"Perfect." Crouching, he laid her against the mound of blankets. Then he dropped to his knees and braced his hands on either side of her shoulders. "You know what I remember? You giving me directions."

She flushed at the memory of her boldness. "You didn't need them. You know what you're doing."

"I still loved having you tell me what you liked. Tell me again."

"You don't remember?"

"I remember everything. Tell me, anyway." His voice grew husky. "Hearing you say what you want gets me hot."

Reaching up, she combed a lock of silky hair back from his forehead. "I'd never done that before."

"Never?"

"That sexy person everyone thinks I am? It's an act. But that night, with you, it wasn't."

His gaze searched hers. "And now?"

"I like letting go with you, Jake. You make me feel safe."

"And you make me feel a hundred feet tall. I didn't know. I thought…"

"Just you."

Leaning down, he kissed her forehead, her nose and both cheeks before looking into her eyes. "I'm humbled."

She smiled. "But now I'm going to get you hot." Her voice became a soft purr. "Start with your tongue."

His eyes darkened. "Yes, ma'am." He slid lower. "Keep talking."

"Circle slowly to the center," she murmured.

He licked her so sensuously that she squirmed against the blankets and began to pant. "Now take...my nipple into your mouth. Suck gently." She gasped. "Then harder...yes, like that, like *that*. And nip me, Jake. Tug on my...oh, yeah, do that...more...again." The pressure began to build.

His breathing was ragged and his hot breath scorched her skin. "What else? Tell me what you want."

"Make me...make me come."

"Gladly." He unfastened her jeans and pulled the zipper down. In seconds his hand was inside her panties and his fingers began working their magic as he continued to suck hard on her breast.

Oh, yes, she remembered the creative play of Jake's fingers, how he would thrust and twist and press and massage until she lost her mind. She was moments away. "Jake..."

"Don't scare the horses."

"I won't." Gritting her teeth, she arched upward. Not making noise as her body convulsed in a Jake-induced orgasm was a challenge. She managed it with only a few whimpers and soft moans. Then she sank down to the pile of blankets in a grateful heap.

He'd said this would help, and it would certainly help her, but she was worried about how such a passionate episode would affect him. She'd spent many naked hours with this man and surely he was frustrated beyond belief.

After she'd recovered her wits, she asked him. "What about you?"

"Don't think about that. I'll be fine."

"I don't believe you."

"My main concern was you. I don't want you to bail on the Christmas Eve celebration because you're not sexually satisfied. Are you okay now?"

"I feel like a limp rag doll. Is that what you were going for?"

He chuckled. "More or less."

"But that doesn't address your condition. Unless I don't know you at all, you have an erection the size of Devil's Tower."

"Not a problem."

Sliding a hand between them, she fondled him, something she'd loved doing when they'd spent the night together. "I think it is a problem. You're erect and ready to rock and roll. What's your plan for that?"

"I'll control the situation."

"Wrong answer. You just gave me a climax so that I could handle the evening without fixating on you all night. It's only fair that I return the favor."

"But you can't. That would ruin your lipstick."

"Believe me, I so regret not thinking ahead on that score. But help me figure this out, Jake. Tell me what I can do for you."

7

JAKE WANTED AMETHYST with the heat of a thousand suns, especially now when he knew that her uninhibited behavior was a special gift only for him. He'd never dreamed that was the case. Later, when he wasn't so jacked up, he'd take time to think about what it meant.

But at the moment he wasn't thinking at all. She was right about his condition, although he hesitated to take the route that was staring him in the face. He'd waited for a discreet moment to dispose of the condom and rinse out the bandanna. He hadn't had that moment until he'd sent Amethyst to the tack room with the caddy.

The damp bandanna was back in his coat pocket. If Amethyst insisted on somehow evening the score, the bandanna was available. He wasn't sure how he felt about using it. Yet she'd been honest about her needs. Was he going to respond with some macho denial of his? That didn't seem fair, either.

"Just a sec." He got up, retrieved his coat and took out the bandanna. Asking for what he needed wouldn't be easy. He hadn't felt this vulnerable in a very long time. Dropping down beside her on the pile of blankets, he held out the bandanna. "I—" He paused to clear his throat. "I washed this out. You can—"

"Brilliant." Her blue eyes shone. "I certainly can. Lie back."

He stretched out on the blankets with a soft groan. Then he had to clench his jaw against coming as she pulled down his zipper and freed his aching cock.

"I felt a little cheated this afternoon, too," she murmured as she wrapped her warm fingers around the base. "You're magnificent."

"And desperate."

"I know." She began to stroke him with a touch that was light but devastatingly effective.

In no time he began to tremble. Her lipstick issue was minor compared to his idiocy in packing one lone condom. He should have remembered that having her once would only mean he'd want her again, and soon. He should have learned that last summer.

His chest heaved. "Almost…there."

"Don't scare the horses." A hint of laughter rippled through her words.

"Won't." He gasped and swore. *"Now."* Fists clenched, he did his best not to thrust upward, not to yell and not to cuss. He failed in that last part as he came, and came, and came some more. The force of his orgasm was so overwhelming that he barely felt the cool bandanna.

Eyes closed, he lay panting and completely undone. He'd never asked a woman to perform that maneuver. He'd either foregone the pleasure or taken care of it himself once he was alone.

Her breath whispered against his ear. "Be right back." By the time he figured out she was going to rinse out his bandanna, she was already gone. He wondered if she'd traversed the length of the barn topless. Even if she hadn't, he hoped she wouldn't run into anyone.

The horses already had been given their evening meal, which was why he'd decided fooling around in the tack room would go unnoticed. Because it could be locked from the inside and was normally left open, a closed and locked door had come to mean something specific to Thunder Mountain guys.

Zipping his pants and getting to his feet, he noticed that Amethyst's coat was gone but her bra and shirt were still there. She'd obviously hurried to accomplish the chore. That touched him.

She walked in and gave him a smile. "Feeling better?"

He laughed and walked over to her. "Yes, ma'am. The patient is gonna live, after all. Thank you." He caught her around the waist with one hand and reached behind her to lock the door. "Good thing you didn't run into anyone while you were on walkabout."

"I had my story ready. I was going to tell them I had a little motion sickness on the sleigh ride."

"I remember that from high school. No Tilt-A-Whirl for you." He unbuttoned her coat and slipped his hands inside to caress her plump breasts. "Pretty flimsy story, though. A sleigh ride isn't exactly the Tilt-A-Whirl."

"They might have believed me, depending on who it was. I can be very convincing."

"Apparently." He gazed into her eyes and watched them grow smoky with desire as he fondled her. "All along I thought you were way more experienced than me. It seemed so obvious from watching you perform. Your songs can be really hot."

"Sex sells."

"But then we went up to the room and you were amazing in bed. You suggested positions I'd never heard of."

"Because I read." She sighed and leaned into his touch. "With you, I could finally relax and try some of those things I'd read about. And if you keep that up much longer, I'll want to do them with you right here and now."

"So will I." Reluctantly he let her go and stepped back. "We should get going. We've already been gone long enough that someone might start to wonder where we are."

"And come looking for us." She slipped out of her coat and reached for her bra.

She obviously wasn't trying to be provocative by doing that. He'd told her they should get a move on and she was complying. But her unconscious sensuality fired his blood. He turned away, unable to watch her dress without reaching for her. Even the sound of her bra hooks locking into place got to him.

"You're good for my ego, cowboy."

"I hope so." He kept his back to her while he took a steadying breath. "Because you're hell on my package."

"Do you think you'll be able to slip away and drive to my place later tonight?"

His laugh was strained. "That's a priority."

"Did I give you the address last summer?"

"Yep."

"You can turn around. I'm covered up."

He faced her and blew out a breath. "You were right about not having sex in the sleigh. I should have listened to you."

"Why? Do I look mussed, after all?"

"No, you look perfect. That's not the problem. Until we got friendly in the sleigh, I'd convinced myself that having sex with you was great but probably not as great as I remembered. Time plays tricks on us sometimes and we imagine something was better than it actually was."

"But that's not true with us."

"No, it isn't. Which means that instead of throwing myself into this Christmas Eve party, I'll be counting the minutes until I'm in your bed."

She held his gaze. "Me, too, Jake."

AN HOUR LATER Jake felt reasonably in control of himself. He'd managed to hold up his end of conversations without constantly searching the room for Amethyst. As if by mutual agreement they'd spent very little time together but awareness of her was a constant stimulant, as if he'd had way too much caffeine.

Early in the evening Grady Magee had showed up with Amethyst's sister, Sapphire. They were clearly in love and Jake was happy for them, but talking to Sapphire turned out to be a challenge. Certain mannerisms reminded him of Amethyst and as they talked he couldn't shake the notion that she knew about the episode last summer. He couldn't blame Amethyst for confiding in her. In a way it was flattering that she'd wanted to, but that didn't keep him from feeling slightly uncomfortable.

A second beer would have helped, but because of the drive he intended to make after the party wound down, he'd decided not to drink much. He didn't think anyone had noticed until Cade drew him aside.

"Been watching your alcohol intake, Fireman Jake. Or rather, your lack of it." Cade's smile was teasing but there was brotherly concern in his eyes. "Can't help concluding that you have plans tonight."

"I might."

"That sleigh sat empty for quite a while this afternoon."

"Guess so."

"Listen, I get the attraction, bro. Any guy would. But she has big plans."

"I know that. She's very talented."

"Then you're just having a little temporary fun?"

"That's right."

Cade sighed in obvious relief. "Glad to hear it. The way you look at her, I was afraid it was more than that."

"Nope." Jake clapped him on the back. "Not everyone is as focused on that walk down the aisle as you and O'Roarke."

"I know. I wasn't worried that you were that far gone. But you seem to like her and I overheard her telling Chelsea she was seriously thinking she'd give LA a shot."

"Huh." He hadn't seen that coming. The distance between Jackson Hole and Sheridan was an obstacle that could be managed. LA would put her out of reach, but it would definitely give her more opportunities to land the recording contract she wanted.

Putting his selfish motives aside, he should be all for it, but thinking of her going to LA by herself made him uneasy. Did she know anyone there who'd watch out for her and show her the ropes? She was beautiful, and even though her sexy persona was a bluff, it could get her attention from the wrong kind of guy. Sure, that could happen anywhere, but he considered Wyoming a safer bet.

"I take it she hasn't mentioned that to you."

He realized he was scowling and forced himself to relax. "No, but why should she?" He shrugged. "Like you said, we're just having fun. No commitment whatsoever."

Cade studied him. "Are you sure? Because I don't think this LA news is sitting well with you."

"Nah, I'm good." He managed a smile.

"Time for presents, you two." Lexi, who'd sprinkled silver glitter in her short, curly hair, walked over and slipped her arm through Cade's. "Everyone's curious about all those hardware store bags, Jake, but since you stapled the top together we can't peek."

"You're not supposed to peek." He gave her a mock glare of disapproval. "You'll ruin the surprise."

"I'll bet I know what it is."

"Bet you don't. So why did you put glitter in your hair? That doesn't seem like a Lexi thing to do."

"Exactly. I wanted to shake things up, be a little more festive this year. Turns out it makes a hell of a mess. I'm shedding glitter everywhere."

"I can testify to that." Cade brushed it off his sleeve.

"Think of it as me showering you with my love."

Cade grinned at her. "Nice save. Now let's go see what Fireman Jake bought us at the hardware store."

Traditionally for the opening of presents, everyone sat on the floor in a wide semicircle around the big tree. Jake felt he could risk choosing a spot next to Amethyst for this part of the evening. The LA plan had cooled his jets somewhat, anyway. He'd thought they'd have a lot more time together in the coming months but maybe not. He'd have to take that into consideration going forward.

Damon brought over a chair for Philomena, although she didn't seem happy about using it. "I appreciate the added comfort," she said, "but I feel kinda funny perched up here above all of you."

Damon gazed up at her from his position on the floor. "I could say you look kinda funny from this angle, too, but—"

"But he won't," Lexi said, "because in his eyes you are the most beautiful, glamorous, mommy-to-be in the world and the queen of his heart. Isn't that right, Damon?"

"Absolutely. That's exactly what I was going to say before you took the words right out of my mouth."

Phil gave him a withering look. "Be careful, daddy-o. My sense of humor disappeared sometime during the third trimester."

"I wouldn't mind having a chair," Rosie said. "I'll sit next to you, Phil. We can be royalty together."

"I'll get it." Herb, who always wore his Santa hat on Christmas Eve, went to fetch Rosie a chair. With his gray hair covered by the cap and a big smile on his face, he looked years younger.

Although Jake hadn't thought he was homesick for the ranch and his foster family, he felt a wave of it as he watched Herb get Rosie settled next to Phil. If the fire department in Sheridan had been hiring when he'd gone looking for a job, he never would have left. Instead he'd ended up in Jackson Hole, which certainly was a beautiful place to live. He liked the people he worked with, too, but Sheridan was home. Maybe he should check on the job situation again and see if he could get back here.

He vividly remembered his first Christmas at the ranch when Herb had explained what he called the November Project. The older guys had jobs in town and could buy small gifts for everyone, but Jake had been fourteen and dead broke. Normally the boys didn't get paid for doing chores, but in November that changed for the younger ones.

Herb found all kinds of odd jobs for them and by the first week in December they each had enough cash to pick out something inexpensive for Rosie, Herb and every foster brother. Herb would take them into town and turn them loose. That first Christmas had been the best one of Jake's life.

As Herb distributed presents and the recipients started opening them, Jake saw that others had chosen his one-size-fits-all solution. Damon and Phil gave everybody eight hours of home maintenance work, collectible after the baby was born. Cade and Lexi had come up with a group trail ride into the mountains next spring complete with a catered lunch.

"You'll have to put in for time off so you can go, too," Cade said to Jake. "And you're welcome to bring a guest." Significantly he didn't suggest bringing Amethyst.

Finn and Chelsea had brought everyone glassware etched with the O'Roarke's logo on one side and a small but sentimental TMB logo on the other. Grady and Sapphire had come up with a creative pairing of their skills. Sapphire had made colorful serving platters, no two alike, and Grady had designed a decorative metal holder so they could hang on the wall when not in use.

Jake's smoke alarms brought laughter but sincere thanks, too.

"This is a very loving gift," Rosie said. "Thank you, Jake."

"I really need this." Amethyst smiled at Jake. "Thank you. I've been meaning to ask the landlady to replace ours with a better one, but now I don't have to."

"You're welcome." He gave her a quick smile. Damn

it, now when he looked at her he couldn't help thinking she could be gone in a matter of weeks. Earlier he'd worried that he should have bought her something more personal, but now he was glad he hadn't. He'd be wise to dial back on the sentimentality.

"I apologize that I have no gifts for any of you," Amethyst said. "But if you're up for a song, I could give you that."

"That would be lovely," Rosie said.

"Definitely." Lexi got to her feet. "But before Amethyst gives us a song, I have a special gift for Cade."

Jake held his breath. This had damn well better be a proposal.

"Should I stand up?" Cade's heart was in his eyes.

Jake *really* wanted this to be a proposal.

"Yes." Lexi took a deep breath. "Please."

Cade got to his feet. To Jake's surprise, the guy was steady as a rock while Lexi seemed a little shaky.

She reached in her pocket and pulled out a small jewelry box. Then she dropped to one knee. "Cade Gallagher, I love you more than life itself and I would be honored if you would agree to marry me." She popped open the box, which contained a man's gold wedding band.

He peered at it. "I can't put that on yet, can I?"

"Not yet. It's for the ceremony." Lexi's jaw tightened. "But I couldn't very well give you a diamond engagement ring. So what's your answer?"

Cade rubbed his chin. "I'm thinking."

"Cade Gallagher, if you don't accept this proposal I swear I'll..."

"What?"

"Get glitter all over you!"

"Ah, Lexi, you will anyway." Reaching down, he pulled her to her feet. "You know I'll marry you, woman. Thank God you finally asked." And he kissed her as everyone in the room stood and cheered.

Sometime in the middle of all that Jake had taken Amethyst's hand. What a stupid thing to do.

But she laced her fingers through his and gave his hand a squeeze. "I love this," she murmured.

"Yeah, me, too." And the worst part was, the scene with Cade and Lexi had showed him that he wanted more from Amethyst than she was willing to give.

8

JAKE'S BEHAVIOR TOWARD her had changed and Amethyst wasn't sure why. He'd pulled back, retreated into some kind of protective shell that reminded her of their high school days. Then he'd taken her hand during Lexi's memorable proposal and she'd thought maybe things were okay, after all.

They weren't, though. The minute the kiss had ended and Cade had called for champagne, Jake had released her hand.

"I need to go help," he'd murmured before hurrying toward the kitchen.

She'd thought it was an excuse, but now wasn't the time to ask him what was going on.

Champagne flowed and everyone congratulated the newly engaged couple. Amethyst felt out of sorts but she knew how to fake looking like a party girl. When Rosie reminded her that she'd promised everyone a song, she asked Cade and Lexi what they'd like to hear. After all, this was their special night.

They picked a sentimental tune from their senior prom and she sang it a cappella, giving it all she had.

Halfway through she glanced at Jake. He looked destroyed. Obviously the happy fling they'd planned was no longer going smoothly. She wondered if he'd changed his mind about driving to her house tonight.

If he had, she might never find out what the deal was. Talk about déjà vu. He'd acted this way in high school and she'd had to pry the reason out of him, which had turned out to be that she'd supposedly flirted with another guy.

That couldn't be the situation tonight. Every man in the room was taken and she wouldn't have cared if a gorgeous eligible male had appeared. She was with Jake. Until recently she'd thought he was with her, too. Now she wasn't so sure.

Eventually she maneuvered him into a quiet corner and asked him the pertinent question. "Are you still planning to drive to my house?"

His reply was short and to the point. "Yes."

"Is something wrong?"

"I don't know. Is there?"

She got right in his face. "Don't do that, Jake Ramsey. Don't answer a question with another question. Is something bothering you? If so, spit it out."

"Cade told me you were going to LA."

Aha. That explained it. "I'm *thinking* about it. Nothing's been decided." She liked Cade, but she wished he'd kept his mouth shut.

"But that's what you ultimately need to do, isn't it?"

"Quite possibly. Chelsea's comments made me realize I should consider it. She's a marketing whiz and I need to listen to her. Then Rosie told me about Matt Forrest, who took off for LA three years ago and, after toughing it out, he's up for a major role. I began asking myself if

I'm being cowardly to keep performing in my Wyoming safety zone in hopes someone will discover me here."

"Do you have contacts in LA?"

"Not yet. That's the purpose of going, to make some. Hire an agent."

"But what if you run into some sleazy characters? What if they make promises they never plan to deliver? What if they—?"

"I'm not seventeen years old, Jake. I've learned something about judging people and making good business decisions. I might have fallen for some fast-talker when I was younger, but I'm not as gullible now."

His chest heaved. "I'm sure you're not."

"I promise I'll be smart about things." She searched his gaze and saw the uncertainty there. He was concerned about her on a more visceral level and she got that. She was a small-town girl considering a move to the big city. "Look, I'm not leaving next week. Probably not even next month."

"But you will go."

"After listening to Chelsea, I think I should if I'm serious about my career." She took a steadying breath. "I realize that affects…us."

"There is no *us*."

"Yes, there is, Jake. We might not have planned it that way last summer, but clearly what we feel for each other goes beyond sex. We might as well acknowledge that and deal with it."

"What's to deal with? You're leaving. End of story."

Although he sounded angry, he was probably mostly worried about her and maybe a little hurt, too. He wouldn't want to admit that last part, especially in the middle of a family party. "Tell you what. I'll go tell everyone goodbye and head on out. You probably want some private time with your brothers."

He sighed and rubbed the back of his neck. "Hey, I'm sorry. Don't go yet. We'll drop the subject."

"I'm not leaving in a huff," she said softly. "I don't do that."

He gave her a rueful smile. "No, I do that."

"Sometimes." She touched his cheek. "I really think it's time for me to go home."

He looked as if he might want to argue, but then he nodded. "I'll get your coat while you make the rounds."

"Thanks." Amethyst made her way through the room collecting hugs and Christmas wishes. Grady and Sapphire said they'd see her tomorrow and Sapphire gave her an extra hug and a whispered "good luck."

Jake waited by the front door loaded down with her stuff, including the bag containing the smoke alarm. That gift made her smile. Naturally he had his coat and hat on, too. She would have been surprised if he hadn't walked her to her car. He was both gallant and protective.

He was also beautiful to look at. As she came toward him, her heart stalled. He'd been a cutie-pie in high school, but since then his shoulders had broadened and his chest had filled out. His face had lost its smooth-cheeked boyishness in favor of rugged masculinity emphasized by the slight shadow of his beard. He fought fires for a living, a heroic job she'd always admired, and tonight his sheepskin coat and gray Stetson added a layer of cowboy appeal.

Moving a thousand miles away from Jake wasn't going to be easy. The miles would be a major barrier between them, but the psychological distance would be the relationship killer. Living in LA would change her in ways she probably couldn't imagine. She'd told him the move wasn't imminent, but the longer she delayed, the tougher she'd make it on both of them. As a kid she'd preferred ripping off a bandage to end the pain faster.

He helped her on with her coat before handing over her purse. "I don't know what was going through your mind just now, but you didn't look happy."

"Just thinking that transitions aren't a lot of fun." She hooked her purse strap across her body.

"Nope."

"But it's the only way to grow." She wound the scarf around her neck and reached for the hat he held out.

"Assuming you choose the right ones."

"Which is something you can't always know in advance." She pulled on her hat and took her gloves from her coat pocket.

"Guess not. I'll carry your smoke alarm." He pulled on his gloves before opening the door. Cold air slammed into them as they both hurried out and he wrapped his free hand around her shoulders. "Be careful on the steps. They're slippery."

She considered telling him that she had slippery porch steps, too, and she'd been navigating them just fine on her own, but she didn't have the heart. Jake's protective instincts ran deep and were the main reason he'd chosen to become a firefighter. No wonder the thought of her going off to LA alone was pushing all his buttons.

But maybe they'd be able to talk it through. "Look, I know you're not crazy about my plan."

"I'm not, and it might seem like I'm being selfish, but there's more to it than that." Their boots crunched through the frozen snow as they walked to her SUV.

"This may sound chauvinistic, but I'm not convinced LA is a safe place for a single woman who doesn't know anybody, let alone one who looks like you."

She didn't know if it was chauvinistic but it sounded exactly like Jake. If he could manage it he'd send her with a bodyguard. "Have you ever been to LA?"

"Actually, I have. Several of us went for training in crowd control. Jackson Hole is getting more popular with celebrities all the time, and our chief wants us to be prepared in case a situation gets out of hand."

She had to admit that gave his opinion more weight. Other than a family trip when she was a kid, she'd never been. "Did you consider it a dangerous city?"

"Not if you're hanging out with a bunch of firefighters."

They'd reached her SUV and she turned to face him while she dug in her purse for her keys. "Would you feel better if I took a self-defense course?"

"Yes. But mostly I wish you knew someone there."

She found her keys and glanced up at him. "I just thought of something. I do know somebody. Matt. Rosie could put us in touch. I'll bet he'd have all kinds of tips on living in LA."

"You should definitely contact him, but you'd better do it soon. Rosie said if he gets the part he'll be shooting on location in Utah for the next few months."

"I hadn't heard that. So much for that brainstorm."

"Maybe he won't get the part, but if he does, you could hold off going until he's back."

She hated seeing the spark of hope in his green eyes because she was about to douse it. "I don't think that's a good idea."

His jaw tightened. "Then you'd better sign up for a self-defense class."

"I'll look into it." Taking hold of his arms for balance, she stood on tiptoe and dipped under his hat to give him a quick kiss. Belatedly she realized a peck on the lips probably wouldn't satisfy either of them, even if they were standing in sub-zero weather.

Sure enough, he groaned and pulled her close. Then he angled his head so he could kiss her more thoroughly without losing his hat.

She'd forgotten that he'd perfected that technique when they'd dated in high school. His kisses had been hot then, too, but he'd never completely lost control, much to her disappointment. Tonight all restraint was gone. Backing her against the side of her SUV, he thrust his tongue deep.

She gripped the collar of his coat and hung on as he ravished her mouth. He poured equal parts longing and frustration into a kiss that surrounded them in a cloud of steam. His arms shielded her from the cold metal of the SUV, but he was still holding the smoke alarm and it pressed against the small of her back. She was sandwiched between the alarm on one side and his erection on the other. Great sex and constant vigilance—the two elements epitomized Jake Ramsey.

The cold air lost its punch as she began to heat up. She imagined opening the door and making love in the backseat. If he'd thought to bring a condom out here, she could easily be talked into it.

Panting, he lifted his mouth from hers. "God, how I want you."

"Let me open the car. We can—"

"Not *here*." His laughter was choked. "Damn, woman,

they'd find our frozen bodies in the morning if we tried a stunt like that. But I'm so done with this party." He released her and stepped back, his chest heaving. "Stay here with the motor running while I let everyone know I'm following you home."

"You are? I thought you'd want to stay longer and hang out with your family."

"I thought so, too, but I have a more urgent issue that needs to be dealt with. I'll be with them in the morning while you're at your folks' house. Get in the car and wait for me. I'll be out in a sec." He handed her the bag and backed away.

She gulped. "Okay, if you say so."

"I do. When you see my truck's headlights, pull out ahead of me." He turned and started for the ranch house, his long strides covering the frozen ground much faster than when he'd been walking with her.

She gazed after him until the cold penetrated her sensual fog and she began to shiver. Without his warmth encircling her, the breeze sliced right through her coat. Climbing into her SUV, she tossed her purse and gift bag on the passenger seat. Then she started the motor and continued to shiver while she waited for it to warm up so she could turn on the heater.

His headlights swung into view not long after she'd done that. He'd really hustled to get here so fast. Putting the SUV in gear, she pulled out ahead of him and started down the winding road that led to the highway.

Once they reached the main road, driving to her place became a kind of vehicular foreplay. Hardly anyone was out at this hour on Christmas Eve, so she could concentrate on the headlights in her rearview mirror and picture Jake impatiently waiting for the moment they were alone in her house.

He'd said the box of condoms was in his truck. He'd likely bring some in with him but if not she'd bought his favorite brand this morning. Thanks to their interlude in Jackson Hole she knew what that was. They'd had to make a trip to the gift shop before heading up to her room.

Judging from his comments today, he'd been under the impression she was used to spontaneous sexual encounters while on the road. Although she'd had plenty of offers, she'd never taken a man to her hotel room after a performance until she'd invited Jake. She'd only done it then because she'd known him.

She'd expected to have fun because they'd always had chemistry. She hadn't expected to have such an incredible sexual experience that she'd turned down every guy who'd asked her out since then. Without consciously admitting it, she'd been saving herself for Jake. That made no sense, especially now that she'd pretty much decided to move to LA.

Or maybe it did make sense. She'd laid all her cards on the table so he knew she was career focused and he wanted her anyway, for whatever time they could be together. He'd initially questioned her new plan but now he seemed to have accepted it provided she got some martial arts training.

That left them free to enjoy passionate sex for the next couple of nights. She'd forgotten to ask him when he had to drive back, but if he'd been given the holiday off he wouldn't be leaving until at least the twenty-sixth. That was more time with Jake than she'd had last summer and she was grateful.

The two-story Victorian that she now shared with Arlene was dark inside. When she'd left earlier today she'd planned to come back, change clothes and freshen up before the party at Thunder Mountain. But the multicolored Christmas lights she'd draped along the porch railing were on a timer so they were glowing and illuminated the fresh pine wreath she'd hung on the front door.

She'd also figured on having an opportunity after the party to prepare a seductive welcome for Jake by turning on the Christmas tree lights and lighting some scented candles. That hadn't happened, either, but judging from the way he'd kissed her, he wouldn't need atmosphere to get him in the mood.

She pulled into the driveway and left enough space for him to park behind her. Anticipation tightened her chest and sent her pulse into the red zone. Until now they'd had to be somewhat cautious, but once they were inside her house, they had almost no restrictions.

They'd have more freedom tonight than they'd had in her hotel room. Her windows were closed and so were her neighbors'. They could yell all they wanted.

By the time she opened her door and climbed out holding her purse and her gift bag, he was there to grab her hand and tug her toward the porch. "Got the key?"

She held it up.

"Perfect. Your lights are festive, by the way."

She laughed. "I'm surprised you noticed."

"I'm trying not to behave like a sex-starved man."

"I appreciate the effort."

"What kind of flooring do you have?"

"Hardwood. Is that a firefighter kind of question?"

"No."

"Then it's a weird thing to ask me, Jake."

"Not if you're in my condition. I need to know if the floor would work or if the sofa is a better option. Do you have a sofa?"

"Yes, and you're insane." She opened the door.

"I'll admit to it." He propelled her through the door and kicked it shut. "Oh, good, you have a rug. Come here."

"Jake, this is crazy. My bedroom's just up the—" But the trip upstairs that she'd been about to suggest became a moot point as his eager mouth captured hers. She dropped her purse and the smoke alarm as he pulled her down to the flowered carpet she'd found on sale last year.

After getting it home, she'd been pleased with how it echoed the Victorian theme of the house. She'd never envisioned that she'd be pinned to it while a virile cowboy unzipped her jeans and thrust his hand inside her panties, but she enjoyed that maneuver.

She enjoyed it even more when his nimble fingers coaxed an orgasm from her quivering body. As she lay gasping from that unexpected pleasure, he pulled off her boots and divested her of her underwear and jeans. Then he lifted her hips and gave her another climax, this time using his mouth and tongue with devastating effect. But she was still wearing her shirt, her bra, her coat, her scarf, her gloves and her knit hat.

She tore off the gloves and hat and tossed them away, but that didn't solve the issue. "I'm burning up." She unbuttoned her coat and yanked her scarf from around her neck.

"Me, too." A zipper rasped in the darkness followed by the crinkle of foil.

"No, really, I'm burning up. The top of me is dressed for a blizzard and the bottom of me is in Tahiti."

"Oh." Breathing hard, he loomed over her. "I see."

She reached up and gripped his sheepskin coat. "Don't you want to take all this off before we continue?"

"Okay." Sitting back on his heels, he wrenched off his coat and tossed it aside. Something spilled out of the pockets that sounded like a barrage of condoms. Then he helped her sit up so she could wiggle out of her coat.

"I have a nice bed upstairs."

"Couldn't make it. Grab on to me."

His desperation sent lust spiraling through her again. She got a grip on his shoulders and he spanned her waist with his big hands. His upper body strength allowed him to lift and position her so his cock nudged the spot where his mouth had recently given her such pleasure. Then he let gravity take over.

She'd never loved a sensation more than she loved this one. There were other techniques for getting and giving satisfaction and they'd tried quite a few. But as Jake slowly filled the aching space that was so ready for him, she felt a special joy that only happened when they connected in this basic way. Once her knees reached the floor, she was able to help him create that sweet friction they both craved.

He groaned. "So good."

"Mmm." She moved faster, yearning for the climax that hovered just out of reach.

His breathing roughened and he tightened his hold on her hips. "Slow down."

"Don't want to."

"I'll come."

"That's the idea." She dug her fingers into his shoulders. "Turn me loose."

With a soft oath he let go and she rode him fast, and faster yet, until she came in a rush. The moment she did, he thrust upward with a strangled cry of triumph. He held her in place as his cock pulsed and he gasped for air.

Gradually their bodies relaxed and they sagged against each other until their breathing quieted. Then Jake began to chuckle.

Leaning back, she looked at him. "What's so funny?"

"Me. I barely made it through the damn door before I was on you. I'm pretty sure I scattered condoms everywhere. Not particularly cool of me."

"I like it when you lose your cool." She cupped his face and gave him a tender kiss. "Remember August? Remember what happened the minute we got into the room?"

"I backed you up against the nearest wall and we did it standing up. Couldn't make it to the bed that was only ten feet away. You make me go wild."

"How does that feel?"

"Great." He took her mouth gently, almost reverently, before lifting his head again. "Thank you for inspiring me to go nuts."

"My pleasure." Maybe this was what Jake needed from her, the chance to abandon his cautious nature and surrender to his underlying sensuality. She'd known all along it was there. She'd had a small taste of it when they'd been teenagers and she'd had solid confirmation now that they'd shared hours of adult pleasure.

How ironic that she wasn't any bolder than Jake and yet, because he'd believed she was, he'd become more sexually adventurous. That might carry over into his next relationship or it might not. Until now she'd avoided imagining him with someone else but she had to be realistic. If she didn't want to be tied down, then of course he'd move on. What a depressing thought that was!

9

JAKE STILL COULDN'T believe his lack of restraint with Amethyst. Mr. Smooth he was not and now he had a little problem. "Wild and crazy is fun and all, but it's left me sitting in the middle of your fairly dark living room wondering where I can dispose of the—"

"Oh!" She gently lifted her hot body away from his. "Stay put. I'll bring you a trash can and a box of tissues." She was back in no time. "There you go."

"Thanks." His eyes had adjusted so he could see a little better, but fortunately he could do this job blindfolded. Getting to his feet, he took care of the condom. Then he pulled up his briefs and zipped his jeans.

"Don't you want to just take everything off? I'm still roasting."

He glanced over at her and noticed she'd taken off her shirt. "And walk around your house naked?"

"Sure. Ah, that feels so much better." She whipped off her bra, too. "I really worked up a sweat."

"If you're going to strip I want to be able to see you. Mind if I turn on a lamp?"

"No, but I have a better idea." She walked over to the

shadowy branches of the Christmas tree she'd placed in front of the windows that looked out on the porch.

Seconds later colored lights bloomed on the Christmas tree and bathed her in a rainbow that took his breath away. "You're gorgeous."

She smiled. "I love being naked with you, Jake. Take off the rest of your clothes, okay?"

He thought about it. "Not gonna work for me."

"Why not? You were fine being naked in the hotel room."

"That's different. We were either in bed or in the shower most of the time. Here we have an entire house to have sex in."

"So what?"

"We can do it anywhere." And the longer he looked at her, the more ideas he had. "On the kitchen table, on the stairs, in the hallway, against the front door, under the Christmas tree, up against the—"

"Okay, I get the idea, but if you're naked that makes those episodes so much easier."

"The shirt can go, and the boots, but not the jeans. I need pockets." Speaking of which, he needed to reload. Sure enough, the carpet was littered with condoms. He gathered them up and transferred several to his jeans before putting the rest in his coat pocket.

She watched him with a smile on her face. "Think you have enough, there?"

"Maybe not." But he sat on the sofa so he could pull off his boots and socks. They definitely weren't necessary.

"I have more of those little raincoats upstairs in my bedroom, where the bed is, hint, hint."

"Patience." He dropped a boot on the floor and glanced up with a lazy grin. "We'll get there."

That made her laugh. "See, you're not the only eager one around here. And I admit I hadn't thought of the storage issue, especially if you want to have sex all over the house."

"It's not your job to cover the equipment." And his equipment was really interested in some action now that she was standing there in the glow of those Christmas lights. Her silky skin was dappled in soft shades of red, green, yellow and blue. He committed the image to memory because chances were good he wouldn't be enjoying this view a year from now.

As he stood and walked toward her, he noticed that her nipples were rigid. Could be either a response to him or to the temperature. "Are you cold?"

"A little, now that we're not having sex. I guess we can't exactly be doing it *all* the time."

"Now there's a challenge." He pulled her into his arms. "Can I keep you heated up enough that you don't feel the need to put on clothes? I just might take that challenge."

"No, don't. It sounds exhausting." She gave him a quick kiss. "Let me throw on something that's a good compromise. I know what I need. It's in a basket of clean laundry on top of the dryer. Want to come with me to fetch it?"

"You bet. Then I can check your wiring."

She batted her eyelashes at him. "Mmm, laundry room sex. What sort of position do you need me in so you can check my wiring?"

He groaned. "Any position works to get me hot. But you'll hate hearing I meant the wiring in your house."

"Well, damn."

"But after that I'll be happy to check out your personal wiring."

"Okay, then." She tossed a smile over her bare shoulder as she sashayed through her kitchen and into the small room adjacent to it.

He took a quick glance at the kitchen on the way through. It looked recently remodeled, which was a good sign if the remodelers had known what they were doing. He'd check it out later, but apparently they'd installed refurbished antique appliances. Nice touch.

Amethyst flipped on an overhead light and gestured toward her washer and dryer. "Check away."

He leaned over the back to study the outlets. "They're fine. Sometimes older houses aren't set up to handle newer machines but this one seems to be. I'm assuming you clean out the lint trap regularly."

"Yes, Fireman Jake, I clean out the lint trap regularly."

"Good." He turned around to find her wearing a red flannel sleep shirt trimmed in faux white fur. Although it covered her up, knowing she wore nothing under it created a whole new level of tension.

She walked over and snuggled against him. "You like?" She lifted her face to his.

"Sure do. It's very soft." Reaching down, he pulled up the fur-trimmed hem so he could fondle her firm little butt. "But you're softer."

"And you're harder." She wiggled against him. "I can feel your pride and joy. Did you want to check my wiring?"

"I do." He leaned down and nuzzled the curve of her neck. "I really do, but I also want to evaluate the appliances in your kitchen. I promise to make it fast."

"So I'm getting my own personal safety check?" She massaged his chest in slow, sensuous strokes.

"That's the idea." He breathed in the coconut scent of her shampoo. Coconut had become a trigger that made him think of her long, dark hair sweeping over his naked body. "If I can keep my mind on the subject."

"You'll feel better once you've made sure I'm not living with any fire hazards, won't you?"

"Yes." He forced himself to stop nibbling on her smooth shoulder and lift his head.

She stepped back. "Then let's take care of that. I want you to feel loose and carefree, not uptight about any dangers lurking in my house."

"You don't know how much I appreciate that."

"I think I do. You're very sweet, Jake."

"Sweet?" He winced. "You sure know how to hurt a guy."

"It's a compliment!"

"Not to a member of the Thunder Mountain Brotherhood. We prefer strong and courageous." He grinned. "But I'm sure you meant well. Let's go look at your retro kitchen."

She turned and led the way. "I love it. The landlady wanted it to appear as if it might be more than a hundred years old, and in some ways it does. I feel as if I step back in time when I come in here."

"I wonder if women a hundred years ago used to walk through their kitchens naked."

She leaned against the counter, temptation personified. "Depends on whether they were lucky enough to have a lusty man who enjoyed watching them do it."

"That counter is the perfect height for…"

"What?"

He blew out a breath. "Never mind." With great effort he looked away from her seductive smile and continued his inspection of the kitchen. "It's well-done. No complaints."

"Want to see my roommate's area?"

No. But once he'd realized she lived in an older house his first thought had been faulty wiring. If he didn't check it out, he wouldn't be doing his job as a firefighter. "Might as well cover the entire bottom floor before we head upstairs." That was another issue he had with her moving to LA. She wouldn't have a lot of money and rents were high. She could end up living in some firetrap because it was all she could afford. "If you ever think of renting a place and the windows are painted shut, please don't move in, okay?"

"I won't."

He made a cursory examination of the bedroom her roommate Arlene used and he found no frayed cords or overloaded outlets. "Looking good. Upstairs we go."

She preceded him up the wooden staircase. "I'm glad I've passed inspection so far."

He couldn't respond to that because he was mesmerized by the view as he followed her. The soft flannel outlined her body and aroused him almost beyond his endurance. The possibilities of the staircase taunted him. They could connect on multiple levels and create all kinds of positions. He filed the information away for later because he really wanted to check out the second floor. That's where Amethyst spent most of her time and a person could become trapped in such a situation.

Her bedroom was the primary source of concern because she slept alone up here—at least, that's how he preferred to picture it—and she might not be aware of a fire breaking out on the first floor. He studiously avoided looking at her bed while he opened the window to make sure it was functional.

Closing it quickly to shut out the cold air, he pulled the curtains closed and turned to her. "If you had a fire and the stairs were blocked, you could climb out this window and onto the front porch roof."

She gazed at the window as if imagining the scenario. "You know, I never thought of that."

"Then I'm glad I mentioned it. Sometimes in an emergency we don't think of the obvious. If you had to, I'll bet you could hang from the porch roof and drop to the ground without doing major damage to yourself."

"I'm sure I could." Her blue eyes darkened. "You're really sexy when you're being official."

He tossed that off with a laugh because he hadn't finished his inspection. If he responded to the invitation in her gaze, he never would. They'd wear each other out in the bed that was steps away and then fall into an exhausted sleep. "I'm not trying to be sexy. I'm trying to—"

"Keep me safe. I know. I guess what I'm saying is that this job you have, where you protect people from the dangers of fire, is super important. Watching you look at everything with a practiced eye turns me on."

"Nice to know." His cock began to throb. "If I remember right, you made the other bedroom into a studio."

"I did. It's at the back of the house." She led the way down the hall and pointed out the bathroom on the way. "I promise I have no frayed cords dangling anywhere."

"I believe you."

"But this is the smoke alarm I'd like to replace with

the one you gave me." She gestured toward the ceiling of the hall.

He glanced up at it. "Yeah, that's definitely an older model. I'll replace it before I leave in the morning."

"Thank you. I don't have your diligence but I wasn't kidding about wanting a better one. I spend most of my time up here." She walked through the doorway at the end of the hall and flipped on a light. "This is where the magic happens, or what I hope is magic. Time will tell."

When he walked in, he was hit by the dedication to her craft that had produced this studio. He didn't know a lot about electronics but he suspected her setup had required some serious money. Besides the recording equipment and two computers, she had an elaborate keyboard that looked expensive. Several autographed pictures of popular singers decorated the walls. He circled the room to read the names and recognized some but not all.

"I was the opening act for a few of the lesser known ones," she said. "The really famous ones are from my fan-girl days when I went to every concert within driving distance."

"This is impressive, Amethyst. I can tell a lot of effort went into creating it."

"It did. Finding the equipment at a reasonable price wasn't easy, but then I had to get the landlady's permission to soundproof the room. And before you ask, the panel over the window lifts off. I realize now that I could climb out that one, too. There's even a little porch roof over the back stoop, although the thought of a fire never occurred to me. I just wanted to be able to open the window on nice days when I'm composing but not recording."

"I feel a lot better about you spending so much time

on the second floor." He shoved his hands into his pockets so he wouldn't reach for her. Being here in her studio surrounded by the evidence of her talent forced him to see the heartbreaking truth. She needed to make her bid for the big-time. Sure, he'd be worried about her when she went to LA, but only a very selfish person would try to talk her out of going.

"I love it up here, especially now that I have my studio organized. I can work any time of the day or night and not disturb anyone. But the outlay was substantial, so that's when I decided to give voice lessons to bring in more cash." Her expression became more animated. "The kids are a riot and they *love* this studio. We put together a Christmas album they're each giving to their folks."

"Great idea. Could you give voice lessons in LA to bring in more money?"

"Maybe. I wouldn't have the same setup, though, and here it's easy to get students because a lot of people already know me. There isn't much competition." She smiled. "This fall one kid's mom took a few lessons because she wanted to sing 'Santa Baby' to her husband on Christmas Eve. I guess people remember that Christmas show."

"I sure do. I watched you perform that song and cussed myself out for being a damned fool."

"You could have said something."

"Yeah, I know." He sighed. "But I'd never expected to hold on to you for long, anyway. I figured you were too hot for me."

"Oh, Jake." She walked over to him and slid her hands up his bare chest. "But I can't blame you for not recognizing it was all for show. I didn't want anybody to see through me, not even you. I still put on that sexy girl persona like a suit of armor before every performance. It let's me go out there without being scared."

He put his arms around her and massaged the small of her back. "Thank you for letting me in on the secret."

She gazed up at him with a sparkle in her blue eyes. "I have an idea."

"Me, too." He smiled. "I wonder if it's the same idea."

"Probably not. I want to sing you a song."

"You do?" He hadn't seen that coming.

"Sit right here in my office chair." She led him to a cushy black-leather chair on rollers.

He settled into it. "What song?"

"You'll see." Stepping away from him, she cleared her throat and moistened her lips. "I've never performed this without accompaniment, but it could be better that way. More intimate." Looking into his eyes, she began singing in a soft, sultry voice.

He should have known the minute she'd suggested it what she'd choose for her serenade. Gripping the arms of the chair, he vowed that he would not leave it until she was finished, no matter how hot he became. And guaranteed he would become very hot for her. No one could sing "Santa Baby" like Amethyst.

10

AMETHYST HAD NEVER tried to seduce a man with a private solo, but, wow, was it effective. Jake had a death grip on the arms of that chair and his powerful chest rose and fell more rapidly with each stanza. This was way more fun than she'd imagined it would be.

Quite a bit was going on behind his fly, too. She couldn't resist teasing him even more by perching on his knee and running her fingers through his hair as she sang. Then she toyed with his chest hair and lightly pinched his nipples.

His low moan of pleasure nearly caused her to abandon the performance. She didn't want to do that, but she was turning herself on, too, and her normal breathing techniques weren't working very well. Fortunately the song was supposed to be delivered in a breathy, slightly husky voice. She certainly had that down.

Toward the end, when she was afraid she'd end up gasping out the last lines because she needed him so desperately, her professional pride kicked in. She regained control of her breathing long enough to finish with the cute, pouty ending, a final touch that made his eyes darken and his nostrils flare.

Desire pulsed within her and tightened a coil of need that demanded release. If he didn't take her in the next five minutes, she might burst into flames all on her own. Quivering, she brushed a kiss over his mouth. "Thanks for listening."

In response he scooped her into his arms and stood, kicking the chair away as he strode out of the room and down the hall.

"Did you like it?"

His reply was strained and succinct. "Yes."

Judging from the way he was barreling down the hall toward her bedroom, she almost expected him to throw her down on the bed. Instead he laid her on the comforter with exquisite tenderness and gently worked her out of her fur-trimmed sleep shirt. No movement was wasted, though, as he pulled a condom from his pocket and shucked his jeans and briefs. He was obviously a man on a mission.

He rolled on the condom before climbing into bed and moving between her thighs.

Looking into his eyes, she found the heat she knew would be there, but another emotion lurked in his steady gaze, one far more potent. Her heart answered with a surge of fierce joy, even though allowing such feelings to take root was a huge mistake for both of them. She stroked his muscled back and felt him tremble beneath her touch. "I'm glad you liked my song."

He started to speak but had to pause to clear his throat. "I didn't just like it. I loved it. And, dear God, how I need you." He plunged his cock deep.

She arched off the bed, a wild cry of joy rising from

her throat as Jake pounded into her again and again. The bed rocked with the force of his thrusts. She lost control in seconds and clung to him as her world shattered into a million brilliant pieces. With a roar that echoed off the walls of her small bedroom, he drove in once more and his big body shuddered in the aftermath of his climax. Gasping for breath, he remained braced above her with his eyes squeezed shut.

At last he opened them, but he still looked dazed. He shook his head as if to clear it. "I have never...wanted anyone so much."

When she reached up to cup his cheek she felt the prickly beginnings of his beard. "I guess it was the song."

"Not just the song, although it really got to me." He took a shaky breath. "It's knowing you've let down your guard for the first time and I'm the lucky SOB you've chosen to do that with. Knowing what you've told me about your suit of armor, I'd bet my badge you've never performed that song for a guy before."

"Nope. Just you."

"That's a powerful aphrodisiac."

She smiled. "Apparently."

"Take my word for it." He leaned down and gave her a gentle kiss. "Don't go away. I'd like to wash up a little."

"I remember that about you. And I can't imagine why I'd leave when I have a seriously ripped fireman spending Christmas Eve in my bed."

His gaze flickered. "Glad I could be here." Easing away from her, he left the bed and walked out into the hall.

While he was gone she got up and pulled the covers back. After all, she'd bought sheets decorated with brightly wrapped Christmas packages so she might as well make the rest of the evening festive. She hadn't expected anyone to enjoy the holiday bedding except her, but after meeting Jake in the hardware store she'd washed everything and put it back on.

She considered lighting the candles she'd arranged on her dresser but after being around Jake in this setting she realized he might not be enamored of that plan. She'd ask him when he came back. In the meantime she could turn her bedside lamp down a notch before stretching out on her Christmas-themed linens.

When he walked into the bedroom looking his usual manly self, she was reminded again of their rendezvous in Jackson Hole. She'd loved having a chance to admire and explore his body that night. Now she had another golden opportunity.

He glanced at the bedding and grinned. "Don't tell me you bought the sheets after we talked in the hardware store."

"Nope. Picked them up a few weeks ago, but they're freshly laundered for the occasion." She gestured toward the dresser. "I have candles, but now I'm thinking you might not be a fan."

He looked over at the dresser. "I'm not crazy about candles in the bedroom. Dinner by candlelight is one thing, but we could forget these were burning. I don't know about you, but I forget my own name when we're—"

"Say no more. We need to concentrate on orgasms, not candles."

"Thank you for that." He climbed into bed beside her. "These sheets remind me I didn't wrap your present up nice and fancy."

"I don't care. The smoke alarm is perfect. Besides, the best gift is you, and I like you much better unwrapped." She ran her fingers through his thick hair. "I remember your hair as being lighter."

"I'd been out in the sun a lot. Did some hiking in the Tetons." As if following her lead, he picked up a lock of her hair and drew it over her shoulder. "Did you cut some off? It used to reach to your nipple. I remember tickling you with it."

"It's a little shorter. Now I wish I hadn't cut it."

"That's okay. It'll grow back." Then he paused, as if realizing he wouldn't necessarily be around once it did. "I mean—"

"For New Year's I'll bring feathers."

He shook his head and grinned. "You'd do it, too."

"I would. I've never played around with feathers but it could be fun. Maybe I'll bring a little satchel of stuff, get creative."

"Mmm, I like that idea." He lazily brushed his finger over her nipple. "I hope I can get the night off. I can't remember for sure, but I'll bet the chief scheduled me for New Year's Eve. It wasn't important so I didn't notice before I left."

"It doesn't matter if you'll let me stay in your apartment when I drive over. I can hang around until you're off duty."

"You'd do that?"

"Why not? Driving to Jackson Hole and not seeing you makes no sense, especially if I don't have to pay for extra nights at the hotel."

"Of course you can stay with me. I'd love that. It's not a bad little place. Not as nice as this house, but I think you'll like it."

"If you're there, that's all that matters." For the first time she noticed a bruise on his shoulder. It had faded quite a bit, but something heavy must have hit him there to make a grapefruit-size mark. She outlined it gently with her finger. "I've been hanging on to you quite a bit recently. I hope I haven't hurt you."

"Didn't even notice. That bruise is almost gone, anyway."

"How'd you get it?"

"Beam collapsed. Reaction time was too slow."

She swallowed a cry of alarm. After hearing his speech about tough Thunder Mountain guys she figured he wouldn't appreciate that reaction. But the image of him dodging a collapsing beam would probably haunt her for some time. "It could've hit your head."

"But it didn't." He stroked her hip. "That's all that's important."

She looked into his green eyes and shivered at the thought of dangers he faced on a daily basis. "And you're worried about me moving to LA."

"I'm trained to avoid being hurt or killed. You're trained to sing and write music, not navigate your way through a busy urban environment. Logically you'll be performing at night in places where guys could get drunk and disorderly. Instead of taking the elevator to your hotel room, you have to make it back to your apartment without being accosted or followed."

"Ugh. You're making me think of things I hadn't before."

"That's my goal."

"I'll take a self-defense course. I'll figure this out, I promise."

He cupped her chin and stroked his thumb over her

lower lip. "Make friends, get a roommate, travel in groups whenever you can." He grimaced. "Ideally you should have a menacing-looking boyfriend, but I can't bring myself to suggest that."

"I don't want a boyfriend. You've spoiled me for anyone else." She'd meant it as a teasing comment.

Judging from the way he looked at her, he hadn't taken it that way. His eyes shimmered with an emotion that could lead to trouble. "Likewise."

Much more of this and they were liable to say things they couldn't take back. Time to change the mood. She began by massaging his warm chest. "You know what? I think you've developed more muscles since last summer."

He smiled. "Unlikely."

"I think you have. Lie flat and let me take inventory."

"Not gonna argue with that plan." Laughing, he rolled onto his back. "But nothing's changed. I've been doing the same workout at the gym since then. Wait, that's not quite true. When my shifts allow it, I've added some early morning or late evening runs through town. Depending on how many times I go around the square, I probably clock about five miles a day."

"Why did you start doing that?" She swung one leg over his hip so she could start at the top and work her way down over his gorgeous body. By the time she was finished, they'd both be ready to rock and roll. That's what tonight was supposed to be about.

"Nostalgia." He cupped her breasts. "Hey, I want to explore, too."

"Let go, please. You'll get your turn later." Grasping his wrists, she pushed them down to his sides. If he hadn't let her do it she never would have been strong enough, but they'd established the routine last August. All requests were granted without question. "What sort of nostalgia?" She leaned down and kissed the hollow of his throat.

"When I first settled on firefighting as a career, I knew I had to get in shape." He sucked in a breath as she licked her way down to his pecs.

"You've certainly done that." She took his nipple between her teeth and was gratified by his soft groan.

"I used to run on the Forest Service road." He drew in another sharp breath as she swirled her tongue over his warm skin. "Lots of great memories connected with that road. Today we added another one."

"Yeah." She glanced up to discover he'd propped a pillow behind his head so he could watch her progress. "I'll never forget that, Jake."

"Crappy sleigh."

"Didn't matter."

"Nope." His green eyes glittered and his attention drifted to her breasts. "Are you about done? Because if you are, I have some plans for you."

"I'm not even close to done." She returned to the vast erotic territory that was Jake. Besides his impressive pecs, he had a six-pack that could make grown women weep with longing. He might claim that nothing had changed, but she thought his abs had gained more definition since August. She kissed her way across them.

He chuckled. "You're tickling me."

"Then let me move to less ticklish areas." His cock had already risen to the occasion. Although she'd meant to save that for last, she couldn't resist the proud jut of his obvious desire for her. Any girl with access to that primo equipment should be grateful. Grasping the base, she began licking the velvet length of him.

His choked response indicated he hadn't expected that. "I thought…you were going to gradually explore."

"Something caught my attention along the way. Do you mind?"

"Are you kidding? I've spent months dreaming about being in bed with you again, fooling around while we… ah, that's so good."

"How about this?" She closed her mouth over the sensitive tip.

He gasped. "I might lose my mind."

She lifted her head. "Are you saying you want me to stop?"

"God, no."

"That's what I thought." She loved making him come this way. He lost his cool whenever he had sex with her, but oral sex seemed to bring out his most primitive instincts. So she threw herself into it, licking and sucking until he thrashed against the mattress, panting and desperate.

"Tell me what you want," she murmured as she blew against the damp underside of his cock.

He groaned. "Finish this before I go insane."

"I can do that." And she did, pleasuring him until his hips bucked and he erupted. She swallowed all he had to give.

When it was over, he pulled her up so that he could kiss her. Despite everything, he still had the strength for that. "You've said you drop your armor for me," he murmured.

"Because I do." She snuggled against his warm body

and held his gaze as she traced the sculpted line of his cheekbones.

"I've dropped mine, too."

Her heart turned over at the vulnerability revealed by that statement and the trust glowing in his green eyes. "I can tell."

"The feeling's new for me, but I like it."

"Good. It suits you." She kept her tone light, but the conversation tore her apart. He'd offered her a precious gift, one he hadn't possessed years ago. Much as she'd wanted him back then, they wouldn't have been happy together. But now he'd evolved into a man capable of loving her. And the kindest thing she could do was walk away.

11

JAKE HAD EVERY intention of returning the favor Amethyst had granted him, but she snuggled close and talked him out of it. Her argument was perfectly reasonable. The next day she'd be spending Christmas with her folks and he'd be out at the ranch with his foster family. If they didn't sleep for a few hours, they'd both be zombies, not to mention they'd be too worn out to enjoy each other later on.

But curling up with a naked Amethyst and then trying to sleep was more of a challenge than he'd figured on. Although she drifted right off, he lay in the darkness mulling over a couple of nagging problems. Interestingly enough, arousal wasn't the more troublesome of the two. He'd dealt with that before and knew that by focusing on what she needed, namely sleep, he'd reduce the urgency to a manageable level.

Once he'd accomplished that he was free to deal with the second issue. He knew he had to stand by and watch her leave for LA. Yet imagining the terrible things that could happen to her had already driven him crazy and she wasn't even there yet.

A self-defense course was a good idea but not adequate, at least in his view. He started entertaining wild ideas, like going with her. Then what? Would she even let him do that—leave his family and job for her?

Ironically, if she hadn't told him that her sexy persona wasn't the real Amethyst, he might not be as worried. Until she'd admitted that today, he'd thought of her as fearless and bold, even a little intimidating.

Until she'd talked with Chelsea and had become inspired by Finn's migration to Seattle and Matt's struggles in Hollywood, she'd apparently been content to stay in Wyoming and see whether some talent scout found her.

In the meantime she'd put great effort into building a studio in a renovated Victorian that she loved. That implied that she expected to stay awhile. She hadn't been poised for flight. Instead she'd been feathering her nest in Sheridan and making forays around the state to give performances in familiar venues.

While they'd sat having drinks and flirting in the resort's bar last August, she'd described her life. She hadn't sounded frustrated by her lack of fame and fortune. She'd seemed to be having fun while she waited patiently to see whether something more would happen.

What if she was heading to LA because she thought that was the expected thing, the intelligent thing, instead of going because she couldn't help herself? Jake had seen Finn's single-mindedness firsthand. The guy had settled on opening a microbrewery in Seattle and couldn't be dissuaded. Rosie had tried.

Jake hadn't been around when Matt had announced he was leaving to become a Hollywood star, but no doubt the same dynamic had been at work. It sure didn't seem like Amethyst was driven to succeed at that level or she wouldn't be building herself a studio and taking in students. But he didn't think she'd appreciate having him say so. Matter of fact, she'd probably hate it.

Even worse, she might think he'd concocted his theory out of a misguided attempt to keep her safe. He'd always walked a thin line between being protective and overprotective. She'd likely accuse him of crossing it.

So he couldn't talk to her about this. He could only be there for her, love the daylights out of her, and hope that a solution would present itself before she made what could be the biggest mistake of her life.

Exhausted from the intensity of their lovemaking and the hamster wheel his thoughts had been running on, he fell into a restless sleep. Nightmares involving Amethyst being pursued by burly guys through dark streets tortured him until morning light edged through a break in the curtains.

He'd been an early riser ever since he could remember. As a kid seeking refuge in various hidey-holes each night, he'd had to wake up and get out before someone discovered him. The habit of becoming instantly awake at dawn had stuck with him even when he'd tried to break it.

Amethyst had really conked out. He managed to get out of bed without seeing even an eyelash flutter. He was happy to let her sleep. It was bad enough that she might have aches and pains today from all their extracurricular activity, but at least she'd be a little bit rested.

He hadn't thought that through very well, not this time or back in August. Sending her out on the road last summer after very little sleep could have resulted in a tragedy. When she came to Jackson Hole over New Year's he'd make sure she didn't drive away until she'd had a decent night's rest. Just because he'd learned to function on a few hours in the sack didn't mean he should expect her to.

Once he'd exited the bedroom without waking her, he quietly shut the door. Her razor gave him a halfway decent shave and he went downstairs to get the smoke alarm and his shirt. He put it on to ward off the slight chill in the house but left the tails hanging out.

He started to turn off the Christmas tree lights they'd left on the night before but decided against it because she might enjoy looking at them when she came down. Besides, they were LEDs. With luck he could install the alarm without making a lot of noise. Since he'd be installing it without a power drill that shouldn't be difficult.

She was still snoozing away when he finished, so he went downstairs, made coffee and took a cup into the living room. He wished he had another gift for her that he could tuck under the tree since this was Christmas morning, but he didn't. He sank onto the sofa to drink his coffee and dream of what life could be like if he came back to Sheridan and Amethyst didn't leave. A lot of *ifs* in that dream scenario.

Her bare feet on the stairs made his heart click into high gear. Turning, he watched her come down in her red sleep shirt. Whatever makeup she'd been wearing yesterday was gone and her hair was a tangled mess. He'd never seen a more beautiful woman.

She paused on the bottom step. "Merry Christmas."

"Merry Christmas to you, too." He wanted to go to her and sweep her up in his arms, but he could tell she wasn't quite awake and that might startle her.

"You installed the alarm."

"Tried to be quiet about it."

"You were. I didn't hear a thing. I woke up when I smelled coffee."

He rose. "Come sit and I'll get you some."

"No, you stay there. I'll get my own. I have a package of chocolate doughnuts in the pantry. They're full of preservatives and not the least bit good for us. Want some?"

"Absolutely." He waited until she came back with her coffee and the doughnuts. "Firehouse favorite."

She smiled and sat next to him, her thigh touching his. "My folks cook an elaborate Christmas breakfast, but I like to start with these." She popped open the lid and held out the narrow box.

"Thanks." He took one. "Rosie makes a big breakfast, too, but there's nothing wrong with a few chocolate doughnuts as an appetizer."

"How soon should you be there?"

He glanced at an old-fashioned pendulum clock that hung on the wall. "Soon. Ranch people get up early to feed the animals. But we can have another cup of coffee and a couple more doughnuts before I leave."

"My family won't expect me until a little later." She settled back against the sofa. "Is it terrible of me to wish we didn't have to go somewhere today?"

That comment warmed his heart more than she could know. "If it is, then I'm terrible, too."

"You wouldn't get the holiday feast if you stayed here with me."

He took another doughnut. "What would I get?"

"Tomato soup. Toasted cheese. Lots of sex."

"Sold."

She glanced at him and sighed. "But you drove here so you could hang out with your family for Christmas.

I've always made it a point to be around for Christmas with my folks, and this year it's more important because Sapphire is there and I don't see her all the time like I used to."

"Does she know about your plan to move to LA?" He was trolling for allies and thought Sapphire might be one.

"I'm not sure. She might not have been around when I was discussing it with Chelsea. I'll talk to everybody about it today. Grady's been a few times for gallery openings. He might have some useful info for me."

"He might. Good idea." He wished that some of her contacts had knowledge of the LA entertainment scene. A roommate who was a street-smart woman who'd lived there for years would be an even greater blessing. "You know what? I should go. If I don't, I'll make love to you again, and God knows when we'll leave this house."

That made her laugh. "I hate to admit it, but you're right. I'm sitting here thinking about how many condoms you have left in your jeans' pocket."

"Three, but we're not using them until tonight." Setting down his empty coffee mug, he leaned toward her. "Do we have a plan? What time can you get away?"

She cradled his face in both hands. "You shaved."

"With your razor. Tell me when to show up here because at the moment that's all that I care about, when I'll be able to hold you again."

"Let's say eight. Everything should have wound down by then."

"I'll be here."

"Me, too." Bending toward him, she gave him a soulful kiss that didn't last nearly long enough. "Until then."

"Until then."

She scurried up the stairs. He took their coffee cups into the kitchen, rinsed them and unplugged the pot. Then he walked back into the quiet living room and put on his coat, hat and gloves. He heard the shower come on upstairs and fantasized going up there.

Shaking his head, he discarded the idea. For one thing, he'd probably scare her to death. For another, leaving wouldn't be any easier after he'd made love to her again, so he might as well locate his keys and vamoose.

His keys were AWOL, naturally. When he'd searched the living room, he concluded they were quite likely dangling from the ignition. He'd been out of his ever-lovin' mind last night.

He'd managed to calm down after having a lot of sex and some good conversation. They'd actually slept together for a little while. If he could stay here for the day, they might settle into a less frantic pace. He'd like that.

But she had her obligations and he had his. The word *obligations* didn't fit, though. He loved his family and she obviously loved hers, so there was no resentment involved, only sadness that they couldn't be together.

Despite feeling bonded with her, he wasn't on track to become a permanent part of her life. Climbing into his very cold truck, he started the engine and the music came on. He sat there listening to her sing to him and fought the urge to go back in there. Damn it, leaving her seemed wrong. But he pulled out of her drive and drove away.

His funky mood lasted until he turned onto the ranch road. The hand-carved hanging sign for Thunder Mountain Academy always gave him a lift. Damon and Phil had made it with some design advice from their saddle maker friend Ben Radcliffe. Rosie had decorated the sign with a fresh pine wreath.

Yeah, he needed to be here today with the two people who'd literally saved his life. At the time he'd been hiding out in vacant houses and storage sheds every night. He hadn't realized how dangerous it was.

When he pulled into the circular drive in front of the ranch house, the Christmas lights were all on. He wouldn't have been able to see that if the sun had been shining, but heavy clouds had moved in. He vaguely remembered that someone had mentioned snow in the forecast.

Herb and Rosie would have a big electric bill but not as big as it could have been if he hadn't arrived in the nick of time. He pictured himself moving back to Sheridan and supervising the Christmas lights project every year. Right there was another excellent reason to check into job openings. He might drive over to the fire department tomorrow morning before he left town.

As he climbed out of the truck he took a deep breath and savored wood smoke combined with cinnamon rolls baking and bacon frying. Christmas morning at Thunder Mountain Ranch. Rosie and Herb would have been up for a couple of hours already, but Rosie always delayed Christmas morning breakfast until after the chores were done. That way everyone could sit around the table, drink coffee and have an extra cinnamon roll instead of rushing off to feed and water.

He spotted a car he didn't recognize and wondered who was joining them for Christmas breakfast.

About that time Cade came out onto the front porch, a mug of coffee in one hand. He was wearing a sheepskin vest that looked new. "Thought I heard you drive up! Was a little worried you'd bail on us this morning. Having other activities on your schedule and all."

"Wouldn't miss it."

Cade grinned. "I'm guessing she kicked you out 'cause she had better things to do today."

"Something like that." Jake climbed the steps. "Nice vest."

"Christmas present from the in-laws, or soon to be in-laws. They came for breakfast. Lexi was afraid to let 'em come last night because that would have tipped me off for sure."

"So that's who the car belongs to."

"Yep. Listen, we need to get inside before I freeze my tokus, but is everything okay?"

"So far."

"Still just fun and games, right?"

Jake hesitated a beat too long.

"Oh, buddy, you don't want to fall for her. That's a heartache waiting to happen."

"Probably, but I'll see it through."

"I hate hearing you say that. Even Mom thinks she's not right for you."

"That's because she doesn't know Amethyst like I do."

"Well, I should hope not!" Cade slapped him on the back. "Come in and have some chow. Then we'll shoot some pool while I talk you out of this self-destructive path you're heading down."

Jake followed him into the house. Cade was right that falling for Amethyst would likely put him in a world of hurt. But it was too late now.

12

AFTER GOING THROUGH the opening of presents and an elaborate brunch with no mention of the LA move, Amethyst concluded that Sapphire and Grady hadn't heard about it at the party the night before and therefore hadn't mentioned it to her parents. She took a deep breath. "Since we're all here, it's the perfect time for me to announce my plan for the New Year. I've decided to move to LA."

She was greeted with stunned silence. "Surely it's not a surprise," she said. "I've been rattling around in Wyoming and no talent scout has shown up. I've sent out demos but nobody's come knocking on my door. After talking with Chelsea yesterday—she's Finn O'Roarke's fiancée and a marketing whiz—I decided to become more proactive."

"Wow." Sapphire was the first one to speak. "I guess it's not a total surprise, but I thought you'd decided to stay here where the cost of living was cheaper until you'd made something happen."

"That was the plan, but I'm convinced I can't make something happen from here. I might have an amazing stroke of luck and be discovered at some Wyoming venue, but it hasn't happened yet and I've been doing this for three-plus years."

"It's a very exciting idea." Her mother's tone was cautious. "You know how much I believe in you."

"Same here," her father said. He normally wore black turtlenecks and jeans but in honor of Christmas he'd added a sweatshirt with Santa playing a sax. "You have a boatload of talent. The competition's tough over there, but you can handle it. You'll knock 'em dead."

"Thanks, Dad."

"You will for sure." Her mom looked especially regal in a dark green outfit that had been a gift from Sapphire. "I'm not the least bit worried about that. I'm thinking of the stuff moms always imagine, like whether you'll get mixed up on the freeway and wind up in a terrible neighborhood, or whether you'll move in next door to a drug dealer."

Amethyst laughed. "Oh, Mom. Have a little faith. You sound just like—" She caught herself before saying his name. "A typical mom. I'll be fine." She avoided looking at Sapphire who'd probably known whose name she'd bleeped out.

"And I'm a typical dad," her father said. "Do you have any friends over there? People you went to college with?"

"Not really, but—"

"Wait!" Her mother sat forward. "There's what's-his-name, the one who went over to become a big star a couple of years ago."

"Matt Forrest."

"Right. I talked to Rosie last month in the grocery store and he was still there trying to make it. You could get his contact info."

"I will, but from what I hear, he might be on location for the next few months. Besides, I'll make friends. No worries."

Sapphire looked over at Grady. "You've been to LA several times for gallery shows. Any advice for my big sister?"

"You know, this is so not my area." He gazed at Amethyst. "I totally agree with the logic of making this move, but I'm a Wyoming boy. If living in LA was the only way I could make it with my art…" He shook his head. "I'm not sure what I'd do. City life is not for me. It may turn out that you love it, though."

"I don't know if I will or not. But if I expect to make any progress in my career, I need to give it a shot."

"I'll bet Matt's made some good friends while he's been living there," her mom said. "Even if he won't be around, his friends could be of some help."

Amethyst smiled at her. "I'll contact him. If he offers his friends' help, then I'll consider it, but I don't want to give him the impression I need babysitting. Anyone who's trying to make it in the recording business needs to be able to stand on their own two feet."

"I'll go over with you for a week or so," Sapphire said. "Just until you're settled."

She was tempted but that would be selfish. "Thank you, but I can't let you do that."

Sapphire lifted her chin. "Try and stop me. I'm going."

"I like that plan," her mother said. "The two of you are a force to be reckoned with. I'd feel much better if you spent that first week there, Sapphire. Maybe two weeks."

"I can't accept it." Amethyst held her sister's gaze.

"It's a lovely offer, Sapphire, but you don't have enough time to plan your own wedding let alone spend a week or two making sure I don't move in next to a drug dealer."

"But—"

"Give it up, sis. I really won't let you go over there with me."

Sapphire rolled her eyes and sighed. "Okay, I won't force myself on you, but if you change your mind…"

"I won't. This is my plan and I'm not going to inconvenience other people in order to make it happen."

"As long as I don't have any gigs scheduled," her dad said, "it wouldn't be an inconvenience for me. I set my own schedule."

"I'm not letting any of you interrupt your lives." She glanced around the table. "I appreciate your generous offers, but I can't predict exactly when the move might take place so it's best if I don't get anyone else involved. I'll need to sublet my half of the house and that could be a last-minute arrangement. Once I find the right person, I could be gone within forty-eight hours. I'll need to stay extremely flexible."

Her mother and father exchanged a look. She'd seen it a thousand times. It meant they would drop the subject for now but it was by no means forgotten.

Sure enough, her dad challenged her to a game of chess that afternoon. They often played on Christmas, so that wasn't unusual. He'd taught both her and Sapphire but she'd been the only one who'd kept up with it. Still, she suspected he had ulterior motives for wanting some time with her.

They were well into the game, which they'd set up in front of the fire, when he broached the subject. "I'm not saying you shouldn't go to LA." He captured a pawn.

"But you seem to have made the decision based on what Finn's fiancée said. How well do you know her?"

"We just met. Judging from what everyone says, she's largely responsible for Finn's success with his microbrewery. Her mention of LA was very casual, but something clicked for me. I knew it was what I should do." She moved her knight. "Check."

"Nice job." He maneuvered out of the tight spot she'd put him in. "So this is something you think you *should* do?"

"Bad choice of words. I meant it's something I *want* to do."

"I hope so, because when it comes to anything creative, the word *should* doesn't work well at all."

"You're right."

"I keep thinking of that music prof you liked so much. What was his name?"

"Professor Edenbury." If she could pull this off and actually get a recording contract, he was one of the first people she'd tell once she'd notified her family.

Her father hesitated, his hand poised over the board. "Do his expectations have anything to do with this?"

"Now that would be silly, wouldn't it? He may not even remember me."

"Oh, I'm sure he does. He had big plans for you."

"Well, I'm not doing this for Professor Edenbury, Dad. I'm doing it for me. By the way, did you and your jazz buddies ever talk about going over there and trying your luck? Before you met Mom, of course."

"Sure we did." He made his move. "Check."

"Oh, good one." But she'd anticipated it and weaseled out of his trap. "So why didn't you?"

"Great question, Amie." He'd shortened both his

daughters' names because he was a nickname kind of guy. Her mother hadn't been pleased, but he'd stuck to his guns on the matter. "One night after a gig the four of us got moderately toasted."

She smiled. "Only moderately?"

That made him laugh. "That night, yeah, because once we got on the subject, we knew if we were going to do it, we needed to hop in the car right then and drive to California. We were young and unattached. We could live on the beach if we had to."

"Did you go?"

"No. We argued the question six ways to Sunday and we didn't come to a conclusion until after four in the morning. We'd listed every pro and con we could think of and we went through several six-packs and bags of Cheetos."

She gazed at him, the game forgotten, as she imagined her father as a young man hanging out with his buddies and deciding their future. "Why did you decide to stay?"

"Because we all agreed we loved this silly place called Wyoming. We might never be rich and famous, but we'd have mountains to look at and minimal traffic. Country living was in our blood and we didn't want to give it up. Then I met your mother and knew I'd made the right choice. When you came along, and later Sapphie, I really knew it."

"That's a great story. Any regrets?"

"Not a one. Staying local and playing gigs here and there has worked for me. But I'm not suggesting it would work for you. I just hope you give the decision the same amount of attention that my buddies and I did that night. Checkmate."

She looked at the board and realized he had her beat. She glanced up. "You win, Dad."

"Considering I have you, Sapphie and your mom, I can't lose."

JAKE RESISTED THE urge to text Amethyst during the day although he desperately wanted to know how her family had reacted to news of the move to LA. Surely he wasn't the only one who was worried. He turned his sound off but he checked the screen every once in a while to see if she'd sent him a message.

But when Cade announced the traditional Christmas snowball fight was about to commence, Jake left his phone on the kitchen counter. Grabbing his coat and gloves, he headed outside, eager to work off some tension.

Although Thunder Mountain's foster care program had ended quite a while ago, the temporary financial crisis Rosie and Herb had endured recently had brought many of the brothers back to Sheridan. They'd helped set up Thunder Mountain Academy to make the ranch solvent again and they'd reinstituted many of the nostalgic activities Jake had cherished as a teenager. The Christmas Day snowball fight was one of them.

In the old days it had been all guys manning the barricades, but times had changed. Lexi and Chelsea wanted in on it and Phil vowed she'd be on the front lines next year assuming she could talk Rosie into holding her kid. Rosie promised she would.

Chelsea and Lexi wanted to be on the opposite team from their fiancés, so Jake volunteered to join them and face off against Cade, Damon and Finn. After listening to the women outline their battle plan, Jake figured it would be at least an even fight, and his team might actually win. The women were focused while Cade's team spent the preparation time joking around and acting macho.

While Cade and Damon wasted precious minutes arguing about the correct way to build a fort, Jake's team worked smoothly to create a sturdy barrier with an impressive stockpile of ammunition. As Jake crouched in the middle between the two women, he took inventory of their skills. "Either of you play softball?"

"Was on the state championship squad," Chelsea said.

"Me, too." Lexi exchanged a high five with Chelsea.

Jake hunkered down. "We're going to whip their butts."

The fight didn't last very long because Cade's team ran out of premade snowballs and Jake's crew charged their flimsy barricade armed to the teeth. Lexi's parents, along with Phil, Rosie and Herb sat on the porch scoring the hits. Jake assumed that trampling over the other team's fort pretty much gave his team the win, but tradition meant leaving it up to the judges on the porch.

They all voted for Jake's team. Laughing, he hugged his teammates.

"Foul!" Cade cried. "The judges were prejudiced!"

"No," Phil said, "you three were treating this like a slam dunk you couldn't lose, and the opposing team took advantage of your overconfidence. We stand by our decision." She turned to Rosie. "Am I right?"

"Yes, ma'am." Rosie gave her a big smile.

"All righty, then." Cade abandoned his protest. "Drinks for all! Except Phil, who's on the wagon until she drops that kid."

"Don't remind me." Phil linked her arm through Damon's as they filed into the house. "Good thing I'm excited about this baby because our decision to have her has seriously impacted my life."

Jake took note of that comment. He'd never considered the sacrifices required of a pregnant woman, but Phil was making it very real. Amethyst might never want marriage, let alone a baby. He hadn't thought much about the concept of having kids. His childhood had been traumatic and he couldn't imagine bringing an infant into the world until he had a stable relationship with a woman who wanted the same things he did.

On the surface, that woman wasn't Amethyst. If he took her at her word, she'd be overjoyed to live in LA and be a star with hit songs and regular concert tours. Yet spending the night in the cozy Victorian had given him a glimpse of a life that seemed at odds with that scenario.

After the snowball fight he found himself momentarily alone with Chelsea in the kitchen when she went to fetch a cup of coffee and he wanted to retrieve his phone. He picked it up and shoved it in his pocket. He couldn't have asked for a better opportunity to talk with Chelsea so he'd check his phone later. "It looks as if Amethyst really is moving to LA."

"Good for her." Chelsea poured her coffee into a mug. "Although I admit I was surprised at how quickly she jumped on the idea after my casual remark yesterday."

"She respects your expertise."

"I'm no expert in this area, but it makes sense to me that if she wants a recording contract she'll do better if she can meet with people face-to-face."

Jake hesitated as he considered how to approach the issue. "She'd hoped that a talent scout would discover her in Wyoming."

"She told me that. But waiting for success to come to you isn't a very good strategy."

"No." Jake could tell she was ready to head back out to the porch. "Before you go, let me ask you something."

"Sure." She paused and leaned against the counter.

"What if she only thinks she wants this? What if everyone's been telling her she has a shot and now she feels as if it's put up or shut up time?"

"In other words, she might have the talent but not the drive?"

"Right. Waiting for a talent scout to show up doesn't sound like someone who'll do whatever's necessary to make a dream come true."

"No, it doesn't." Chelsea's gaze was sympathetic. "You really care about her."

"I do. And I'm worried."

"Let me think." Putting down her coffee, she paced the length of the kitchen while she ruffled her damp hair, making the multicolored strands dance around. Finally she turned to him. "I'm guessing you'd like me to talk to her, maybe invite her for coffee before Finn and I leave town."

"Would you?" A ray of hope pierced the gloom.

"I would if I thought it would help. But it won't. She's announced to everyone she's moving to LA. How do you suppose she'd react if I tried to convince her not to go because she's missing that fire in the belly?"

"She'd say you're wrong, that you don't know her well enough and she's highly motivated."

"Exactly. No way would she listen carefully and then admit that I'm right. Unfortunately this isn't something I can tell her. You obviously know her better than I do, but I question whether you or anyone can tell her without creating an explosion. You'll come off as someone who doesn't believe in her."

He groaned. "I believe in her. She's amazing. But she's *happy* here. You should see the studio she's set up in her house. She loves giving voice lessons to little kids. What if she tears her life apart and it doesn't work out? Or even worse, what if it does work out and it's not what she wants, after all?"

"Then she'll suffer and you'll go through hell knowing she's made a terrible mistake. You'll ask yourself if you could have prevented it, even though you understand intellectually that people have to learn for themselves. It's no fun watching someone you love barreling down the tracks toward a potential train wreck. Believe me, I know."

"Who did you go through it with?"

"Finn."

"Finn?" Jake stared at her. "I thought you two met, fell in love and got engaged. Nobody mentioned any train wreck."

"Then I guess you didn't hear about his first marriage."

He thought back. "You know, I vaguely remember something like that, but I was in Jackson Hole by then and didn't get home much. What happened?"

"We had chemistry from the day we met but he was afraid I'd tempt him to ignore his business obligations. So he married someone else, someone who didn't have the power to distract him."

"Wow, I gave him credit for being a lot smarter."

"It was an emotional decision. He was afraid to do the wrong thing so he did something worse. If I'd tried to tell him, he wouldn't have listened. I doubt Amethyst will listen to you, either, even if you have the purest of intentions."

"Which I don't." He sighed. "I'm thinking of her, but I'm also thinking of myself. Tomorrow I'm planning to check for openings at the fire department here. I want to move back."

"Because of her?"

"No. That much is clear in my head. I want to live here again whether she goes or stays."

"Does she know you're moving back to Sheridan?"

He shook his head. "I thought it would complicate things."

"You could try mentioning it. At least then she'd have all the facts before she heads off to LA."

"I don't know. She might think I'm doing it in hopes she'll stay."

"Just tell her the truth. Once you have a job, you're moving back regardless of what she does. You can't control what she chooses to believe. But when she's balancing what she hopes to find in LA against what she's giving up here, you'll be included in her calculations. You never know. That might tip the scales."

"I'll think about it." He gave her a weary smile. "Thanks for the heart-to-heart."

"Sorry I don't have a magic solution."

"Yeah, I was hoping you would, but you're right. There isn't one."

When she left the kitchen he stayed behind and pulled out his phone. His pulse jumped when he saw the text from Amethyst: Change of plans. Mom and Dad want us all to go caroling at 5 and dinner here afterward. You're invited.

13

AMETHYST THOUGHT CURIOSITY was at the bottom of her mother's caroling and dinner plan. Maybe she'd noticed her daughter checking her phone several times during the day and had figured out that Jake Ramsey was back in the picture. Getting him under the Ferguson family roof and at their dinner table was a time-honored way to confirm those suspicions.

That was fine with Amethyst. She wasn't deliberately keeping Jake a secret, but they weren't heading for a fairy-tale ending so there seemed to be no reason to include him in her family's plans. Her mother obviously felt differently.

Jake arrived looking more gorgeous than any man had a right to be. He was freshly shaved, but then, he would be. He knew what was scheduled after the family togetherness time.

Her mother suggested that Jake should leave on his coat and hat because everyone else could be ready in a jiffy. Amethyst couldn't blame her mother for not wanting to alter the picture he made standing in their entry hall. He'd turned up the collar of his sheepskin coat against the night air and his perfectly creased gray Stetson, snug jeans and polished boots made him look like an ad for Western wear. Once again she was amazed that the single women of Jackson Hole hadn't lined up outside the firehouse.

Because he was ready to go, he was free to help her with her coat and he managed it with polite chivalry as if they were only good friends and not passionate lovers. He charmed her parents with his winning smile and thanked them for inviting him. He called them Mr. and Mrs. Ferguson because that had been protocol when he'd dated her ten years ago.

Her mother asked him to use Jane and Stan instead, and he slipped right into that without awkwardness or hesitation. Amethyst couldn't help contrasting the self-confident person he was now with the high school senior who'd been so unsure of his place in the world. His work as a firefighter had given him an impressive physique, but it had also matured him. He appeared completely relaxed, as if he didn't consider it the least bit strange that he'd received a last-minute invitation to join a family Christmas activity.

At one point Amethyst's mother glanced over and lifted her eyebrows as if silently asking why her daughter didn't snap up this paragon. That gesture was enough to convince Amethyst why her mom had issued the invitation. She hadn't said much since breakfast about the LA plan. She must be frustrated that her teaching job at the high school would keep her from checking on the safety of Amethyst's apartment until at least spring break. She probably hoped that a romance with Jake would postpone the move or maybe even cancel it.

Neither of her parents could be blamed for their nervousness about LA. She wasn't entirely calm herself. But that didn't mean she wasn't going.

"I should warn you that I'm not much of a singer." Jake glanced at Amethyst's parents. "I hope the rest of you will be really loud so nobody can hear me."

Her mother patted his arm. "I'm not much of a singer, either, Jake. I count on Amethyst and Stan to help me stay on pitch. Sapphire can hold her own, but I've never heard Grady sing."

"I have." Jake grinned at his foster brother. "He's got a halfway decent voice but—"

"Hey!" Grady threw back his shoulders. "I have a fully decent voice. There's nothing halfway about it."

"You know, that's a fact." Jake tugged his Stetson a little lower. "Now if you could only remember the words, you'd be all set. If anyone hears a person going 'Silent night, holy night, something something, something something,' that will be Grady."

"Not anymore." Grady whipped out his phone. "Times have changed, bro. Thanks to the modern age, I have the words at my fingertips."

Jake pointed to Grady's thick gloves. "Those don't look like the kind for handling a phone. In essence you have no fingertips."

"Oh. Yeah, that's true." He pocketed his cell. "Didn't think of that. Guess I'm back to mumbling."

"Never fear. I've got you covered." Amethyst's father held up a sheaf of papers. "When we came up with this idea, I printed out a few carols." He passed them out. "Here's the plan. We walk to the end of the block. Jane and I will take the lead and you four will follow. At the end of the block we'll cross the street and serenade the people who bought the Blakely's house. It's a young couple with a baby. I've met them and they seem nice. Then we'll cross back to Mrs. Gentry's."

"Does she still live there?" Sapphire asked.

He nodded. "Yes, but she's at least ninety and she's hard of hearing so we'll have to belt out those tunes. Anyway, we'll crisscross the street and end up back here for dinner. Everybody ready?"

"Ready as we'll ever be," Amethyst said.

"Then let's go surprise the neighbors."

"Surprise them?" Jake asked. "This isn't a family tradition?"

"Used to be," her dad said. "Back when we could corral the girls and bribe them with promises of hot cocoa and Christmas cookies afterward. Then the day came when they flatly refused, regardless of the bribe."

"Because it was embarrassing, Dad," Sapphire said as they headed out the door. "Nobody else did it and we had friends living around here. We'd hear about it when we got back from Christmas vacation. They called us the Trapp Family Singers. It was not cool."

"And none of our neighbors knew how to react." Amethyst suspected it would be even more confusing to them this year after a thirteen-year hiatus. "They weren't sure whether to invite us in for dinner, give us money or bring out a platter of Christmas cookies."

"No kidding," Sapphire said. "They were completely bewildered. Mrs. Lester wanted to give us the poinsettia she had sitting in her entry."

Amethyst started laughing. "Yeah, and you almost took it until Mom made you put it back. Oh, and remember the Danforths and the bowl of candy?"

"The candy they started throwing at us like they were on a parade float?" Sapphire rolled her eyes. "But that was better than Mr. Johannsen trying to make us eat some *surstromming*."

"Eeuuww, yes! That was gross!" Amethyst could still remember the smell of the fermented fish.

"Hey, Dad," Sapphire called out. "Could we skip his house? Just in case he still eats that awful stuff?"

"He's moved," their father said over his shoulder, "so you don't have to worry about it."

"That's a relief." Sapphire motioned Amethyst and Jake to the back of the parade. "You two bring up the rear." She lowered her voice. "I'm sure you have things to talk about."

"Um, okay." Amethyst glanced at Jake. "Sorry about this," she murmured.

"No problem." He took her hand. "I can't wait to see how this caroling gig turns out. I'm a little sorry Mr. Johannsen moved away."

"Trust me, you would not want to get anywhere near that stuff. But thanks for accepting the invitation." She glanced over at him. "Did I pull you away from anything important at the ranch?"

"Not really. Playing poker and pool, watching basketball, eating leftovers. They all thought it was hysterical that I was coming here to go caroling."

"I'm guessing you've never done it before."

"Good guess. But it seems kind of nice, growing up in a neighborhood where you knew most of the people."

"You probably didn't have much to do with the neighbors when you lived with your dad."

"Sure didn't. He was the most antisocial person I've ever known and if I talked to anybody who lived around there I was in big trouble."

"I never asked you before, but do you know where he is?"

"No, which is fine with me. Rosie used her connections in social services to keep tabs on him for a while. I was petrified that he'd try to take me away from the ranch. Then he left town, thank God. Never heard from him again."

"Good."

"Yeah, really. I have my family, now, and they're great." He glanced around. "This is nice, though, walking along looking at all the Christmas lights. We didn't get to do that when we were dating."

"Nope. That's what happens when you break up right before Christmas."

"There should be a rule—no breakups right before Christmas. That was one of my worst holidays ever."

"Mine, too."

He squeezed her hand. "Sorry. Entirely my fault. I promise not to go stomping off like that in the next twelve hours so we should be okay this Christmas."

"Good to know." She tugged on his hand so he'd slow down. "I should probably warn you that my parents aren't completely in favor of my going to LA and I think they're hoping you'll be a factor in changing my mind."

"Which is why I got the sudden invitation, right?"

"Yes."

"I kind of figured that. And I need to tell you something in case it comes up in conversation. I'm going to see if I can get on with the fire department here."

She sucked in a breath. "Because you're hoping I'll change my mind, too?"

"No, not at all. Whether you leave or stay, I'm still

doing it. If you change your mind and decide to stick around, that would be wonderful, but that's not the deciding factor."

She probed his statement for any hidden agenda and didn't find one. He'd never lied to her, so she was inclined to believe him. "So what is the deciding factor?"

"Simple. I'm homesick. Rosie and Herb are the only parents I have, and I want to be able to see them on a regular basis. I didn't realize how much I'd missed the ranch and being with them until I came back this Christmas. Cade and Damon have moved back, too, so I can hang out with them. When others visit, I'll be around."

"You'd live at the ranch?"

"No, that's not practical. The Academy students are staying in the cabins now, except for vacations, and I don't want to move into one of Rosie and Herb's guest rooms. I'm too used to being on my own. Besides, a place close to the station makes more sense."

"My house isn't that far from the station." She wasn't sure how she felt about him living in the space, but at least he could be trusted not to trash her studio.

"That's true."

"My half of the rent's reasonable."

"You think I should take over your lease?" He sounded surprised.

"I don't know. Arlene might freak out if I said a guy was moving in. Or she might like it from a security standpoint, although we don't have much in the way of crime around there. I'd have to ask her."

"I love that house, but there may not be a job opening for me. I'm going to check on that in the morning before I leave town, but I won't move until I have something lined up."

"Tell you what, I won't go looking for someone to sublet it until you find out about the job."

"Thanks. The idea's growing on me." He took a deep breath. "Although moving in there after you're gone would be…a little weird."

"I'm sure. Knowing you were moving in would be weird for me, too. But I'd love it if I didn't have to tear out my studio."

"But why would you want to keep it if you're never going to use it again? You could take some of the equipment to LA and sell the rest, which would give you extra money."

She thought about it and knew he was right. If she sublet her space to anyone besides Jake, they'd expect her to dismantle the studio. Finding a musician to move in was unlikely, and it would have to be the right musician, someone who'd treat the studio with respect. She should take it apart and sell what she couldn't use. The soundproofing she'd done would be wasted, but moving on meant sacrifice.

"If I ended up renting from you, I'd let you take everything out gradually," he said. "That way you wouldn't have to rush to strip it all away. That could be stressful."

"It could, and I appreciate the offer. But I'm a rip-off-the-bandage kind of girl, so if that studio is destined to go, then I might as well get it over with."

They walked in silence for a little longer.

"You know, on second thought," he said, "what if you left everything the way it is? I don't need that second bedroom for anything. You could rent a furnished apartment until you see how it all goes. Then you'd only have to take your clothes and what few other things you'd need."

"You mean leave all my furniture, too?"

"Sure. Or I could buy it from you if you want. It's nicer than what I have. That way you don't have the hassle of renting a truck and hauling furniture into your new apartment."

"It would be a heck of a lot easier, wouldn't it?"

"Seems like it to me."

"Let me think about it. First, you have to get a job with the fire department."

"If they have an opening, you could pack up and leave whenever you want."

"I could." Her stomach began to churn with a combination of excitement and anxiety. If Jake's visit to the fire department in the morning produced a job, she was free to simply take off. Then she remembered her New Year's Eve gig and was relieved that she couldn't go immediately even if Jake did get hired right away. She wanted to go to LA. She really did. But leaving next week seemed a little hasty.

"I couldn't go until after New Year's," she said. "I agreed to perform in Jackson Hole and canceling at this late date would be unprofessional."

"You're right. You can't cancel now. Anyway, I'm selfish enough to want to see you again before you take off."

She squeezed his hand. "I want that, too. And, by the way, I appreciate this gesture on your part."

"It might not work. It all hinges on the job situation."

"I know, but you're still attempting to help me get there even though you don't think it's a great idea. Or have you changed your mind?"

"Not really. But if that's what you want, then you need to give it a shot."

"Thank you. That means so much to me."

"Okay, troops!" her dad called out. "Time to cross the street. Watch for cars."

"There aren't any cars, Dad," Sapphire said.

Her father laughed. "Sorry. Force of habit."

Amethyst's heart swelled with affection as she thought of all the times her parents had cautioned her and her sister to watch out for this and that. No wonder they were worried about this move. They couldn't be expected to simply turn off that impulse, no matter how old she was.

Once they were all on the other side of the street in front of what used to be the Blakely house, her dad arranged them in a semicircle. Then he gave out the stapled sets of lyrics and hummed the opening note of "Joy to the World." Jake fumbled with the pages and finally let go of her hand so he could deal with them.

As the six of them launched into the carol, she discovered that Jake wasn't such a bad singer. His deep baritone was untrained but he had a good ear and stayed on pitch. This was going to be fun, after all.

They were partway through the song when the door opened and a woman and a man came out wearing their coats. The woman held a blanket-wrapped bundle that was probably the baby swaddled against the cold. A second woman with long blond hair stepped onto the porch and closed the door behind her. She hugged a furry coat to her body instead of fastening it and she kept looking at Jake.

Amethyst couldn't blame her. He was gorgeous. She'd been spoiled the past couple of days because she hadn't had to deal with watching attractive women ogle Jake. This one was subtle about it, but she clearly found him appealing. Well, she was out of luck, at least for the time being.

When the carol ended, the women both applauded and the blonde called out, "Jake, is that you?"

Amethyst's jaw tightened. Damn.

Jake hesitated a moment. "Marla?"

"It's me! I've moved to Sheridan!" She made her way down the porch steps toward Jake. "It's so good to see you. I thought we'd lost touch forever. Are you back in town, too?"

"Not permanently yet, but I hope to be soon. Let me introduce you to my friends."

Friends. Amethyst winced at the casual term that didn't come close to describing how she felt about Jake and how she believed he felt about her. But, under the circumstances, she couldn't claim to be anything else.

14

Talk about rotten timing. But he couldn't introduce Amethyst as his girlfriend because she wasn't. He knew she wasn't happy about the chance meeting with an old flame, but then, neither was he. On the other hand, he didn't want to be rude to Marla. They'd had a good thing going for a while.

At the time he'd taken the job in Jackson Hole, she'd been immersed in her accounting courses. She'd made a couple of trips to Jackson during breaks in her schedule and he'd made a couple to Sheridan, but in the end the relationship hadn't survived the separation. She'd sent him a wedding invitation to a ceremony down in Cheyenne two years ago but she wasn't acting married now.

She didn't specifically mention a divorce, but when they all tromped up to the porch to meet her sister, brother-in-law and the baby, Marla said she'd moved to Sheridan to be with them. Her brother-in-law worked for the bank and had recommended her for a job.

While everyone goo-gooed at the baby, Marla asked for his cell number so she could text him hers. He couldn't figure out any way to refuse. It wasn't as if he had a commitment to someone else. He was sure Amethyst had heard the entire exchange, damn it.

He wasn't interested in Marla. He wanted Amethyst, but she might eventually be lost to him. He didn't intend to stay celibate for the rest of his life and mourn the loss of his one true love, so if the time came when he had to accept that Amethyst would never be with him, he'd take comfort elsewhere. If Marla was still available, well… he might take comfort with her.

Amethyst had probably figured all that out. Women were quick to do that. He had a strong feeling the subject would come up once they were alone, but Amethyst was a fair person. She'd know that she didn't have a leg to stand on. That didn't mean she had to like this turn of events. In a way, he found her irritation encouraging.

Other promising signs had cropped up tonight. He was serious about renting her half of the Victorian if he got a job, but he had ulterior motives. So far she hadn't called him on it, but she was smart so she might before too long.

If he was right that she was ambivalent about the move, having the chance to accomplish it right away with a minimum of fuss might be startling enough to make her question her decision. If that backfired and she hightailed it over to LA thanks to his help, then coming home would be really easy if it didn't work out for her.

He wanted a job in Sheridan for many reasons, but securing the Victorian and keeping it ready for Amethyst's possible return was now high on his list. She'd guess his motives at some point and he'd be happy to confess if she did. He hoped that eventually she'd want to come back to the house and to him, but if not, he'd live with the memories they'd shared for as long as he could stand it.

Finally the carolers extricated themselves from the very nice couple, their sweet baby and a woman Jake had not expected to deal with tonight. They all crossed the street to Mrs. Gentry's, the lady Stan had said was going deaf.

Jake had never had a grandparent in his life and he thought that was sad because he'd be an excellent grandson. He'd check on them to see if they needed anything and be tolerant of their infirmities. Maybe being a foster kid without the normal advantages had contributed to his tenderness toward older people. When a person had experienced being at a disadvantage, they understood how it felt.

Because of that, he suggested ringing the doorbell before they started singing. Rosie had once told him that people who lived alone and were hard of hearing often increased the volume on their doorbell chime and their telephone ring. Jake had taken a personal interest in providing Mrs. Gentry with a Christmas carol tonight.

In fact, he stayed at the door until she came in response to the doorbell. He glanced down at a plump little lady with wispy white curls framing her round, pink-cheeked face. She wore a Frosty the Snowman sweatshirt, gray sweatpants and bunny slippers.

He smiled and touched the brim of his hat. "Merry Christmas, Mrs. Gentry!"

She shouted right back at him. "Merry Christmas to you, cutie-pie! Looks like you're here with the Fergusons! What can I do for you?"

"We want to sing you a Christmas carol!"

"Wonderful!" She clapped her hands.

"Want to bundle up so you can come out and enjoy it?"

"Of course! Whatcha gonna sing?"

"What's your favorite?" He hoped Stan had included it in the mix.

"'Grandma Got Run Over by a Reindeer.' I'll get my wrap!"

Jake turned back to Stan, who was cracking up. "Do you know it?"

"Not all of it. You had to ask, didn't you?"

"No worries." Jake grinned as he returned to the group. "I know it. We used to drive Herb and Rosie crazy with that song. I'll bet even Grady knows most of the words."

Grady nodded. "Yep, sure do."

"So do we." Amethyst exchanged a smile with her sister.

"Then you four take the lead." Stan glanced at his wife. "The old folks will mumble along."

"You can mumble if you want," Jane said. "I know the words. Sapphire and Amethyst drove *me* crazy singing it."

Stan looked confused. "I don't remember that. Where was I?"

"Traveling the state doing Christmas shows," she said gently. "We needed the money a lot more back then."

"Guess I've sort of blocked those years."

"Here I am!" Mrs. Gentry came out to the porch and closed the door behind her. She was still wearing her bunny slippers but she'd added a bright red parka and a Santa hat. "Sing away!"

Jake turned to Amethyst. "You're the professional. You'd better start us off."

"Okay." She hummed the opening note. "On three. One, two…"

And they were off, everybody except Stan belting

out a song about poor Grandma's fatal encounter. Stan jumped in each time they reached the chorus, and Mrs. Gentry sang it all at the top of her lungs while she danced a jig on her porch. Hysterical as that was to watch, Jake hoped she didn't slip on an icy patch and fall down.

Fortunately she didn't. When they were finished she insisted everyone had to come in for a mug of hard cider that she guaranteed would put hair on their chests. Jake immediately accepted, which meant everyone else had to go along, but judging from the laughter and smiles, he didn't think they minded.

Mrs. Gentry's artificial tree was loaded with delicate-looking ornaments and large clumps of tinsel. Jake steered clear of it but even so the tinsel shivered as he went by. Christmas-themed knickknacks covered every available surface and Jake moved carefully as he helped Amethyst with her coat and took off his own. One wrong move and he could take out an entire nativity scene.

Jane offered to help with the cider but Mrs. Gentry told her to find a seat and get comfortable. The men hung the coats on a wooden coat tree that already held Mrs. Gentry's red parka although she'd left on the Santa hat. Keeping the coat tree from falling under the load took some balancing, but they managed it while they waited for the women to sit.

When Jake turned around, all three ladies were in a row on the sofa. That left a recliner, probably Mrs. Gentry's spot since it faced the TV, and two dainty armchairs with seats that had flowers stitched on the seat cushions.

Jake wasn't going to take the recliner and he was afraid he'd break those chairs, plus, there were only two. "You guys go ahead." He gestured toward the chairs. "I'll stand."

Grady shook his head. "I'm not taking a chance on one of those."

"Oh, for goodness' sake." Jane moved over to one of the chairs. "Stan, you take the other one. It'll hold you. Your mother had some just like this."

Sapphire scooted to one end of the sofa. "We can fit both of you guys on here with us."

"Definitely." Amethyst moved to the other end.

Grady and Jake looked at each other, shrugged and wedged themselves in between the women.

"I won't be able to drink cider." Grady began to chuckle.

"Why not?" Sapphire glanced at him. "You're not driving anywhere."

"I can't move my arms."

"Oh, for heaven's sake. Put your arm around me. That'll give you more room."

"Now there's a concept." Grady looked over at Jake. "I'll go first and then you. If we tried to do it at the same time, odds are we'd tip this sofa backward into the teeny, tiny snow village."

"Understood."

Moments after they'd finished the maneuver, Mrs. Gentry wheeled in a tea cart loaded down with mugs of cider and a huge plate of decorated sugar cookies.

Stan got up and Jake started to do the same because that was his training when a lady entered the room.

"Don't try it," Grady warned in an undertone. "You'll throw off the equilibrium and make a mess."

"Right." Jake raised his voice a couple of notches above normal conversational level. "Don't mean to be impolite, Mrs. Gentry, but Grady and I will disrupt everything if we stand."

"Heavens, don't do that." She handed Stan two mugs and the plate of cookies before turning toward the sofa. "One of you big boys could have had my chair."

"Thank you, ma'am," Jake said. "But we're fine right here."

"You look mighty squished up to me, but when you're courtin', that's probably how you like it." She gave Sapphire a mug of cider. "Is that an engagement ring on your finger, Sapphire Ferguson?"

"Yes, Mrs. Gentry, it is. I'd like you to meet my fiancé, Grady Magee."

"Pleased to make your acquaintance, young man." She beamed at Grady. "Well done. Sapphire's a catch."

"Yes, ma'am, she is."

"When's the big day?"

"We're working on that," Sapphire said. "We have tight schedules."

"Tight saddles? Then you need Ben Radcliffe to loosen them up. He's—"

"No, *schedules*."

"Oh, *schedules*. I see that problem a lot with young people these days. I hope you find the time, but at least you've found each other. That's the important part."

When the older woman turned her attention to the other half of the sofa's residents, Jake could guess what was coming. He wondered how Amethyst would handle it. After all, he had his arm around her and he was out caroling with the family. He must look suspiciously like a significant person in Amethyst's life.

Apparently, Amethyst decided to take the initiative. She had such amazing voice control that she could subtly turn up the volume without shouting. "Mrs. Gentry, this is Jake Ramsey. Remember I dated him in high school?

He lives in Jackson Hole now, but he came over for a couple of days so we invited him to go caroling with us for old time's sake."

"That's nice." Mrs. Gentry handed him a mug of cider. "Enjoying yourself, Jake Ramsey?"

"Yes, ma'am."

"Thought so." She gave him a wink before taking the plate of cookies from Stan and offering them to the couch sitters. At last everyone had been served, so she took her cider over to the recliner.

Once she was settled in, she lifted her mug. "To love!" When everyone echoed her toast, she smiled. "Nothing else matters, you know. Now, drink up. I have plenty more where this came from."

The cider turned out to be delicious and sneakily potent. Two mugs of the stuff and Jake could feel the effects, so he wondered if Amethyst, being much lighter, might be getting smashed. That would explain why her conversation had become more animated and she'd allowed her free hand to rest lightly on his thigh. Fine with him.

Jane was the one who finally got them all moving toward the door. Mrs. Gentry insisted they take a Tupperware container of cookies and Jane accepted it with a smile and a loud thank-you. Miraculously they all donned coats, hats and scarfs without dumping the cookies or breaking any of the fragile items crowding the room. But the coat tree would have fallen into the Christmas tree if Jake hadn't grabbed the top at the last minute.

"Yay, Jake!" Amethyst blew him a kiss. "My hero!"

Yeah, she was definitely toasted. That meant they'd hang out at her folks' house longer than he might have planned because he didn't want her driving until the cider had worn off. Food would help a lot, though.

At last they were all standing on the sidewalk and, once again, Jane took charge. "I propose we end this caroling gig and go fix some dinner."

"Good idea." Stan wrapped an arm around her shoulders and headed down the sidewalk toward home. "That cider packed a punch."

Sapphire and Grady followed, arms around each other's waists. Sapphire started giggling. "But it sure beats the heck out of *surstromming*! I'll carol at Mrs. Gentry's any old day."

"Me, too." Stan called back to her. "But next year we're reversing the order and ending with her house."

"Works for me." Amethyst gazed up at Jake. "How 'bout you?"

"I'd go along with that." He'd had his arm over her shoulder the whole time they'd been on the sofa and he saw no reason to hesitate now. He tucked her against his side as they followed Grady and Sapphire.

Amethyst slid her arm around his waist as naturally as if they'd picked up where they'd left off when they'd dated in high school. "Although I might not be able to come home for Christmas next year." She didn't sound very tipsy now.

"I know." He wondered if the cold air had sobered her up. Or it could be the realization that she couldn't blithely make plans with her family if she intended to follow through on her move.

"Because I've kept my overhead low by living here, I've had the luxury of turning down any gigs that would take me away over Christmas. My parents could have avoided having my dad work through the holiday if they hadn't had kids."

"I'm sure neither of them regrets that."

"I'm sure they don't, either. I probably won't regret giving up Christmas with my family if it means I'll get my big break."

"Probably not." But he was glad she was taking the necessary sacrifices into consideration.

"I just happened to think of something. Do you stand to make more money if you stay in Jackson Hole?"

"Quite likely. It's been a vacation playground for the rich and famous for a while, and chances are the area will grow faster and bigger than Sheridan because it's so close to Yellowstone. I considered that a plus when I got the job, but money isn't everything."

Amethyst chuckled. "So I've heard. I hope you know I'm not into this music thing for the money."

"I've never thought that. But I may not be clear on what you do want out of this career."

"To fulfill my potential."

That sounded like something a teacher might have said to her. "And what does that mean, exactly?"

"I've been told I have the voice to be a major recording star, so, obviously, since I'm not a major recording star, I haven't fulfilled my potential."

He didn't know how to respond without risking the fight Chelsea had warned him about. Amethyst must not value the contribution she was making now or she wouldn't say something like that. He thought what she was doing, entertaining locally and teaching kids, had great value, but he hesitated to tell her. She might take it the wrong way, as if he wanted to keep her here for his own selfish purposes.

"So what's the deal with Marla?"

He almost said Marla who? He'd forgotten about her already, which wasn't fair to Marla. He made a mental note that he couldn't let his old flame think he was interested when he clearly wasn't. If and when they communicated again, he'd make sure she understood that he was…what? Unable to focus on anyone but Amethyst? No, he couldn't say that even if it turned out to be true.

"You don't have to tell me. It's none of my business."

"It is while you and I are still involved. Marla and I dated for a while. It didn't go anywhere."

"In case you didn't pick up on it, she's ready to revisit the idea."

"I picked up on it. I didn't want to be rude on Christmas night with everyone standing around listening. I'll handle it later."

She was quiet for a while, but finally she spoke. "I'm a bad person."

"You're absolutely not, so why are you saying it?"

"Because I'm happy that you have no plans to get it on with Marla once I'm out of the picture. But that's completely unfair. We both know that if I achieve what I'm going for in LA, it will be the end of anything between us. If I care about you, and I do, I should *want* you to find someone else!"

Sapphire turned around. "Everything okay back there?"

"Yeah, fine," Jake said. "Just having a deep discussion."

"Okay." Sapphire smiled and hooked her arm around Grady again.

Jake envied the hell out of them. He wanted to be like Grady, who was walking down the street knowing that he had a future with the woman nestled against his hip. Instead Amethyst wanted to discuss his plan to replace her after she'd moved away.

He sucked in a lungful of cold air. "Let's take one thing at a time, shall we? You haven't even left yet. I'm not going to troll for a new girlfriend while you're still in Wyoming. As for Marla, when I saw her tonight I had the fleeting thought I should probably stay in touch in order to hedge my bets."

"Aha! See, I knew—"

"But then the evening continued, and we had a great time with Mrs. Gentry, and you sat on her sofa with your hand on my thigh and—"

"Hang on. I did no such thing!"

"Sorry, but you did."

"I put my hand on your thigh in front of *everybody*?"

"Yes, but it's possible nobody else noticed. I couldn't very well miss it. My thigh is extremely sensitive, especially when you're stroking it."

Her voice rose. "I was *stroking* it?"

Sapphire glanced over her shoulder again. "Just so you know, I'm getting little snippets and my imagination's going wild up here."

"Mine, too," Grady said. "I must've been drunker than I thought if I missed stroking action going on."

"Calm yourselves," Jake said. "It's not what you're thinking."

"Then what is it?" Sapphire asked.

"Nothing," Amethyst said. "Absolutely nothing."

Sapphire laughed. "Yeah, okay. We'll talk later."

"Good idea, sis."

In the silence that followed, Jake hoped she'd forgotten all about his ex-girlfriend.

She cleared her throat. "So. Back to Marla."

No such luck. "What about her?"

This time she kept her voice low. "Look, it's fine and perfectly logical for you to keep her number in case you might want to call her later. Why wouldn't you do that?"

"Because she's not an option, regardless. Taking up with her after being with you would be like dealing with a brush fire in somebody's backyard after battling a two-thousand-acre forest fire in Yellowstone."

"I'm a two-thousand-acre forest fire? That doesn't sound like a good thing."

"In terms of firefighting, it's not." He hugged her close. "But in terms of passionate loving, it's a very good thing."

15

AMETHYST HAD MORE fun at her parents' dinner table that night than she'd had in ages. She'd always enjoyed hanging with her folks, but having Grady and Jake there changed the dynamic in ways she couldn't have imagined. The foster brothers couldn't help teasing each other, which fit right in with her dad's sense of humor.

He'd held his own in a house full of women for years, but tonight he clearly got a charge out of having male allies. She had a rare glimpse of what he must have been like when he'd been a single guy traveling with a band. Yet when he'd had a chance to make that his life, he'd chosen a different path.

She was at that same crossroads, and her parents and her sister and Grady provided a live demonstration of what she would be giving up. Dedication to her art, especially when it involved popular music, required sacrifice. Professor Edenbury had drummed that into her. But sitting at the dinner table surrounded by love, she felt a twinge of doubt that such a sacrifice would make her happy.

Then again, Mrs. Gentry's cider might be making her

more nostalgic than usual. It definitely had been a factor in loosening everybody up. As Amethyst wiped away tears of laughter while Jake and Grady danced around the table singing "Grandma Got Run Over by a Reindeer," she knew she'd remember the moment for the rest of her life. She wanted to be alone with Jake, but when the hour grew late and it was past time to leave, she lingered. Given her plans, this kind of evening might never happen again and she hated to see it end.

When she and Jake finally stood in the entry with their coats on, her mom handed her a bag full of Mrs. Gentry's cookies and gave her a fierce hug. "All I want for you is happiness," she murmured.

"I know, Mom." She hugged her back with equal doses of love and gratitude. "Thank you for inviting Jake tonight. It was special."

Her mother gazed at her with affection shining in her eyes. "It was. I enjoyed seeing him again." She paused, as if about to say something else, but gave a little shake of her head as if deciding not to. "How about having coffee at Rangeland Roasters before you head off to Jackson Hole for your gig?"

"Sounds great." She wouldn't be meeting her mom for coffee every week, either. Change was hard, but progress couldn't be made without it. She hugged her dad and then preceded Jake out the door. "Hey, it's snowing!" she called over her shoulder to her parents.

"Drive carefully!" her dad said.

"Want me to drive you?" Jake followed her down the porch steps. "I can bring you back here to pick up your car on my way out of town in the morning."

That was so Jake, wanting to keep her safe. "Thanks,

but I'd rather drive it home now. It's not too bad, yet. We'll go slow."

"Okay. I'll follow you."

On the way back to her house she navigated the road with extra care because she didn't want Jake to worry. That was ironic, because he would worry himself to death when she left for LA. But of all the hazards in that city, both real and imagined, driving in snow wouldn't be one of them.

She could try pointing that out to Jake and her family but she doubted it would have any effect on their misgivings. Driving in snow was a known quantity that everyone in Wyoming had learned how to handle. LA was full of the unknown. She was scared, too, and unfortunately her nearest and dearest weren't helping.

By the time she pulled into her driveway, the snow had let up a bit. Big flakes drifted lazily down for a snow-globe effect. She'd never minded snow. As a kid she'd spent hours playing in it, and sometimes she and Sapphire still did. Or they used to before Sapphire moved to Cody.

She and Grady were staying another day before heading back, so if this snowfall kept up all night, they might be up for building a snowman. Amethyst wanted to grab such opportunities while she could. Although she missed her sister now, it would be worse once they were more than a thousand miles apart.

Jake's light rap on the window startled her and she jumped.

"Are you okay?" His voice was muted by the closed window, but she could tell from his expression that he was concerned.

She nodded and quickly unfastened her seat belt. Then she grabbed her purse and the bag of cookies.

He opened the door as she started to climb down. Then he lifted her out and into his arms. "You were just sitting there. I thought something was wrong."

"Sorry if I scared you. I got caught up in memories of making snowmen with Sapphire when we were kids."

"You were still building them when we were dating." He reached around her and nudged her door closed. "I remember a really elaborate one you two made over the Thanksgiving weekend of our senior year."

"The pilgrim couple! I'd forgotten all about that. Sapphire was the mastermind behind it. I just did what she told me. It's no wonder she and Grady get along so well. Two peas in a pod."

He drew her closer. "I hear California is chock-full of musicians. Maybe you'll find your matching pea over there."

He might be teasing but she didn't think so. At least she could put his mind to rest on that score. "That's not the goal. I'm going over there to see if I can make it as a recording artist, not look for a soul mate. Besides, that life is hard on relationships. I can't imagine how tough it must be to maintain a connection with someone when you're completely focused on the work."

"Sounds like you've made peace with that."

"I have, Jake." She looked into his eyes. "I may never live like my folks or Sapphire and Grady. That doesn't mean I won't cherish every moment I've spent with you."

"Same here." He searched her expression a moment longer before he visibly pulled himself together. "You know what? We have more of those moments available before I leave. Give me those cookies." Wrapping his other arm around her shoulders, he hurried her toward the porch and up the steps. "First thing in the door, boots off."

"Aw, no wild sex on the floor with our boots on?" She fished out her key and inserted it in the lock.

"Yes to wild sex on the floor. No to doing it with our boots on." Once the door was open he hustled her inside and leaned against the wall to remove them. "It's Christmas night. We should make love under the tree."

"We won't fit unless you plan to lop some branches off the bottom."

"Literal woman, aren't you? *Near* the tree. I want to see the lights make a rainbow on your naked body like they did last night." He put down the cookies, shrugged out of his coat and threw it on the sofa. "But your floor is hard. We're bringing bedding down here this time." He helped her out of her coat, grabbed her hand and started toward the stairs.

She had to hustle to keep up with him. She was gasping by the time they reached the landing. "Hang on a minute. I don't go for five-mile runs like some people."

"Oh, sorry. I was thinking with my dick."

"Just let me catch my breath."

Glancing back at her, he gave a short nod. "Right. I should've done this in the first place." In one smooth motion he hoisted her over his shoulder and carried her the rest of the way with her ass in the air.

"Jake!"

"What?" He set her back on her feet and smiled. He wasn't even breathing hard. "Everyone should experience the fireman's carry at least once in their lives, so there you go."

"You're showing off."

"Yes, ma'am." He walked into the bedroom, pulled off the comforter and thrust it into her arms. Then he piled a blanket on top of the comforter, nearly blocking her view. "If you'll take that, I'll get the pillows and the sheets."

"You've obviously put a lot of thought into this fantasy."

"I had some thinking time while I was following you over here." He began stripping off the holiday sheets. "We only have a few hours left and I want to make them count."

"Does that mean you have other schemes in mind once this is checked off your list?"

"Maybe." He bundled up the sheets and added them to his pile. "How about you?"

"I haven't fully accepted that this will be our last night together in this house. The reality hasn't hit me yet."

He turned toward her. "It doesn't have to be the last night." His tone was casual but there was an underlying tension in his words. "If I rent from you, you're welcome to come back and visit anytime."

"You make it sound as if you'll have my room ready and waiting for me."

"Not just your room." He gave her a wicked grin.

Oh, yeah, she could picture coming back to visit Jake and the hot time they'd have. "I appreciate the invitation, but that's not fair to you."

"Why not?"

"Because, as we've said, you need to be free to date someone else. Maybe I didn't like the idea that you'd immediately hook up with Marla, but I also don't want to think of you living in the house waiting for the day when I…" She stared at him as the realization struck. "Is that the idea, Jake? You'll keep this place ready for my eventual return? Because you think I probably *will* be back?"

"No."

"Because if that's your motivation for renting from me, you can forget about it."

He divested her of the comforter and blanket before drawing her into his arms. "I don't want you to come back. Not permanently, anyway."

"Liar."

"Yeah, well, I do, but that's not what *you* hope for, so I'll be rooting really hard for you to make it big over there." He rubbed the small of her back. "Please believe me, Amethyst. I want whatever you want. I'm not trying to sabotage you."

She knew him now, knew she could trust him not to lie to her. "Okay, I believe you."

His shoulders relaxed. "That's a relief, although I don't want to be misleading, either. I expect you to succeed. God knows you're talented enough, but we both know life isn't fair. So I thought if I kept the house the way it is, then if the unthinkable happens and something goes wrong…"

At first she was touched, but the more she thought about his plan the less she liked it. It wasn't good for either of them. Then she remembered something else Professor Edenbury had said. "I'm supposed to burn the boats."

"What?"

"It's a military strategy but it applies whenever a goal is set. First you land the army on the beach. Then you burn the boats so retreat isn't an option."

"Did Chelsea say that?"

"No, it was my voice teacher and he made an excellent point. Your reason for keeping the house unchanged is very sweet and so like you, but I just realized that I can't let you rent this place."

He frowned. "What if you take out the furniture and turn the studio back into a bedroom like you talked about before? Would that do it?"

"Not if I know you're living here. I'd still have a connection to the house. And you'd still have a connection to me, and you really need to move on. You might hesitate to do that if you're staying in what used to be my house."

He held her gaze for several seconds. Then he sighed. "Let's forget it."

"I'm sorry. I know you like this place but—"

"I can find something else. You're right. I didn't want you to burn the boats. You built that studio with loving care and I hated to think of you ripping it apart. I see now that you have to give up the house entirely."

And Jake, too. She had a feeling that unless she made a clean break with him he'd imagine they could keep this thing going somehow. He hadn't dated anyone else since August, which should have told her this was more than a fling for him. She hadn't dated anyone, either. Clearly they weren't suited for casual sex.

"Hey." He hugged her closer. "You don't have to burn any boats tonight. Let's carry this stuff downstairs and burn up the sheets instead."

She allowed the passion in his eyes to make her forget everything but this moment. When he looked at her like that, nothing else mattered. "Great idea."

After they carried the bedding downstairs, Jake took over the arrangement and she stood back to watch.

"I wouldn't be upset if you ditched your clothes while I'm doing this," he said. "You'd save us time."

Laughing, she undressed, but she kept an eye on the proceedings as he made up the bed quickly and efficiently. "You've done this before." Her stupid heart felt a pang of jealousy at the idea he'd lovingly made up a similar bed for another woman.

"When I was a kid."

Oh. Not for another woman, after all. Her chest tightened. He'd probably smuggled bedding into whatever secret place he'd used to get away from his father every night. He might still associate a bed on the floor with an escape from reality.

They could both use an escape tonight. As he shook out the top sheet, she finished taking off everything except her bra and matching panties. They were Christmas red, with holly embroidered on them—a sprig over each nipple and one strategically placed on the front of the panties. He'd asked her to undress herself, but these last items were his to remove.

"Done." He tossed back the top sheet before glancing at her. "Hel-lo, Christmas fantasy." He unsnapped the cuffs of his Western shirt as he came toward her. "Humor me and say you bought that combo strictly for my benefit."

"I did."

"Really?" He took off his shirt and dropped it to the floor before reaching for her. "When?"

"Yesterday morning, before I came out to the ranch." She nestled against him and ran her palms up his sculpted chest. "I saved them for tonight. They're not exactly a Christmas present but—"

"Oh, yeah, they are." Heat flared in his eyes as he stepped away from her and held out his hand. "Come on, fantasy lady. Time to unwrap my present."

16

Jake was doing his damnedest to keep from saying or doing anything that would set off an explosion, but it wasn't easy. That little speech about burning the boats sounded idealistic and noble, but it didn't fit this situation, at least not in his opinion. Besides, had this professor who'd spouted off on the subject burned any boats or did he or she simply stay in the safety of the classroom and pass out that advice to impressionable students?

But it wasn't Jake's place to question the strategy or anything else, for that matter. In fact, his impromptu invitation to have her come back and visit had almost ruined everything. He'd managed to contain the damage, but now she didn't want him to rent the house, which sucked.

For the next few hours he'd better concentrate on the one thing they definitely agreed on. He doubted he'd change her mind with great sex, but he'd have a hell of a good time trying.

She stretched out on the bed he'd created, tucked a pillow under her head and the effect was outstanding. Christmas lights splashed color over her delicious-looking skin and his mouth watered.

The house had been chilly last night when she'd been naked beside the tree, but it was warmer now. He'd be willing to bet she'd turned up the heat before leaving for her parents' house today. He appreciated the advance planning because he intended to use his tongue on every inch of her.

That program would go better in a warm room. She'd bought her outfit for him, too, and he intended to pay special attention to the places currently being covered by red satin decorated with holly. Her erect nipples pushed at the holly decoration, giving it a 3-D effect. Nice.

He stripped off his jeans and briefs and laid the jeans within reach because of the condoms tucked in the pockets.

"You look good in Christmas lights," she murmured. Her attention was fixed on his package and her tongue swept over her plump lips. She crooked a finger at him. "Come down here."

His balls tightened. He'd spent enough naked time with her that he recognized that husky tone. He had a game plan but she might have one, too. Tonight he would deny her nothing.

He dropped slowly to his knees beside her. "What can I do for you?"

Her blue eyes were smoky with desire as she wrapped her warm fingers around his cock. "I want this."

He nearly came. "And just how do you want it?"

"I want to taste you."

Although having him above her for this particular pleasure was new, he didn't have to be a genius to figure it out. Responding to her gentle tug, he straddled her. "Don't make me come."

Her soft laughter tickled the sensitive tip, already moist from wanting her. "Why not?"

"I'll be out of commission for a while."

"Not for long. I know you. Now, lean forward. I want to play."

He flattened his palms on either side of the pillow and surrendered to her mouth. Sweet heaven, the woman knew how to play. His fingers curled into the sheet as her tongue danced and her cheeks hollowed. Then, because she was in the perfect position for it, she cupped his balls and began a slow massage.

He groaned, hoping that would relieve the pressure building as he fought the urge to come. But the vibration in his chest only increased the erotic sensations swirling around him. He gasped as she raked her teeth along the underside of his cock.

He'd probably known from the moment he let her take the lead that he was done for. She loved giving him an orgasm as much as he loved giving her one. As his control slipped away, he abandoned himself to extreme pleasure. She seemed to know exactly how to touch him, when to squeeze, how to lick, where to bite.

At the moment when he completely let go, it was with the knowledge that she was the best thing to ever come into his life. He might lose her. In fact, he probably would. But as he whirled in the grip of a shattering climax, he knew the eventual pain was worth this. Oh, yeah, *this*.

Eventually the roaring in his ears subsided and his muscles responded to his commands. He managed to flop down on his back beside her on the makeshift bed, but his breathing was still ragged. "That wasn't how I intended this adventure to go."

"That's how I intended it to go."

"Oh, really?" He turned his head to find her gazing at him. "Since when?"

"Since you threw me over your shoulder like some modern-day caveman. I felt the need to create a balance of power."

"But you've always had the power."

"I don't *think* so. You're the one who broke up with me in high school, remember?"

"Self-preservation. Even then I knew that you had the power and it freaked me out."

"But not anymore?"

"Oh, no, it still freaks me out, but for a blow job like that I'll deal with it." He wanted to lighten the mood and he'd succeeded.

She laughed and rolled to face him. "When this started between us in August, I—"

"It started long before that." He mirrored her position so he could look into her eyes.

"Okay, when we were juniors, planning for the junior-senior prom."

"Bingo. I volunteered to help and there you were. I was toast."

"I never got that impression." She reached over and traced the curve of his eyebrows. "I thought you were mildly interested."

"I was a heat-seeking missile, which scared the crap out of me because I was a virgin and terrified of getting a girl pregnant."

"I was a virgin, too."

"I never guessed. I believed I'd fallen for the sexiest, most experienced girl in the junior class. I thought about you all summer."

"I thought about you, too."

"You're kidding."

"No, Jake, I'm not. I kept hoping that I'd run into you that summer, but you were out at the ranch and I was in town. It never happened."

"My bad luck."

"Or not. By the time school started I was determined to ask you out. If I hadn't been so persistent I'm not sure we would have dated."

He sighed. "Forgive me for being an idiot." He skimmed her hip with a light touch. "You wanted me and I loused it up."

"No you didn't." She cupped his face in both hands. "If you hadn't broken up with me, you would have been my first, and we would have attached so much significance to the experience at that age. Instead my first was someone I didn't love and I never went out with him again."

"What's good about that story? That first time is supposed to be special."

"Was yours?"

"No, but that was my own fault. There was a party and I was slightly drunk. Never should have happened but she was persistent and I was stupid. We never went out again, either."

"See? Let's say you hadn't broken up with me and we'd done the deed senior year."

"It would have been special." And, damn it, he wished he could rewrite history.

"I'm sure it would have been, and we could be married by now. We might have kids. Maybe you wouldn't be a firefighter and I definitely wouldn't be moving to LA. It all worked out for the best."

Obviously he was supposed to agree with her. He swallowed his initial response, something along the lines of *bullshit*, and confirmed the part that he did happen to agree with. "Yeah, we were too young for that kind of intense relationship. At least I was. I had a lot to learn." Although he'd known couples that helped each other grow up. One of his buddies at the station had married his childhood sweetheart and after twenty years they were closer than ever.

"I had plenty to learn, too." She smiled at him. "I still do."

"Not me. I've achieved total perfection."

Her eyebrows arched. "Is that so?"

"Ask anybody." He pulled her close. "I know all, see all. I can even read minds. Right now you're thinking *a little less talk and a little more action*. Am I right?"

"No, you're not, smarty-pants. I like talking to you."

"Of course you do, because I'm a brilliant conversationalist." He rolled her to her back, which was fun to do when they were both laughing. "But let's be honest, that's not the most spectacular thing I can do with my mouth. And I know you, Amethyst Ferguson. You want some of that."

Her blue eyes sparkled with a mixture of laughter and lust. "Yes I do, you conceited man. Lay your amazing perfection on me immediately."

"You've got it." Capturing her wrists, he stretched them above her head and manacled them with one hand while he looked into her eyes and stroked her warm skin. "I can't wait to play with my Christmas present."

Her breathing changed. "I hope you like it."

"I know I will." Lowering his head, he nibbled on her mouth while he stroked the sleek satin covering her breasts. "When you put this on this morning, did you think of me touching you here?"

"Yes." She arched upward so she could thrust her breast into his palm. "And now I want it off."

"Are you going to tell me how to unwrap my present?"

"I'm only making suggestions as the owner of the bra. There's a front catch, so if you..." She sucked in a breath as he flipped it open and pushed the fabric away so he could massage at will. "Mmm, like that."

"Glad you approve."

"Turn me loose and I can take it all the way off."

"Okay." He couldn't help smiling. "Still giving directions, I see." He loosened his hold on her wrists and helped her out of it.

"Once it's unfastened it serves no purpose."

"I wouldn't say that." He grabbed the bra before she could toss it aside. "I've always believed in reusing Christmas wrapping."

"For what?"

"A game." He captured her wrists again and drew them over her head. Then he wound the bra several times around her wrists.

"Jake Ramsey, are you getting kinky on me?" Her breathy question sounded as if she sincerely hoped so.

"A little bit. Hold still while I fasten the hooks. How does that feel?"

"Like I'm no longer in charge of this operation."

He cupped her cheek while he feathered a kiss over her mouth. "Yeah, you are. Do you want it undone?"

"No." Her voice vibrated with excitement.

"See, I knew that because I can read your mind." He ran his tongue over her lower lip as he pulled the flimsy material of her panties aside so he could explore.

"Then why ask me?"

"It turns me on to hear you say you like it."

"I've never let anybody do this before."

"But you let me." He slid his fingers into her wet channel.

"Because you're... Jake." She gasped out his name as he circled her clit with his thumb.

He left the velvet softness of her mouth and kissed his way to her full breast. "Perfection." Drawing her nipple into his mouth, he rolled it over his tongue while he pumped his fingers in a slow rhythm.

"Perfection...perfect—oh...ohhh." Lifting her hips, she silently asked for more.

He delved deeper and found her G-spot as he continued to suck on her tight nipple. Her soft whimper became a wail, then a series of panting breaths and finally a lusty cry that made him shiver with happiness. Her orgasm undulated across his fingers and he savored the pleasure of knowing he'd made her come.

She was still shuddering in reaction when he moved down and wedged his shoulders under her hips. He sacrificed one precious moment to admire the play of Christmas lights over her quivering body. Then he lifted her to his waiting mouth, nudged her panties aside and coaxed her to come again. Gasping and moaning his name, she writhed against the sheets.

His bed was coming undone but so was she, and that was all that mattered. He'd vowed to drive her crazy tonight and, judging from her wild cries, he was succeeding. As she lay panting beneath him, he made a slow journey back up her moist, hot body, kissing and licking a pathway to her breasts, her throat and, finally, her lips. The flavor of her climax was still on his tongue as he thrust it deep.

She kissed him back with such heat that he knew she was ready for more. Sliding his hands up her arms, he unbound her wrists. She responded by gripping his head, her fingertips pressing against his scalp as she held him steady so that she could ravish his mouth.

"Take me." Her urgent plea was followed by equally urgent kisses.

The pressure in his cock was almost past enduring. He fumbled blindly for his jeans and by some miracle snagged his finger in a pocket. The condom seemed to leap into his hand. Breaking away from her hungry kiss, he pushed back onto his knees. No condom in the history of birth control had been rolled on this quickly.

She reached for his hips. "Now, Jake. I want you inside me."

"I want that, too." His words were choked with the intensity of his need for her. "More than you could ever know." Poised between her welcoming thighs, he allowed the tip of his cock to slip easily into her wet channel. Then he leaned down and locked his gaze with hers. "Hang on. This might be intense." Before she could respond, he pushed his hips forward and did exactly what she'd asked. He took her.

The phrase implied vigorous action, so he gave her that. Full throttle, no holds barred. Her breasts trembled with the force of his cock driving deep.

But he wasn't a conquering hero. He was her lover, at least for this brief space of time. So he paused, gasping. "Talk to me. Are you okay?"

She gulped for air. "Never better. Go for it."

So he did, but then as he felt his orgasm approaching and knew hers was very close, too, he felt the need to slow things down. Words welled up inside him, words he'd never allowed himself to say. Yet if he didn't say them now, he might never have the chance.

Vaguely he understood that saying those words would change everything. But she'd told him to go for it, and that could be interpreted more than one way. Orgasms were wonderful, but without the words he longed to say, what did they mean?

So instead of rocketing forward to a blazing mutual climax, he eased back on the throttle. Sure, his cock protested, but he was in charge, not the bad boy who only cared about instant gratification. A great deal was at stake, and leaving things unsaid was not a good strategy.

Amethyst, being a very smart woman, noticed the change in mood immediately. She glanced up at him. "Is something wrong?"

"No, but I need to tell you something." He maintained a steady rhythm, but it was nothing like the balls-to-the-wall pace he'd kept up before.

"Can't it wait?"

"I don't think so."

She must have had a hint of what was coming, because her blue eyes became a little misty. "I have a feeling this is something best left unsaid."

"You're probably right." He rocked forward, settling into her warmth before instinct made him ease back to create the same friction all over again. Sometimes he wondered why this connection between a man and a woman had to be so complicated. These were the basics. The rest was just details.

"Then don't say it." She bracketed his hips and held on tight. "Just concentrate on the pleasure we give each other." She rose to meet his thrust. "Isn't that enough?"

"Not anymore. You don't want to hear it, but I have to say it. Amethyst, I love you."

Her gaze filled with longing. "Oh, Jake."

"I can't help it. Every minute, every second, with you feels so right. I used to think we didn't belong together, but not anymore."

She reached up to cradle his face in both hands. "We don't belong together," she murmured.

"Why? Because you don't love me?"

"I didn't say that."

"You can't say it because it's not true." He kept up his lazy rhythm, loving her, wanting her to feel and acknowledge the unbelievable connection between them. "Admit it. You're in love with me."

"What if I am?" Her words were tinged with regret. "That doesn't change anything."

He paused to gaze down at her. "It doesn't?"

"No." Her voice was husky with emotion. "I was in love with you in high school. I'm in love with you now. That won't affect my decision to leave."

He knew she meant what she was saying. She thought herself capable of sacrificing love for her music career. She imagined herself burning those boats. Not tonight, but soon.

But as she lay warm and succulent in his arms, he had a hard time believing it. She loved everything about her life in Sheridan. She loved him. The woman he'd come to know wouldn't throw everything away because some college professor had told her she should.

17

AMETHYST HAD NEVER been loved so well or so thoroughly, and she knew why. Jake was right. They did belong together, except for one small detail. She'd decided to walk a different path.

When he left their cozy bed to dispose of the condom in the kitchen, she lay gazing up at the lights on the tree. Then it hit her. The problem was Christmas. The holiday brought out emotions, both good and bad, that lay buried the rest of the year. People expected so much of Christmas—marriage proposals, meaningful gifts, declarations of love.

She'd thought meeting Jake in the hardware store was a happy coincidence. Why wouldn't she be thrilled at the prospect of enjoying some hot sex with him during a holiday filled with joy? The timing had seemed perfect, especially after they'd worked out the logistics.

Instead, they'd created the perfect storm. Without Jake's arrival, she wouldn't have met Chelsea or learned about Matt Forrest, a guy who'd spent three years pounding on doors in Hollywood. Meanwhile she'd spent the same amount of time gallivanting around Wyoming hoping to be discovered.

Matt's story had showed her the risk she'd been unwilling to take. Problem was, in the midst of getting clarity on that issue, she'd fallen in love with the man she had to leave behind.

Last summer's encounter had been about sex. Really good sex, too. The kind that made her reluctant to get naked with anyone else while that vivid memory still simmered in her mind and body. But it hadn't been love. That development could be blamed entirely on Christmas.

She'd started to fall when she'd discovered him checking out smoke alarms. Until that moment she hadn't thought much about his occupation or his dedication to it. Then she'd watched him coming in backward in that broken-down sleigh and had eventually realized that he'd invited her for a sleigh ride without being in possession of one.

With each change of scene, the facets of his personality had gleamed in a way she might not have noticed without the Christmas festivities. She'd had a chance to observe him interacting with his family and hers, and she'd admired how easily he fit into either situation. She'd watched him handle a deaf old woman's request with humor, grace and compassion.

She'd learned more about him in the past two days than she had in weeks of dating him in high school. And she'd revealed more about herself. Her family knew that her sexy persona was an act, but she'd never discussed that with anyone else. Dropping that mask had seemed like a natural thing to do with Jake. After all, she'd been falling in love.

The subject of her musings, gloriously naked, walked back into the living room. Only the Christmas tree lights were on, which gave him a mysterious, almost other-worldly appearance as he made a slight detour and picked up something from an end table. Then she recognized what it was and smiled.

"I thought it was time for some of Mrs. Gentry's cookies."

"Excellent thought." She sat up.

"I didn't want to rummage through your refrigerator without asking, but do you have any milk?"

"I have milk and I also have eggnog. Take your pick."

"I'd love some eggnog."

"Me, too." She started to get up.

"Nope." He laid a hand on her bare shoulder. "You stay there and relax. I'll take care of it."

"Glasses are in the top cupboard next to the stove."

"Thanks." He walked back into the kitchen and she admired the view. She'd been too blissed out on great sex to think of it the first time he'd left the room. Wide shoulders, narrow hips, tight buns, muscled thighs and calves—she couldn't imagine a man who would appeal to her physically as much as Jake did.

Even better, he'd developed that body so he could be a better firefighter. Knowing that he'd probably carried people and animals to safety the way he'd hauled her up those stairs made him quite a hero. He deserved a woman who would be there for him, who would want to have children, assuming he did. She hadn't ever asked him and wouldn't. Not a good subject for them.

He returned with the eggnog and a couple of glasses. "I didn't know you liked eggnog."

"Love it. I'm always sad when Christmas is over and it disappears from the shelves."

"I know!" He handed her the glasses and sat on the blanket, facing her. "Why couldn't it be available all the time?" He gave the carton a vigorous shake. "It's not like they couldn't keep making it."

"True." She held out the glasses while he poured. "It could be marketing. If eggnog's available all year, then it wouldn't be special. Think about how wild we were for each other last night. We're much calmer tonight. Give us another week and we'd be watching TV instead of having sex."

"Wrong." He clinked his glass against hers. "To love."

"You and Mrs. Gentry. Both incurable romantics." She sipped her eggnog.

"Whereas you're a flinty-eyed realist." He dug in the bag and handed her a cookie.

"I'm not sure about the flinty-eyed part, but I think I'm pretty realistic." She bit into the cookie, which was shaped like a Christmas tree and covered with green frosting and little candies to simulate ornaments. "She put a lot of work into these."

"She did. When I move back here I plan to go see her."

"And check out her house for fire hazards?"

"That, too. She had a couple of cords that looked compromised and I wonder what kind of wiring she has in that house. It's been there awhile. But mostly I just want to pay her a visit, find out if she needs any errands run, things like that."

She melted. If she hadn't been totally in love with him, that little speech would have done the trick. "What a fabulous idea. I'm sure she'd love having you visit."

"And I'd love doing it." He finished off his cookie and glanced at her. "You're not eating your snack."

"I was imagining you making friends with Mrs. Gentry. If I weren't leaving, I'd go with you."

His gaze sharpened. "You would?"

"Sure. She was always nice to Sapphire and me. Once I moved out of the neighborhood I didn't make the effort to see her very often. Now I wish I had."

"Having you come along would be great."

"Obviously it's not possible, but if I could clone myself, I'd hang around and watch her reaction. She'll get such a kick out of you, Jake."

"I already get a kick out of her."

"That's why you'll be so good for the community. You're focused on helping others and we need people like that."

"Hmm."

"What?"

"Nothing. I just noticed that you...never mind." He took a deep breath. "Do you want the rest of that cookie?"

"You can have it." She handed it to him. "The eggnog filled me up. They're big cookies. I was thinking of offering them to my students. I scheduled a couple of lessons for the twenty-seventh because they'll be bored with vacation by then, anyway. But one of those and they'd be on a sugar high. I'll have to come up with something else because I like giving them a little treat after the lesson."

"You won't have to worry about it much longer, though."

"That's true." She sighed. "I'm not sure what to do about those kids. Nobody else in town is offering private voice lessons and I hate to see them quit. You should hear those cuties sing, Jake. They're amazing!"

"Wish I could."

"They're all coming along so well, too, but there's no one to take over after I leave. Well, there's one person but he's not good with the little ones. He yells. They'd be better off with no one than him. The elementary school music teacher has her own children and really doesn't have the time."

Jake drained the last of his eggnog and set the glass aside. "But that's really not your concern. You can't let those kids keep you from going to LA."

"I won't. I'm just worried about them."

He gazed at her for quite a while. "I can see that."

"Something's bothering you."

"Let me ask you a question. After you graduated with your music degree, after you'd heard that advice about burning the boats, why didn't you pack up and move to LA?"

Her chest tightened. "Because I wasn't ready."

"Then why didn't you go last summer?"

"You know why." She began to shake. "I'd figured out how to live on what I was able to make and every time I performed somewhere, there was a chance someone would be in the audience who could make it happen for me."

"But you've decided to abandon that strategy. You're ready to burn the boats. Why now?"

"Because I've been procrastinating! I realized that after talking to Chelsea. Professor Edenbury was right. I have to risk everything and just go!"

"Why?"

"Haven't you been listening? I have the talent and I'm wasting it!"

"I don't see it that way." He reached for her.

She wiggled away. "Don't. Don't try to hold me and soothe me like you would an agitated horse. I'm getting a picture here and it's not a pretty one. I thought you were on my side, but you're not, are you?"

"I am! I want the best for you, but is your plan to charge off to LA what's best? You love it here. You have family, friends, students and a recording studio. What's wrong with building a career out of that?"

"What's wrong? I have the ability to be so much more."

"Yes, you do. But will achieving that give you more satisfaction, more happiness? After watching and listening for two days, I doubt it. What if you forget about what some professor put in your head and think about what *you* want? If it's fame and all that goes with it, then fine. But if you really wanted that, it's likely you would have been on the bus for LA the minute you graduated."

"Not necessarily!" Rage coursed through her. "How dare you say such a thing? You don't know a damn thing about this, Jake. So butt out, okay?" She scrambled to her feet and hurried over to the sofa to grab her coat. It was the fastest way she could think of to hide. She hadn't felt naked before, but she sure as hell did now.

He sighed and hung his head. "Damn me for a fool. I kept telling myself not to say anything, to enjoy the sex and keep my mouth shut." When he looked up at her, his eyes were filled with misery. "But I love you, and I think somebody should tell you the truth. You're not wasted here. You're in your element. You can perform, and teach, and hang out with your family. What could be better?"

She hugged her coat around her. "You know the worst part of this? I can't even accuse you of saying this for your benefit because that's not who you are. You're saying this for *my* benefit. You're trying to clip my wings for my own good."

"I'm not trying to clip your wings, damn it!" Getting to his feet, he began pulling on his clothes. "There are different ways to soar, Amethyst. You don't have to top the charts to have liftoff, to affect people's lives in positive ways. You're doing it now and you love every minute of it."

"You think I can't make it."

"Oh, no, I think you can." He paused to gaze at her. "And that would be the real tragedy."

She swallowed. "Let yourself out. I'm going up to my studio."

"Amethyst…"

"It's over, Jake. It would have been eventually, so maybe this is better. Goodbye." She ran up the stairs and adrenaline gave her the necessary boost to make it to the top without stopping for breath. The memory of Jake throwing her over his shoulder hurt like hell, but she'd get past it. Besides, she wouldn't be in this house much longer anyway.

JAKE STARED AFTER her and debated going up there. Then he heard a lock click and knew he'd have to break down her studio door, and that wouldn't help matters. He'd caused the explosion he'd been trying so hard to avoid, but her comments about her students had been the final straw.

As he'd listened to her rave about those kids, he'd realized that if everybody danced around the issue of her leaving, she was liable to do it. She'd hurt herself, her family and those children she was mentoring. She'd also hurt him, but he'd been willing to take the blows. He wasn't willing to stand silently by and let her do this to herself and others. So he'd said what was in his heart.

Chelsea had predicted she wouldn't like it and she definitely hadn't. She'd ordered him out of her house and locked herself in her studio so there was no recourse. She'd soundproofed the walls, but the vibration of a heavy bass made the whole house shiver.

After he finished dressing, he folded all the bedding and laid it on the sofa. Then he rinsed the glasses in the kitchen sink and closed up the bag of cookies. At least he had a place to go. In the old days he would have had to break into a vacant house to find a safe place to sleep. But a key to one of the ranch's log cabins lay in his pocket.

So did several condoms. He grimaced. Wouldn't be using those anytime soon. Before he left he turned off the Christmas tree lights. Even though they were LEDs, he didn't like the idea of leaving them on when nobody was downstairs.

Although he couldn't lock the dead bolt on his way out, he could at least engage the one on the knob. He was out the door before he fully realized how hard it was snowing. He had to fight his way to the truck and wrench the door open. His windshield wipers struggled with the snow piled on them, but they finally cleared a small space that would allow him to drive away from there.

The trip back to the ranch took forever, which gave him way too much time to think. He kept his cell phone on the seat in case he got stuck and had to call someone.

The plows hadn't come out yet and likely wouldn't until morning. Sensible people wouldn't be out on the road at this hour on Christmas night, or rather, the morning of the twenty-sixth.

Christmas was officially over and he'd ended his and Amethyst's holiday with a bang. But when he considered what he'd said to her, he didn't regret a word of it. He deeply regretted that those words had driven a wedge between them, but he'd heard somewhere that it was a tradition to kill the messenger. Come to think of it, he did feel sort of dead inside.

But at the very least, he might have given her something to think about. She was furious now, but when her anger faded, she might remember some of the things he'd said. She might even wonder if any of those ideas held water.

Or maybe that was too much to hope for. He'd have to accept the fact that he could have ruined everything between them and destroyed any happy memories she had of their time together, all for nothing. She could go to LA, after all, cursing his name the whole way.

If she did make the move, he wouldn't hear from her, but he had ways to find out what had happened. He could go through Grady because Sapphire would be dialed in to Amethyst's progress. He wondered if someday he'd turn on the TV and see her, or he'd be listening to the radio and one of her songs would come on.

If so, he prayed she'd be happy with the choices she'd made. He couldn't see how she would be, but she might prove him wrong. She might never forgive him for what he'd said tonight. He'd live with that, just as he'd live with the knowledge that he'd never stop loving her.

18

JAKE WAS UP early the next morning after getting very little sleep in a narrow bunk bed. As a teenager he hadn't minded them. They'd been a hell of a lot better than the makeshift beds he'd created in his hidey-holes. But he'd grown considerably larger since then and he didn't fit anymore.

The bunk hadn't been the main problem but it gave him something to blame for his lack of sleep besides worry over Amethyst. She'd been really upset. Although he was glad he'd said his piece, he hated to think of her in pain, especially when he couldn't do anything about it.

Peering out the cabin window, he saw that the snow had stopped. He had just enough light to do some shoveling before getting cleaned up for breakfast, and shoveling was great for clearing the mind. He used to do a lot of it when he'd lived here—either snow or manure. There had always been plenty of both.

In winter each cabin had been supplied with a snow shovel and apparently the tradition had continued because he found one leaning in the corner. After bundling up, he grabbed the shovel and headed out. Nothing marred the blanket of snow, so he must be the first person out this morning.

Pushing his way through knee-deep drifts, he trudged up to the ranch house and started there. A path from the house to the barn was the first priority. By the time he finished he could smell wood smoke, which meant Rosie had lit a fire and Herb would be coming down to the barn soon. Jake felt good about making that an easier trip for him.

Next he returned to his cabin and cleared the way to the bathhouse. He added a side path for Finn and Chelsea. The lack of footprints on their snow-covered stoop indicated they hadn't ventured out yet.

When the cabins had been built, a communal bathhouse had been the cheapest solution. Braving the cold walk on winter mornings had become a source of pride for the foster brothers and now for the teenagers enrolled at Thunder Mountain Academy. Chelsea hadn't been part of either tradition and yet she seemed fine with it.

The exercise had warmed Jake up enough that his trip to the bathhouse to shower and shave wasn't bad at all. He made it up to the house in time to help Rosie cook breakfast.

His foster mom looked a little surprised to see him but then she handed him a carton of eggs, a bowl and a whisk. "I love having company when I cook." She gave him a bright smile.

He set to work cracking the eggs into a bowl. "I know I told you I wouldn't be around for breakfast."

"Things change." Rosie started the bacon.

"If Amethyst moves to LA, I doubt she'll be keeping me informed about how it's going, but if you hear anything, would you let me know?"

"Of course." She glanced his way. "Maybe you'd better add another dozen eggs to that bowl. I just remembered that Cade and Lexi are coming for breakfast."

Jake went to the refrigerator and took out another carton. "Has Lexi finally moved in with Cade?"

"Yes." Rosie sounded very happy about that. "She promised me they wouldn't eat all their meals with us, but I don't care if they do. It's fun having them."

"Yeah, but from what I heard, she wants Cade to be more domestic, take on his share of the cooking and such." He added more eggs to the bowl. "I saw the cabin Damon and Phil built for him. Great kitchen."

"I know, and they'll have some of their meals there, I'm sure. Maybe they'll even invite Herb and me up for dinner, which would be fun. But I'm used to feeding a crowd, so it feels normal to have a full table."

"Then I'll be sure and invite myself over once I move back."

Rosie spun away from the stove. "You're moving back?"

"I didn't tell you?"

"No, you did not!"

The excitement in her eyes made him smile. "Nothing's for sure, so don't get too excited, but I plan to if I can get on with the fire department. I'm going over there on my way out of town to see what's up."

Rosie put down her spatula and came over to hug him. "That's wonderful news, Jake."

He hugged her back. "Like I said, don't get your hopes up yet. They may not have an opening. But this time I have years of experience to offer, so that should help my cause."

"I have a good feeling about this." She stepped back to gaze at him. "I've missed you."

The love in her eyes brought a lump to his throat. "I've missed you, too, Mom."

"Hey, there, Jake!" Herb walked into the kitchen. "I didn't think you'd be joining us this morning."

"He's moving back to Sheridan!" Rosie turned to her husband. "Isn't that great?"

"You bet!" He came over to give Jake a hug, too. "Does this have anything to do with—"

"No, it doesn't," Rosie said. "This is all about Jake missing us and wanting to come home." The note of finality in her voice was a clear signal that the subject of Amethyst was closed.

The knot of tension in Jake's chest loosened. He might never have Amethyst in his life, but he'd have his foster parents and his foster brothers. That made him one lucky guy.

RANGELAND ROASTERS HAD windows all along the street side of the shop, so Amethyst could see her mother sitting at one of the tables, waiting for her. Her mom smiled and waved. Amethyst's eyes filled with unexpected tears and she dug in her purse for a tissue.

She'd been doing a lot of crying lately and over silly things, like the way her little five-year-old student mispronounced a word in a song and ended up in a fit of giggles. Yesterday she'd been fixing breakfast and sunlight had come through the kitchen window and caught the crystal she'd hung there a couple of years ago. That dancing rainbow had made her cry, too.

Now she was all choked up because her mother had smiled and waved through the coffee shop window.

She'd like to blame her emotional state on Jake, but after crying her eyes out the night he'd left, she hadn't shed another tear on his behalf. Then again, maybe it was his fault.

Just like the angel in *It's a Wonderful Life*, Jake had pointed out all the ways she was connected to this town she called home. She would be missed when she moved to LA and that was a bigger deal for her than she'd acknowledged when she'd made her decision. It wasn't a two-way street, either. She'd miss everything and everybody, especially her sweet mother. And that brought on another bout of tears.

Her mom left her purse to hold the table and stood so they could walk up and order. But then she took a closer look at her daughter and sat again. She motioned Amethyst to do the same. "What's wrong?"

"Nothing. Everything." She dabbed at her eyes.

"Is it Jake?"

"Not exactly." She sighed. "I thought I knew what to do. If I want to make it as a singer, I need to go to LA, right?"

"Probably. If you want to be a really big success, that's quite likely the way to go."

"I'm scared."

"Oh, honey." Her mother reached over and squeezed her hand. "You'll be fine. You have a good head on your shoulders. I shouldn't have said that about the drug dealers living next door. I'm sure that won't happen."

"I'm not scared about what I'll find there. Well, maybe a little, but that's not what's bothering me." She swallowed. "I'm not even scared of failing, although I understand that's a very real possibility. Mostly I'm scared of losing what I have here."

"You can't really lose that. If it doesn't work out, you can always come home."

Amethyst shook her head. "But, see, that's the problem. If I go, I have to do it with all my heart. I can't be thinking about running home at the first sign of trouble. I have to be totally committed to overcoming every obstacle, the way Finn was when he moved to Seattle and Matt was when he went to Hollywood. I have to want it so much that nothing else matters."

Her mother took a deep breath. "You're right."

"So the way I figure it, I have to know in my gut that I'm willing to make the necessary sacrifices and right now I'm not sure if I'm willing to do that."

"Nobody said you had to leave tomorrow. If you need more time to think about it, then I say take what you need."

She nodded. "That's good advice. And before you drive yourself crazy wondering whether to ask about Jake or not, let me put your mind at rest. I won't be seeing him when I go to Jackson Hole. We called it quits."

"I see."

"I know you liked him."

"That has no bearing on the matter."

"It has all kinds of bearing, Mom. I wouldn't want to get serious about someone you hated."

"I doubt that you would, but thanks."

Amethyst sighed with relief. She never remembered loving her mother more than now. "Since we've made it through all that, let's get some coffee. And a doughnut. I ate all Mrs. Gentry's cookies and I crave something loaded with sugar, something that's really bad for me."

The mood lightened considerably after that and she was able to describe the antics of her voice students without bursting into tears. They talked about the art project her mother planned to assign her high school students when classes resumed in January.

As they hugged goodbye outside the coffee shop, her mother glanced at her. "You said you wouldn't be seeing Jake when you go to Jackson Hole, but couldn't he come to your performance if he wanted to?"

"He won't. He knows I wouldn't like that."

Of course now that her mom had planted the idea, she kept thinking about it during the time leading up to her departure for Jackson Hole. The prospect of Jake showing up at her gig didn't horrify her. She wouldn't ask him up to her room again, but seeing him wouldn't be the worst thing in the world. She'd missed him.

On the day she had to leave, she put her suitcase in the car and turned back to look at the Victorian. How would it feel to leave this house for the last time? She'd have to turn over her key to whoever rented her half of it and that would be the end of making breakfast in the kitchen, working in her studio, enjoying the front porch in the summer.

Her stomach hurt at the thought of giving up this house. A few months ago she'd even considered approaching the landlady about selling it to her. She probably had enough savings for a down payment. Except that was the money earmarked for her first few months in LA.

She climbed into the SUV and backed out of the driveway. One thing she knew for sure—if she went to LA she'd take her crystal. But she might not have a spot where it would work. Her kitchen was on the east side and the double window was perfect. No telling what she'd find in LA.

She had to drive down Main Street to get to the highway and she pictured the SUV loaded with all her stuff instead of just one small suitcase. She'd really be leaving. No more coffee dates with her mom and no more shopping in the stores she knew so well. No more recognizing people she knew and stopping to chat.

Usually she played music when she drove, but on this trip she preferred silence. She needed to think. The closer she came to Jackson Hole, the more she wanted to talk with Jake again, but she didn't have time before the show. If he came to the performance, that would be great. She had something important to tell him.

LA was a dream she'd nurtured ever since Professor Edenbury had told her that she had the necessary talent to be a star. Everybody wanted to be a star, right? She'd imagined it from the time she'd been a little kid with a karaoke machine.

Professor Edenbury had given her dream the stamp of approval but, come to think of it, what had he ever done that was brave or risky? He had a great voice but he'd never tested himself on Broadway. He'd never moved to LA to explore the possibilities there. Near as she knew, he'd never recorded a single song.

Instead he'd expected Amethyst to do that. She'd seen him as a powerful mentor, but now she viewed him as a puppeteer, manipulating his most gifted students to achieve what he'd never dared to try. She was herself, not a puppet.

Because she was her own person and not some mannequin to be shoved around according to her mentor's ambitions, she could rethink her career path. She could realize the value in teaching kids, although she'd learned the hard way not to push them into venues that didn't work for them. She could begin to value the gigs she booked even if they were within the state and not in some exotic location.

She had to face the truth. She pulled great satisfaction from performing in front of a crowd of Wyoming natives. A sophisticated crowd in an LA nightclub didn't excite her at all. Even Jackson Hole was a little rich for her blood, although she recognized the opportunities in such a cosmopolitan town.

Then why was she angling for a lucrative recording contract, a fifteen-city tour and international fame? She'd been taught to want that. She'd been conditioned to believe that if you had the necessary talent, you were obligated to take that ability as far as you could.

Her father had that kind of talent. She'd heard him play and he was easily as good as the big names. But he'd chosen a different path. At one time she'd viewed that as copping out, but she didn't see her father's decision that way now.

Success came in all sizes and shapes. Sometimes it flashed on the giant screen in Times Square. Sometimes it came in the form of enthusiastic applause from the crowd at the local Elks Club. Amethyst thought about how Jake measured success—a family saved from a house fire, a child plucked from a backyard swimming pool.

She thought about Professor Edenbury and the fire in his eyes as he'd dictated her marching orders. *Go out there and knock 'em dead, Ferguson! Make your old professor proud!*

A weight lifted from her shoulders as she realized that she didn't have to obey his marching orders, didn't have to live his dream. Instead she could live her own. She could stay in Sheridan.

The decision made her giddy with relief. She jabbered away with the registration clerk while checking into the hotel. Smiling, he agreed with her that Wyoming was a fabulous place to live. Then he gave her the room key and an envelope with her name on it.

Her heart leaped. Jake? She tore into it while she was still at the desk and glanced at the signature without reading the note. Not Jake. It was from the guy in charge of booking entertainment at the resort. Damn.

She stuffed the unread message into her purse and wheeled her suitcase over to the elevators. After she'd settled into her room, hung up her dress and taken off her shoes, she pulled the note out of her purse.

Amethyst—a guy from LA named Gerald Kincaid will be in the audience tonight. He's heard one of your demos and wants to talk with you. I gave him a table near the stage. Thought you'd want a heads-up. Bob

IT HAD BEEN a busy night at the fire station with numerous calls, which was tough luck for the people involved but a blessing for Jake. If he'd had to sit around watching TV or playing cards, he'd have been tortured with thoughts of Amethyst. She'd been on his mind during every idle moment since leaving Sheridan, but tonight was worse because she was a short drive away.

So he'd welcomed the sound of the alarm because whenever he climbed on the truck, nothing else mattered. After an easily contained kitchen fire that was more messy than dangerous, he returned in a state of exhaustion, which was also welcome.

Sleep had been elusive the past few nights but maybe

he could sneak in an hour or two in the firehouse after a hot shower. As he was putting away his gear, his buddy Steve grabbed him by the shoulder.

"Somebody's here to see you."

"To see me?" He used the front of his T-shirt to wipe some of the soot from his face. "At three in the morning?"

"Yeah. A woman. Said she needed to talk to you. Chief stuck her in his office so you two could have some privacy."

Dear God. Had to be Amethyst. "Thanks."

His exhaustion vanished as adrenaline kicked in. Maybe she'd come to ask for the key to his apartment because she'd changed her mind about spending time with him. She might want another sexy encounter before they said goodbye forever.

He wished he had the willpower to reject the idea, but he'd take what he could get. He'd missed her like the very devil ever since driving away from Sheridan the day after Christmas.

Whenever he was working in the sooty stench of a fire, he forgot about Amethyst. But the minute the crisis had passed, his brain was flooded with images of her.

Seeing her again was like a mirage in the desert. He wanted to believe she was here but couldn't quite accept the reality of it.

Hurrying to the chief's office, he walked through the open door. Because he didn't know what to expect from this meeting, he closed it behind him.

She leaped up and tears glistened in her eyes. "Oh, Jake." Flinging herself into his arms, she peppered his grimy face with kisses. "I love you so much."

"I love you, too, but I'm filthy." Catching her around

the waist, he eased her away from him. "You'll ruin your sparkly dress."

"I don't care." She gazed up at him, her mascara smudged and her makeup streaked with tears. "I came over here as soon as I could, and you were gone, and I've been waiting, and I had the most horrible thoughts about something happening to you."

"Nothing's going to happen to me. I'm tough and I'm careful."

"I know, but...did you get the job in Sheridan?"

"I did, as a matter of fact. I start in two weeks."

"Good. That's so good."

He took a deep breath and tried to calm his racing heart. "Why are you here?"

She swallowed. "A talent scout from a recording studio came to my performance."

"Is that right?" He pumped as much enthusiasm into his response as he could manage. She'd come to share her good news and he would, by God, be happy for her. It was what she wanted. "That's great! Do you have an offer?"

"He made me one and—"

"That's terrific!" Love was so weird. His own heart was breaking but he could still feel joy for her. "You did it. Now you'll have—"

"Jake, I didn't take it."

The statement was like a smack upside the head. "Why not? Was it a crap deal?"

"No, it was a very good deal." She drew in a shaky breath. "That's what I came to tell you. I'm not going to LA. I want to stay in Sheridan."

He stared at her as he tried to process that. "But if you'd be earning money from the get-go, that takes away a big part of the risk. Why the hell aren't you going?" He had an awful thought. "Is something wrong with one of your parents?"

"No."

"Then why not go?"

"Because I don't want to. Professor Edenbury's dream is not mine." Smiling, she tucked a finger under his chin. "You'll catch a fly."

He closed his mouth but he was still stunned that she'd refused a contract. "Are you sure about this? Going there with no guarantees was one thing, but this deal is exactly what you wanted."

"I know. But on the drive over I realized that you were right. I've let Professor Edenbury's expectations have too much power over me. I love Sheridan, love being near my parents, love teaching my students, recording in my studio and living in that house. Why would I leave everything I love?"

"Beats me." He began to understand the enormity of her decision. And the rightness of it. This could be good, very good.

"I have a great life. And I'm telling you that because I'm not staying just because I want to be with you."

"I'm glad. Then you'd be trading your professor's expectations for mine."

"I promise that's not the case. But unless you've made other living arrangements, you can be my roommate if you want."

"Oh, I want." A surge of incredible joy made him forget about her sparkly dress and he pulled her close. Then he realized what he'd done and released her again. "Maybe this should wait until I'm—"

"Oh, no, you don't." She plastered herself against him.

"I realize you're on duty and all I can have is a kiss for now, but I'm hoping for more later. Lots more."

"Count on it." He lowered his head and brushed his mouth over hers. "I'm all yours."

"Then I have everything I could ever want."

"Me, too." He kissed her with tenderness, gratitude and as much passion as he dared. But mostly he kissed her with all the love in his heart.

Epilogue

MATT FORREST HAD made some very good friends during his three years in Tinseltown, but when he signed a contract for his first major movie role, the two people he most wanted to tell were a thousand miles away. Thank God for cell phones.

He called his foster mother first because she was better at keeping her phone nearby. His foster father seldom carried one while he handled his daily chores, but Rosie liked being able to get calls wherever she happened to be. She would love getting this one.

"Matt!" She sounded excited already.

"Hey, Mom! Are you at home?"

"I most certainly am and I've been on pins and needles waiting for the news. Did you get it?"

"I did!" He'd gone back to his tiny apartment to make the call so they could hear each other. But he had to hold the phone away from his ear for a while because the only mother he'd ever known was going apeshit on the other end. He sat there grinning while she whooped and hollered. Yeah, this was the reaction he'd been looking for.

His friends would be happy for him. Some might

be jealous, but they'd be nice about it. The peripheral friends might wonder if they could capitalize on this development. But Rosie had pure joy going on without a single agenda.

Finally she wound down enough to have an actual conversation. "Okay, tell me everything."

"It's a Western. I think I mentioned that before."

"Yep."

"We'll be shooting on location in Utah beginning next month."

"How about Wyoming? We have great scenery for a Western and we'd get to see you!"

"Logistics. Economics. Utah's closer."

"I suppose."

"My costar is Briana Danvers."

"Wow! She's a big deal!"

"You're telling me. I still can't believe it. A big-budget film with a costar like Briana. I'm so flying you and Dad out for the premiere."

"Oh, my God, Matt, a *premiere*. This is incredible. Can I tell your dad or do you want to call him yourself? I know he's hard to get on the phone."

"You can tell him. You can tell anybody you want. It's official!"

"I can't wait to spread the word. Everyone is going to be so excited! Briana Danvers as a costar! I really like her, but I've had a crush on her husband for years. Talk about a gray fox. Clifton Wallace has it going on."

"People around here really love him, too. From what I hear, he's a class act. I'm hoping he visits the set once in a while. I've never met him but I admire his work."

"People are going to admire your work, too! This is

such wonderful news and you deserve it after all you've been through."

"Thanks, Mom. It feels really cool." He sighed. "Very cool."

"I'm sure it does. And I'll bet you have some other calls to make and some partying to do."

He laughed. "You know me too well."

"Go have fun! We'll celebrate the next time you make it home."

"We sure will. Give my love to Dad."

"I will."

"Love you, Mom."

"Love you, too, sweetie."

He disconnected and sat for a minute savoring the thrill of being able to make that phone call. He'd envisioned it for so long and had started to wonder if he was kidding himself about his prospects. At his lowest point he'd seriously considered moving back to Sheridan.

He could forget about that now. But this day would never have arrived without the years spent at Thunder Mountain Ranch and his foster parents' belief in him. Although they'd be proud of whatever he accomplished, he loved being able to give them something to really brag about. Their son was about to become a movie star.

* * * * *

COMING SOON!

We really hope you enjoyed reading this book.
If you're looking for more romance
be sure to head to the shops when
new books are available on

Thursday 21st November

To see which titles are coming soon, please visit
millsandboon.co.uk/nextmonth

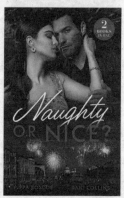